C0-ASL-164

Featured Alternate Selection of
Doubleday Book Club and Rhapsody Book Club

Praise for

Connie Lane's

outrageously readable novels

GUILTY LITTLE SECRETS

"A fast-paced, humorous tale about the
underside of the country's glitziest city."
—*Booklist*

"Hidden agendas and undercover missions make this tale
of romance and suspense fun and inviting."
—*Romantic Times*

"The suspense was nail-biting and the
characters . . . likable."
—*All About Romance*

"Fast-paced and absorbing. Connie Lane has written
a marvelous . . . romance."
—*Romance Fiction Forum*

ROMANCING RILEY

"Sassy and stylish . . . this past-meets-
present tale will help Lane (*Reinventing Romeo*) win over
a younger generation of romance readers."
—*Publishers Weekly*

DISCARD

WAKARUSA PUBLIC LIBRARY

"Lane's fast-paced story is a lot of fun, and the electricity between Riley and Zap crackles."
—*Booklist*

"The very talented Ms. Lane does a great job in building romance. . . ."
—*Romantic Times*

REINVENTING ROMEO

"Irresistibly witty . . . a page-turning tale of adventure and romance. It's an engaging ride well worth the price of admission.
—*Milwaukee Journal Sentinel*

"A delightful laugh-out-loud book."
—*Rocky Mountain News*

"*Reinventing Romeo* is a delightful tale, full of heart-stopping anticipatory scenes and witty dialogue. You'll find yourself in a reading frenzy while you devour the last pages towards the exciting conclusion."
—*Romance Reviews Today*

WAKARUSA PUBLIC LIBRARY

Connie Lane

Dirty Little Lies

A DELL BOOK

BT. 6.50 3/04

DIRTY LITTLE LIES
A Dell Book / April 2004

Published by
Bantam Dell
A Division of Random House, Inc.
New York, New York

This is a work of fiction. Names, characters, places, and incidents either are the product of the author's imagination or are used fictitiously. Any resemblance to actual persons, living or dead, events, or locales is entirely coincidental.

All rights reserved
Copyright © 2004 by Connie Laux
Cover art by Bunky Hurter

No part of this book may be reproduced or transmitted in any form or by any means, electronic or mechanical, including photocopying, recording, or by any information storage and retrieval system, without the written permission of the publisher, except where permitted by law. For information address:
Dell Books, New York, New York.

If you purchased this book without a cover, you should be aware that this book is stolen property. It was reported as "unsold and destroyed" to the publisher, and neither the author nor the publisher has received any payment for this "stripped book."

Dell is a registered trademark of Random House, Inc., and the colophon is a trademark of Random House, Inc.

ISBN 0-440-23747-5

Manufactured in the United States of America
Published simultaneously in Canada

OPM 10 9 8 7 6 5 4 3 2 1

For Maureen Child and Amy Fetzer,
great writers and good friends.
Thanks for listening, brainstorming,
and reading!

Dirty Little Lies

1

Just because Lacie Jo Baxter was a beauty queen didn't mean she was a pushover.

At least that's what she told herself.

It was pretty good advice when it came to the upbeat, look-for-the-silver-lining-in-every-gray-cloud department. Almost as good as the cheery little speech about self-esteem, personal responsibility, and the use of God-given talent she'd made only a short time earlier at the grand opening of the new Mercer's Drug Store in downtown Klaber Falls.

Too bad all that talk about the sunny side of life was a little hard to swallow at the moment. Just like the possibility of the kind of warm and fuzzy, joy-to-the-world happy ending she'd always believed in was looking more and more remote by the second.

It wasn't like her to be so negative, but then, she figured that for once she had a good excuse.

Being locked in the trunk of a speeding car had that sort of effect on a girl.

"Not a pushover. Not a pushover." Lacie did her best with the I-am-woman-hear-me-roar chant. Better to listen to that than to the nagging, terrified warnings inside her head that threatened to overwhelm her. Her breathless voice bumped over the words while the car—as badly in need of shock absorbers as it was of a muffler and a serious tune-up—smacked into a pothole and flew back up again. Lacie's rhinestone-studded tiara banged against the inside of the hood, and when she smacked back down on the thin, scratchy fabric that passed for carpeting on the floor of the trunk, it felt as if every single one of the beads and sequins and pearls on her perfectly fitted, perfectly styled, perfectly breathtaking evening gown were being drilled into her skin.

She didn't have a whole lot of time to think about it. The car made a sharp turn, and if Lacie's five-foot-seven body hadn't been folded into a four-foot-eleven space, she would have rolled with it. As it was, there was barely room to move and her legs were cramped. She could feel the telltale tug of what was surely the beginning of a run in a brand-new pair of pantyhose.

Lacie was tempted to grumble one of the curses she'd heard her sister, Dinah, use. She actually might have done it if her face hadn't been shoved up against the spare tire, so close that she could taste the rubber on her lips. Then again, if she were anything like Dinah, even a mouth full of steel-belted radial wouldn't have stopped her from letting loose with every expletive in the book. But if she were anything at all like Dinah, she wouldn't be Miss Kansas Summer Squash in the first place.

And she wouldn't have been making that personal appearance at Mercer's Drug Store this evening.

And she wouldn't have stayed around long after the store closed to talk to the nice folks who'd shown up to meet her live and in person.

And she wouldn't have left after the crowd was already gone.

And she never would have been in the parking lot alone.

Which meant she never would have been grabbed and

tossed into the trunk of this car before she ever had a chance to let out a scream for help.

None of which was the least bit of consolation.

Not when the baton she'd used to give the crowd a demonstration of her mean twirling technique poked her ribs, a tire jack jabbed her thighs, and the tall, thin heel of her left shoe was hooked at a funny angle on the wires of the car's rear lights.

Those same lights flicked on and off when the driver stepped on the brakes, then let up on them again. The car slowed, turned, and Lacie heard the crunch of gravel beneath the wheels. The next second, the car skidded to a stop.

So did Lacie's heartbeat.

The engine cut off. The driver's side door scraped open. Lacie held her breath.

Not a pushover, huh?

Now all she had to do was convince the six-foot-whatever, two-forty-something gorilla in the ski mask who had snatched her.

The trunk lid popped open and Lacie craned her neck to see what she could see. What she could see wasn't much of anything except a faint sprinkling of stars in a pitch-black sky. The view didn't last. Her kidnapper stepped around to the back of the car and even that little bit of starlight was blocked. Without a word the man grabbed her, and running on instinct—not to mention fear—Lacie reached for her baton like it was a security blanket and held on tight.

She was not so lucky with her left shoe. It was still caught on the taillight wire, and when the man hauled her out of the trunk and set her on the ground, her shoe—and her foot—refused to budge.

"Excuse me!" It wasn't ladylike to interrupt, and a beauty queen was nothing if not a lady. Still, Lacie figured there was an exception or two to every rule. Kidnapping certainly was one. Shoes she'd gone all the way to Kansas City to buy were another. Especially when those shoes fit like a dream and looked divine.

"Excuse me, but these are my best shoes. I'd really rather not leave one of them in the trunk of your car." Just to be sure he was listening, she glanced over her shoulder at the guy. He didn't say a word and because of the ski mask, she couldn't read his expression. Big points for him, though, he kept a firm hold on her. Kind of a bad thing, considering she didn't appreciate being manhandled by a stranger with the manners of a troglodyte. Kind of a good thing, since she was trying to balance on one thin heel at the same time she did her best to unhook the other.

"I can't exactly afford to twist an ankle, either. The national Miss Summer Squash pageant is just a few weeks away and . . ." Lacie stretched to reach her left shoe. Not an easy thing, considering her evening gown was form-fitting enough to show off her perfect-in-every-way size-six figure. Luckily, the gown was slit far enough up one side to show a hint of legs that were as well proportioned as the rest of her. She had just enough room to maneuver. It wasn't easy, but after a couple of seconds, she managed to snag the taillight wire with one finger. After that, it was a cinch to loop the wire away from her heel.

"Thank you." Breathing a sigh of relief, she settled herself on both feet. "I mean it, really. Thanks. Not that I have a great deal of experience when it comes to this sort of thing, but I can't imagine there are many kidnappers who would be considerate enough to—"

The rest of the compliment was lost in an *oomph* of surprise when the man pinned her arms to her sides and propped one hand firmly on her sequin-encrusted behind. None too gently, he march-stepped her toward the hulking shape of a house on the other side of the driveway.

Whipple Farm.

Lacie recognized the dilapidated front porch, the rotted stairs, the roof caved in over what used to be the living room.

But though she made a mental note of the location, she didn't dare speak the words out loud. Something told her kidnappers didn't appreciate their kidnappees knowing where they were.

And where they were, Lacie knew, was in the middle of nowhere.

Whipple Farm. Seven miles outside of town and nothing between here and there except seven miles of blacktop fringed by seven miles of cornfields. No neighbors within hailing distance, and if the Whipples were as deep in debt as everyone said they were, something told her they'd disconnected the phone long before they skipped town and the foreclosure notice that was waiting for them at the bank.

If she was going to get out of this predicament, she was going to have to do it alone.

At the same time Lacie gulped down a breath of apprehension, she reminded herself that it wasn't the first time she'd found herself out of options and on her own.

There was the time she was headed down the runway at the Miss Future Farmers of America pageant and her bathing suit strap popped.

And the never-to-be-forgotten occasion when she was all set to go on stage for the talent competition at the Miss Midwest Football Conference finals and couldn't find her baton.

There was the episode when a desperate Miss Wichita paid Dinah to put blue color in Lacie's hair gel on the morning of the important Holiday Spirit pageant.

And then, of course, there was the whole ugly incident with Jake McCallum.

As quickly as the thought formed, Lacie put it out of her head. This was not the time for self-recrimination or for soul-searching. This time, like all those times before, she needed to pull out the big guns: the smile that never failed to captivate. The charm that was as legendary in Midwest pageant circles as big hair and speeches about world peace. The personality plus that meant that in spite of blue hair gel and ripped bathing suit straps and the one guy who had broken her heart and nearly ruined her pageant career forever, Lacie Jo Baxter always came out the winner.

"It's a beautiful night, isn't it?"

So far, so good. Lacie's kidnapper was surprised enough by her comment to stop at the bottom of the rotting steps.

"I mean, look at all those stars!" She glanced around and her kidnapper automatically looked up at the night sky, too. "Every one of them is a little messenger, you know. Twinkling to us about courage and hope and love and—"

The man grunted, lifted her off her feet, and struggled up the steps with her.

When he propped her against one hip and grabbed for the handle on the back screen door, Lacie tried again.

"Old farmhouses." It wasn't easy to sigh when a bruiser with arms like steel bands was squeezing all the air out of her lungs. Somehow, Lacie managed. "Farmers are the backbone of America. They're true heroes. Why, if it wasn't for the farmers of this great land—"

Without loosening his hold, the man stumbled inside the house, kicked the door closed behind him, and dropped Lacie down on her feet.

"Thank you." She smoothed her gown and straightened the Miss Kansas Summer Squash banner that used to be draped elegantly over one shoulder and was now crushed and twisted. When she was done, she brushed a shiny and sweet-smelling curl of hair as bright and as yellow as the Kansas sun behind her ear. Right before she adjusted her tiara.

"It was kind of you to help me inside." She turned up the wattage on a smile that was known to sway pageant judges from Illinois to the Colorado border and from South Dakota to Oklahoma and beyond.

Maybe the man couldn't see her smile through the gloom. Or maybe he could and he didn't care. Maybe he—unlike so many thousands of others over the years—was just immune.

Whatever the reason, he took a step toward her and Lacie swore she heard him growl with annoyance.

She took a step back. "If you're looking for an autograph," she said, "I could—"

The man took another step in her direction.

And Lacie would have retreated again if the corner of the kitchen countertop hadn't poked her in the back.

Though she was tempted, she refused to let her smile wilt around the edges. It was the only thing keeping her from complete panic right now.

"I've got some eight-by-ten glossies back at the house," she told him. "You know, the usual sort of stuff. Various poses in evening gowns. Even a couple of bathing suit shots, though I'm not especially fond of those. Not to say you shouldn't be. If you are." She looked his way, hoping to see some hint of something in his eyes that would tell her if she was on the right track.

Instead, all she saw was a flash of raw emotion that made her stomach swoop and her heart beat so hard, she was sure they could hear it back in Klaber Falls.

Who could blame a girl for losing control?

When the man took another step nearer and grabbed her left arm, Lacie reacted on nothing but adrenaline, blind impulse, and pure panic.

"Sorry," she said, not because she was particularly, but because she knew it was the proper thing to do.

And a beauty queen was nothing if not proper.

"Sorry, sorry, sorry." And holding tight to her baton, she swung at the man for all she was worth.

It was hard to ignore Miss Kansas Summer Squash.

Especially when she was eighteen feet tall.

With a low whistle, Ben Camaglia slowed his standard-issue sedan to a crawl, pushed his Chicago Cubs baseball cap a little further back on his head, and glanced up at the billboard that dominated this stretch of road between Sutton Springs and Klaber Falls.

"Summer squash à la Lacie...beautiful!"

He read the words written in flowing script above the head of a blonde in a pink evening gown who was holding a bubbling casserole of summer squash in what looked like cream sauce.

"Beautiful is right," Ben mumbled.

He wasn't talking about the summer squash.

Traffic in these parts was pretty much nonexistent, but always careful when it came to the safety of others even though he was notorious for not caring a whole heck of a lot about his own, Ben checked the rearview mirror and pulled the car onto the berm. He stopped, put on the flashers, and punched the gearshift into park, then hit the button for the automatic window. It slid down and at the same time the summer heat poured in and the AC-cooled air gushed out, he propped one elbow on the window frame. He settled back and took a long look across the two-lane blacktop at the woman whose smile was as bright as the sparkling tiara that crowned her head.

Eyes of the same blue as the sapphire earrings he'd once chipped in with his brothers to buy for their mother's September birthday. Lips the exact red of the cherries that grew on the tree outside the front door of his rent-by-the month rooms back in Sutton Springs. Cheeks touched with a splash of color that reminded him of the strawberry milkshake on the menu at the fast food place down the road where he'd stopped for a breakfast sausage sandwich. A body—at least what he could see of it behind the steaming casserole she offered to every single driver who passed by—that was nothing short of perfection.

"Lacie Jo Baxter, Miss Kansas Summer Squash." These words were in smaller letters right there at the place where the casserole ended and the smooth line of one of Lacie's hips showed. Ben read them out loud, automatically comparing what little he knew about Lacie's disappearance with the beautiful young lady who invited drivers to enjoy the bounty of a Kansas summer squash harvest.

And the first small glimmer of hope he'd felt in the last few months started a buzz through his bloodstream.

Before he had a chance to think about it or fantasize about where it all might lead, his cell phone rang and Ben let out a grumble of annoyance. "If it's Wednesday and it's ten-thirty in the morning..."

He grabbed the phone from the empty passenger seat next to him and checked the caller ID. He wasn't surprised to see the familiar number of the Washington office. What did surprise him was when he realized that for the first time in exactly three months, four days, and three hours, he wouldn't mind talking to Ryan Kalinowski.

Smiling in anticipation of a little one-upmanship, Ben punched the little green button on the front of the phone. "Camaglia."

The second of hesitation on the other end was enough to let him know he'd caught Ryan off guard.

"Camaglia?" If Ben needed any more proof, it was there in Ryan's voice. He didn't even try to disguise his skepticism. "You're not supposed to say 'Camaglia' like you're on the job and rarin' to go. You're supposed to say exactly what you've been saying every time I've called you for the last three months. You're supposed to say—"

Ben gave in with a long-suffering sigh. "Kalinowski, you're way too predictable. There. I said it. Happy now?"

Ryan laughed. "Damn straight. And now what I always say is, 'Hey, farm boy, what's been happening?' And you say—"

"'Nothing.' The same nothing that happened last Wednesday and the Wednesday before and the Wednesday before that and—"

"And then what I always say is, 'And what's going to be happening?' And you say—"

"What I've been saying is, 'Not a thing.'"

There was a catch of disbelief in Ryan's voice. "What do you mean, 'What I've been saying.' Don't play games with me, buddy. I didn't get a whole lot of sleep last night."

"And that's my fault?"

"Sort of." Ryan yawned. "You remember Gretchen Harrison, right? She's that—"

"That looker of an ATF agent I introduced you to last Christmas." Ben remembered Gretchen, all right. With a little more time and not a whole lot more effort, Ben was sure he would have had her in his bed before the end of the summer. If only he'd stayed around Washington long enough to give it a little more time.

It might be the first Wednesday morning in three months that he was happy to be talking to Ryan, but that didn't do much for the bitterness that surfaced out of nowhere like the shark in *Jaws*. Just like that hungry fish, this one had teeth and they were plenty sharp. The feeling that cut through Ben's gut had nothing to do with Gretchen Harrison. And everything to do with his life as Ben had once known it.

Naturally, the last thing he was going to do was admit that to Ryan.

"Yeah, I remember Gretchen," Ben told his friend, careful to keep his voice as cool as he was sure his feelings toward Gretchen would have become after the first few hot weeks of hot sex. After all, for all her sultry looks and come-on-like-gangbusters personality, Gretchen wasn't any different from any of the other women he'd met in D.C. or New York or in any of the cities where he'd been assigned. Great when he met them. Fun while it lasted. And never enough of whatever that elusive something was to keep his interest for very long.

With a twitch of his shoulders inside his starched white shirt, Ben got rid of the thought. "Gretchen Harrison, huh? Don't tell me you two are—"

"Officially. As of last night."

"I thought she had better taste than that."

Ryan laughed. "That was when you thought she was hot for you. She came to her senses. Officially. Last night."

"You don't need to rub it in." Exactly why Ryan was doing it, of course. "Get yourself another cup of coffee, my friend, and listen up. I've got things to tell you."

"Got my second cup right here. Consuela's coffee."

Consuela Lopez's coffee was another thing Ben didn't want to think about. The department secretary back in the D.C. office made the most kick-ass coffee on the East Coast. It was a far cry from the watery brew they served at the Morning Star Diner across from Ben's office in Sutton Springs. And another thing he missed about D.C.

The coffee. The women. The chance to actually do something that didn't involve staring out the window of his cramped office. Used to be he could look up from his desk and see the panorama of Washington, D.C., outside his window. Now the only thing he could see when he glanced out his office window was the squat clock tower that looked down on Main Street from the facade of the remodeled convenience store across the street. The one someone with a sick sense of humor or delusions of grandeur had the nerve to call the Sutton Springs Civic Center.

Of course, all that had changed early this morning when he stopped at the Morning Star.

Holding as tightly to the thought as he was to his excitement, Ben flashed another look at the billboard. "So..." He switched his phone from one ear to the other. "Before you decided to take a detour into your sex life and your coffee drinking habits, you were saying..."

"I was saying..." Ryan got himself back on track. "I was saying what you were saying. And what you were saying was, 'What I've been saying.' Those were the words you used, Ben. As in, *What I used to say but I'm not saying anymore because something has changed.* Are you telling me—"

"That I've got a case?" It was Ben's turn to laugh. There

was only so long he could string Ryan along, especially when he was anxious to discuss what was going on. "Damn straight."

Though Ryan may have been surprised, it was obvious he wasn't completely convinced. He chuckled. "What is it? Crop circles? Cow tipping? Or maybe somebody in that sleepy little town is fixing the every Tuesday night Ladies League bingo game?"

"How about a missing person?"

Ben heard the telltale squeak that told him Ryan had sat up in his desk chair like a shot. "No kidding?" The amusement was out of his voice. "It's not a kid, is it? Tell me it's not a kid because when these things involve kids, it makes my insides feel like—"

"I know." Ben could relate. Because when he heard about crimes against kids, his insides felt like that, too. "No kid this time, thank goodness. This time, it's a beauty queen."

There were a couple of seconds of dead air on the other end of the line before Ryan let out a snort of disbelief. "A Miss America type, huh? Give me a break, Camaglia. You can't tell me that out there in the middle of the cornfields—"

"Out here in the middle of the cornfields is one of the most wholesome-looking beauties I've seen in a long time." Ben gave the billboard another look. "Eyes like the summer sky," he said, and because he knew Ryan was a sucker for blondes, he was sure to add, "Hair as golden as an ear of corn. She's good-looking, all right."

"Body?" Ryan's question was as penetrating as Ben knew his eyes would be if they were shaking down an informant.

"Can't see a whole lot of her body," Ben admitted. "She's wearing a pink sort of gown thing. Skinny straps. Cut low in the front..." As if it might help him see what was hidden by the casserole of summer squash in Lacie's hands, he strained for a better look. "But not low enough."

He heard a little gulp of envy from the other end of the phone. Right before Ryan slapped his professionalism firmly back into place. "How much do you know about the woman?"

Ben got himself back on track, too. After all, the sooner he got started, the sooner he'd be finished and with any luck, the sooner he'd be out of Kansas. "What I know about her," he said, "is that she made a personal appearance at the grand opening of a drug store last night."

"Sounds exciting."

"Right." Ben could only imagine, and since it was something he didn't want to do, he went right on. "Never made it home. They found her car this morning, still parked behind the drug store."

"And let me guess, no one saw a thing."

"No one saw a thing. No one heard a thing. And at least according to the folks I talked to this morning, Lacie Jo Baxter doesn't have an enemy in the world. From the girls at the diner to the lady over at the Sutton Springs library who keeps a scrapbook all about Lacie. Everyone says the same things. Bright. Attractive. Well-mannered. Compassionate. Considerate."

"Mother Teresa in an evening gown, huh?"

"Pretty much. You name an adjective, and they used it to describe her."

"But only complimentary adjectives."

"But only complimentary adjectives," Ben conceded. "It's hard for me to believe that someone could dislike her enough to want to hurt her."

"Unless that someone is jealous."

"Or that someone likes her a whole bunch more than he should in a sick and twisted, I'm-a-stalker sort of way."

It was a sobering thought, and not for the first time that morning, Ben turned it in his head and took a look at it from all angles. "It just doesn't add up," he told Ryan and himself. "Not with what I heard from all those people. Lacie's been in beauty pageants for years and she's never had trouble before. Not until last night. Why all of a sudden—"

"The *why* is what you need to figure out."

Ben knew that.

Of course, that didn't make it any easier to work his way through the mess. It also wasn't a reason for him to waste any more time.

He turned the car flashers off and checked his rearview mirror before he eased back onto the road. It was only natural that he take one long, last look at the billboard. What he hadn't anticipated doing was sighing with admiration when he did.

Leave it to Ryan not to miss that little detail. "Hey, you're looking at a picture of her right now, aren't you?" Ryan's curiosity was piqued and Ben knew from long experience that the only thing that would satisfy him was the truth.

"Yep." He raised his window and turned the AC to high. "Looking right at the lady."

"Is she tall?"

Tall was another benchmark that was important to Ryan, and realizing it, Ben laughed.

"She's tall, all right. I'd say about eighteen feet tall."

"Eighteen—" Ryan grumbled a word he probably shouldn't have said at the office. "You've been out in the prairie sun too long, Camaglia."

"You bet I have." At the same time Ben clicked off the call, he hit his accelerator and shot past the billboard. Exactly three months, four days, and three hours too long.

And finally, that was about to end.

Because beautiful or not, dead or alive, Miss Kansas Summer Squash was about to become his ticket out of there.

2

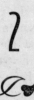

Ben nearly got creamed by a bundt cake.

"Holy—!" He slammed on his brakes just in time to avoid running into a white-haired lady with a chocolate cake in her hands who didn't notice his car. Her head high and a crusading fire in her eyes, she stepped off the curb and hurried across Mapleshade Street.

Just like everyone else in town.

More than a little amazed, Ben looked around. The street was jammed with cars. Even more than he'd ever seen back in Sutton Springs during what folks generously called their rush hour, that fifteen-minute window when the high school started for the day, the feed mill got its morning delivery, and the senior citizens' van dropped its riders for their daily visit to the Food Emporium.

He tried a couple of sharp blasts on the horn. It didn't work. There were cars parked on either side of the street and crowds of people blocking what little room there was to squeeze through. People stood in knots of six or seven, talking. Kids ran back and forth in the street and up across the well-manicured lawns. There was an eager-beaver reporter—notebook in hand and camera over one shoulder—

stationed near a white frame house where cotton-candy-pink geraniums spilled out of window boxes and an American flag hung from a pole on the front porch.

Ben didn't need to check the address. He knew he'd found what he was looking for.

Grumbling, he shoved the gearshift into reverse and backed up until he found an empty parking spot behind a pickup truck filled with straw. He whisked off his Cubs baseball cap and tossed it onto the passenger seat, then combed his fingers through hair that was the same color as the black and bloodred of the aged-to-perfection Chianti his Grandpa DiNardo made in the basement. Grabbing for his suit jacket, he got out of the car.

He locked the door behind him and shrugged into his suit jacket, stopping just short of slamming into an old lady headed down the street carrying an apple pie.

". . . found her car this morning, you know. Right outside Mercer's. That first space nearest the door where I always park when—"

". . . waiting for the phone to ring, I imagine, and knowing her, just losing her mind. Poor dear! Heard she was already asleep and she didn't know—"

". . . not that Dinah would tell her. You know that one. Never a nice thing to say about anyone and especially not about her sister. Why, just last week—"

Ben listened to the bits and pieces of the conversations going on around him while he dodged around women with strollers and old men smoking pipes and even one guy who, though he was within thirty feet of the place, was staring at the Baxter house through a pair of binoculars.

"See anything interesting?"

It was meant as a rhetorical question. That didn't stop the guy with the binoculars from answering. "Nothing," he said, never bothering to put down the binoculars. "Sheriff Thompson arrived about two hours ago and he's been in there ever since but no one's come out and no one's saying a word."

"That means they haven't found her yet."

Even as the words left his mouth Ben wondered if the man noticed how edgy he sounded. Or how hopeful. Had Lacie Baxter returned home? At the same time he waited for the man's answer, he prayed she hadn't. After all, if she was still missing, it meant Ben had a chance to find her.

As if he noticed the undercurrent of expectation in his statement, the man slanted Ben a look. "Guess not."

It wasn't exactly the ringing endorsement Ben was hoping for, but for now it was enough. The thought burning through him the same way the morning sun was heating the back of his neck, he hurried toward the house. He got there just in time to see a sullen young woman break away from the crowd and head into the backyard.

Ben had read a couple of files about the Baxters back at the office. He'd talked to people at the Morning Star earlier that morning. He knew enough to put two and two together, and it didn't take two and two to figure out who the girl was.

Torn jeans. Black T-shirt. A tattoo of something that looked like a cross between a snake and a poorly drawn goat around her right wrist. The girl's hair had been dyed so many times, it was hard to say what color it was. Sort of brown, Ben decided. Kind of purple.

Skirting the crowd, he followed her around to the back of the house. He started talking even before he was all the way up the flower-lined sidewalk that led over to the picnic table where she was perched.

"You must be Dinah."

There was a flicker of some emotion that might have been surprise in her eyes, but she wasn't about to let him know that he'd caught her off guard. "No shit, Sherlock. What was your first clue?"

It was supposed to sound hard-assed. Exactly why Ben chuckled. "I'm taking that for a *yes*." He stopped three feet from Dinah Lynn Baxter, who was doing her best to look tough and sophisticated in an I'll-kick-your-teeth-in sort of way that didn't exactly jibe with the white picket fence or the sunflower wind sock that hung near the back door.

Dinah had porcelain skin, a small nose turned up slightly on the end, a heart-shaped face, and eyebrows that were as ruler-straight as the road Ben had taken from Sutton Springs to Klaber Falls. There was no way she could ever be described as pretty, but she actually might not be bad-looking. If only she'd lose the scowl. And the pack of Virginia Slims she dangled in one hand. Oh, yeah, and the nose ring.

"Some excitement, huh?" The hubbub out front sounded more like a dull roar back here. Ben glanced toward the front of the house. "Nice of all these folks to come out and show that they're worried about your sister."

Dinah shot a look toward the front yard, too. One that would have flash-frozen the citizenry of Klaber Falls had the house not been in the way. "They think they can help with food."

It was the kind of self-defense statement he'd heard from scared kids a hundred times before, and in spite of the tattoo and the cigarettes, Ben realized that Dinah couldn't have been older than twenty. "Sometimes when you're hurting," he told her, "even a little thing like food shows you that other people care."

"Hurting? Is that what you think?" She laughed and showed off her tongue piercing.

Was it supposed to gross him out? Or turn him on?

Ben wasn't sure. He only knew that after all he'd seen in New York and D.C., little girls playing at being gangsta-rap tough didn't exactly send fear into his heart. At least no more fear than the whole America's heartland, amber waves of grain, boring, boring, boring middle-of-nowhere Kansas already had.

"So you're not really worried, huh? About your sister, I mean. Does she drop out of sight often?"

Dinah's top lip curled. "What are you, the FBI?"

"Well, actually, yes." Just to prove the point, Ben reached for the credentials in his back pocket and flashed them in front of Dinah's nose. It was more than a little satisfying to watch the way her eyes widened. She was just a little scared, just as he was counting on, and once he was sure she'd had a good look at his picture ID and gold badge, he tucked them back in his pocket. "You look surprised to see me."

She shrugged, and for the first time, Ben noticed that her T-shirt just happened to be one size too small. The better to show off the fact that she wasn't wearing a bra.

Though he was itching to jump in with both feet and find out exactly what Dinah knew about where her sister might be and who she might be with, Ben knew the approach wouldn't work. Not with Dinah. Instead, he leaned back against the picnic table. "I figured all those folks out front might be well-intentioned, but they don't really know anything. That's why I followed you back here. I'm hoping you can tell me something about what happened last night."

Dinah ripped open the pack of cigarettes and picked one out with two reddish-brown fingernails. She propped the cigarette between her lips and got a thirty-five-cent disposable lighter out of the back pocket of her JC Penney jeans. "I wasn't here last night," she said, daring him to ask where she was instead of at home. When he didn't give her the satisfaction, she flicked the lighter and hauled in a lungful of smoke. She let it out slowly. Right in Ben's direction.

"Did you talk to your sister at all before she left the house? About where she was going? Who she was going to see?"

She wrinkled her nose in what might have been a childlike expression but for the silver ring that glinted from her left nostril. "Did you?"

"Obviously not. Why? Do you think if I did, she'd tell me something interesting?"

"Only if you're interested in mascara and shampoo and

how many fat grams there are in a cheeseburger. You're not, are you? Interested in mascara and shampoo, I mean. I mean, I know the Army, they have that don't ask, don't tell policy. But I figure you cop types—" she gave him the kind of thorough once-over that would have made a lesser man squirm. "Well, they wouldn't exactly want any fags in the FBI, would they?"

They would have a talk some other time about being politically correct—not to mention socially tolerant. For now, Ben returned her look with one penetrating enough to make her glance away. "So I guess what you're saying is that you don't have anything to tell me." It wasn't a question and he didn't wait for an answer. He knew she'd never answer a direct question, so he pushed off from the picnic table and walked toward the back door.

He was halfway there when he heard Dinah reply anyway. Just as he expected she would.

"Leave it to Lacie," she said, and Ben glanced over his shoulder just in time to see her hop off the picnic table. The lot next door to the Baxters' was empty, and behind it, he could see the street that ran parallel to Mapleshade. A late-model pickup turned the corner on two wheels and squealed to a stop, and the young driver revved his engine as a signal to Dinah that he was waiting.

"How much you want to bet that her picture is on the front page of the paper this morning?"

It wasn't. Ben had already checked.

He didn't bother to tell Dinah, mostly because it was pretty obvious that she didn't care but also because she cut across the backyard and disappeared before he could. Looked like Dinah's mind was pretty much traveling in the same direction as Ben's. For all different reasons.

Though Lacie's picture didn't grace the front page of this morning's paper, he had no doubt that it would tomorrow. After all, the disappearance of a local celebrity had it all over the usual kind of news he'd seen in the Sutton Springs *Intel-*

ligencer for the last three months: Who was visiting whom from out of town. Whose prize bull was breeding with whose blue-ribbon cow. What recipes would make the family sit up and take notice at the dinner table. How many different kinds of chicken feed were on special at the grain store.

A missing beauty queen was way more interesting.

And the federal agent who found her would get just as much press. With any luck at all, Ben's picture would be on the front page of the paper sometime soon, too.

Once it was, he would send a copy of it and the details of his investigation back to headquarters in D.C. And somebody there would realize that they had made a big mistake when they relegated him to a one-man field office where the only fields in sight were filled with corn, soybeans, and summer squash. And the Powers That Be would forget this ridiculous lesson they were trying to teach him.

And call him back to the land of the living.

The thought sparked a thrill of anticipation. And the first glimmer of hope he'd seen in a very dark tunnel that was already three months long.

"Don't get ahead of yourself, Camaglia." Ben took a deep breath, reminding himself that the *get ahead of himself* part was what had landed him in Kansas in the first place. Just so he wouldn't forget, he told himself to count slowly to ten.

By the time he got to three, he was already knocking on the back door.

"Shit!"

Dinah jerked open the truck door and hopped inside. Too bad if her language offended Miss Winston, who was standing out on her front porch craning her neck to see what was happening at the Baxters'. Miss Winston couldn't hear much of anything, anyway. And Dinah wasn't about to curb her tongue just to keep some cranky-assed old lady happy. A bad day had just turned way worse, and if there was one thing Dinah knew, it was that the only way to deal with the *worse* part was to let the world know how she was feeling. Better to do that than fall into the every-cloud-has-a-silver-lining bullshit trap her sister was always preaching.

She slammed the door closed behind her and punched her fist against the imitation leather seat. "Shit! Do you know who that is?"

Wiley Burnside looked over his shoulder and under the gun rack that hung in the back window so that he could see across Miss Winston's yard. "Who?" He glanced at Dinah out of the corner of his eye. He wasn't about to argue or ask why she was talking crazy. Three years of dating Dinah had taught him to choose his words—and his fights—carefully. Dinah Baxter might be the hottest little honey in the state of Kansas, but she was nobody's fool.

"Ain't nobody there." Wiley gave her the little one-sided smile that always made her heart beat faster and her insides turn to mush. At least when she wasn't totally pissed. "Didn't see anybody when I pulled up, either," he told her. "Who you talking about?"

Dinah twisted in her seat. When she left, the guy in the suit had been headed toward the back door. There was no sign of him now. "He must have gone inside." She turned around and plopped back in her seat, her brain working furiously over the problem. "And shit.... Shit, Wiley, he's an FBI agent."

"FBI!" Wiley sat up and looked back at the Baxter house. "FBI? Dinah, are you telling me there's an FBI agent—"

"In my house. Right now. That's exactly what I'm telling you. He's looking for Lacie."

"Of course." Wiley's jaw was rigid, his spine was straight. He was over six feet tall and when he sat up like that, his shaved head brushed the inside roof of the truck.

Wiley had the handsomest face, the widest shoulders, and the sexiest brown eyes this side of Oklahoma. That—along with the fact that he was so hot in bed, she sometimes wondered if she'd need to be hosed down—was just part of the reason Dinah was nuts about him. Wiley wasn't afraid of anyone or anything, and that was a big turn-on, too. She'd seen him go up against muscle-bound Buddy Folsome in a bar fight. She'd seen him outrace Sheriff Thompson's cruiser even before he souped up the truck engine back at Carson's Garage, where he worked. She'd even seen Wiley manage not to barf when her sister was being her bone-headed, old-fashioned, corny self.

She should have known that a little inconvenience like having an FBI agent in town wasn't enough to make her Wiley shake in his work boots. Of course, that didn't keep him from giving the Baxter house another long look. "You don't think—"

"That he's on to us?" Dinah laughed. It was better than admitting that when the guy flashed his badge and she caught a glimpse of the gun he was wearing in a shoulder holster under his suit jacket, she got a little worried, too.

"No way," she told Wiley and herself. "He's looking for Lacie, and from the questions he asked, he doesn't have a clue where she is. But, shit, it's the last thing we need. Some FBI agent snooping around and asking questions and, hell, doing I don't know what else. We don't need him getting in our way."

"Maybe he's asking questions because he's playing dumb. You know, trying to catch us off guard." Wiley drummed his fingers against the steering wheel in a rhythm that reminded Dinah of the drumbeat in her favorite Godsmack song. For the first time, she realized her heart was pounding to the same furious drumming.

No surprise there. She and Wiley were like one soul in two bodies.

Wiley chewed on his lower lip. "Maybe we should just forget the whole thing."

"What!" Dinah sat up like a shot. Love him or not, she could have done some major damage to Wiley at that moment. She would have, too, if she hadn't remembered the stupid saying she'd heard Lacie use more times than she cared to remember: You catch more flies with honey than with vinegar.

For all her faults, maybe Lacie was on to something.

It wasn't easy, but Dinah tucked away her anger. It was a little less hard to scoot closer to Wiley. Closer to Wiley was one place she never got tired of being.

She skimmed one finger up and down his right arm and over the series of tattoos that marched from where the short sleeve of his black T-shirt ended down to his wrist. She brushed a tiger with only one ear and a lopsided mouth. She whirled a feather-light touch over a half-done American eagle that even to her looked a little like Barney the Dinosaur on a really bad day. She tapped a fingertip against an elaborate heart outlined in red where the letters of her name— the *D* and the *I* bigger than the rest because they wouldn't all fit—proclaimed Wiley's love for all the world to see.

"You don't really mean that," she told him, daring him with a sexy glance and a quick kiss, to contradict her. "You wouldn't—"

"I wouldn't. I mean, not normally. You know I wouldn't." He twitched her hand away and chewed his lip again. "But, Jesus, Dinah, we're not talking about stupid Sheriff Thompson or that no-brain deputy, Clete Harter. This guy's the real deal. We're talking the FBI."

Pouting was for girls who were too moronic to know how to use their heads at times like this. Girls like Lacie. Dinah gave it a try anyway. She leaned forward, too, so that her breasts brushed against Wiley's arm.

"I won't be the real deal," she said, her voice as low and husky as when she had Wiley in bed and was making him crazy by talking dirty. "I'll never be the real deal, Sugar Lips." She tickled a finger along his thigh and over to the button fly of his jeans. "Not without your help."

Wiley glanced down when Dinah popped the top button

out of its hole. He swallowed hard. "And I want to help," he said. "You know I do. You know I'd do anything for you."

"Anything?" Another button and another quick breath from Wiley. One that caught in his throat when she slipped her hand inside his jeans. She smiled at the way he hardened the second she touched him, but as much as she enjoyed teasing him, she knew Wiley well enough to know exactly when to pull away.

"I don't think you mean that, Wiley Burnside." Dinah sat back. Just like she was counting on, Wiley looked a little dazed and confused. And a whole lot disappointed, too. "If you meant it . . . if you really meant it, you wouldn't let something like one little FBI agent scare you away."

"But if he—"

"If he what? What if he sees us together? What if he follows us around? That wouldn't prove anything, would it? And besides, if he's so busy looking for Lacie, he won't have time to pay any attention to us." Just so he knew she wasn't kidding, Dinah opened the truck door and turned, ready to get out.

"You wouldn't leave me here like this, would you?"

She stopped and pretended to reconsider.

"I would . . . I will . . . if you're going to let this guy scare you away from what you promised you would do." She glanced over her shoulder to where Wiley was weighing his options. If he loved her as much as he said he did—and Wiley said he loved her very much—there never really was a question about which one he would choose. "Are you, Wiley? Are you going to let this guy get to you?"

Wiley edged closer. "I'll let you get to me, Snuggle Bunny."

He knew she couldn't resist. Not when he called her Snuggle Bunny.

But that didn't mean she was going to fold.

Dinah looked away. "That's not what I need to hear, Wiley."

He leaned across her, closed the door, and moved her hand onto his lap. "What is it you need to hear?" he asked, his words no more than a growl against her lips.

"I need to hear . . ." He nipped a little kiss against her bottom lip, and Dinah reminded herself that she couldn't get distracted. Not yet. Not until she got exactly what she wanted.

She braced her hands against Wiley's shoulders and pushed him away. "I need to hear that we're not going to let this stop us, Wiley. We can be careful. And we can be smart. This guy doesn't have to get in our way."

Wiley pressed her back against the seat and unzipped her jeans. "And if you hear that?" he asked.

"If I get what I want, then you get what you want."

"Deal." Wiley grinned and got ready to settle himself over her.

Dinah stopped him dead in his tracks with one look. "Except that I haven't heard it yet," she told him.

He gave in with a sigh. "I told you I'd help you, Snuggle Bunny." Wiley inched her jeans down over her hips. "And I will." He tugged the elastic band of her hot-pink panties down. "And nothing—and no one—is going to stop me."

Dinah didn't have one ounce of doubt that he meant what he said. But she wasn't about to take chances. Not when it came to something this important. "Wiley!" When he leaned in nice and close to kiss her, she grabbed his chin and looked him in the eye. "I'm not kidding about this, Wiley," she told him, her voice as steely as it had been soft and sexy only a couple of minutes earlier. "If you screw me—"

"Oh, Snuggle Bunny! That's exactly what I want to do!" When Wiley laughed, Dinah couldn't help herself. She realized what she'd said and she laughed, too. Right before she let him do what she'd wanted him to do all along.

There wasn't a better way that she could think of to seal a deal, and a deal was what they'd made, even if Wiley didn't realize it.

After all, Wiley was a guy, and all he realized was that he was getting what he wanted.

Dinah was a woman, and a woman knew better than that. A woman knew that sometimes you had to use a little brains and a lot of sex to get where you wanted to go.

As for Miss Winston, she was so busy still trying to figure out what was going on at the Baxters', she didn't realize anything at all.

Not even when the pickup parked in front of her house started to rock.

3

"The FBI? Really? You're from the FBI?"

Ben did his best not to sigh with exasperation. It wasn't easy. There wasn't any way he could explain things much clearer, and the realization that Krissie Baxter didn't understand was enough to grate on what little patience he had.

Which wasn't a whole lot.

He looked across the kitchen table to where Lacie's mother sat with a coffee mug clutched in one hand and reminded himself to be easy on her. After all, the woman's daughter was missing. And if the redness in her eyes and the nearly raw spot under her nose meant anything, Krissie wasn't taking the news any differently than any other parent would. Krissie was closing in on forty-five, but it was clear from one glance that she wasn't about to surrender to middle age without a fight. She was wearing a pink tank top that made the most of her perky breasts and a neck that was long and elegant. Her jeans were form-fitting enough to show off a too-thin body. Her nails were painted a color that perfectly matched her shirt.

Krissie's hair was almost the exact shade of Lacie's sunny yellow curls, and at the same time that Ben wondered if the color came right out of a bottle, he reminded himself that he didn't know enough about women's hair to say. He also didn't know a whole heck of a lot about hairstyles, but if he had to guess, he'd say Krissie had what was called "big hair." Poufed out at the top. Flipped at the shoulders. Wide as the big blue eyes that looked at him with a mixture of confusion and concern.

"FBI." This time, Ben said it carefully, just to make sure she understood. "I'll be coordinating the search for your daughter from here on in. On my way over here, I called the State Highway Patrol. They've agreed to call a volunteer search-and-rescue organization and—"

"But Eddie...that is, Sheriff Thompson...He told me he had everything under control. He's already been over at Mercer's. That's where we were last night, you know. Me and Lacie. Oh, God!" Krissie sniffed, and touched a lace-edged handkerchief to her eyes. "I never should have left before she did. But I had things to do and...and they found Lacie's car, you know. Sheriff Thompson, he was looking for clues."

It was an argument Ben had expected. "I'm sure the sheriff is doing a fine job." Dimes to donuts, he wasn't, but this wasn't the time to tell Krissie Baxter that. Ben had run into the local sheriff a time or two, and his first impressions were not positive. Thompson was overworked, understaffed, and from what Ben could tell, anything but a stickler for procedure.

The thought that some hick sheriff had a head start on the investigation was enough to add a thread of urgency to Ben's voice. The realization that that same hick sheriff might actually find Lacie before Ben did sealed the deal.

"This isn't the kind of thing a local sheriff is used to dealing with," he told Krissie. "That's why I'm taking over. Case in point: When I called, it was the first the Highway Patrol had heard of Lacie's disappearance and—meaning no disrespect, ma'am—but it's something your Sheriff Thompson should have thought to do first thing. Thanks to my call, they've agreed to send in a team to help. Two helicopters should be here—" he checked his watch, "in just under three hours. And later this afternoon, the search-and-rescue dogs will be arriving from Kansas City along with their handlers."

"Dogs and the FBI? My goodness!" Krissie gave a watery laugh and pressed one hand to her heart. "Color me impressed. You came all the way over here this morning? Just to take care of all this for us? You must have flown in from Topeka or something."

Ben swallowed his pride along with the explanation he didn't have the time—or the inclination—to provide. "Actually, ma'am," he told her, "I didn't need to come nearly that far. My office is in Sutton Springs."

Krissie tipped her head to one side. "Sutton Springs? I didn't know there were FBI agents in Sutton Springs."

"I'm the only one," he told her, and before she could ask for details he didn't want to provide, he added, "I'll be in charge of—"

"They've got him set up there across from the Civic Center."

Apparently, Sheriff Eddie Thompson was enough of a fixture around the Baxter household not to stand on ceremony. He strolled in from the hallway that led from the living room, and headed straight for the coffeepot. "Thought I mentioned it, Krissie. A couple months ago. Agent Camaglia here, he's got an office up there over Zelda McCrea's place."

Zelda's Golden Comb was something Ben didn't want to think about. Not now or ever. Thanks to Zelda and three months of day-in-and-day-out in the cramped and stuffy office above her beauty parlor, he could swear the smell of permanent solution was in everything from his file folders to his six-hundred-dollar suits. As for the troop of elderly ladies who swarmed him whenever he left the office, armed with stories about their granddaughters and nieces who were "just right" for him . . .

Well, that was another reason he needed to get to the bottom of Lacie Baxter's disappearance. Fast.

The sooner he found her, the sooner he could be hailed as the hero of Sutton County, Kansas.

And that meant the sooner he could bid the place farewell.

Reminding himself that there was a chance—however slim—that Sheriff Thompson might actually help him attain that goal, Ben leaned back against the sunny yellow kitchen countertop and watched the sheriff pour his coffee. On his way to the table, Thompson got a carton of half-and-half out of the refrigerator and grabbed the sugar bowl out of a cupboard. He made himself at home in the chair next to Krissie's, his khaki uniform a contrast to her brightly colored top.

Thompson was twenty years older than Ben, was a whole head shorter, and outweighed him by at least sixty pounds. His hair was nearly gone, and even this early in the morning, with the summer heat settling over Klaber Falls like a thick batting of wet cotton, Thompson's high forehead gleamed in the morning light.

He flicked away a bead of sweat and added two spoons of sugar to his coffee. "I've got everything under control here, Ben. You see, that's why I didn't bother to call you this morning and ask for your help." Thompson glanced up from stirring his coffee. The look said more than words. Things like, *Don't need it, don't want it.* "Surprised you made the trip all the way over here for nothing."

It wasn't a game Ben liked to play, but he wasn't about to back down. If Thompson knew enough about him to know he was chomping at the bit in the office above the Golden Comb, he might as well also know that Ben wasn't about to miss this opportunity to dodge the hair spray and the blue-haired ladies. Not to mention the boring-as-hell monotony of three months of inactivity.

"If what I hear is true, your *nothing* might really be something," he reminded the sheriff. "Unless you found something over at Mercer's that proves otherwise, no one knows where Miss Baxter is. I don't want to worry you prematurely, ma'am—" he glanced at Krissie, "but we do have to consider the possibility that she was kidnapped. And after all . . ." Ben raised his eyebrows and shifted his gaze to the sherrif. Just so Thompson wouldn't forget that, like it or not, there were places where local jurisdiction ended. And federal took over. "Kidnappings are us."

"Kidnapping." Thompson waved away the word as if it were nothing more annoying than one of the king-sized mosquitoes that inhabited these parts. "Ain't exactly a kidnapping as far as I can tell. Not yet, anyway."

"As far as I can tell, we don't want to take the chance to find out too late that it is. We need to get organized. And co-ordinated."

"And there are going to be dogs! And helicopters!" Krissie grasped one of the sheriff's arms in both her hands. "I'm so thankful, Eddie. With all the commotion and all the publicity, you're bound to get some leads."

The press was something else Ben didn't want to think about. Bad enough he had to worry about Thompson and his deputy scooping him on the case. Worse if some small-town reporter found Lacie first and stole all the glory.

Still, whether he liked the idea of the press butting in on his case or not, he owed Krissie what comfort he could offer.

"Don't worry about the publicity," he told her. "You're right, sometimes it can actually help. Publicity gets people talking. It might be just what we need to break a case like this."

"Worry? About publicity?" Wiping a hand across her cheeks to banish her tears, Krissie popped out of her chair and tried her best to look brave. "You don't know us Baxter women, Agent Camaglia. Publicity is second nature to us, like breathing in good, clean Kansas air. Wherever Lacie is, I know she has her priorities straight." Krissie's lower lip quivered, her voice shook. "Wherever she is, I'm sure she's thinking the same thing."

It was on the tip of Ben's tongue to tell her he only hoped that Lacie was alive to think it, and only years of ingrained training kept his mouth shut. That, and the knowledge that if there was one thing Ben had learned in the last few months, it was that free speech was never really free.

Before he could say another word, a noise like a roar came from out front. Something that sounded like a cheer. And applause.

"Lacie!" Krissie pivoted toward the sound but Ben made it to the door between the kitchen and the dining room first. At a trot, he headed down the long hallway that cut the house in two and punched open the screen door that led out to the front porch. He was just in time to see the crowd gathered in the Baxter front yard part like the Red Sea in front of Moses. A second later, he saw what the excitement was all about.

As if the move had been choreographed by a pageant producer eager to milk the drama out of each and every moment, Lacie Jo Baxter walked to the spot where the sidewalk met the flower-lined pathway that led up to the Baxter house. Apparently not surprised by the crowd, she paused for a couple of seconds, hauling in deep breaths of the humid air while she got her bearings.

And her balance.

Lacie was wearing one shoe with a broken heel and carrying the other one in her hand. The effect was a little off-putting, and Ben cocked his head, trying to get some perspective at the same time he sized up the woman who'd thrown Sutton County into an uproar.

Miss Kansas Summer Squash might actually be as pretty in person as she was on her billboards. Right now, it was a little hard to tell.

Lacie's face was smeared with dirt, Her hair was a mess. It was dotted with blades of grass and sprinkled with bits of hay and what looked like pieces of cornstalks. A rhinestone tiara sat atop it all at a cockeyed angle.

What had once been a beauty queen banner hung over one shoulder in shreds. Kind of like the right strap of her once-sparkling evening gown, which drooped over one arm and dragged down the front of her dress just enough to hint at breasts that were even perkier than her mother's.

At the same time Ben blasted himself for giving in to sensations that had no place in an investigation, he knew there was no way to fight the thought. Beauty pageants were all about flesh, weren't they? A guy couldn't help but be pulled in by the fantasy.

No doubt she knew that every eye in the crowd was on her. Lacie sniffed and wiped her cheeks. Using one end of her baton, she straightened her tiara and pasted a smile as wide as the prairie sun on her face. Shoulders back, she headed up the sidewalk as if it were a runway in the spotlight.

"Lacie!" Over the noise of the crowd's deafening cheer, Ben heard the catch in Krissie's voice. Before he even had a chance to move, Krissie elbowed her way around him and sprinted down the front steps to meet her daughter.

It was a classic Kodak Moment that made the entire crowd hold its collective breath. And a couple of them cry.

Ben didn't like to think of himself as a softie, but the meeting might have touched a tender chord even in him except that the first thing Krissie did was take the baton out of Lacie's hand. And replace it with a hairbrush.

"Not the back." Krissie fluffed the hair over her daughter's shoulders. "Forget about the back, the back is fine. It's the front . . ." She plucked the brush from Lacie's hands and combed her bangs.

"Lipstick?"

The question from Lacie brought a curt nod from Krissie.

Like a well-trained team of synchronized swimmers going through their routine, they worked without a hitch.

At the same time Lacie beamed a smile toward the photographer who fought his way to the front of the crowd, she slanted a look at the tube of lipstick her mother held out to her. "Not the coral. Cotton-candy–pink, I think. With the daylight and the color of my dress and—"

"Speaking of that—" Krissie stepped back for a better look and clicked her tongue. "You're a fright!" She provided the right color of lipstick, nodded her approval when Lacie applied it, and yanked the drooping gown strap up on Lacie's shoulder. "Everyone was just worried sick. Eddie's here. And—"

"Blush." Lacie held out one hand and Krissie slapped the appropriate item into it. She touched the blush to her cheeks, and if she realized she was putting it over a layer of dirt that went from her right ear all the way across her nose, she didn't let that stop her. Just as she handed the compact and one shoe to Krissie and got the baton back in exchange, an elderly man with a hearing aid stuck out a hand and Lacie took it and gave it a squeeze. A woman who didn't look much older than Lacie darted forward and crushed her in a hug, and Lacie hugged her back and thanked her for coming.

The hugs and kisses and well wishes were repeated all the way to the front porch. Once they arrived, Lacie climbed two of the steps and waited until Krissie was standing beside her. As one, they turned to where the reporter with the camera was waiting for the perfect photo op. They linked their arms. They tipped their heads. They smiled.

"Tell us, Lacie!" As soon as he was done with another few quick photos, Jeff Parkman, the reporter from the *Intelligencer*, flung the camera over his shoulder and reached for a pad of paper. "Tell us everything that happened, Lacie. It will make a great page-one story!"

"Oh, no!" Even if Ed Thompson didn't look like he was going to move a muscle to stop it, Ben knew better than to let things get that far out of hand. The last thing this or any other investigation needed was to have its details spilled to the press before they could be carefully considered by law enforcement. In this case, that law enforcement was him, and the details were something he didn't want to share. Not until he knew what he was dealing with.

In one fluid movement, he reached down, took hold of Lacie's elbow, and tugged her up the steps. Still, the crowd was calling for a speech and Krissie was directing Jeff Parkman as to which angle would provide the most flattering photo of Lacie.

And Ben wasn't about to get entangled in the circus.

"Inside," he said, nudging Lacie toward the house.

"But I—" Lacie looked to her mother for help.

"This is Agent Ben Camaglia." Krissie provided the information at the same time she stepped aside to give Jeff a clear shot. On cue, Lacie turned her head and gave Jeff a smile bright enough to charm the birds out of the trees. "He's with the FBI and—"

"And he's talking to you before anyone else does." Before things could get even more out of hand than they already were, Ben opened the screen door. Propping it with his foot, he let Lacie step inside ahead of him, and before anyone could get any ideas about how public their talk was going to be, he closed the door and locked it behind him.

Lacie had always thought of FBI agents as grim old bureaucrats with gray hair, skinny ties, and horn-rimmed glasses.

Agent Ben Camaglia definitely did not fit the mold.

Old?

Not a chance. Ben was just a couple of years older than she was.

As for the skinny tie and the horn-rimmed glasses...

She did a quick once-over and gave Ben's fashion sense a mental thumbs-up. He was wearing shined-to-within-an-inch-of-their-lives shoes that appealed to her love of cleanliness, and an Italian silk tie splashed with red and yellow that told her he had a flair for style and wasn't afraid of color. His suit was expensive and so well cut, the likes of it hadn't been seen in Klaber Falls in a long while. At least not since the Reverend Teddy Pawtuck (now serving time in a federal penitentiary) came through town with his message of salvation, his fifty-member Praise and Hallelujah Gospel Choir, and one hand dipped into the donations that were supposed to be for a mission in India but turned out to be the down payment on a sumptuous house in Bel Air instead.

Ben's eyes were temptingly brown. His hair was an even darker shade. His haircut (too short around the ears and a tad too long in the back) didn't exactly jibe with the designer suit or the Continental tie until Lacie recognized the handiwork of Gib Allen from over at the Sutton Springs Main Street Barber Shop.

His haircut might have come straight from the county seat, but there was no mistaking Ben's aftershave. Lacie drew in a long breath and felt the incredible scent go right to her head. If she was any judge of fashion, it was Prestige, the latest from one of the up-and-coming New York designers, and it smelled every bit as expensive as the glossy ads in *GQ* made it look.

Though he was no muscle-bound Arnold, Ben was a tad over six feet tall, athletic enough to carry his weight, and obviously, no pushover. Apparently not everyone knew that. His nose had been broken a time or two; there was a funny little hump at the bridge of it that made it look like it was set a little crooked on his face.

Body. Face. Style.

It was a package impossible to resist, and for a moment, Lacie had trouble catching her breath.

Old, gray, and grim?

Hardly.

Except for the grim part.

Ben had that part down pat.

He was also keeping her from her public.

"Excuse me!" Her voice was honey. The smile she aimed

at Ben had been known to melt male hearts—not to mention their resolve—at twenty feet.

It didn't work.

She could tell, because Ben still looked as cheerful as a thundercloud. He also hadn't let go of her arm.

Lacie hid an exasperated sigh behind a sweet-as-sugar smile and a flutter of eyelashes.

"Those people are waiting for me." Just so he didn't miss her message, she gave the front door a pointed look. "Out there. Not in here. And they've been nice enough to be patient and orderly. I owe them an explanation."

"Not before you give one to me."

It was remarkably insensitive, and Lacie couldn't help herself, bad manners always rubbed her the wrong way.

"Really? You? Before them?" She looked into the living room, where a luxuriant bouquet of pink roses (Krissie's favorite) sat on a lace-covered table along with two teddy bears with "Thinking of You" balloons in their furry hands, a box of chocolates, and a single carnation in a bud vase. She glanced the other way toward the dining room, where the oak table was covered with casserole dishes, cakes, a platter of cookies, and no less than three cherry pies.

"Did you bring pies?" she asked him. "Or flowers?" There was an arrangement of snapdragons and zinnias—straight from someone's garden—on the buffet in the dining room. Another one—marigolds Lacie could smell all the way over here—on the table in front of the dining room window. "Did you make fried chicken, Agent Camaglia? Because I know Mary Brown did. I see one of her Tupperware containers right over there. And it looks like Betty Morris came through with her cream cheese brownies. I'd recognize her Pyrex baking dish anywhere. These people brought all this here to make my mother feel better. And they waited for me for God knows how long. They came all this way and they waited and—"

"They can wait a little longer."

"But they brought food!" Didn't the man know anything about how neighbors helped neighbors? Baffled, Lacie shook her head and a sprinkle of grass rained down on her shoulders. "Where are you from, anyway?" she asked him.

It was a question he wasn't expecting. Ben's eyes narrowed just a little bit. His mouth thinned. He stepped back far enough to give her a quick look and his glance landed on the baton she was still carrying in her right hand. "Not someplace where the locals are entertained by a little baton twirling. Is that what your public—" his gaze homed in on the front door. "Is that what they're waiting for?"

Was that a little bit of high-and-mightiness she heard in his voice? A little bit of condescension?

It wasn't the first time she'd run into it. And this time— like the time the opera-singing Miss Sunflower contestant sneered and the time her ballet-dancing Miss Sweet Corn rival smirked and the time the girl who wanted to be Valentine's Kissing Queen came right out and laughed—Lacie wasn't about to be drawn in by the pettiness. This time—like all those times—she knew she'd come out a winner.

The smile Lacie aimed Ben's way was as warm as those two teddy bears in the living room. And just as fuzzy. "Like most decent people, what those people outside are waiting for is word that someone they know and care about is safe. If I need to do a little baton twirling to prove to them that I'm okay, then that's what I'll do. Maybe where you come from—"

"I come from Chicago originally. I've worked in Cleveland. And New York. And D.C."

It explained the suit. And the tie. And the attitude. "Then you must consider yourself very lucky to have finally landed in a place as wonderful as Klaber Falls."

Though she couldn't have known it, these were the magic words. Ben dropped his hand and moved far enough away to give Lacie a little breathing room.

"Oh, yeah, I'm lucky, all right," he said, and only a moron

could have thought he actually meant it. "I'm the luckiest guy I know. I'd be even luckier if you'd quit beating around the bush and tell me what happened last night. Unless nothing happened and that whole crazy scene out there was staged so you could get your picture on the front page of the local paper."

The accusation was so far out in left field, Lacie sucked in a breath of surprise. "Is that what you think? Great! Now all you have to do is tell that to the Incredible Hulk who grabbed me outside of Mercer's and tossed me into the trunk of his car."

"You're telling me it was a kidnapping?"

"Since I'm standing here right now, I'd say it was more like an attempted kidnapping."

"And since you're standing here right now, Ms. Baxter, you're the logical place for me to start my investigation. I can't do that until you stop wasting my time."

Lacie spun around and headed for the stairs that led up to the second floor. "Wasting your time, huh? Looks to me like you can't start your investigation until you talk to me. And you know what, Agent Camaglia? I'll talk to you when I'm good and ready to talk."

"And that will be . . . ?"

The steel in his voice brought her spinning around. Anybody else might have been intimidated by the determination in Ben's eyes. Or the stubborn line of his chin. Anybody else might have been bullied when he put one hand on his hip and nudged his suit jacket back just far enough for her to see the gun in his shoulder holster.

That was enough to make up Lacie's mind.

She drew in a deep breath and let it out slowly. Right before she gave him a smile that would have knocked any other man's socks off.

"That will be after I've taken a shower," she told him. "After I've washed my hair and given myself a hot oil treatment. Do you know how many hair follicles are lost when—"

"Hold on a minute!" He climbed the stairs and stationed himself two steps below where she stood. At that angle, they were just about eye-to-eye. "You can't just disappear for a couple of hours. Not until I have some facts to go on. Not when I'm sitting here spinning my wheels. You said it was a kidnapping; prove it."

"Prove it?" Lacie glanced down at her mud-spattered gown, her tattered banner, the Perfectly Pink nail polish that was so chipped, it wasn't nearly perfect anymore. "You think I usually look like this?"

If he was smart, he would have let the subject drop. Instead, Ben lifted his chin just a fraction of an inch. Enough to make him look more intimidating than ever.

"Well, if it was an attempted kidnapping," he said, "and if your kidnapper was a big guy, explain this to me. How does a woman who's—" he gave her a thorough look, his gaze sliding from her face and briefly to the décolletage revealed by her gown. From there, he glided the look to her hips and back up again. "What are you? Five-seven, one hundred and fifteen pounds?" Another quick look. "No muscles to speak of and obviously, no weapon. Tell me, how does a featherweight in a tight gown and high-heeled shoes manage to escape from a guy like that?"

"How?" Lacie headed up the rest of the stairs. There was plenty of room on the landing at the top of the steps, and when she got there, she did a showy spin and a couple of well-timed dance steps. She gave her baton a twirl, tossed it so that it just missed the ceiling, and caught it in one hand.

She looked down at Ben and grinned. "Let's just say there are a couple of other things a baton is good for besides twirling."

4

Nobody was as perfect as Lacie Baxter. Not for real.

Okay, so the thought was a little cyncial. Ben admitted that much. Just like he admitted that he couldn't help thinking it.

Even before he'd decided to make a career of law enforcement, he wasn't a guy who thought the world was all bright and sunny, sweetness and light. Sure, there were great things everywhere. Family. Friends. Career. The occasional woman who hooked his interest and snared his heart for as long as it lasted. The fact that it never lasted very long.

But he knew there was a flip side, too. Life could be messy. And sometimes, ugly. Anybody with a brain—and cable TV—knew that.

Six years of working with the FBI had done nothing to disprove the theory.

In his time with the feds, Ben had seen everything from skirting-the-edge-of-the-law dishonesty to out-and-out, throw-it-in-your-face corruption. These days, none of it surprised him. Not the lies. Or the cheating. Not the stealing. Or the callous disregard for human life.

Perfection, however, shocked the hell out of him.

Keeping fifteen feet behind her at the Food Emporium, Ben watched Lacie—perfectly dressed in a perfect little black skirt and a perfect sunny-yellow sleeveless top that perfectly matched her hair—maneuver her grocery cart around a display of snack foods and over to where the canned soup was stacked in orderly rows. On her way, she stopped to talk to a weary-looking lady with pink rollers in her hair, and though they kept their voices down and Ben couldn't catch the drift of the conversation, whatever Lacie said, it was—no doubt—perfect. By the time they were done and the woman turned toward the bakery department, she was humming a bit of a tune.

Lacie headed toward Dairy. She smiled at a pimply-faced stockboy and the kid blushed as red as the apron he wore. She stopped, perfectly composed, and waited for a guy in overalls who—between his shopping cart and his size fifty-eight waist—took up most of the aisle. A can in each hand, he weighed the pros and cons of one brand of value-priced coffee against another and grumbled under his breath about how things used to cost less. And taste better.

"Hello, John!"

The cheery greeting from Lacie made the guy look up, and once he met the perfect smile and those perfect blue eyes, he never stood a chance. John's frown dissolved in an instant. Ice melting in the summer sun. He moved his cart to the side and let Lacie pass.

Watching it all in wonder, Ben tossed a couple of bags of potato chips and a bag of corn chips into his cart. It would have been nice to include a jar of salsa, just to shake up his Midwestern meat-and-potatoes diet a little, but as he'd discovered three months earlier, Sutton County folks weren't exactly a salsa sort of crowd.

Resigning himself to the fact, Ben reached for a jar of cheese dip.

When Lacie started up again and headed past the frozen

foods, he added a couple of pizzas (double pepperoni, peppers, extra cheese) to his cart and followed.

They actually might have gotten wherever it was they were headed in something like normal time if Lacie hadn't encountered a young woman carrying a baby. There was a toddler in her shopping cart and another, just-a-little-older child trailing behind her. Once she had them settled and had handed out peanut butter crackers to keep the two older ones quiet, she proceded to pull out not one but three envelopes of pictures. She showed each and every snapshot to Lacie, and each and every time, Lacie asked the perfect question.

"I haven't seen Laura in ages. How is she?"

"Is your Aunt Lettie feeling better since her surgery?"

"Do you know how lucky you are to have such a beautiful family?"

Just right. Every single word of it. And damn, nobody—but nobody—was that perfect!

With a sigh, Ben leaned against his grocery cart. Though he made a mean minestrone, he wasn't much of a baker. Still, the cut-and-bake cookies were close by and he tossed a roll of chocolate chip into his cart. He watched and waited, just like he'd been watching and waiting for all of the last week.

And just like she'd done the day before and the day before and the day before that, Lacie went about her business, apparently oblivious to his presence. When she made one more stop to lean down and say hello to an elderly woman in a wheelchair, he closed in a little. Finally, Lacie made it to the refrigerated section. While she stepped back and tipped her head, checking over the shopping list she carried in one hand, Ben grabbed a pack of each-piece-individually-wrapped cheese food. Lacie reached for a carton of yogurt and read over the nutritional information on the back.

"You know . . ." She looked over her shoulder at him while she set the yogurt in her cart on top of a head of lettuce, two bags of carrots, and a loaf of whole wheat bread. "You really don't have to follow me everywhere I go. I'm sure you have more important things to do."

He didn't, but Ben wasn't about to go there. Instead, he shrugged. "So much for being the unobtrusive type, huh? And here I thought I might have a shot at the CIA someday."

"You weren't unobtrusive yesterday, either, when you followed me to the aerobics class I teach." She added three more containers of yogurt to her cart. "Or the day before, when I conducted the twirling workshop at the high school over in Rogers and you hung around outside the entire time. You haven't been unobtrusive since the day you showed up at our house and began your investigation."

Her yogurt shopping complete, Lacie gripped the grocery cart handle with both hands and her gaze skimmed Ben's charcoal gray suit, the red tie he'd originally bought to wear to his sister Gina's wedding, the haircut that he'd asked Gib Allen to spruce up a bit so that now, it was shorter and weirder than ever.

"You're not exactly the unobtrusive type," she told him. "Especially in a place like Klaber Falls."

Ben wasn't sure if it was a compliment. Or the worst sort of insult. Considering the source and how she always seemed to have the perfect words for every occasion, he would have liked to think of it as a compliment.

Considering that his ego needed the kind of boost it hadn't had since he left D.C., it would have been just what he needed.

But since the last time he'd talked to Lacie was the day she'd showed up on the front doorstep of the Baxter house looking like she'd been dragged through acres of cornfields and miles of mud, and the rest of his questioning hadn't gone much better than their initial, less-than-pleasant meeting, he figured he'd better step carefully.

Too bad stepping carefully also included stepping closer. Lacie lost hold of her shopping list and it fluttered to the

green-and-white tile floor. Instinctively, Ben moved forward
and picked it up. She made a move for the list at the same
time, and when he stood up again, he found himself red tie
to yellow sleeveless shirt with Lacie.

"Thank you." The perfect response was delivered along
with a perfect little smile that almost made him forget that
the last time they'd met, she'd done her best to stall his investigation. And condemn him to this corn-fed hell even
longer.

This close, Lacie's smile was more potent than ever, and
rather than face it—or the idea that he might be just as pow-
erless against it as everyone else in this godforsaken place—
Ben skimmed a look over her. Her yellow top was open at
the neck, and his gaze touched the creamy hollow at the
base of her throat and the bit of freckle-sprinkled skin that
showed just beneath it. It dipped down even farther to
where her breasts pressed against the sunny shirt. Even
though he told himself he was being a little too indiscreet
and a whole lot more aroused than he should be at this time,
in this place, and with this person, he watched the way her
breasts moved against the fabric with each measured breath
she took.

Oh, yeah, Sutton County must be hell, all right.

That would explain why it was getting hotter and hotter in
here.

Though it took more willpower than he realized he had,
Ben forced himself to look back up into Lacie's eyes. "I'm
not exactly following you. Not like some sort of crazed nut-
case." He told himself that he'd better not ever forget it. "It's
just part of the job. I'm just trying to..." He couldn't help
himself, he brushed another look from her eyes to her
mouth and down even farther. "Just trying to keep an eye on
you."

"And I really do appreciate it."

Was it his imagination, or did Lacie sound the tiniest bit
interested?

The thought caught Ben off guard. Kind of the way the realization that he was suddenly thinking he was just a little interested, too, made him feel like he'd been whacked in the kidneys by a big guy with a brand-new set of brass knuckles he was just itching to try out.

Ben pulled in a sharp breath. And reminded himself to get a grip. This was Lacie he was dealing with. Miss Wholesome, Wide-Eyed, Aw-Shucks, Corny, Baton-Twirler. Miss More-Perfect-than-Anyone-in-the-Whole-Wide-World.

Except that the longer he followed her and the less that happened, the more his suspicion grew. Maybe he was right from day one. Maybe the whole crazy kidnapping was staged to get Lacie a little publicity and what seemed to be permanent spot on the front page of the *Intelligencer*.

Maybe she wasn't so perfect after all, maybe she was playing him for a sucker?

Ben swallowed the sour taste in his mouth at the same time he took a step back.

"I just wondered . . ." He held out the shopping list to her. "Just wondered if you'd remembered anything, anything that might be useful to the investigation."

With a tiny shake of her shoulders that made her golden hair shiver around her and her breasts jiggle in ways Ben knew it was best not to watch, Lacie took the list out of his hand. "I wish I could help," she said, and there was so much gee-whiz honesty in her voice and in her blue gaze, Ben felt it was practically un-American not to believe her. "I told you everything. Big guy. Ski mask. I didn't see his face."

"And you don't seem very worried."

Okay, so it was a little early in the game to lay his cards on the table. Ben never was much for poker. He was all for the gambling part. All for taking risks. And putting himself on the line. It was just the whole hiding-his-emotions thing that he never could get past. He didn't like the thought of not sticking it in his oponent's face, especially when he thought he had the upper hand.

"You have to admit, it's a little curious," he told her. "You say this guy grabbed you. You tell me he tossed you in the trunk of his car. You told me where he took you and you said that you whacked him with your baton and left him there. But there was no sign of him when I went out to the Whipple Farm. No sign that he'd ever even been there except for some footprints in the mile-high dust that coated the floors. And in the meantime, you're going about your life like nothing happened." He gave her the kind of no-nonsense look that had been known to make a suspect or two reconsider their half-baked excuses. "I'm thinking after a kidnap attempt, most other people wouldn't be so calm. Just about any other woman I know would be shaking in her high-heeled shoes."

"Just about any other?" There was the faintest hint of a smile in Lacie's voice. "That makes me think you must know some interesting women."

"I don't. Not all that interesting." Ben knew he was being too honest for his own good but that never stopped him from speaking his mind. "You have to admit, it's a little odd. And excuse me for saying it, but it's also a little suspicious. You should be afraid. You could have been killed."

As if she were thinking very hard, Lacie's lips thinned and her brows dipped low over her eyes. "No, not killed." She shook her head. "Like I told you the other day, I don't know what that guy wanted, but I do know he didn't want to kill me. If he did, he would have done it. Right when he first saw me. There was no one around when he grabbed me at Mercer's. Why not do it there? Why not do it as soon as he got me out of the trunk? Why bother dragging me all the way into the house if all he wanted to do was kill me?"

The day she first told him the story, Ben had wondered the same things. Thinking it all through again didn't get him any further now than it had then. The kidnapper hadn't made a move to hurt Lacie, and that might say something about the man's mental state. But it still didn't help explain a thing about hers.

"So what you're telling me is that if he had tried to kill you, you'd be afraid. But knowing he's still out there . . . that he might try it again . . . that doesn't make you want to stay home and hide under the bed?"

Much to his surprise, Lacie laughed. It was a perfect little laugh. Not too loud. Way too feminine. The kind of laugh that tickled up and down a guy's skin like the brush of a feather.

The kind Ben couldn't afford to let distract him.

"Of course I feel like hiding under the bed," she told him, and added, almost as an afterthought, "except that under my bed is packed tight with storage containers for sweaters and shoes and—" She brushed aside the thought with a toss of her head that made the light of the overhead fluorescents gleam against her hair like sunshine on silk. Lacie glanced up at Ben, then glanced away again.

"It isn't easy for me to admit," she said. "I don't like being afraid."

"But if you're really afraid—"

"If I'm really afraid, then that guy, whoever he is, he wins. And though you may not know much about me, Agent Camaglia, you should know that's completely unacceptable. I win. Always."

"So you'll keep right on doing what you're doing because . . . "

"Because that's what people expect me to do." Lacie reached for her shopping cart and headed toward the checkout. "After all," she said, "a beauty queen has duties and one of those duties is to make sure everyone around her is happy. And not worried. If they thought I was afraid, they'd be afraid, too. And no beauty queen wants to be responsible for that!"

"Fair enough." Ben grabbed his cart and caught up to

her. Side by side, they rolled down the bread aisle. "But it's just as important to make sure it—"

When Ben realized Lacie wasn't beside him anymore, he jerked his cart to a stop and turned around. He found her paused right where the bread aisle dissected the snack foods section, and whatever she was watching, she wasn't very happy about it.

Hands on her hips, Lacie abandoned her cart and headed toward the potato chips. Curious, Ben followed along.

He found her standing over a fourteen-year-old boy whose hair matched the carrot-colored shirt he was wearing. The kid was busy stuffing packages of beef jerky into the pockets of his jeans.

"Joey Campbell!"

The kid jumped when Lacie put a hand on his arm, and she looked down at him, her expression a sweet mixture of compassion and concern. "I can't believe it. Not of you, Joey. You're way too good a kid to risk getting yourself in trouble over something as small as beef jerky. What if your mom finds out what you've been up to? Or your dad? He works hard over at the feed mill. You wouldn't want him hearing about this and getting worried, would you?"

"Yeah. Whatever." For a couple of seconds, Joey sized up Lacie, apparently trying to decide what her next move might be. When he realized it wasn't likely to be anything more than a prim look and a lecture he'd let go in one ear and out the other, he knew he could afford to be cocky. He yanked his arm out from under Lacie's touch and backed up a step. The kid wasn't any taller than the five-foot display of pork rinds stacked nearby. What he lacked in size he made up for in attitude. Bad attitude.

Joey's mouth twisted into a mockery of Lacie's gentle smile. "What are you going to do?" he asked. "Run and tell my folks? Or old Mr. Prancy? Some store manager he is! Me and my friends, we come in here a couple times a week and rip the guy blind and he doesn't even know it. Just smiles and nods when we leave. Stupid old fart."

"Joey!" Though the expression on Lacie's face never changed, there was a bit more mettle in her voice. She took a step closer to the boy. "You know you don't mean that. Not about Mr. Prancy. He practically kept food on your table when your dad was sick and couldn't work last year. You know that. And this is how you repay him?"

"Back off!" Joey stood his ground. "Look who's talking, anyway. If you're so worried about saving people, you should start with that sister of yours. You think she doesn't come in here and do the same thing?"

It was news, but it wasn't surprising. Disgusted, Lacie shook her head. "Dinah needs to get her act together. Just like you do. I've known you since the day you were born, Joey. I know you're not the kind of kid who—"

Joey's only response was a grunt.

Not about to give up, Lacie tried again. She put a hand on the purse she had slung over one shoulder. "If you need a couple of bucks—"

"A couple of bucks!" Something told Ben that if Joey were just a little older—and just a bit more sure of himself so that he could afford to be a complete smart-ass—he might have spit on the floor. Instead, he laughed out loud and shot a look Lacie's way that was so mean-spirited, she automatically backed up a step. "You know what you can do, Miss stuck-up Lacie Baxter? You can take your couple of bucks and shove them right up—"

"That's it!" Ben was practically on top of the kid before he could stop himself. And long before Joey even realized he was coming. Before Joey ever had a chance to react, he found himself backed against the nearest shelf. Bags of potato chips crunched under Joey's weight. Pretzels tumbled and scattered all around.

Ben never touched the kid. But just getting in his face was enough to send the right message. Joey's eyes goggled from his head, and Ben reached around to the back of his belt and pulled out his handcuffs. He dangled them in front of the boy's eyes.

"You want to know where you can shove these, smart guy? Shoplifting is a serious crime, Joey. Juvenile or not, you're going to find yourself on the wrong end of a record."

Joey's eyes were as wide as saucers. He swallowed hard. "You..." He looked from the handcuffs to Ben. "You ain't a cop. I know the cops around here and you ain't—"

"That's right. I'm not." Ben whipped out his credentials and flashed them in front of Joey. "I'm FBI. And that doesn't make me a cop, it makes me a super-cop. And because I'm the super-cop and you're not, you're going to do two things for me. First, you're going to empty your pockets and leave everything you took right where you found it. Next, you're going to apologize to Miss Baxter. If you don't, the only beef jerky around here is what we'll make out of what's left of you when I finish wiping up the floor with you."

"Ben!" Behind him, Ben heard Lacie's breathy protest. "He's just a kid and—"

"And this *just a kid* is about to apologize." He looked Joey in the eye, playing the tough-cop role for all it was worth. "Isn't that right?"

Beneath the freckles that covered his face like sand on a beach, Joey went pale. His eyes filled with tears. Automatically, he reached into his pocket and brought out a handful of beef jerky packets. "I'm sorry," he said, glancing over at Lacie. "I didn't mean—"

"Of course you didn't." Lacie moved forward to put a hand on Ben's arm. "He didn't—"

"He did." Ben stepped back, and seeing the opening, Joey was out of there. The only thing left to show that anything had happened was the trail of beef jerky packages he dropped out of his pockets before he hit the door.

Watching him hightail it out of there, Ben laughed. "I think it's safe to say that's the last time he'll shoplift."

"It might be the last time he dares to go out in public."

Lacie wasn't laughing. Her voice was as sharp as icicles, and hearing it, Ben turned around and met a gaze that was just as cold.

"What's that supposed to mean?"

"It's supposed to mean that you didn't have to be so hard on him. He's just a kid and—"

"I never touched him." Ben straightened his tie, smoothed his suit jacket, and put his handcuffs back where they belonged. When old Pete Prancy came around the corner, huffing and puffing, Ben waved him away and told him everything was fine and there was nothing to worry about. Except the potato chips. "Besides, being a kid is no excuse. Kid or no kid, he knows right from wrong and that means he has no right to break the law. No one does. He learned a valuable lesson."

"A lesson about responsibility?" Lacie turned and headed back to her cart. "Or a lesson about how a bully can make you do just about anything?"

"Bully?" Ben followed her. "What do you mean, bully? I could have made things worse for the kid. I could have called Sheriff Thompson. Instead, I decided to teach the kid a lesson and send him on his way. You want to tell me where the fault lies in that?"

Lacie glanced down to where her hand clutched the handle of the shopping cart. Though he hadn't even realized he'd put it there, Ben's hand was over hers, and he pulled his hand away. She drew in a breath and let it out slowly, carefully schooling her emotions.

"You may be right," she said. "You may have taught Joey a lesson he won't forget. But you've also taught him that not all authority figures can be trusted to treat him equitably. And with respect."

"Oh, please!" Ben might have laughed if Lacie hadn't looked so doggone sincere. He settled for a roll of his eyes. "You don't really believe that bull, do you? All that warm and fuzzy stuff about how we should all get along? Let me tell you something, Lacie, I've seen kids no older than that pull out knives and kill the poor suckers who wanted to do nothing more than help them."

Something told Ben that Lacie actually might have stomped her foot if she hadn't thought the gesture too petulant. "Not in Sutton County!"

"Not in Sutton County, huh? And I suppose you're also going to tell me that kidnappings don't happen in Sutton County, either? Unless you're finally willing to admit that it wasn't a kidnapping? That it was nothing more than an attempt to get a little publicity for yourself?"

Lacie's mouth fell open. Her eyes went wide. "You can't possibly think—"

"I think it's mighty peculiar that some big guy in a ski mask goes to all the trouble of trying to kidnap you, fails, and doesn't try again."

"Do you? Do you really?" It must have been a trick of the fluorescent light that was blinking just above them. Ben could have sworn she practically smiled. Lacie grabbed her shopping cart. "Maybe the guy—whoever he is—just doesn't want to take the chance. Not when I've got someone watching over me who's rough and tough enough to pick on a kid half his size."

She headed toward the front of the store, and Ben stepped back. He took a deep breath, waiting for his blood pressure to settle down to a slow simmer while he gave himself plenty of time so he didn't have to see Lacie at the checkout.

"Great," he grumbled. "First you're attracted to the woman even though you shouldn't be. Now you're fighting with her over something as stupid as a teenage petty thief."

Disgusted, Ben shook his head. It was a lot of energy wasted on a lot of nothing, and where had it gotten him?

No closer to solving the case that was looking as if it weren't a case to begin with.

No closer to getting back to where culture wasn't defined by how many square dancing groups you belonged to, how many tons your pickup could pull, or how many head of cattle lived side by side with your soybean crop.

And that was perfect, he told himself. Even though he was feeling like it was anything but.

Just perfect.

5

"Hold still, Wiley!"

"I'm trying to but—ow!"

Like he'd stuck his finger into an electrical outlet, Wiley twitched. He was sprawled over a desk chair with wheels, and it bucked and rolled out of Dinah's reach.

"Well, that's just great." Her lips pulled into a no-nonsense line, her patience just as thin, Dinah frowned at the mess of red pigment smeared over Wiley's skin and the tattooing needle still stuck in his bare butt. "How do you expect me to work when you're moving around like that?" she asked, and because she really didn't think he could come up with an excuse that could possibly make her happy, she didn't give him a chance to answer.

"I'm an artist, Wiley," she reminded him, looking over the tattoo she was inking in on his awe-inspiring butt. "And artists need peace and quiet to work. I also need you to keep still. Unless you want me to mess up."

"You know I don't. You know I never would. It's just that—" Wiley groaned and touched a tentative finger to his backside. "It stings."

"Wimp-ass." Dinah plucked the needle from his butt and

Wiley flinched. "I'm never going to have a chance to practice if you won't cooperate." She put the needle down in the plastic tray she'd set on the desk of the Carson's Garage office. "I need to develop my talent before I apply to a school," she reminded him for the hundredth time. "You've gotta help me out here, Wiley."

"I want to. You know I do. I just wish we could afford to get you a tattoo machine. Doing it by hand takes a long time. Especially when it hurts." His brows low, his mouth tight in his chipped-from-granite jaw, Wiley stood. He craned his neck to see over his shoulder. "How does it look?"

"It looks—" Dinah checked out the half-colored-in picture that covered nearly all of Wiley's backside. The design was one of her originals, and she was as proud of it as she'd ever been of anything. It was an Indian chief in full regalia, complete with a background of rugged Western mountains, a lake, and even a waterfall.

Looking it over, Dinah felt her ego deflate a little, and a thread of doubt creep in to threaten her confidence in herself as an artist. It wasn't that the picture wasn't terrific, it was just that on paper, her Indian looked a little more chieflike. On Wiley's butt, he looked kind of like a hobbit with feathers in his hair and a bad overbite.

On paper, her mountains were majestic. Dramatic. Spectacular. And maybe because Wiley's butt was all those things to begin with, the mountains on his backside looked a little like rolling hills.

On paper, her waterfall was the best thing about the picture and it was still nice and gushy and blue. But because of the way Dinah had transferred the stencil from paper to his body, it had ended up in a sort of weird place. Now the waterfall ran off the mountainside and right into Wiley's butt crack.

"It's awesome," she said, and even if the description didn't exactly apply to the tattoo, it was at least true about Wiley's butt. "Honest, it looks amazing."

"And I can see it . . ." Wiley tried stretching again so he could see what he could see, "when?"

Dinah laid a clean disposable towel against the newly worked area. Her touch was enough to make Wiley grin, and, of course, Dinah had to smile, too. Just thinking about putting a hand on Wiley's butt—or any other part of him—always made her feel like she was walking on clouds. "You can see it when I'm done. And not before. That was our deal, remember? I promised to give you the best tattoo in the universe. And you promised you wouldn't look. Not until I was finished."

"I know. I know." By now, Wiley knew the routine. As he had done when she did each of the tattoos on his arms and the one on his ankle and the other at exactly the place where his chest met hers when they kissed, he waited while Dinah put gauze and nonstick adhesive strips over the area. When she was done, he reached for the silky black boxers covered in red hearts that he'd tossed onto the desk when she first got to work. He slipped them on, being careful not to snap the elastic waistband anywhere near the bandages. "Only, I'm anxious, you know? I know you're doing a great job and I can't wait until everybody else knows it, too."

"Everybody else?" The very thought made Dinah feel like the rubber mat on the floor had been pulled out from under her feet. Her stomach did a little flip. Her eyes went a little bleary. Suddenly, it was hard to breathe. "What do you mean, everybody else? Wiley Burnside, you're not planning on ever letting another woman get a look at it, are you?" Before he could see the tears that sprang to her eyes and think that she was some kind of crybaby, Dinah turned her back on him. "It was supposed to be special. Just for us."

"Of course it's just for us." He came up behind her and wrapped his arms around her waist. He pressed a kiss to her neck. "You know I didn't mean anything by it," he said, in that growly voice that always made her crazy. "It's just for us, Snuggle Bunny. Just for you."

Dinah murmured her approval, both of what he said and of the way he chose to reinforce it. She was glad she'd decided to meet Wiley at the garage tonight. Usually, they worked on her tattoo designs at Wiley's place or at home, but the light was better here in the garage office, and at least here—now that it was late and the garage was closed for business—no one would bother them. More than she could say for either of their homes.

Wiley's mother was a scrawny woman with long, frizzy hair and dresses that hung around her ankles. She was always reading one of those half-baked newsletters she got from the Reverend Teddy Pawtucket's prison ministry and mumbling about the poor unfortunates shut up behind prison walls and how she had to send them whatever she could from the paycheck she earned as secretary of the high school. Krissie wasn't much better, looking in on them all the time, not because she cared particularly what Dinah and Wiley were up to but because she didn't want to miss out on anything.

As for Lacie...

Even Wiley's arms around her didn't make her feel much better when she thought about Lacie with her trophies, crowns, and sparkly dresses that cost way more than a few months of training at a really good tattoo school ever could.

"Hey, whatcha thinking?" Wiley's voice brushed Dinah's ear.

"Nothing much." She spun around in his arms and linked her hands behind his neck. "Just thinking about us. About you. About everything you promised to do for me."

"Aw, Snuggle Bunny!" He cupped her behind with both his hands and gave her a squeeze. "You know I'm working on it."

"I know." It was the truth, and as much as Dinah would have liked to read him the riot act, she knew she couldn't. Some things couldn't be rushed and this was one of them. Still, she wasn't the most easily satisfied person in the world—just ask Wiley—and she hated idling in neutral.

Especially when there was something important that needed to be done.

Dinah pulled out of Wiley's arms and went over to the desk to start packing up her supplies. "You haven't seen that FBI guy around, have you?" she asked him.

"Nah." Wiley walked over to where a grimy mirror hung on the wall just outside the bays where the mechanical work was done. He considered trying to take a peek at his new tattoo in the mirror, but one look at the height of the mirror and another at the rolling chair he would have to stand on to make the maneuver work made him think better of it. He reached for his jeans. "You seen him ever?"

"Seen him *ever*?" Dinah laughed. "When haven't I seen him? He sits in his car outside the house practically all night long. Plus he follows Lacie everywhere. God, if it was me, I'd flip the guy off, but you know Lacie. She smiles and waves and goes about her business, acting like she's the queen of the world and she's got nothing to worry about."

"Think she does?"

Dinah shrugged. "I dunno. Maybe." She tossed the last of her supplies in the plastic Food Emporium bag she'd brought along. "Maybe we have more to worry about than she does," she told Wiley. "You watch the *X-Files*. You know these FBI guys—they can be real sneaky."

"Not sneaky enough to figure out what we're up to."

"I know." Dinah sighed. "It's just that I don't like to wait."

"I don't like to wait, either." Wiley sounded a little winded. Like he did the time a couple years before when he was caught smoking a joint in the men's room at the high school and Mr. Fortnoy, the principal (who was also the football coach and filled in for the home ec teacher when she was drinking again and couldn't make class), made him run around the track twice.

Dinah looked up just in time to see him toss aside his jeans. Grinning, he closed in on her.

"So," he said with a little twinkle in his eyes, "you gonna make me wait?"

Leave it to Wiley to know exactly how to get her mind off her troubles.

As soon as he got within touching distance, she glided her hands over the silky boxers.

"Ouch!" When her fingers touched his backside, Wiley winced.

"Sorry, Sugar Lips!" Since the back hurt, Dinah concentrated on the front at the same time she hiked her short black skirt over her thighs and sat down on Frank Carson's desk. "Guess we better make sure that you stay on top!"

Years on the pageant circuit had taught Lacie nothing if not how to be gracious.

Too bad.

If that was Ben Camaglia she saw through the crowd just inside the door of the VFW hall, she would have liked nothing better than to leave him standing there looking as out of place as a Givenchy original at a Sunday school picnic. After all, it was exactly what he deserved for what he'd said when she ran into him at the Food Emporium. All those crazy things about how she'd made up the story of the kidnapping just to get a little publicity.

As if she needed help to get publicity!

Her hands clutched around a paper cup decorated with stars and stripes and filled to the brim with punch, Lacie automatically struck a pose and smiled when she saw Jeff Parkman raise his camera to get a shot of her.

Was it Ben near the door?

She took a sip of punch, pausing for another photograph at the same time she looked over the rim of her cup at the long line of people filing in. Now and again, somebody moved just the right way and she had a clear shot through the crowd.

Designer suit.

Two-hundred-dollar shoes.

Color-splashed tie.

Bad haircut.

Yep, it was Ben, all right, and though someone had obviously told him there was a dinner dance tonight, they had just as obviously left out the part about how except for the Sweethearts' Dinner in February, Founders' Night in May, and the once-a-year Community Meal of Thanksgiving (held in October so as not to interfere with anyone's holiday plans), dinner dances at the VFW were traditionally casual.

Lacie glanced down at her own neatly pressed jeans and crisp purple T-shirt. She looked at the folks around her and the ones just coming in the door, all of them dressed pretty much the same way. And she really couldn't help herself.

It was part of her nature to be compassionate—not to mention style conscious. As much as she tried not to, she couldn't help but feel sorry for Ben and his fashion faux pas.

Lacie excused herself from the conversation she was having with her mother and Sheriff Thompson and started across the room with every intention of having a quiet little talk with Agent Camaglia. She would simply let him in on the fact—ever so politely, of course—that he was as overdressed as a tuxedo-clad cow at a barn dance. But before she was halfway there, another thought occurred to her: If she had to be nice to Ben, it didn't hurt that he was the hottest thing in these parts since the Lewis house burned to the ground and the volunteer fire department couldn't put out the blaze for two days because of the corn liquor Marge and Buddy had tucked away in their root cellar.

The realization made Lacie catch her breath, and the punch in her cup nearly sloshed over the side. Because she couldn't afford any fruit punch stains—notoriously difficult to get out of cotton/polyester blends—she set her cup on the nearest table, gulped down a breath, and reminded herself that she was on a mission of mercy.

Not on the make.

It all might have been easier to remember if she weren't also remembering that being close to Ben at the Food Emporium a couple of days earlier had made her feel like she was hot enough to melt the butter in the refrigerated case nearby.

That was no excuse for a girl to lose her perspective or her composure, she reminded herself.

But, of course, that didn't explain why, when she finally made it through the crowd and over to where Ben was standing near the door, the words that fell out of her mouth were "You really should get undressed."

Ben's eyebrows shot up and he turned his attention from a group of toddlers running by to Lacie. He stared at her bright white sneakers, his glance brushing over the snug (but not too tight to be trashy) jeans, the T-shirt, the tiny gold earrings. She actually felt relieved when his gaze went to her hair. At least if he wasn't looking at her face, he wouldn't see that her eyes were wide with mortification and her cheeks were burning. Still, it took every bit of control she had—and a little extra that she usually only pulled out and used at pageants—to keep herself from smoothing a hand over the neat French braid she had tied with a purple ribbon at the back of her neck.

It took more than that to keep still when he shifted his gaze to her lips. And her eyes.

"I expected to have a nice time tonight. But I never thought things would start so soon." A barely perceptible smile teased an unexpected dimple to almost showing up in his left cheek. "Tell me, Miss Baxter, was that a proposition I just heard?"

Good thing he made it sound like he was only joking around. Otherwise Lacie wasn't sure she would have been able to answer.

"That was fashion advice." She looked over her shoulder

and into the room where half of the county was gathered. "You're a little overdressed."

"Yeah, I guess I am."

Wonder of wonders! Ben could actually look sheepish when the occasion called for it. Intrigued, Lacie found herself taking a step nearer.

"I hear you live here in Sutton Springs. You could go home and change."

"I'd hate to miss anything."

"Then the tie has to go for sure."

"Think so?" He looked down at his tie, then up at Lacie again. "It was your idea that I get undressed. You want to help?"

It wasn't wise even to think about answering. Then again, it was impossible to resist the twinkle in Ben's eyes.

"You think that's smart?" she asked him.

"Smart?" One corner of Ben's mouth curled into a smile that was half regret, half *go ahead and make my day*. "No, I don't think it's smart at all. But then again, I've never been known for my smarts."

"Not as much as for your looks, huh?"

"Not that, either." This time, he laughed outright. The change in him was remarkable. The man with the gentle gleam in his dark eyes and the smile that made him look as warm and as fuzzy as a field full of sheep on a clear spring day couldn't possibly be the same man who'd taken ten years off Joey Campbell's life with his high-handed tactics.

Could he?

As much as she told herself it didn't matter, Lacie suddenly wanted to find out.

When Mayor Crist came in and started shaking hands with everyone in sight—it was, after all, an election year—she took the opportunity to step closer to Ben. She gave him the kind of thorough once-over he'd just given her, taking her time to check out the breadth of his shoulders beneath his suit jacket and the cut of his trousers that hinted at long, muscular legs. When she was finally done, she looked him in the eye.

"What are you known for?" she asked him.

"Me?" Ben cocked his head. Like he had to think about it. Like he wasn't the kind of guy who was so sure of himself, he never gave that kind of thing a second thought. "There are any number of people who think I'm a jim-dandy G-man," he told her. "And some who actually believe that if I could give up my undying faith that the Cubs are going to win the World Series someday, I might actually lead a normal life. Believe it or not, there are even a few—my folks mostly, and my younger sisters, who I've been fooling for years—who think that beneath this starched shirt beats a heart of gold. There are actually more than a couple women out there who think I'm a darned good kisser."

Kisser?

The single word sizzled through Lacie's bloodstream like bacon on the griddle over at the Morning Star. Her heartbeat staggered, then stuttered. She gulped down a tiny breath of panic and another one to remind herself that he was joking. And she was joking back. He was being coneeited. And way too sure of himself—and of the way he knew she'd react to that sexy gleam in his eyes that looked more dangerous than ever when paired with his little boy's smile.

And she was smack in the middle of falling for it.

It wasn't easy but she managed to keep her voice as airy as her laugh. "Looks like you're something of a Renaissance man. We're lucky to have you here."

"And here I thought I was the one who was going to get lucky."

"Not that lucky." It wasn't often she allowed herself the luxury of indulging in a little bold-faced flirtation, yet Lacie knew she had to draw the line somewhere. Something told her they'd just come to that place.

"You're getting ahead of yourself," she told him, and reminded herself that she was, too. Way ahead of herself. "I'm not the kind of girl who is easily swept off her feet. Especially by a guy I hardly know. And all I know about you is that you have an office here in Sutton Springs, you live and breathe your work, and you don't know how to dress for a small-town Saturday night dinner dance."

It was a less-than-subtle hint, but that didn't stop Ben. His eyes never leaving her, his voice as warm as the honey in one of old Clem Parmalee's hives, Ben slipped off his suit jacket. "Better?"

"Except for the gun." Lacie wrinkled her nose and checked out the holster over Ben's left shoulder. "At the risk of offending the fashion police, something tells me you'd better keep the jacket on."

"Anything you say." He slipped into the jacket again. "That leaves the tie."

"Yeah, the tie." Looking back on it, Lacie would have liked to believe that what she did next was the result of the intoxicating scent of his aftershave. Too bad even she wasn't enough of a fashion slave to believe everything the ads said. The fact that she had the nerve to reach up and tug the knot of Ben's tie loose had more to do with the way her heartbeat sped up. And the way his did, too, the second she touched him.

"You'd better be careful." Ben glanced over her head and toward the crowded dining room. "People will talk."

"Think so?" Lacie glanced that way, too. "You know they do. Talk, I mean. About everything. They talk about what colors of lipstick I wear and how many pairs of pantyhose I buy over at Mercer's."

"And you don't think that's an invasion of privacy?"

"Never did before." It was enough of an insight to make her catch her breath.

And enough of a reminder that she was acting like one of the girls who hung out at the Dew Drop Inn on weekends with the hopes of snagging herself a muscular farmworker.

Lacie dropped her hand and backed away, both from Ben

and from the too-hot-to-handle sensations that shivered around him like the heated air around a fire. She offered him a come-and-go smile that should have made it clear that she had only joined in the fun to be polite.

"We wouldn't want that, would we?"

"You asking?" The way he said it made her wonder if he got the message. "Or waiting for me to say that I don't give a damn what people say?"

"I'm ..." Lacie weighed her options. And decided that although she *was* asking and she *was* waiting for him to say that he didn't give a damn, neither alternative was in her best interest.

"We wouldn't want people to talk," she told him, putting a little more distance between herself and him. And her fantasies. "Guess that means you'll have to take off your own tie."

"Fair enough." With one finger, he loosened the knot all the way. "We can always save that for another time."

Ben sounded awfully sure of himself, and that alone should have made Lacie bristle. It did make her bristle— somewhere beneath the little tingle of anticipation that made her blood pump a mile a minute and the incessant buzz in her ears that made the air sound like it was alive.

If she was smart, she'd extricate herself from the situation before things got even more out of hand. Then again, if she was all that smart, she wouldn't have gotten herself into it in the first place.

She watched him carefully fold the tie and tuck it into his jacket pocket, and because she couldn't think of anything else to talk to him about—anything besides him getting undressed and her helping and why, though it was such a bad idea, it was sounding better and better by the moment—she kept to the one thing they did have in common. Except that they were both acting crazy. "Tell me," she said, "you're not here because you're expecting another kidnap attempt, are you?"

"That's the thing about kidnap attempts. You can never really anticipate them." He gave her a lopsided smile. "I guess that means that's probably why I'm here. Does that bother you? Would you rather have me say I'm here to wine and dine you, dance until dawn, and—even though you claim it can't be done—sweep you off your feet?"

Because she wouldn't admit it, she ignored the second question and answered the first. Even though that one was just as disturbing in its own way.

"Yes, it bothers me. So does you thinking there might be another attempt. Here." She turned enough to look into the dining room where the people she'd known all her life were getting ready to sit down to dinner. "You can't possibly think—"

"I don't know what to think. But I do know that I can't think anything—anything useful—until I have more information. I also know that you're exactly the right person to give it to me. I'm still not sure you're telling me the truth about what happened that night."

If he was looking to throw ice water on all the hot ideas and the even hotter sensations they sparked in her, he'd found the exact right words to do it. Just so there was no mistake about what she thought of the statement, Lacie turned on her heels to head back inside.

He stopped her, one hand on her arm. "Let's just call it an occupational hazard and not a personal opinion, okay? I want to believe you. I want to help."

"And I can do that how? By getting myself thrown in the trunk of another car?"

"That would be the best thing." When her mouth fell open, he laughed. "I'll tell you what, why don't we call a truce instead? Until I find something that makes me think otherwise, I agree to listen to you. And believe you."

"And me?" Something told Lacie she wasn't going to like the answer, but she knew she had to ask. "What do you want me to do?"

Ben wound his arm through hers. "What I want you to do is introduce me to everyone around here. And tell me everything you know about them. After all, if I'm going to investigate—really investigate—I can't do that in the dark. Will you help?"

"Agreed." She nodded.

"Oh, and—" Just inside the door, he stopped and turned her so that she was facing him. "I also want the first dance."

6

"He's bound to get reelected. Everybody knows that. Even though there's no way he should."

Ben wasn't sure who Lacie was talking about. So far this evening, he'd heard about how Stan Fortnoy (the high school principal who was sitting at the next table) had been carrying a torch for years for Miss Nielson (the sophomore English teacher who was sitting in the corner near the kitchen doors). He'd heard the rumors about Mrs. Waterberry (down at the end of the table) who couldn't get her grandson off the couch and to a job. He'd heard so much gossip about so many of the people of Sutton County—people who were as bland as the menu of baked chicken, mashed potatoes, overcooked green beans, and iceberg lettuce with Thousand Island dressing—that he was stunned and more than a little brain-dead.

It took him a second to realize Lacie was looking over to where Mayor Crist and his wife (who, at least according to the heavyset woman sitting next to Ben) was first cousin of the niece of the man who lived next door to Ziggy Burton, who actually knew the governor...

Ben shook his head, clearing it. A hum of voices, laughter,

and clinking silverware echoed through the VFW hall, and he bent closer to Lacie so that he didn't have to raise his voice.

"You mean the mayor of Klaber Falls?"

She laughed the perfect little laugh that even through the rumble of voices all around them was as pleasant as the mashed potatoes were lumpy. Which was more than just a little.

Lacie touched a paper napkin to her lips expertly enough so as not to smudge her lipstick. "Of course I mean Mayor Crist," she said, and for just a second, Ben could have sworn he saw something that might actually be a frown cloud her expression. It must have been a trick of the light. The next second she was the same as ever. Her expression was pleasant. Her voice was as smooth as the stories she'd been telling him ever since the minister from the local Methodist church said grace and they sat down to dinner.

"He's been mayor for twenty years. Ever since his father, the first Mayor Crist, died. But if you ask me..." She glanced around and just to be sure, she lowered her voice and leaned in closer to Ben.

Her arm touched his. The purple ribbon tied at the back of her hair brushed his cheek. And he couldn't help but notice the sweet scent of strawberries that wreathed her hair like a cloud.

"If you ask me, he should never get back in office," she said, and as soon as Ben caught his breath and reminded himself that he wasn't there to think about purple ribbons or strawberries, he saw that she glanced around again to make sure no one was listening. "Because of what he's done."

Purple ribbons and strawberries notwithstanding, old habits died hard. Before he even realized he was doing it, Ben sat up and sent a laser look toward the mayor, sizing him up and not missing a thing, just as he had with countless suspects in his day.

"You mean"—a spark of interest tingled in Ben's voice—"corruption?"

"Down, boy!" Lacie neatly folded her napkin and set it next to her plate. "You've got an overactive imagination."

"You bet I do." Ben crumpled his paper napkin and tossed it onto the plate he'd cleaned of the too-dry chicken, the too mushy beans, and the mashed potatoes that were laced with enough butter to clog even the arteries of a guy who had grown up on Grandma DiNardo's killer Alfredo sauce. "Are you telling me . . . ?"

"I'm telling you that any mayor who forgets to visit Elsie Johnson when she's in the hospital shouldn't be reelected."

"Because . . ."

She tipped her head. Blinked. Gave him a steady look that dared him to refute her logic. "Because Elsie is a nice lady. And she was in the hospital."

So much for sinking his teeth into an investigation of a little hometown political hanky-panky. Ben hoped he didn't sound as disappointed as he felt. "So . . . no corruption?"

"In a small town, some things are even more serious. Like the time Mayor Crist went to the Reverend Moore's Friday night spaghetti supper but didn't stop at Father Sullivan's fish fry. And the time he forgot—and I mean absolutely forgot, if you can imagine it—Al Peterson's one hundredth birthday. The mayor may not think anyone notices those sorts of things, but let me tell you, tongues wagged."

"I can only imagine." Ben's spirits lifted considerably when a volunteer in a crisp white apron whisked away his dinner plate and replaced it with a smaller plate that held a piece of chocolate cake with thick chocolate icing. He dug right in. "So why doesn't someone run against him?"

Lacie pushed back from the table, disassociating herself from the piece of cake that was set in front of her. "Mayor Crist? No one would even think to do that. He's an institution."

"But you said—"

"I said he isn't worthy of his office. He doesn't deserve to be mayor. Not unless he starts thinking about his public image. After all, it is important."

"To a mayor? Or to a beauty queen?"

She glanced at him out of the corner of her eye, and apparently, she decided there was nothing more to the question than heartfelt interest.

There wasn't.

Mostly.

"To both a politician and a beauty queen," she said. "Because a beauty queen isn't all that different from a politician."

Though dinner had been bland, Ben had to hand it to the ladies of the VFW kitchen committee: They made one mean chocolate cake. He finished his piece, and because it looked pretty certain that Lacie wasn't going to touch hers, he raised his eyebrows and gave it a look. She pushed it in his direction.

"So you think a beauty queen has a civic duty? Like an elected official?"

"Of course." As if on cue, someone at the other end of the table waved to Lacie and she waved back. She didn't make it look like a duty. She waved like it was the most natural thing in the world. Like it was something she really wanted to do. For all Ben knew, it was. "Privileges. Responsibilities. I figure in your line of work, you know all about that."

He did. Like the responsibility of being accountable enough for your actions to live with their consequences. Even when the living-with-the-consequences part meant living in Sutton County with the likes of Stan Fortnoy and Mayor Crist, who didn't even have the gumption to indulge in a little corruption. Just to give an FBI agent something to do besides trail around after the county's one and only resident celebrity.

The second piece of cake didn't taste nearly as good as

the first, and Ben pushed it away, half-finished, and shifted his gaze to Lacie. "So, you want to explain?"

"About Mayor Crist?" When someone passed her an eight-by-ten glossy of herself in an evening gown and her Miss Summer Squash banner, Lacie smiled, signed it with a cheery "Keep enjoying Kansas summer squash," and passed it back. "I thought I already did that."

"I was thinking more of why you're being nice to me." Ben watched for any hint of emotion from her that didn't involve smiling and nodding and turning in the right direction to be in just the right light when the guy from the newspaper happened to snap a picture. "You didn't have to meet me at the door and warn me about the dress code. I would have noticed on my own eventually. And you didn't have to have dinner with me. The way I remember it, we didn't exactly part on the best of terms the last time we saw each other."

"And..."

There was that steady look again. Bright and blue and as perfect as everything else about Lacie, from the manicure to the hair, the lipstick to the sneakers that—even though it was as hot as hell outside and it hadn't rained in a week—didn't have even one speck of dust on them.

It was the most sincere look he'd ever seen. The least threatening. And just as pitiless as the one Ben gave to the bad guys who happened to have the misfortune to cross his path.

That probably explained why he suddenly felt so guilty.

"Okay!" He scraped a hand over his chin and looked up at the ceiling, gathering his courage and his thoughts. "I admit it! I wasn't exactly at my best the last time we met."

Though she apparently had an infinite store of patience for other people's foibles, she was not so impractical as to pretend they didn't exist. Lacie nodded. "You mean at the Food Emporium. That's an understatement. You were surly."

Ben would have laughed if she hadn't looked so damned

serious. He was pretty sure he'd never been called *surly* before.

He was saved from thinking about it when a quick blast of music erupted from the speakers placed on the stage.

"You said you'd dance with me." He pushed his chair back from the table and stood.

"Are you sure?" Lacie glanced over to the folks who were getting out of their seats and heading to the dance floor. "Really?"

"Sure. Why wouldn't I be? Or don't you dance with surly guys?"

Lacie rose. "Okay," she said. "You asked for it." And apparently because it was the way things were done when a man and woman were headed to the dance floor (and Lacie was all about doing things just the way they were supposed to be done), she put her hands in his.

The second her fingers touched his, a little crackle of electricity arced between them.

At least, Ben could have sworn that's what happened. It was a little hard to say if Lacie noticed. Before she could react and long before she could say anything, a lady in a flowered dress leaned back in her seat and said hello. A man with a really bad toupee and a moustache that was nothing short of picturesque patted her arm. They sidestepped their way out from between the long tables set up around the dance floor, with Lacie nodding and greeting each and every person they passed. And each and every person they passed whispered as they went by.

"He's that FBI agent. You know, the one from over at Zelda's Golden Comb and—"

"Giving her a little extra attention, of course. I mean after everything that happened to the poor darling and—"

"And don't they look nice together! Why, he reminds me . . . just a bit, and more because of his build than his face, of course. He reminds me of—"

"Jake McCallum."

Taking it all in—and ignoring most of it—Ben followed Lacie to the dance floor. By the time they got there it was already crowded with people shuffling their feet in anxious anticipation.

Static shrieked from the DJ's speakers.

"Sorry!" The disc jockey, the blotchy kid who worked over at the Food Emporium, got red from his neck all the way up to his ears. He fiddled with the buttons and knobs on his audio equipment. "Better?" he asked the crowd, and because there was no more ear-splitting noise, they applauded, and the kid grinned.

"So..." For all his blushing, the kid was a natural ham. He held up a CD jewel case that featured the picture of some tough-as-nails rapper wearing a boatload of gold chains on his chest, a ton of gold rings on his fingers, and a girl in a painted-on gold dress who was draped over his right hip and had one of his legs tucked up between both of hers. "What do you say we start with this?"

There was good-natured booing from the crowd, and it was clear to Ben that this was something of a ritual. Everyone knew the kid's schtick. And everyone played along—even Lacie, who booed and yelled good-natured catcalls along with the rest of them.

"Okay! Okay!" The kid rifled through the rest of the CDs he had on a table. He picked up one after the other and discarded each in turn. "I don't know..." He tossed down the last CD and looked at the crowd. "Maybe I should just ask all of you what you'd like to hear first."

"Bunny Hop!"

The cheer erupted around Ben with all the enthusiasm of true-blue Cub fans greeting a Sosa home run.

"Bunny Hop?" He looked at Lacie, who, like everyone else, was applauding and laughing. "You've got to be kidding. I haven't done the Bunny Hop since I was seven years old and went to my Uncle Dom's wedding. You're not really going to—"

"Gotcha!" She grinned up at him. "We always start with the Bunny Hop," she explained, grabbing his hand again and leading him to the front of the crowd. "It's a good way to get everyone involved. Even the kids."

"Yeah, but..." Ben looked around at the folks forming a loose conga line of sorts. "The Bunny Hop?"

She glanced at him over her shoulder. "Chicken?"

Whether she knew it or not, it was the one thing that was sure to get him to bite.

Ben straightened his shoulders. "I'm not afraid. Not even of the Bunny Hop."

"Then hop to it!" Lacie laughed at her own joke and gave the disc jockey a wink that turned him even redder than before. "Just like the Bunny Hop is always our first dance, I'm always the one to lead it. It's a traditional sort of thing. Started back when I was named Little Miss Sutton County. Probably the same year you went to your Uncle Dom's wedding." She stepped in front of Ben and looked at him over her shoulder.

"What's the matter?" she asked when he didn't do anything but stare at her. "Don't you remember how it's done? Put your hands on my hips."

"Hands? Hips?" It wasn't like Ben to get bowled over by something as simple as a silly dance. But the tingle of electricity that had sparked when she took his hand still sizzled in the air and he hesitated, not sure if the center of the dance floor, the center of the VFW hall, the center of attention, was exactly where he wanted to be when the shock wave hit again.

He didn't have time to think about it. The kid cued the music, and the heavyset lady who had sat next to Ben at dinner and was now standing right behind him grabbed him around the waist for all she was worth.

After he caught his breath, he figured he had no choice; he fit his hands around Lacie's waist.

It was a perfect little waist. And his hands fit around it . . . well . . . perfectly.

By now, he didn't expect anything less.

The rest of the dance was a bit more of a surprise.

The music started and every single person (except for Ben) in the long line that wound around the dance floor and through the first row of tables and over in front of the bar moved as one.

Right foot forward. Right foot back.

Left foot forward. Left foot back.

Hop forward.

Hop back.

Hop. Hop. Hop.

It only took the first set of steps and he knew that if he didn't fall in with the program, he was going to get left behind by Lacie—and mashed by the rest of the line.

When they started again, Ben moved with them.

Right foot forward. Right foot back.

Left foot forward. Left foot back.

So far, so good. Pretty far removed from Uncle Dom's wedding, but some things were second nature. Looked like the Bunny Hop was one of them.

Hop forward.

Hop back.

Hop. Hop. Hop.

Not exactly Ben's idea of fun but not awful, either, especially when every time she stepped forward, stepped back, and hopped, Lacie's body moved beneath his hands as if it had been made for the purpose.

Right foot forward. Right foot back.

And her hip rotated just enough for him to feel it glide inside her denim jeans.

Left foot forward. Left foot back.

And he allowed himself to adjust his hold on her—just a little—so he could enjoy the motion.

Hop forward.

And he moved in a little closer.

Hop back.

And her backside brushed the front of his trousers.

Lacie's head came around and she looked at him over her shoulder, her eyes wide, her lips parted just enough for him to see her tongue flicker across her teeth.

Hop.

Hop.

Hop.

Ben didn't have a clue how long the Bunny Hop lasted. He only knew that it wasn't long enough and that before it was over, he was thinking about things that had nothing to do with bunnies. Things like how Lacie would feel moving beneath him without that layer of denim between them. And how each time he hopped forward, he got just a little closer. And each time she hopped back, it wasn't his imagination. She did exactly the same thing.

By the time the music ended and the crowd clapped, Ben was pretty sure they were applauding the simple fact that he had enough willpower (not to mention good sense) not to toss Lacie on the floor and have his way with her. Right then and there.

It wasn't nearly the next best thing, but when another song started up and it was slow and sung with a country twang, Ben couldn't have stopped if J. Edgar Hoover himself had been up in front of the crowd issuing him orders to cease and desist.

He swung Lacie into his arms and pulled her close.

Lacie couldn't catch her breath. And something told her it had nothing to do with the Bunny Hop.

She wasn't the type who was prone to the jitters. If she had been, she never would have come so far in the looks-way-easier-than-it-really-is pageant world. But she wasn't the type who often had to deal with a man like Ben, either.

And she could still feel the thrill that danced over her skin when she thought about his arm brushing hers at the dinner table. And his voice whispering against her cheek when they bent their heads together to discuss Mayor Crist. She could still feel the tingle of electricity that had zapped her out of nowhere when she put her hand in his.

The one that still skittered along her skin. Each and every place he touched her.

And now that she thought about it, that was more than she was doing to him.

Lacie realized that though Ben's arm was around her waist and his hand was on her arm, she was frozen in place like a first-timer in a Miss Swimsuit competition spotlight. She smiled an apology and put her hand in Ben's. When she put her arm around him, though, it was right at the spot where he wore his gun inside his jacket.

Instinctively, she pulled back. "Sorry. I'm all for constitutional rights, but I don't think I've ever danced with a guy who was carrying a gun. Takes a little getting used to." She repositioned her hand but there was no getting around it. Whatever kind of gun he carried, it was a big one.

Lacie wrinkled her nose and slanted Ben a look. "Do you take that thing with you everywhere?"

He chuckled. "Pretty much," he said. "Though there are a couple of places..."

She didn't pursue it. She could well imagine where those couple of places were. Just like she could well imagine that thinking about them on the dance floor of the VFW wasn't the smartest thing to do. Instead, she adjusted her hold to avoid the gun as much as possible and fell into step.

It took her only a couple of bars of Patsy Cline's *Crazy* to realize Ben knew exactly what he was doing.

"You're good."

"Yes, I am." Something told her that though she had

clearly steered the subject to what should have been a safe discussion of dancing, he was back to talking about those places where he didn't wear his gun.

"I meant good at dancing."

"Yeah, that, too."

He smiled down at her, and even if she didn't have twenty-some years of pageant training to fall back on and a sense of congeniality so ingrained she sometimes found herself smiling even before her eyes were open in the morning, she had no choice but to smile back. It was impossible not to when that little dimple in his cheek winked at her. Impossible not to when the feel of him moving next to her sent a sudden rush of heat coursing through her. Like the time her Miss Christmas Pageant rival spiked the fruit punch with one hundred proof rum.

Just to show off, he let go of her waist and whirled her around, one arm over her head, and she figured that explained why, when he was done and she was eye to eye with him again, she felt off balance. "You never answered my question, you know when I asked why you decided to treat me like your date for the night."

"Did I? Am I? Treating you like a date, I mean."

"I don't know." When they did a spin around the bar on the far side of the room, he hitched his arm a little tighter around her, and when they were done spinning, he didn't let go. "I guess that all depends on how you treat your dates."

The breathlessness was because of all the whirling and twirling. It was because—though she made sure she danced with any man kind enough to ask her at functions like this—she couldn't remember the last time one had made her as hot as a hornets' nest in the dead of August.

Another thing it was definitely not in her best interests to think about.

Lacie shrugged and tried not to notice the way Ben

watched her breasts brush against his chest. "What with personal appearances and baton practice and exercise classes and dance lessons...my schedule is pretty full. I don't have a lot of time for dating."

"That's not what I heard. What about Jake McCallum?"

1

Hearing Jake's name out of the blue like that was a whole lot like finding a rattlesnake in a bottle of pink bubble bath.

Not something that happened often.

Plenty surprising when it did.

And as scary as anything Lacie could think of.

She stopped dancing and would have tripped and gone down on her nose if Ben hadn't been quick enough to scoop her up and hold her tight.

For a couple of seconds, she didn't move and he didn't, either. The couples who were out on the dance floor with them smiled politely and stepped their way around them, glancing at them over their shoulders when they glided by. More than a few times, Lacie heard what sounded like "Isn't that cute?"

It wasn't.

Through the sudden blinding haze that clouded her vision and blinded her reason, she scrambled for something to say that wouldn't make her look like a complete idiot. And wondered if it was already too late for that.

"Jake McCallum?" It was amazing that she could say the name without choking on it. She got her feet moving again and looked Ben in the eye. "Funny you should mention his name. I was just thinking about Jake."

She couldn't believe she could lie so effortlessly or so coolly.

As far as Lacie could remember, she hadn't wasted even one brain cell thinking about Jake McCallum in years. At least not until the night of the kidnapping when she was scared to death—and in way over her head. It was only natural that Jake had come to mind.

She tucked away the thought along with the queasy little feeling that started up in her stomach because of it, and somehow, she managed to make herself sound like they were having the most natural conversation in the world.

"I haven't heard anyone mention Jake in a long time."

"I hear he's a nice-looking guy."

"Fair to middling."

Ben winced, and Lacie couldn't help herself, even though Jake's name still hung in the air between them like some sort of poisonous cloud, she had to laugh.

"Let me guess, you heard someone say that you remind them of Jake."

Not surprising. Back in the old days, people around here were used to seeing Jake and Lacie together. Constantly. The folks who'd known her forever just naturally made the connection.

Lacie couldn't blame them. Ben did remind her of Jake. He wasn't as tall as Jake. He wasn't as thin as Jake. He was way better-looking than Jake.

Still, there were plenty of similarities. Ben reminded her of Jake because when he was holding her close like this, she was tempted to forget everything but how good it felt to be near him and how his mouth looked delicious enough to kiss. When she was dancing with him, nothing else mattered except the magic that was somehow happening in his arms.

If she let herself, she could fall again. Hard. Like she had for Jake. And just like that time, she could easily lose her mind, her common sense, and every shred of perspective on the fool's bet of falling in love.

It was hard to hold on tight to a realization that left her feeling empty and cold deep down inside. Lacie managed. She forced a laugh that mingled with the last words of the song and the smattering of applause from the other dancers around them. "I haven't seen Jake in a long, long time. No one has. He moved away from Sutton County the summer after we graduated from high school. California. Or so I was told. And don't bother doing the math. Let's just say it's ancient history."

Ben didn't look disappointed. "So I don't have any competition?"

"If you mean—"

"I mean exactly what I said." The dimple in his cheek showed up and disappeared again in a jiffy. "That's one thing about me you'll have to get used to. I always say what I mean. And I always mean what I say. So the question is, do I have any competition?"

"Competition?"

Lacie was so busy trying to extricate herself from a situation she wasn't sure how she got into that she didn't notice Krissie and Ed Thompson come up behind them. At the sound of Krissie's voice, she jumped.

"No one knows more about competition than my Lacie." Krissie beamed a smile at her daughter and fluttered around her, brushing an errant strand of hair out of Lacie's eyes, untying and retying the purple ribbon in her hair to make sure it was just right.

Lacie breathed a sigh of relief. The cavalry. Just when she needed it!

"Let me guess...you're talking about beauty pagents. Agent Camaglia, I'm willing to bet you're astounded by how much success Lacie's had in her career. I'm just as willing to bet my daughter here is being modest about the whole thing. She always is." Krissie wrapped Lacie in a brief heart-felt hug and when she was done, she made sure to smooth any wayward wrinkles from the sleeve of Lacie's T-shirt. "I've got to warn you, though," she said, her voice warm with admiration. "She may not look it, but she's the toughest little competitor in the entire state of Kansas. And a real hard worker. She's amazing!"

"I don't doubt that for a moment." Ben's polite smile never wilted, and the careful attention he gave Krissie and everything she said never faltered. Still, he managed to send Lacie a look that told her he wasn't thinking about beauty pageants. Or what a tough competitor she might—or might not—be. He was still thinking about those places where he didn't carry his gun.

One place in particular.

Lacie knew that from the gleam in his eye. And the tiny smile that teased the corners of his mouth. And the way he brushed a look over her that grazed her mouth and her breasts and her hips. He was still thinking that he wouldn't mind if she joined him in one of those places where he didn't carry his gun.

One place in particular.

And Lacie was thinking that if she wasn't careful, she'd find herself not minding, either.

While the thought did wonders for her ego—not to mention her libido—she knew it was a sure way to wreak havoc on her heart. Call her old-fashioned, but she was one of those women who believed in love. At least she always had until Jake came along and proved it was nothing more than a fairy tale.

She didn't need an affair with Ben to write a postscript to the story. Or to remind her that happily-ever-after was nothing more than wishful thinking. And impossible, to boot.

"We were just talking about competition." Ben eased back into the conversation. "I was just asking Lacie if—"

"Excuse my French but . . . oh, fudge!" Krissie's smile fell

like an overbeaten meringue and Lacie followed her horrified gaze to the door.

She was just in time to see Dinah and Wiley walk in, and
it didn't take more than one look to see why Krissie had
turned beet-red and hurried away. No doubt, she was
headed straight to the ladies' room to splash cold water on
her face.

No doubt, Dinah was the reason why.

Lacie's sister could be a lot of things. Subtle wasn't one of
them. Tonight Dinah was dressed in a tiny black skirt, a
teeny little halter top that was the exact color of the new
neon-blue streak she'd added to her hair, and backless shoes
with heels that were pencil thin and high enough to put her
in the nosebleed section.

She looked cheaper than usual. Trashier than ever. Vulgar
enough to make all the upstanding, right-minded, and God-
fearing Baxters who had ever come before them turn over in
their graves. Twice.

And Lacie was never so happy to see anyone in her life.

At least if she had Dinah and Wiley to worry about, she
wouldn't have to think about the way her heart beat double
time when Ben gave her that little smile that made her feel
as if the soles of her sneakers were melting into the floor.

"Your sister, huh?" Ben followed her gaze over to where
Dinah dropped her fringed leather purse on a nearby table
and waited while Wiley brought her a drink. When the disc
jockey started the next song, Dinah grabbed Wiley's hand
and together they trotted out to the dance floor.

The song was the up-tempo version of "MacArthur Park"
that Lacie used for one of her baton routines, and before she
even realized she was doing it, she found herself moving to
the beat.

No big surprise, Ben moved right along with her. He po-
sitioned himself to keep an eye on Dinah, but he kept right
on dancing.

"Is she always so . . . ?"

"Trashy?" Lacie laughed. It was working! Think about Dinah, she reminded himself. Not about how Ben moved around the dance floor smoothly, as if to prove how comfortable he was with his body, how right he felt inside his own skin.

Think about Dinah. Not about the little smile he shot Lacie's way when he saw how smoothly she could move, too.

When someone from behind bumped Lacie just enough to nudge her closer to Ben and her thigh brushed his, a zap that felt like prairie lightning flashed through her insides and heated her blood and—

Think about Dinah.

Lacie tamped down her temperature with a cold dose of reality. "I'm afraid Dinah doesn't have much fashion sense," she confessed.

"That's an understatement." Ben shook his head. "She must be hell on wheels."

"She's just a kid." It was an argument Lacie had been making in Dinah's favor for as long as she could remember and though it never changed a thing, she believed it as steadfastly as she believed in the benefits of cucumber lotion for the sensitive skin around her eyes. "She's still trying to find herself."

"That's not all she's trying to find." Lips pursed, Ben watched Dinah and Wiley bump their way around the floor. It didn't take them more than a minute to go from the this-is-fun stage straight to the dirty dancing. Wiley's groin brushed Dinah's. Dinah's thighs rubbed his. Dinah turned her back to him and Wiley wrapped his arms around her. His fingers bounced up and down her ribs and over the little ring she wore in her belly button. He inched them down even farther.

And Lacie felt herself get red all the way from her chest to the roots of her hair. She turned her back on her sister just in time to see Ben's eyebrows climb.

"We could try that."

She wasn't even sure what he was talking about until she realized that he was still watching Dinah and Wiley.

"Not a chance." Lacie shook her head. Partly to get the thought out of her head, because she'd had it herself before he even mentioned it. And because it was as crazy an idea as she'd ever heard.

She bundled her embarrassment along with her runaway fantasies and tucked them beneath a layer of righteous indignation. "Imagine! Acting that way. In public!"

"How about in private?"

For all her aw-shucks honesty, Lacie apparently wasn't used to someone laying it on the line quite so bluntly. Her eyes widened and she sucked in a sharp breath that pressed her breasts against her purple shirt.

And Ben realized that he wasn't sure if he wanted her to take him up on his offer or not. Getting her in bed—soon— sounded like a mighty fine idea. But there was something about just watching Lacie that was nice, too. Something about the thought of a leisurely seduction that appealed to him. As long as it wasn't too leisurely.

He leaned in closer. "So what do you say?"

"I say..." Her tongue flickered across her lips and for just a second, he was sure she was going to ask, "Your place or mine?" Instead, Lacie glanced across the dance floor toward the bar.

"I say that you should stop trying to be funny. Because it isn't working. I also say that I could use something cold to drink."

"You mean I've been shot down?"

She smiled that perfect smile that showed her perfect teeth. "In flames."

He offered her his arm and promised himself he'd try another day. "Beer?"

She contained her horror. But just barely. "Too many carbs. I'll take a diet soda, please."

Ben got a soda for himself, too (high-test, not diet), and

sipping it, he watched Dinah and Wiley go through their gyrations.

As if she could feel his eyes on her, Dinah glanced his way. She recognized Ben right away and her cheeks went ashen. But it was the look she shot Lacie's way that made Ben step back and check out Dinah with new interest.

"She doesn't like you."

Lacie discarded the thought with a little lift of her shoulders. "Don't be silly. Everyone likes me."

It didn't look like *like* to Ben. It looked more like *can't stand the sight of you and your big smile and your cheery voice and your house full of trophies*.

A new thought occurred to him and he stood up and gave Dinah's date a long, hard look. "What's his name?"

"Wiley. Wiley Burnside." Lacie took another drink before she set her plastic cup down on the bar. "His mother is the secretary over at the high school. His dad's been gone as long as anyone can remember. He's—"

"Trouble?"

"Did I say that?" Lacie smiled a hello to a group of ladies who sidled by to give Ben the once-over. "Dinah just won't listen. To Mom or to me." There was more wistfulness than aggravation in Lacie's voice and in the look she gave her sister, who was now down on her knees in front of Wiley and making more than one of the gray-haired ladies nearby choke on her iced tea.

"She won't listen when we talk to her about clothes. That's pretty obvious, isn't it? She won't listen when we talk to her about makeup. I wish she would because then she wouldn't even dream of wearing that color of eye shadow with her skin tone." She shook her head, getting rid of the thought. "If she won't listen about all that, you can be pretty sure she also won't listen when we talk to her about Wiley."

"And you talk to her about Wiley plenty."

"You would, too, if she were your sister." Her eyes bright with emotion, Lacie picked up her cup. "It's not that I want to interfere. I don't. It's not that I like to interfere. I'm a firm believer that we all control our own destinies. And that's the problem, don't you see? Dinah is in control of her own destiny. But instead of steering her life in the right direction, she's heading straight for disaster. I love my sister. And I don't want to see her make the same mistake as—"

As if she'd said too much without realizing it, she swallowed the rest of whatever she was going to say along with another sip of soda. Set down her cup. Folded her hands at her waist. "He's all wrong for her," Lacie said.

Even that much of a show of emotion was enough to catch Ben's interest. Especially when it came from a woman who was usually so good at hiding how she was feeling with a smile wide enough to encompass the state and every single person in it. More intrigued than ever, he leaned an elbow on the bar. "How so?"

"How?" She looked at him like he'd just asked her to explain something that was both simple and staring him in the face. Which, now that he thought about Dinah and Wiley, probably was pretty simple and staring him in the face.

But that still didn't explain Lacie's comment about Dinah making mistakes.

And whose footsteps she would have been following in if she did.

"He's not her type." Lacie's voice rang with conviction. "Not at all."

"That's funny, they look perfectly matched."

"In whose opinion?" A frown drew her golden brows into a vee. "He works at a garage."

"Is that a little bit of elitism I hear?"

The very idea horrified Lacie nearly as much as the thought of nondiet soda. "Not at all. I'm all for hard work. Why, if it weren't for the working men and women of this great land . . ." She caught herself just as she was about to launch into a speech and got herself back on track. "What Dinah and Wiley have—"

"What they must have is one hell of a good time." Watching them on the dance floor, Ben shook his head in wonder. "Man, look at the energy between them! You can just about see it crackle in the air."

Lacie was apparently not willing to consider the energy. Or anything else that might put Dinah and Wiley's crazy little love life in anything even close to a favorable light. The song finished and they headed over to a table along the far wall. When Dinah picked up the beer bottle she'd left there, Lacie's lips thinned.

"Proof positive," she said. "They're drinking beer. He's twenty-one. That's all well and good for him. But she's only twenty." She took a step in that direction. "Somebody needs to have a serious talk with—"

"Lighten up!" Ben stopped her, one hand on her arm. "Let them have a little fun and blow off a little steam. It's only a beer."

"Only a beer, huh?" Lacie glanced from her sister down to where Ben's hand was on her arm. "I would have expected a little more from you. Aren't you supposed to uphold the law?"

"Not that kind of law. Besides, it's not like they're dropping acid or anything. They've only had one beer each and that's not going to hurt anybody or anything." He signaled the bartender. "Maybe you could use one yourself."

"No, thank you," Lacie told Ben, and the bartender. "Miss Summer Squash doesn't drink alcohol."

"All right, then, if you won't look at your sister through a nice alcohol buzz, try looking at her as if she weren't your sister. Like you didn't know her or Wiley. Personally, I think they're kind of cute."

"You're kidding, right?" As if to distance herself from the very thought, Lacie pulled her arm out of Ben's grasp. "Dinah and Wiley are a disaster waiting to happen. She's going to end up with her heart broken. In case you don't get it, that's why I object to their relationship. Dinah may not see it but I do. Wiley Burnside isn't the man for her."

"Unless it's not just Wiley's bulging muscles and Wiley's manly tattoos she's after." Ben dangled the idea in front of Lacie like a fat worm on a hook, and when she didn't bite, he set down his cup and leaned back against the bar, his arms crossed over his chest. Another song started up, and Wiley and Dinah headed back to the dance floor. "How tall did you say your kidnapper was?"

The question caught Lacie off guard. But only for a second or two. She didn't have to think twice about her answer. "Over six feet," she said. "I could tell because of where my head hit his shoulder when he dragged me out of the trunk of that car."

"Muscular?"

"I suppose so. It didn't seem to be that much of an effort for him to lift me out of the trunk. That would take some muscle."

"It was hot that night, remember? I do, because the AC in my room wasn't working and I had all the windows open. I'm a city boy. The sounds of the crickets chirping their heads off just about drove me crazy. Hot. Really hot. Humid. Sticky. Uncomfortable. But you told me the guy was wearing a ski mask."

"That's right."

"You think that might be because he didn't want you to recognize him?"

This was clearly a new thought to Lacie. She considered it for a couple of moments, and when she still couldn't work her way through it and down the path where Ben was leading, she looked at him in wonder. Finding him still watching Wiley, she looked that way, too. "You mean someone I—" She took a sharp breath. "Don't be ridiculous."

The protest came out of her so fast and so vehemently that Ben couldn't help but want to pursue it.

"Why?" he asked. "Why is it ridiculous?"

"Because—" She picked up her cup. Took a drink. Set the cup down again. "It's ridiculous because...because it's ridiculous. That's why. There isn't any reason in the world for Wiley to want to—"

"You said it yourself. You said he was trouble."

"I never did. You said that. I said he was wrong for Dinah."

"And what if Dinah's the one who put him up to it?"

Her mouth fell open and she pulled herself up to her full height, raised her chin, and gave him a look that would have frozen the insides of a lesser man. Luckily for Ben, though it did chill him a little, it wasn't enough to make him let go of his theory. "How dare you? How dare you accuse my sister of—"

"I'm not accusing anyone of anything. I'm just saying that your sister isn't fond of you. That's easy to see. And don't forget, I've met her. I've talked to her. The girl doesn't have a kind word to say about you or anyone else."

"Because she's young. Because she's mixed up. That's all. She sometimes feels neglected because of all the time Mom and I spend together at pageants and dinners and grand openings and...and who can blame her? I try my best to make sure she feels included. What you're seeing here is teenage rebellion. Nothing more than that."

"Except that she isn't a teenager anymore. And kidnapping goes way beyond the rebellion stage."

"Kidnapping!" Lacie gave him one of her trademark sparkling laughs. "Your imagination has run away with you. Obviously, you've been out in the prairie sun too long."

It wasn't the first time Ben had been accused of thinking under the influence of heatstroke. And just like last time, when Ryan had dared to suggest it, he knew otherwise. His instincts told him so. His gut agreed. And he wasn't about to fight it. Not any of it. Not when his instincts and his gut and that strange sixth sense that cops have about good guys and bad guys and motives that were invisible to civilians had shown him the way to solving more cases than he could remember.

Not even because of a beautiful lady with a sparkling laugh and a sunny smile.

"I'm not accusing anyone." It went without saying, yet somehow, Ben found that more often than not, he needed to clarify that with folks. "I'm just exploring the possibilities."

"And one of those is the possibility that my little sister sweet-talked her bulky boyfriend into kidnapping me?" If Lacie had been a little more human and a little less perfect, she actually might have snorted. "You'll have to excuse me," she said. She pushed away from the bar and headed across the dance floor. "I think I've had enough for one night."

Ben had had enough, too.

Of course, that had never stopped him before. .

Before she was through the crowd and out the door, Ben was following. It might have been easier to catch up with Lacie if the Hokey Pokey hadn't started. Ben sidestepped his way through the crowd of folks putting their right feet in and their right feet out. He apologized his way around an old woman with thick-soled shoes who was so busy turning it all about that she danced right over him. By the time he got to the door and slapped it open, Lacie was nowhere to be seen.

"Damn!" Ben stepped out into the night and let the door swing closed behind him. It was still as hot as blazes and as humid as it sometimes was back in his hometown of Chicago. The air felt like a wet towel against his skin.

He undid the top button on his shirt and took a look around. There were a couple of kids coming out of the pizza place across the street and a couple more he could see over near the parking lot, but other than that, downtown Sutton Springs was as quiet as a tomb.

Except for the slim woman in jeans and a purple T-shirt who was pounding down the pavement over on the other side of Freedom Park.

Ben jogged to catch up with her.

"Hey!"

Lacie didn't stop and she didn't turn around. Ben ran a little faster. He was right behind her before he decided to try again. "I didn't mean to—"

"Of course you did." Lacie kept right on walking, her arms close to her sides, her hands folded into fists. "It was exactly what you meant. How can you accuse Wiley of anything? You don't even know Wiley."

"And you don't even like Wiley!"

"That doesn't mean I think he's some kind of felon."

"And he might not be. But if someone put him up to—"

Lacie ground to a stop and turned to face him. "Just come right out and say it, why don't you. Just come right out and say that you think my sister talked her boyfriend into kidnapping me. While you're at it, you might want to come up with a motive, too. What's Dinah going to do, get me out of the way so she can take my place at the National Miss Summer Squash pageant? Pardon me for sounding a little too sure of myself, but I think we both know there's not a chance in h-e-double-toothpicks!"

"H-e-double-toothpicks?" Ben actually might have laughed if he hadn't been so busy getting angry. "You mean—"

"I mean that a beauty queen doesn't swear." Lacie squared her shoulders and kept her voice even and far lower than Ben's. Like it or not, his was gaining in volume with every word he spoke. No wonder, in light of every ridiculous word that came out of Lacie's lips.

"A beauty queen doesn't have to swear. She's more articulate than that. More together. She's more—"

"More annoying than just about anybody I've ever met." Ben slapped his thigh and turned away. He spun back around just as quickly. "No wonder your sister wants to kidnap you! You're absolutely the most uptight, hokey—"

"Oh, please!" Lacie turned and headed back the way they had come, covering the distance in record time. "I don't need a lecture from you, Ben. As a matter of fact, I don't need anything at all from you."

"That's where you're wrong. What you need from me is protection. That's what I'm here for and that's what I'm trying to do. Only it seems mighty odd to me that when I bring up a theory that might actually have something to do with protecting you, you reject it out of hand."

"Because it's ridiculous."

They were nearly back at the VFW hall, and Lacie paused right where an alley separated that building from the dress shop next to it.

"Not so ridiculous," Ben told her. "You can't tell me you never suspected—"

"Never."

"So explain this to me. Explain why just hearing me mention that Dinah and Wiley may have somehow been involved in your kidnapping made you go off like a Fourth of July rocket. You don't like either one of them. Why are you trying so hard to defend them?"

"Number one: I do like them. At least one of them. I like my sister very much. That's exactly the reason I don't want to see her throw her life away with some guy who can't get out of his own way and isn't good at much of anything except playing video games and letting her ride roughshod over him. Number two: I'm defensive because you're talking about my sister. And that's how people in families feel about each other. Or at least that's how they're supposed to feel about each other. Even when one of them doesn't know that cream beige foundation makes her look sallow or that while basic black might be perfect for some occasions, it can also be trashy when it isn't paired with the right accessories. And number three . . ." She hauled in a deep breath.

"Number three: I don't need your protection and I don't want your protection. I'm tired of you following me around. I'm tired of seeing you everywhere I go. I can't believe you don't have better things to do. So go do them!"

"I can't. It's part of my job to—"

"What if I told you it was all a hoax? Then what?"

Though it was a theory Ben had trotted out and examined a time or two, he'd never actually believed that Lacie had it in her to string him along. Partly because she was just too goody-goody to do it. Mostly because he wasn't easily fooled.

He cocked his head and gave her the look that had made more than one scumbag shake in his shoes. "Are you telling me—"

"I'm telling you I made it all up! I spent the night in Rogers with a friend. I tore my own gown to make it look like I'd been out in the fields all night. I messed up my hair. And it got me a ton of publicity, didn't it? Just like I wanted. I'm telling you that you don't have to follow me anymore because there's no reason for you to follow me. I'm telling you that you don't have to be suspicious of Dinah and Wiley because they didn't do anything. No one's trying to kidnap me. Not Dinah or anyone else. No one's trying to hurt me."

"And you aren't scared?"

"Nope." She looked away. Like people did when they were lying. "Because there's nothing for me to be scared about. Is it a crime to make a false police report? Here!" She stuck out her arms. "Put the cuffs on me. Or browbeat me like you did poor Joey Campbell. Send me off to jail. But stop following me!"

"Fine."

But that didn't explain why Ben was feeling anything but.

Just so she wouldn't notice it, he turned and headed to the parking lot where he'd left his car. That's what he got for being a jerk. That's what he got for being taken in by the smile that wouldn't quit and the body that was as to-die-for as any he'd ever seen. That's what he got for thinking he could hook his investigative wagon to the star that was Lacie Baxter and find his way back to civilization on the coattails of her celebrity.

That's what he got for almost falling for her.

Halfway to his car, Ben stopped, rocked by the thought and all it meant. He glanced over his shoulder to where Lacie stood in the halo of a street lamp, and as soon as she looked his way, he turned around so she wouldn't know he was watching her.

He started off toward his car, mumbling to himself. "Don't need it to help me pass the time in this two-bit town. Or to get me out of here. Don't want it messing with my head and with the rest of me just because you're playing some publicity game or trying to protect your sister and her dumb-ass boyfriend so that—"

"Ben!"

He wouldn't have stopped mumbling to himself and whirled around if the voice screaming his name hadn't sounded so desperate.

He wouldn't have started running like a madman if he hadn't been just in time to see a man sprint by, latch onto Lacie's arm, and pull her into the alley.

He wouldn't have thrown the first punch if he'd had time to think, but there wasn't a whole heck of a lot of time to think.

"Ow!" Even through the gloom, Ben saw the guy who'd grabbed Lacie drop her arm and back away, both his hands over his nose. "Ow, you hit me and—"

"Jeff?" Lacie gave the man a look before she turned another, much more scathing one on Ben. "It's Jeff. Jeff Parkman. From the *Intelligencer*. You punched him in the nose."

Ben backed Jeff against the wall. "I'll hit him again if he doesn't tell me what he's up to."

"Nothing. Nothing." Jeff wiped a finger under his nose and when he saw a trickle of blood on it, he went as pale as the sliver of moon that shone above them. "I wanted to talk to Lacie. About...about the dinner dance. That's all." He glanced at Lacie, his look pleading. "I'm sorry I caught you by surprise, but I saw you talking to Agent Camaglia here and he didn't look very happy and I didn't want him to see us

together and get the wrong impression and...ow!" Jeff
fingered his nose. "All I wanted to do was get a couple of
quotes and maybe another picture or two. I didn't mean—"

"Of course you didn't." Lacie pulled a lace-edged handkerchief from the back pocket of her jeans and dabbed it
under Jeff's nose. "And I shouldn't have screamed. I was just
surprised."

"Yeah. Right. You were surprised, all right." Ben stepped
back, but only after he gave Jeff another sharp push. Just for
good measure. That wasn't nearly what the guy deserved for
scaring Lacie like that. It wasn't nearly what he had coming
to him for making Ben gallop all the way over here like he
actually cared about Lacie enough to come running to her
rescue.

He swung his gaze from Jeff to Lacie. "You panicked because you don't have anything to be afraid of. Because you
made up the story about the kidnapping and no one's trying
to hurt you. Not Dinah. Not anyone."

"That's right." Lacie wound her arm through Jeff's. "Let's
get inside and get some ice on your nose," she told him.
"And then we'll have a long talk and you can have an exclusive interview. It's the least I can do for you. For exposing
you to Attila the Hun here."

Jeff brightened instantly. "And a couple more shots—"
He glanced at Ben warily. "I mean...pictures?"

"All the pictures you want." Lacie patted his arm. Before
she could walk away, Ben grabbed her hand, holding her in
place at the same time he let Jeff by so that he could head
toward the mouth of the alley.

"You sounded pretty scared to me."

"I..." Lacie glanced away, then glanced back at him. "I
was startled and..." She lifted her chin, and though she may
have claimed not to be scared, there was no mistaking the
unshed tears that shone in her eyes.

Ben felt gratified. He had been right all along. She *was*
lying when she said she'd set up the kidnapping. She *was*

trying to protect Dinah and her boyfriend. She *was* suspicious that they were behind the thing. Just like Ben was.

"You can let go of my hand now." Lacie's gaze never wavered. "And then you can say *good night*. And throw in *good-bye* for good measure."

As if it were on fire, he dropped her hand. "Can't think of anything else I have to say right now. Not to a woman who isn't bright enough to know when she's in danger."

"That's my decision, isn't it? For now . . ." She turned and headed over to where Jeff was waiting for her, his face paler than ever now that it was illuminated by the streetlight. "I think it's safe to say we don't have anything else to say to each other. Now or ever. Good-bye, Agent Camaglia. I'd say your investigation is over."

Ben watched her go, her arm wound through Jeff's, and it wasn't until he saw them go into the VFW hall and head straight for the bar in search of ice that he stepped out of the alley and headed to his car.

This investigation? Over?

It just proved that Lacie didn't know him very well.

Because now that he had a fresh scent to follow and the chilling realization that she was just as suspicious of ol' Wiley Burnside as he was, there was no way it was over.

Not one chance in h-e-double-toothpicks.

8

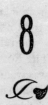

"Yes, I'm saying scared. Really scared."

"So you don't believe her? About the whole kidnapping thing being nothing but a hoax?"

Ben tucked the phone between his shoulder and his ear, trying his best to hear Ryan over the chatter of female voices that seeped through the heating ducts from Zelda's Golden Comb along with the smell of permanent solution, coffee, and the unfiltered Camels that Zelda puffed on in the back room where she washed the towels.

"No way." He scraped a hand through his hair and cringed when he realized that it was growing out in funny clumps that stuck up at odd angles all over his head. "You should have seen her face, Ryan. You should have heard her voice when she screamed. All that doofus from the newspaper did was tug on her arm and she was scared, all right. She must be teetering on the edge of a nervous breakdown, just waiting for the kidnapper to try again. And how she's able to hold it together..."

Thinking back to the incident of the night before, Ben shook his head in wonder. "Maybe she just doesn't realize that her life is in danger. Maybe it comes from breathing in too much hair spray."

"Maybe. But she's beautiful, huh?"

Ryan's voice held a note of wistfulness that made Ben chuckle. "What's the matter, buddy? You get dumped by that ATF agent already?"

"Not exactly dumped." Ryan swore under his breath. "She got transferred. To Miami, of all places. Miami! Makes me shudder just thinking about it. Besides, I'm not any good at long-distance relationships."

"The way I remember it, you're not any good at close-up relationships, either!" Ben laughed, mostly because Ryan didn't need to know that if last night proved anything at all, it proved that Ben wasn't much good at close-up relationships, either.

"So . . . you were saying . . ." Ryan waited for some kind of response, and it took Ben a second or two to remember that he'd asked about Lacie. About Lacie being beautiful.

"Hell, yes, she's beautiful." Because Ben didn't want to think about it, he spun his chair away from his desk and toward the window that looked out over Main Street, Sutton Springs. Across the street and just behind the Civic Center, a guy with a long pole was smoothing a new ad in place on the billboard that took up most of the side wall of the Food Emporium.

Cow
Sum
Squa
Sen

The already-in-place left side of the ad didn't make any sense without the still-missing right side, and that only served to pique his curiosity. He watched while the guy with the pole pasted another long roll of paper on the empty side of the billboard and smoothed it up little by little.

A bit of blue jean appeared at the very bottom of the picture, then a hint of a hip. The corner of a belt buckle. A tin dish filled with what looked to be a weird combination of vegetables in a sort of barbecued bean concoction.

Ben found himself rapping his knuckles against the windowsill, impatient to see more.

A red, white, and blue flannel shirt, sleeves rolled up, open just enough at the neck to reveal a tantalizing peek of skin the color of peaches and cream. A piece of the right side of the advertising slogan along with a chin that was flawless.

And before Ben even realized he was doing it, he found himself holding his breath.

A little more of the slogan. And a mouth that looked moist and ripe enough to kiss and gave the world a smile that was a mile wide. A nose that was turned up just the tiniest bit on the end.

And those eyes.

"Hey, did I just hear you sigh?"

Ryan's voice snapped Ben back to his senses. "Don't be ridiculous. I never sigh." He sat back and read the words on the billboard: "Cowpoke Summer Squash . . . Sensational!"

"Well?" Ryan might not know exactly what was going on, but he was always willing to play along. "Is it sensational?"

Ben took a look at the finished picture. In it, Lacie's hair was pulled up off her neck and tucked under a cowboy hat. Like on the Summer Squash à la Lacie billboard that graced the road between here and Klaber Falls, she was smiling and holding out the dish of steaming vegetables.

Eve with summer squash instead of an apple.

And Ben didn't need to remind himself that for a couple of minutes the other day at the Food Emporium and for more than a couple of minutes last night at the VFW hall, he had been all set to follow in Adam's footsteps. Even if it meant heading for a fall.

"Oh, yeah. It's sensational, all right." He knew his voice sounded sour, he just didn't care.

"And something tells me we're not talking about summer squash anymore."

"Wrong!" Ben reminded himself that, sensational or not, Lacie was his ticket out of Kansas. If he kept his mind on his investigation instead of letting it stray to Lacie's hot little body, he'd be far better off. "You get that information I asked you to check for me?" he asked Ryan.

"Got it right here." Ryan's voice faded when he reached across his desk. "Only I don't see why—"

"Let's just say they don't move like greased lightning out here in the heartland. My Internet line will be installed. Someday. Until then—"

"Until then. Anytime I can help. Only I hate to tell you, but I didn't find anything. No marriage licenses. So there goes that theory. No connection of any kind to anybody in our database."

Even though Ryan couldn't see him, Ben nodded. "That pretty much agrees with what I've found out by talking to the folks around here. Doesn't look like there's a disgruntled lover, no ex with an ax to grind. It all leads me back to the same place."

"The sister's boyfriend." It wasn't a question. Ryan was too good an investigator to miss something that obvious. Even from the other side of the country. "And you think she doesn't want you looking at him because . . ."

"Because she's empty-headed and illogical," he grumbled both to Ryan and to himself. "I don't care how beautiful the woman is, she's also as dumb as a rock. Imagine trying to protect her sister's big, stupid boyfriend! Why? Where's that going to get her except stuffed into the trunk of a car again? And next time, she might not be so lucky to get away. She's brainless, that's what she is. And clueless." Too agitated to keep still, he spun his chair back the other way. "She's—"

"She's sorry, that's what she is."

Standing in front of Ben's gray metal desk listening to him catalog her weaknesses wasn't exactly Lacie's idea of a good time. Still, she stood her ground, and when he realized she was there and his mouth dropped open and he hung up the phone without so much as saying good-bye, she held on tighter to the package she'd just picked up at the Sutton Springs Post Office. It was that, or he was sure to see that her hands were shaking.

"I don't often have anything to apologize for."

Ben just might have been on the verge of offering an apology himself. He changed his mind and snorted instead. "There's a great way to start an apology. I accuse you of being self-centered and you have the nerve to be self-centered enough to say—"

"Will you just listen?" She was always polite, but Lacie figured that this situation called for an exception to the rule. "If I don't come out and say what I came here to say, then I won't say it at all." She shook her head, ordering her thoughts. "What I mean to say is that if you don't let me just say what I came to say, I might not say—"

"Say it."

He sat back, waiting, and Lacie realized that even in the dingy little office with its murky green walls, its government-issue furniture, and its completely-lacking-in-personality photo of the President on the wall to his right, Ben looked together and completely in control.

It was the starched white shirt, she told herself. It was the tie she'd seen him wear once before, the one with the splashes of red that most guys wouldn't have been brave enough—or fashion-conscious enough—to wear. Ben's suit jacket was off and his gun was in his shoulder holster and, like it or not, she had to admit there was something about a guy carrying a gun that automatically made her think *power, manliness, sex.*

Not sex!

She slapped the thought aside.

It was the aura of confidence that made Ben look so

authoritative. It was the undeniable energy that hummed in the air around him like an electrical field.

It was not his haircut.

Even though her stomach was jumping like a grass-hopper in a wheat crop and her knees felt rubbery, Lacie couldn't help her first impulse.

And her first impulse was always to offer advice.

"You know, a hot oil treatment would do you wonders."

"You think so?" He ran a hand over his hair and made it look worse. "So would you mind explaining what you're doing here. The way I remember it, you said—"

"I said I never wanted to see you again. I said I wanted you to stop following me around. I said I wasn't scared because I didn't have anything to be scared about." Lacie swallowed her misgivings along with her pride. "I lied."

"Really?" Ben sat up in his chair and propped his elbows on his desk. "You lied about which part of it? About the not being scared part? Or about the part about not thinking that your sister and that beefy boyfriend of hers could ever wish you anything but blue skies and sunshine, puppy dogs and rainbows?"

"Sarcasm will get you nowhere." Lacie set her package on the desk. "I lied about all of it," she told him. "And it's not what I usually do. Lie about anything, I mean. It's not in my nature and, frankly, it's not in my job description. It's just that when you said that Dinah might be behind the whole kidnapping thing…well…it isn't something you like to think about, is it? About your sister disliking you so much that she would actually do something to hurt you? I lied about being scared, too. But I guess you know that." She glanced at the beige phone on his desk. "Otherwise, you wouldn't think I was brainless and clueless and empty-headed and illogical and—"

"Brainless, clueless, empty-headed, illogical, and as dumb as a rock." He didn't sound the least bit embarrassed by what he'd said, just really certain that it was the God's honest truth. "Only a woman who is brainless and clueless

and empty-headed and illogical and as dumb as a rock
would—"

"All right! I get the message." Lacie laughed, not because
it wasn't true or because she thought that Ben didn't mean
it. He meant it, all right. Every word of it. He wasn't the type
who minced words and he wasn't the type who accepted excuses for behavior he thought was foolish. In his book, the
way she had acted the night before was about as foolish as
could be. "I already said that I was sorry."

"You did." He gave her a look thorough enough to make
her quake in the sensibly priced pink leather sandals that
matched her pink-and-white cotton sweater and her pink
capri pants. "You want to explain why?"

Lacie let go of a long breath. There was a rather uncom-
fortable-looking chrome and black vinyl chair in front of
Ben's desk, and she dropped into it and moved aside her
package so that she could see him. "A woman in my position
can't afford to lie," she told him, and when he had the nerve
to smirk, she clutched her hands in her lap and gave him a
look firm enough to wipe the smile off his face.

"I'm not kidding," she told him. "Not even a little. We
talked about it. About responsibilities and obligations. Well,
being honest is every beauty queen's responsibility. Especially Miss Kansas Summer Squash. Why, the people of this
great state—"

She caught herself on the brink of starting in on the
speech she'd used at the state Summer Squash finals and decided Ben didn't really need to know any of it. It probably
didn't matter and, besides, he probably didn't care.

"I felt guilty about lying to you," she said, firmly leaving
out the part about how one of the reasons she'd lied to him
was simply to get away from him. To make sure he left her
alone. To put some distance between herself and the sensations he set off inside her. Fourth of July sparklers. Waves of
wildfire. Crazy ideas that cascaded through her head and
made her skin tingle and her insides go molten.

Before she could look into Ben's chocolaty eyes and get lost in the fantasy again, she got herself back on track. "I still feel guilty," she reminded him and herself. "About lying. I spent all night thinking about it and I knew it wasn't right."

"And every beauty queen always has to be right."

"Not to *be* right. To *do* right. Even if she feels uncomfortable about it."

"And you feel uncomfortable about—"

"About ratting on Dinah and Wiley." Too uncomfortable even with saying it, Lacie got up and paced to the door and back again. The office was small and it didn't take her long. "If I am ratting on Dinah and Wiley. I mean, it's not like I have any evidence or anything—"

"But it's not like you haven't thought of the possibility. Just like I did. From day one, you wondered if Wiley was the guy in the ski mask."

"I have. I did." Once again, she dropped into the chair. "I'm ashamed to admit it, but I have thought of it. Dinah's my sister and—"

"And stranger things have happened. Believe me. I've seen them. Have you mentioned your suspicions to your mom?"

Lacie shook her head. "She's upset enough. She loves me like crazy and—"

"And she doesn't love Dinah?"

It was one of the subjects Lacie hoped they'd never get around to discussing. She tried for a smile that didn't last long enough to be convincing—to Ben or to herself.

"Of course she loves Dinah," she said. "It's just that . . ." She cringed. Airing the family dirty laundry wasn't something she enjoyed doing. Then again, she suspected that if he really wanted to, Ben would find it all out anyway.

"Dinah and I have different fathers," Lacie said. "Not that that's any big secret or some kind of big bad news, but that's part of the dynamic between Mom and Dinah. She was what's euphemistically called an *unplanned pregnancy*."

"And your mom holds it against her."

"No." Lacie shook her head. "It's not as simple as that. She loves Dinah just like she loves me. But she loves beauty pageants more. More than anything. My mom loves the spotlight and the excitement. She loves the glamour and the competition and the sparkle and the applause. She was a pageant winner, too, you know. Mom was Sutton County Homecoming Queen and Miss Sweet Corn and Miss Valentine and even Miss Kansas Summer Squash long before I was. She was a shoo-in for the national Summer Squash title but instead of entering the pageant, she got married and got pregnant. With me. She traded in her dreams to be a mom."

"And then she turned around and sunk all those dreams into you."

"In a way." Lacie tried never to think of it exactly like that. When she did, it made her feel as if she'd robbed her mother of her rightful place in the spotlight. But she knew that wasn't true. Krissie had stepped out of the spotlight of her own accord to follow another, different dream. "By the time Dinah was born, I was almost six and I'd already been in pageants for years."

"Years?" Ben grimaced. "You mean those little girl—"

"Yes. By then, my folks were already divorced. We never saw my dad again. So you can understand, I was my mother's whole world. It isn't cheap to compete in pageants and it isn't easy. Our life revolved around getting ready for a pageant and traveling to the pageant and winning the pageant. And then starting all over on the next pageant. Then along comes Dinah and suddenly, Mom's got more to worry about than baton routines and evening gowns."

"She could have started Dinah onto the pageant circuit."

It was always amazing to Lacie that guys could never see their way past the obvious when it came to women. "Dinah? Not a chance. She doesn't have the height. She doesn't have the style. She doesn't have the cheekbones."

"So Dinah grew up resenting both of you. And Krissie resented Dinah for getting in the way."

"Not resented. My mother isn't like that. She only wants what's best for both of us. She knew Dinah would never stand a chance in the pageant world so she knew better than to even try. She knew I had potential and she's worked two jobs just to afford my pageant dresses and such. She's a clerk at the county library, you know. And she does a weekend shift at the video store just to supplement what I make teaching baton and dance. All her hopes rested on me."

"And you grew up carrying that burden."

"It's not some kind of death sentence." Lacie twitched her shoulders, getting rid of the thought. "It's an honor. And a privilege. And I'm finally going to get the chance to repay my mom."

"Summer squash?" The twinkle in Ben's eyes told her he was kidding.

Then again, he probably didn't realize just how serious the business of beauty pageants was.

"Mom is going to be a pageant coach," Lacie explained, and before he could question her further—and she knew he would—she added, "She's starting her own business. As soon as the national Summer Squash pageant is over. She's a natural."

"A natural to—"

"To teach girls the right way to walk. And the right way to talk. She'll help them choose the right costumes, find their strongest talents. You know, that kind of thing. It's the perfect opportunity for her to put her experience to work. Her own titles give her the perfect qualifications and everybody knows she's coached me all these years, so my pageant wins will really put her in demand."

"So both you and your mom have a good thing going here. That doesn't say much for Dinah. I'll bet she's never been happy with the whole pageant thing."

"It's not easy having me for a sister."

"I'll bet!" Ben stood and leaned forward a little, his palms flat against the desktop. "So tell me, why have you suddenly decided to come clean about all this?"

"I told you. I felt guilty." It wasn't easy for Lacie to admit. Just like it wasn't easy to force herself to look up and into Ben's eyes. Bad enough that she was there eating crow. Worse when every second they were together, she thought about how good being with him last night had made her feel.

Until she remembered how bad it was bound to turn out.

"I figure I owe you," she told him.

"For?"

She looked away and immediately regretted it. Most of last night and all of this morning, she'd practiced what she was going to say to Ben. How she was going to explain. She'd reminded herself that she wasn't here for anything except his help. It was silly to feel nervous.

"For following me. For watching over me."

"Following you and watching over you were exactly what you were complaining about yesterday."

"You sure don't make apologizing easy." Lacie stood, too, mostly to dispel the nervous energy that built inside her every time Ben looked at her. And he was looking at her now.

"You're doing your job. I understand that. Even when you're accusing Dinah and Wiley, you're doing your job. Just for the record, let's set everything straight. There really was a kidnapping. I didn't make it up. I didn't tear my own dress. I didn't spend the night in Rogers. I said all that last night just so you'd leave me alone."

"And—just for the record—how do you think Dinah and Wiley fit into the whole thing?"

"They don't. I've thought about it and thought about it. And I still don't think they had anything to do with the kidnapping."

"Then who did?"

"I honestly don't know." Lacie sucked in a breath and let it out slowly. "You see, that's exactly why I'm so scared. If I really thought it was Dinah and Wiley...well, let's admit it. If I really thought it was Dinah and Wiley, I'm pretty sure I could handle it. They're not exactly the brightest bulbs in the box. Even if they did try again, I don't think they'd get it right. Dinah may be a mess physically, but honestly, I don't think she's mentally unstable. Or dangerous. Even if she wanted me out of the way or she wanted to prove she was smarter than me or even if she just wanted to kidnap me to scare me...even if she was behind it, I don't think either she or Wiley would ever really hurt me."

"And if she's not behind it?"

Lacie picked up her package, then set it down again. "I've got a personal appearance," she said. "The Summer Carnival in Rogers next week. I thought..."

He knew exactly what she was going to say. Lacie could tell from the little satisfied smile that tugged at the corners of Ben's mouth. She also knew he wasn't going to let her off the hook. He was going to make her come right out and say it. No matter how much pride it cost her.

She hurried through the words she'd been practicing on the drive from Klaber Falls. "I'd appreciate it if you'd come to Rogers with me. It's a couple of hours away and I'll be gone all day. Mom has offered to go. She comes to most of my personal appearances with me, of course, but...well, it's Ed Thompson's birthday and I hate to make her miss the celebration. Besides that, if the kidnapper tries anything..."

"If the kidnapper tries anything and if that kidnapper isn't big, dumb Wiley Burnside, then you might be in serious danger."

"Exactly." Lacie let go of a breath along with some of the tension that had been building in her ever since the night she'd left Mercer's and ended up in the trunk of that car. Funny how sharing what she was feeling took some of the fear out of the situation. How knowing that Ben would be there to keep her safe made her feel better. "Mom is great company but...well, if there really is any danger, I don't want her exposed to it. And, frankly, I don't think she'd be much help if it came to a fight."

"You could always use your baton."

From the gleam in his eye she knew he was teasing. As much as she appreciated what he was doing to lighten the mood, she wasn't about to succumb. Considering the way she'd treated him, she didn't deserve it.

Considering the way he made her feel, she couldn't afford it.

"Yes," she said, "I could use my baton. But let's face it. We both know that the only reason I got away from that guy was because he didn't expect me to fight back. Next time, I might not be so lucky."

His expression sobered. "I'm glad you finally realize it. The carnival is—"

"Next weekend. My appearance is scheduled for Saturday. I'll be leaving early in the morning and staying until late. I could pick you up on my way."

"Or I could come and get you." It wasn't a suggestion, simply a statement of fact.

"Thank you." Their business was done and it had gone well, considering. Still, Lacie was reluctant to leave.

"It's the hair!" The words fell out of her mouth before she could stop them and before she even knew what was holding her there. "If you'd just let me—"

"What's wrong with my hair?" Funny that a guy carrying a gun that big and that lethal-looking could sound so defensive. Ben ran a hand over his hair.

Lacie called on years of training in the gentle art of even gentler criticism. "There's nothing *wrong* with it. Not really. Not exactly. It's just that . . ." She ripped into the package she'd brought with her from the post office. "Here." She held out a little tube filled with pumpkin-colored oil. "I get this from a boutique in San Francisco. It's a mixture of oil and herbs. Half a tube. Once a week. In another few weeks or so—"

"In another few weeks or so, I am happy to say that I'm

going to get my hair cut by a barber who isn't as scissor-happy as that guy down the street." Ben declined the hot oil treatment with a shake of his head that made his hair droop over his forehead and a smile that warmed Lacie down to her toes. "My sister's getting married," he explained. "Back in Chicago. If I can hold out until then . . ."

"By then, the best haircut in the world isn't going to help if your hair is damaged beyond belief. And, believe me, I've seen the results of Gib's work. I don't know what he does, but he has a way of manhandling even the healthiest hair. After a few cuts, most of the guys around here are hopeless. Come on." She offered him the tube again. "It's the least I can do, considering that you're going to come to Rogers with me."

"I'm not allowed to accept bribes in return for doing my job."

"And I'm not allowed to offer any bribes. After all, that would be unethical and every pageant contestant always has to be—"

"Ethical."

They finished the sentence in unison and laughed.

"Let's not call it a bribe, let's call it a work of mercy." She set the tube on the desk. "Trust me, you'll love it. And so will your hair. By the time you get that haircut in Chicago, you'll be your old self."

"I doubt that."

No way had Ben intended the statement to come out with quite so much honesty. Chalk it up to the heat and the AC that was cranking away and doing pretty much nothing at all. Blame it on the early hour and the fact that after Lacie had made his blood boil the night before—first in good ways by treating him like he was the only man in the world, and then in not-so-good ways because she was so hardheaded and unreasonable—he hadn't gotten much sleep. It was the only reason he'd nearly come right out and announced that he was bored, miserable, and just counting down the days until he could spend a weekend in Chicago—and away from Sutton County.

Either that, or today was a day for confessions.

Ben considered the thought along with all it meant while he studied Lacie. In her cheery pink outfit, she looked like a garden flower. Bright and beautiful. Sunshiny and—he had to admit it, even though he knew it was best not to—as sexy as hell. But, bright or not, there was the slightest trace of stress on Lacie's face. He could see it in the way her lips thinned when she talked about Dinah and Wiley and the things her mother expected from her. He knew it because, whether she realized it or not, she leaned just to one side every once in a while, hiding behind her package. He could tell because, though she'd used an expert hand to hide it, he'd been trained to look for such things. Even the makeup under her eyes couldn't disguise a smudge of sleeplessness.

It had cost her a lot to come here and admit that she was scared. That she was wrong.

The least he owed her was a little honesty in return.

"I guess it doesn't take a psychic to see that I don't have a lot to do around here to keep me busy."

She nodded as if she understood. "That explains why you've stuck your nose into this kidnapping case even though the FBI—"

"The FBI has traditionally been the point man, so to speak. For kidnapping cases." Ben sounded a little too quick and defensive, even to himself. Still, he wasn't about to pull back. He knew he was right and besides, it was too late. "Kidnapping is in our jurisdiction, after all."

"When the kidnapper crosses state lines."

She had him there, and there was no use pretending she didn't.

He waved a hand over his desk. It was as clean as a whistle. "Look at this! Back in Washington, I had stacks of papers on my desk. Miles of reports. Tons of information I needed to sift through. Lots to do and all of it interesting. And here—"

"Here, you're bored." Lacie nodded briskly, as if she'd known the ugly truth all along. "That explains the bags, of course."

"Bags?"

"Under your eyes."

Ben leaned down and peered at himself in the monitor of the computer on his desk. He couldn't see much with the way the light was streaming in through the window behind him. Before he could even begin to offer a protest, Lacie was already digging through the package she'd ripped open just a few minutes earlier. She fished out what looked like a fat tube of toothpaste and grinned. "Sit down." She waved him toward his chair.

"But I don't—"

"Stop being a baby." Lacie was the least likely general he could think of. Especially in those short pink pants, that cute summer sweater, and the sandals that showed off the pink polish on her toes. That didn't stop her from issuing the command as if she were used to being in charge. "Sit down," she said again, and the ring of conviction in her voice was so unexpected, Ben had no choice but to obey. He dropped into his chair.

"A little bit of Mrs. Allen's Secret Formula Eye Rejuvenating Emollient under your eyes for just a few minutes and—"

"Under my eyes?" He ran a finger over his face. "I don't need to put anything under my eyes. I don't have bags under my eyes. And besides, guys don't—"

"Of course they do!" She twisted the top off the tube and squeezed something that looked like lime-green slime onto her fingers. "Head back," she ordered. "And if you could turn just a little so that the light is better…"

She whirled his chair toward the window and before Ben knew it, she was spreading the green ooze on the skin just below his right eye. Mrs. Allen's Secret Formula Eye Rejuvenating Emollient was cool; Lacie's fingers were warm.

Though Ben had no intention of doing it, it wasn't long before he found himself closing his eyes.

"That's better. Just relax." Slowly and carefully, Lacie smeared the stuff over his skin until he could feel it in a semicircle under his eye. "You're so tense—no wonder you look so awful."

"Awful?" He popped open one eye just to see if she was serious, and when he saw that she was, he closed it again. Better to look at nothing at all than have to face the satisfied look on Lacie's face.

"Awful," she said again. Maybe just because she wasn't sure he heard her. Maybe just to rub it in. "You've heard people say that your eyes are the windows to your soul? Well, your skin is, too. It's a sort of barometer that can tell a trained person how you're feeling."

"And you're a trained person?"

"You bet I am." Ben heard her step back and he could only imagine that she was taking a look at her handiwork. Apparently deciding it was just right, she moved on to the other eye. "Your skin is screaming tension. Loud and clear. It's screaming dissatisfaction. Lack of interest. Lack of enthusiasm. I suppose that makes sense considering that you said you're bored. Still..." He could tell she had paused with her hand just inches from his face because he could feel the ripples of warmth that rose off her skin and smell the flowery perfume she'd touched to her wrists before she left the house.

"You do have good coloring," she told him. "And very nice skin. I'll bet your mother is a redhead."

"It's my dad, actually. And it's more mahogany than red. His great-grandparents were from Milan."

"Ah, that wonderful northern Italian coloring!" Lacie sighed in appreciation, and because she was leaning over him, her breath rippled the funny clump of hair that hung over his forehead. "And your mother?"

"My mother?" It wasn't exactly easy for him to talk about

his mother. Not when Lacie leaned even closer and her breasts brushed his arm. His mother? His mother—who was as famous for speaking her mind as she was for her home-made pizza—would have told him flat out that he'd better mind his p's and q's and keep his wits about him.

If only Mom were here, he would have told her that what she was asking was next to impossible.

Ben opened his eyes—just a little—so he could get a look at Lacie, up close and getting more personal by the moment. "Mom's parents are straight from Sicily. I've got my Grandpa DiNardo's hair. Minus the bad haircut, of course."

Lacie daubed goo below his left eye. "I'll bet you have his temperament, too."

Bad enough he was sitting there like a Ken doll in train-ing, getting more aroused by the moment thanks to Lacie's perfume and the touch of her skin against his. Worse that he had to listen to a criticism of his personality while he did. He sat up straight and opened his eyes, and Lacie stepped back and out of his way. "What's that supposed to mean?"

Lacie was standing no more than a foot away, the index and middle fingers of her right hand smeared with green gunk. She tipped her head to one side, then the other. "The way you're always so impatient, of course. I mean, far be it for me to believe in stereotypes, but Italians do have a repu-tation for being—"

"What?" Ben's jaw went rigid. "What are we?"

"Stubborn. Headstrong. Always itching for a fight." She tipped her head back the other way at the same time she closed in on Ben. With one finger of her left hand, she nudged his chin and, like it or not, he had no choice but to tilt his head back and look up at the ceiling. That, or come across looking stubborn and headstrong.

"Then there's quick-tempered, of course," Lacie said, smoothing the glop under his left eye. "You've proven that a time or two."

That wasn't all he'd like to prove. Especially when she

was standing so close and all it would take was one quick move to hook an arm around her waist and pull her onto his lap.

After that?

She was right about one thing. Italian ancestors or not, Ben was impatient. After he had her on his lap, he wouldn't wait another second. Stuck-up and as dumb as a rock? She sure was. But Ben could hardly wait to kiss her silly.

Just like he'd been wanting to kiss her silly practically since the moment they met.

"There." Was it Lacie's imagination or did she sound winded? Like she'd just run through her most strenuous baton routine. Or pushed herself too hard and too fast through her aerobics exercises. Like she was standing too close to a man who was too hot for both her fantasies and for the reality she should have been smart enough to recognize when it was staring her in the face.

She backed up one step, then another, putting some distance between herself and the temptation that was Ben Camaglia. Even when he did have half-circles of chartreuse gook under his eyes.

"Let that set for ten minutes." She hurried around to the other side of the desk and picked a handkerchief out of her purse with her clean left hand. She wiped her gooey fingers. "Then just wash it off with cool water and—"

"Camaglia! You here?"

Before either of them could react to the voice, Sheriff Ed Thompson gave a quick rap on Ben's door and pushed his way into the office. He looked surprised to see Lacie there, but only for a moment. He looked surprised to see green goo under Ben's eyes, too, but that surprise didn't last long, either.

Thompson pointed at Ben and grinned. "Mrs Allen's Secret Formula Eye Rejuvenating Emollient. Krissie swears by the stuff."

"That's because it's so good." Lacie knew a gift from the

gods when she saw one, and this one was about as welcome as one could be. Before she could stop and think of how close she'd come to indulging in the fantasies that popped out of her subconscious every time she made the mistake of getting too close to Ben, she grabbed her package and her purse and headed for the door.

"I'm sure you two have law enforcement things to discuss." She stepped her way around the sheriff. "So I'll just be leaving. Remember, cool water," she told Ben, and she hurried out the door.

Out in the hallway, the smell of permanent solution and Zelda's cigarettes was even stronger than in Ben's office. Lacie didn't much care. She leaned against the wall outside his door and drew in a long breath.

"Nothing to get all upset about," she told herself in the little half-whisper she used to psych herself out before pageants. "You came to apologize and you apologized. You came to ask for help and you asked for help. So you see..." She stood up straight, tugged her sweater down into place, and headed for the stairs. "Everything turned out just the way you wanted. You've got an escort, a knight in shining armor. And you don't need to worry about that kidnapper anymore."

Even before she was all the way down the stairs and out onto the street, she saw the error of her reasoning.

Sure, she didn't have to worry about her kidnapper. But now she was stuck with taking Ben on the long trip to Rogers, and that gave her more serious things to worry about.

Like the way Ben Camaglia made her feel.

The fact that she was getting used to it.

And the way she was enjoying it.

Way too much.

9

"I'll tell you what, my friend . . . I have never in my life seen anything that looked as delicious as that!"

The words coming from the old bald guy standing at Ben's side snapped him out of his fantasies and back to reality.

Delicious?

The man, whose skinny legs stuck out of his denim shorts and whose arms were as thin as broomsticks, wasn't kidding.

Only something told Ben he wasn't thinking about the same thing Ben was thinking about.

Uncomfortable with the thought, Ben pushed off from the outside wall of one of the Rogers Summer Carnival exhibition buildings. He slanted the old fellow a look and saw that the man—the senior citizen center badge hanging from his neck said his name was Hank—was still watching what was going on ten feet or so in front of them. "Delicious, huh?"

Hank nodded his appreciation. "You bet! Haven't seen anything that looked that good since my Wilma up and died. You know what I mean?"

"Not about Wilma, no. I do know what you mean about not seeing anything that's looked that good in a long time."

Hank, apparently, was more observant than Ben could have imagined—and a better judge of Ben's wistful looks than he thought any stranger could be. He gave Ben a good-natured elbow to the ribs. "I'm talkin' about this here cookin' demonstration we're watchin'. About those there vegetables that young lady's cookin' up," Hank said with a laugh. "Not about the young lady herself."

"I'm talking about the young lady." No one was more surprised than Ben that he was willing to admit it. Then again, there was something about baring his soul—along with the figments of his runaway imagination—to a stranger that was far easier than admitting the truth to a friend. Or to himself. "She may be a complete airhead, but she's as pretty as a picture."

"I'll say." Hank sighed with appreciation and pulled a container of chewing tobacco out of his pocket. He put a pinch of chew between his cheek and gums. It was only a little after eleven in the morning and already, the sun was high in a clear blue sky and the temperature was flirting with ninety. Hank moved a little farther back into the scrap of shadow thrown by the exhibition building and watched Lacie toss a bowlful of diced summer squash into a sizzling skillet.

Though there wasn't a soul in the crowd not dripping with sweat or using the tractor pull timetables that were being handed out at the turnstiles as a fan, Lacie looked as fresh and as cool as a salad. She was wearing a short-sleeved green and white flowered dress and a little white apron embroidered with tiny summer squash. As much as the whole retro look reminded Ben of the women he'd seen on TV sitcom reruns from back in the antediluvian Fifties, he couldn't help but admit that it was also as sexy as hell.

White pumps. A hairstyle that was as neat and as prim as the way she wiped her hands against the linen towel on the countertop next to her. A smile that was as wide as the sky above them. And a personality that just about jumped out into the crowd and had each and every person there glued to the spot and smiling right back at her.

Lacie had it all.

Including, apparently, summer squash recipes the likes of which every person in the audience couldn't wait to get their hands on.

"See? Wasn't that easy?" Lacie finished off the squash in the skillet with a drizzle of lemon juice, added a handful of almonds, and tipped the pan so that her audience could see. "Ten minutes," she told them. "Cutting board to dinner table." She handed the pan to the representative of the Summer Squash Board who was assisting her, and went on to the next recipe.

"Summer sqaush isn't just a side dish," she told the crowd. "It can also make a dramatic main dish. See . . ." She pointed toward a platter of cut-in-half, degutted squash that was slowly wilting in the sun. "You can always try Summer Squash Surprise. Just fill your Kansas summer squash with . . ."

"You like summer squash?" Ben didn't know why the question seemed so important, but he asked Hank anyway. "I mean, would you go through all the trouble of having so many different recipes for—"

Hank spit tobacco juice on the ground. "You've never had a garden, have you, young fella? Stuff multiples overnight. Like those danged rabbits that used to roam around in my soybean fields like they owned the place. You plant it in hills, you know? Little mounds." He demonstrated with both hands, rounding the imaginary dirt on top of an imaginary little hill.

"And each and every mound . . ." Hank whistled low under his breath. "Got so Wilma had to get pretty darned creative with the stuff. Squash bread and squash casserole and squash pie. Even tried one of them there quiches once. Imagine that!" A shiver ran across the old guy's scrawny shoulders. "Not the kind of thing a man eats, after all, and I told her as much. She didn't take it too hard. Went back to the squash bread, the way I remember it."

Squash bread was something Lacie had yet to demonstrate, and as much as Ben was tempted, he knew better than to be impatient for her to get the whole squash thing over with. She had explained all about it on the ride from Klaber Falls to Rogers.

One morning appearance. Summer squash recipes.

One evening appearance. Something more flashy, apparently, because she'd brought a long clothing bag that contained a gown.

In between . . .

Ben thought back to the conversation they'd had in the car that morning.

In between the summer squash recipes and the evening gown appearance, Lacie anticipated spending the day smiling and pressing the flesh. She knew there would be photographs to sign, and people to meet and greet. She'd promised to have lunch with members of the Summer Squash Board and told Ben that he was more than welcome to join them.

A grueling schedule under the best conditions.

Even more so, considering the temperature and the press of the crowd. And, of course, though neither of them had said a word about it on the way from Lacie's house to Rogers, they both knew that this was an ideal situation for the kidnapper to try again.

Plenty of people.

Plenty of noise.

Plenty of confusion, with people coming and going, and that meant there were plenty of chances for everybody and his brother to get close to Lacie. Maybe even close enough to grab her.

And if it happened?

Ben twitched away the thought.

"Not on my watch," he mumbled to himself, and when he

saw Hank look at him out of the corner of his eye, he dismissed the comment with a wave of his hand. "Talking to myself," he told Hank. "About—"

"About her, I bet." Hank nodded as if he understood. For all Ben knew, he did. "Can't say I blame you, though I have to say, you don't exactly look to be her type. She's a local girl, you know. Born and raised in these parts. The pride of Sutton County." Hank turned just enough to give Ben a long, careful look. "You ain't from around here. I can tell that. Even if Gib Allen over in Sutton Springs does cut your hair."

Defensively, Ben ran a hand over his head. After two applications of the pumpkin-colored oil Lacie had insisted on giving him, he thought his hair looked pretty good. Apparently, it still had a long way to go. He reminded himself that his haircut—good or bad—was not the most important thing he had to think about.

"You know a lot of the people from over in Sutton Springs?" he asked Hank.

"Pretty much all of them." Hank spewed a long stream of brown tobacco juice on the ground. "It's a big area, mileage-wise, but there aren't many of us left around here. Not like it used to be. These days, the kids finish over at the high school and head off somewheres else. Big cities. Everyone wants to live in big cities. Can't understand why."

Ben could. The building just behind them housed the 4-H exhibits, and when the wind shifted, the smell of livestock was as thick in the air as the chatter of appreciative squash watchers. "There's one young guy who hasn't left," he said, wading into the topic casually so Hank wouldn't be suspicious. "Kid by the name of Wiley Burnside. You know him?"

"Burnside?" Hank tugged on his right earlobe. "Knew his father. No-good son-of-a-beet. The mother's a nice lady, though. Works at the school. Drove my grandson home once. When he missed the bus. Saw her here a little while ago. Over near where they're milkin' the cows."

"And Wiley?"

"Big kid, right? Lots of muscles. Really bad tattoos, the way I remember it."

"Seen him around?"

"Here?" Hank chuckled. "Maybe later. At the tractor pull or when that loud music group from over in Wichita is supposed to perform. Or maybe even later than that, when the vendors aren't so careful about who they're selling beer to or how much they're pouring. But this afternoon . . ." Hank glanced around. "Lamb judgin' in thirty minutes," he said. "Summer squash recipes now. I hear there's a pie-eatin' contest sometime around three. That sound like the kind of stuff Wiley Burnside might be interested in?"

"It isn't that kind of stuff I think he might be here for."

Hank looked at Lacie. "You mean her."

"How—"

The old man brushed away the question. "I ain't no mind reader, if that's what you're thinkin'. Like I said, everyone around here knows everyone else. And everyone around here knows everyone else's business. Since you're wearin' one of them Goo-chi suits while the rest of us is in our play clothes, all I did was put two and two together. You're that FBI fella. And you must be keepin' an eye on Lacie. I'm glad, I'll tell you that much. Wouldn't want to see anything happen to the girl."

Like everyone else in the crowd, Hank applauded when Lacie finished preparing Summer Squash Surprise.

"Haven't seen Wiley. Not all day," Hank said. "If I were you, though, I wouldn't waste too much time thinkin' about him. Wiley doesn't have the brains to get in out of the rain. Besides, I don't think you'll find your kidnapper anywhere around here. Has to be one of them nutcases. You know, hitchhikin' and drugs and booze and rock 'n' roll. Somebody just passin' through."

It was a possibility Ben had thought about a time or two, but this time, like those times, he wasn't convinced. "Why here, then? And why Lacie? How did the kidnapper know the Whipple house was empty?"

"Pure, dumb luck." Hank nodded, as sure as can be. "Only explanation that makes any sense at all. Look at her. And think about it. Ain't nobody in these parts would wish Lacie bad."

Hank's theory fit in light of what Ben had found out from Sheriff Thompson the day Lacie came to his office. A lady walking her dog had found an abandoned car near the picnic grove on the far side of Sutton Springs. The car had been reported stolen somewhere in Nebraska just a couple of days before Lacie was kidnapped. Ben had checked, of course, and no one could remember that Wiley had ever left town to go to Nebraska. No one could even remember Wiley ever talking about going to Nebraska. Several folks swore that if you spotted him the *N-e-b-r-a-s* and *k,* Wiley couldn't even spell Nebraska.

Ben was back exactly at square one.

A movement on the fringes of the crowd caught his attention and Ben glanced that way. "What about him?" he asked Hank. "That guy over there. The one with the potbelly and the greasy hair."

Hank followed his gaze. "Randy Holcomb?" He spit his wad of tobacco on the ground. "Seems strange you should ask about Randy."

"Not so strange, the way he's been acting all day." Ben had kept an eye on the guy in shabby blue jeans and a blue windbreaker. "Saw him soon after we got here this morning and it seems like everywhere Lacie goes, he does, too."

"No surprise there, if you take my meaning. You said it yourself: She's a delicious little thing."

Ben thinking about Lacie as delicious didn't seem nearly as disgusting as some middle-aged guy with blotchy skin and long, thinning hair thinking of Lacie as delicious.

He got rid of the thought with a grunt. "You think—"

"Nah!" Hank chuckled. "Randy might be a little off in the

noodle—" He tapped his forehead with one finger. "But it ain't Lacie he's watching. It's Crystal over there." Hank wasn't a tall man and he craned his neck. He saw who he was looking for and pointed toward a woman on the far side of the crowd. Crystal was small and as round as a haystack. She had bleached blond hair and was wearing tight black shorts and a bright red tank top. With one hand, she fanned her face with the tractor pull schedule. With the other one, she hung on to a little boy who looked to be about four. The kid was chomping on a cone of cotton candy that, thanks to the sun, was getting gooier by the moment.

"She dumped him, you know. Not a surprise to anybody but Randy. She took up with that Slim Pepboy from over at the truck stop. Dumped Randy and convinced the judge not to let him have any visitation with Tyler, neither. Not right, if you ask me. A boy needs his father. Even when that father is as loony as Randy Holcomb. But you know how it goes, what a judge says is gospel."

"And so now Randy follows Crystal around."

And wears a windbreaker even though it's hot enough to cook summer squash on the pavement.

Ben glanced down at his own Goo-chi pants and the suit jacket he was wearing to hide his shoulder holster and the forty-millimeter Glock in it. He made a mental note to himself to keep an eye on Randy Holcomb.

Not as easy as it sounded.

Lacie finished her presentation and the crowd burst into appreciative applause. People hurried forward to talk to her and get one of the free samples of her cooking that was being handed out by the lady from the Squash Board.

And Randy Holcomb was lost in the commotion.

"You are going to get one, aren't you?" Hank tugged on Ben's arm. "She's givin' out them free cookbooks. Come on, young fella. My Wilma, she would have loved one of those."

By the time they fought their way to the front of the crowd, the cookbooks were nearly all gone. Luckily, there was one left for Hank, and when Lacie signed it and handed it to him, the old guy beamed like a bridegroom.

"So what do you think?" Lacie waved a hand over the area where the dirty pots and pans were being whisked away by a Squash Board gofer. "See anything you like?"

"Oh, yeah!" Ben glanced over at the dainty apron and wondered how it would look if Lacie were wearing that— and nothing else at all.

He batted the thought aside and waved when Hank walked away. He used the opportunity to take another look at the crowd.

"I think things are going well," he told Lacie. "Doesn't seem to be much interest in you."

Lacie's shoulders shot back and her chin came up. "Excuse me? What do you mean there doesn't seem to be much interest in—"

"I mean in an I'm-going-to-kidnap-you sort of way." Ben made sure he kept his voice down so that the people milling around wouldn't hear. "I mean that there doesn't seem to be anyone hanging around who looks dangerous. Or crazy."

"Except for you!" Lacie laughed and gave Ben's wool suit a long look. "You get extra pay for wearing that thing in these temperatures?"

"Do you?" He looked at her outfit again. "The high-heeled shoes, the dress, the apron. You must be broiling!"

"All part of the job." She grinned. "Duties and responsibilities, remember?"

"Same here." Ben ran a finger around the collar of his white shirt. "Though if you're done, I sure could use something cold to drink."

"I can do better than that!" Lacie leaned down and opened a Styrofoam cooler and brought out a bowl with a scoop of ice cream in it. "Francie..." She bestowed a smile on the lady from the Squash Board. "She brought this for me but, well..." Lacie lowered her voice. "Too many fat grams," she whispered. She handed the bowl to Ben. "That ought to cool you down."

Ben accepted the ice cream and scooped up a spoonful. It was a pale color somewhere between yellow and green, and at the same time he wondered if it was pistachio or butter pecan, he decided he didn't really care. Hot was hot, and it was definitely hot. And the ice cream looked nice and cold.

He popped the spoon in his mouth and made a face. "What the heck!" It was impossible to do anything else, so Ben swallowed before he pushed the dish back at Lacie. "What's that supposed to be?"

"Summer squash ice cream, of course!" She laughed. "What else did you expect?"

"Thank you, and keep enjoying Kansas summer squash!"

Lacie signed the eight-by-ten photo of herself and handed it—along with a bright smile—to an elderly woman.

"Thank you, and keep enjoying Kansas summer squash!"

The next photo and smile went to a fifteen-year-old girl with bad hair and worse skin, who looked at Lacie with nothing short of unmitigated adoration.

"Thank you, and keep enjoying Kansas summer squash!"

When she handed out the next picture, Lacie took the chance to check out the line. It fanned out from the table where she sat and snaked all the way between the Ferris wheel and the Tilt-O-Whirl, at least forty people long. The last thing she wanted to do was slight anyone, but Lacie picked up the pace just a little. The hog-calling contest had just concluded over in the grandstand; she'd heard the winner announced. That meant it was just after six and she needed to change out of her green-and-white dress and into the evening gown she'd brought along. She was scheduled to hand out the blue ribbons for pies, cakes, and cookies in a little less than an hour.

"Thank you, and keep enjoying Kansas summer squash!"

Automatically, she signed another picture and glanced up. "Randy?" Lacie wasn't exactly surprised to see Randy Holcomb. Crystal and Tyler had been in line only a couple of minutes earlier, and though Randy had always been quiet and more than a little withdrawn, it wasn't much of a secret that he'd spent the day following them.

"I haven't seen you in ages, Randy! How are you?"

Randy shuffled his feet and looked over Lacie's shoulder toward the tent where the senior citizens were playing bingo. He looked to his right, to where Crystal and Tyler were waiting in line for the Tilt-O-Whirl. "I'm ... I'm okay, Miss Baxter." His fingers worked over the snaps on his windbreaker. "And how are you and ... and your family?"

"We're fine, Randy. How nice of you to ask." Like everyone else in a hundred-mile radius, Lacie knew the story of how Crystal had cheated on Randy with Slim Pepboy. She knew it was a touchy subject, but like everyone else, she also knew that a little nutty or not, Randy Holcomb had gotten the short end of the stick when it came to the custody battle in court.

"I saw Tyler earlier," she said because there wasn't any use pretending Randy didn't know that Crystal and Tyler were at the carnival. "He's grown a foot since last winter! He's a handsome boy."

"He is, ma'am." Something that wasn't exactly a smile touched Randy's face and was gone again in an instant. "He's got his mother's eyes."

"And his father's mouth." His mouth was actually the only part of Randy's face that was anywhere even close to attractive, so Lacie didn't feel guilty offering the compliment. "You should be proud of him."

"I am." Randy glanced toward the Tilt-O-Whirl again, and when he saw that Crystal and Tyler were just getting on, he looked away. "I just miss him is all."

"I know." Lacie reached across the table and gave Randy's hand a quick squeeze. Embarrassed, he backed away. "Don't forget your picture." She held out the glossy photo to Randy and gave him the teasing sort of smile that she often used to help shy people open up just a little. "That is what you came for, isn't it?"

"I ..." Randy moved back another step, bumping into the person behind him. "I just came to say hello and ... well ... and good-bye."

He hurried away and Lacie found herself holding a photo out to the person who was in line behind Randy.

"Thank you, and keep enjoying Kansas summer squash." She waited for that person to step aside, and signed another picture. "Thank you and keep enjoying—"

"What did he say?"

Ben's voice at Lacie's shoulder startled her just a bit. The last time she'd seen him he was standing over near the french fry cart. Still, even that wasn't enough to distract her from her duties.

"... Kansas summer squash."

She handed over the picture and looked at Ben out of the corner of her eye. "He didn't say much of anything, just hello." She swung her gaze to the next person in line. "Thank you, and keep enjoying Kansas summer squash."

"Hello? He stood in line all that time just to say hello? Do you think he's tall enough to be—"

"Thank you, and keep enjoying Kansas summer squash." Lacie's smile faded when she turned from the person in front of the table to Ben. "Yes," she said. "He is tall enough to be my kidnapper. But Randy is the last person who—"

"Randy isn't the kidnapper. Wiley isn't the kidnapper. What, you got kidnapped by the Invisible Man?" Ben bent closer, one hand on the table next to Lacie's. "The guy's been following you. All day." He had to keep his voice down, and that meant he had to lean in close.

Not a good idea, considering the heat.

Really not a good idea, considering that when Ben was

this close, the outside temperature was nothing compared to the heat that built inside.

"Thank you." Lacie pulled herself back to reality and held out another photo, adding almost as an afterthought, "And keep enjoying Kansas summer squash."

The next folks in line were Rita and Dave Johnson, who Lacie had gone to high school with. She waved and waited when Rita Mae, their five-year-old, dumped her iced tea and the line stopped while they cleaned it up.

"Randy hasn't been following me and you know it," she told Ben. "He's been following Crystal. And Tyler. I told you that at lunch."

"Well, I didn't see Crystal and Tyler anywhere near where we had lunch. But I did see Randy. He's wearing a windbreaker. I don't like it."

Lacie laughed. "What? So now you're the fashion police? I don't like it, either. Not exactly high style but then, this isn't exactly—"

"That's not what I mean." Ben had to back off when the paper iced tea cup was finally cleaned up and the ice cubes were kicked aside. Rita, Dave, and Rita Mae made their way to the table. Since Lacie had just seen Rita at a church potluck, they didn't have much catching up to do and she was on to the next person in line in record time.

"Thank you and—"

"So if he's following Crystal and Tyler, what's he doing here in your line? Crystal and Tyler are already over there." Ben looked toward the Tilt-O-Whirl.

"Thank you, and keep enjoying Kansas summer squash." Lacie wondered how it was possible to smile at the same time she spoke to Ben from between clenched teeth. "He wanted a picture."

"Yeah, but he didn't take one."

"Thank you, and—" She stopped and turned in her seat so that she was facing Ben. "You're right. He didn't. He said he just wanted to say hello. And good-bye. Strange, considering we see Randy a lot. He stocks the shelves over at Mercer's and—"

"Was he working the night you were kidnapped?"

It took a second for the question to register and another second before Lacie felt calm enough to answer it. She handed out another picture along with another cheery greeting and was relieved to see that Junie Morgan was next in line. Old Mrs. Morgan used a walker to help her get around. With any luck, it would take her a while to make it to the table.

"Yes," she said, and the way Ben was standing, she had to look up to look him in the eye. "He was working. Mom was there, too, of course. She was helping me hand out keychains with the Summer Squash Board logo on them. Randy helped us carry the box of keychains in from the car."

"Did he help you carry them back out to the car, too?"

Lacie thought back to the night of Mercer's grand opening. "No. Randy wasn't around when I left. It didn't matter since the keychain box was just about empty by then. I left the extra keychains on the counter and threw the box away. I figured Randy was just finished working for the day, and—"

"Finished working but maybe not gone." Thinking, Ben rapped his knuckles against the table. He looked over the crowd and Lacie looked that way, too. Because she was sitting, she couldn't see nearly what Ben could see, but she knew he didn't see Randy. She could tell from the way he pressed his lips into a thin line.

"Maybe I should back off a little," Ben said. "You know, make myself scarce. Maybe if I weren't around he'd try something and—"

"Randy? Try something?" Okay, so it was ill-mannered of her to laugh. Lacie admitted that much. She also admitted that it was a little hard not to when Ben looked so serious while he said something so ludicrous. "Randy's quiet and he can even be a little weird, but he wouldn't hurt a soul. Not even that no-good Slim Pepboy and, Lord knows, Randy's had plenty of opportunities and plenty of good reasons why he'd want to try. He's not exactly normal, depending on your definition of normal, but deep down, Randy's good people."

She never had a chance to find out how Ben intended to argue the point. He opened his mouth, all set to come back at her. But before he could say a word, there was a commotion from over near the Tilt-O-Whirl and Ben stood up straight and tall to check it out.

Somebody screamed. Somebody else started running, and even though they couldn't have known what was going on, a lot of other folks in the area started running, too.

"You stay here." Ben put a hand on Lacie's shoulder just as a woman ran by the other way.

"It's Randy!" the woman screamed, pointing to the Tilt-O-Whirl. "Randy Holcomb! And he's got a gun!"

10

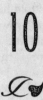

It had been a long time since Ben had had SWAT training. Fortunately, some things were second nature. Especially when it came to life and death.

With one last look at Lacie and one last order for her to stay put and keep calm, Ben raced toward the disturbance. Not as easy as it sounded, considering that everybody else at the fair was screaming and running in the opposite direction.

"Good," Ben mumbled, dodging in and out of the crowd. "The less people around, the less chance of anybody getting hurt."

By the time he got closer, the area was just about deserted. Still, he wasn't going to take any chances. There were a couple of brave souls (or maybe they were just stupid) who were hanging around to see what the excitement was all about, and he waved them back and called over the rent-a-cop security guard who was standing near the ice cream concession looking like he didn't know which end was up.

The guard wasn't much older than Dinah, a thin kid with a pale face and, thanks to the sun, cherry-red cheeks.

"Get these people out of here," Ben ordered him. "And

keep them back at least—" He looked over his shoulder, gauging the distances. "Over there near the Ferris wheel. When you're done with that, call Sheriff Thompson and tell him to send SWAT if he's got 'em and that lazy-ass deputy of his. And—" Ben reached into his pocket for his car keys, tossed them to the kid, and told him his license plate number. "Fourth car in the seventh row just outside the main entrance. There's a bulletproof vest in the trunk. And a hat. Bring that, too. And don't forget the rifle. The cartridges are in a case next to it."

"Vest. Hat. Rifle?" The kid's voice broke over the words. "You want me to—"

There was no time to explain. Ben flashed his badge and added a not-so-friendly "Now!" just to make it clear that he wasn't kidding. That done, he headed for the Tilt-O-Whirl.

Even if he wasn't familiar with the amusement park ride where teacup-shaped cars turned and whirled one at a time while the whole series of them turned and whirled as they moved around a track, he would have found the place without any trouble. Hard not to when Crystal was standing near the turnstile that led into the ride. She was screaming her fool head off.

"Crystal!" Ben figured the only way he was going to be heard above the screeching was to raise his voice. It didn't work and he tried again. "Crystal!"

Crystal didn't stop.

"Great." Ben grumbled the single word and stalked over to where she stood. He grabbed her arm and startled her enough so that her screaming quieted to a loud blubber. "Out of here," he told her.

"But . . ." Tears streamed down Crystal's cheeks. Not exactly a nice sight, considering that her mascara was running with them. Her face was sloppy with the stuff. Her lower lip trembled. "But he's been following me." She sniffed and pointed toward the ride. "All day long, he's been following me and now he's up there and—"

"Right." Ben wasn't blind. The ride was stopped and he could see Randy Holcomb sitting in the Tilt-O-Whirl car farthest from the turnstile. Randy had his left arm wrapped around little Tyler. And a .38 Smith and Wesson in his right hand.

"Did he say what he wants?" Ben asked Crystal.

"Wants?" She blinked. It didn't do a whole bunch for her mascara. She tossed a look over her shoulder toward her ex that was every bit as deadly as Randy's weapon. Her voice was no more friendly. "That son-of-a-bitch wants to see me suffer, that's what he wants. He wants to see me in pain so he can laugh at me. Ain't nothing he'd like better than to see me beg. He wants me to take him back. That's what he wants. He wants me. He's always wanted me. He can't get enough of me, the sick bastard."

"The way I'm reading it, you're not the one sitting next to a guy holding a gun." All right, so it wasn't exactly fair to be so hard on Crystal at such a stressful time. Ben really couldn't help himself. Tyler was crying quietly. His face was pale. His little chest heaved with every breath he took.

And Crystal's only thought was that Randy couldn't get enough of her?

Ben shook his head, reminding himself that right now, whatever soap opera Crystal imagined herself in didn't much matter. What mattered was little Tyler. And the cold, hard reality that Randy Holcomb was in way over his head.

"I'll tell you what, why don't you go right over..." Ben looked toward the midway just in time to see the security guard trotting toward them, out of breath and redder in the face than ever. Grateful for even that little bit of backup, he hurried Crystal away from the ride and behind a nearby lemonade concession stand. He handed her over to the security guard. "Get her out of here but don't go too far. He might want to talk to her. And did you talk to Sheriff Thompson?"

"I called." The kid had a hand on Crystal's meaty arm and

he didn't quite know what to do with it. He slid it to her shoulder. Slipped it to her elbow. He finally ended up holding her hand. "Sheriff's in Plankville. Actually had to walk away from his birthday luncheon over at the Morning Star because of an emergency call. There's a missing cow over at the Prentiss farm, see, and—"

"Missing cow." Ben massaged his forehead with the tips of his fingers. "You left him a message, I hope?"

"Sure." It was the first thing the kid had said that he was sure would please Ben, and he nodded vigorously just to emphasize the point. "Told him to get here as fast as he could. That there was a crazy guy with a gun and—"

"And he wants to kill me." Crystal broke away from the security guard and threw her arms around Ben's neck. She burrowed her mascara-smudged face into his white shirt. Snuggled her more-than-a-little moist nose into his tie. She rubbed her ample breasts against his chest. "I just know he wants to kill me." She looked up at Ben, wide-eyed and with a little pout. "He's always said I'm the absolute best he's ever had. He's always wanted to—"

"Shut up, Crystal." Ben stood her on her feet and pushed her an arm's length away. Though he never raised his voice, the command worked wonders. Crystal clamped her mouth so tight, her jaw trembled.

"Get her out of here," Ben repeated to the security guard. He slipped into his bulletproof vest, then put on the navy-blue baseball cap with FBI written on it in fat yellow letters. He left the rifle behind the lemonade stand where Randy couldn't see it and put the ammunition into his own pocket. "I'm going to go have a talk with Randy."

Ben slipped his suit jacket back on and tucked his Glock into the back waistband of his slacks. Talking or not, it was stupid not to be prepared.

Now that Crystal had stopped her wailing, it was blessedly quiet back at the Tilt-O-Whirl. Ben looked over the scene quickly.

Randy hadn't moved and neither had Tyler. It was clear the kid didn't understand what was going on and just as clear that it didn't make any difference. Tyler knew something was wrong. He sensed it in the quiet, and because he was suddenly alone with a man he didn't see very often. He felt the tension in the air, just like Ben did. He saw it, no doubt, in Randy's rigid posture, his bright eyes, the tilt of his chin that was so determined, it was chilling.

The little boy's eyes were wide. His face was smeared with cotton candy and tears. Randy, on the other hand, was as still as a statue.

Except for his gun hand. That was shaking like a leaf in a Chicago windstorm.

Ben paused just outside the metal railing that ran all around the ride. "I'm unarmed." Keeping his eyes on Randy, he raised both hands and pushed his way through the turnstile. "As long as you're willing to be reasonable, we can talk. What do you say, Randy?"

"I say I don't want to talk to you." Randy might have looked as cool as a cucumber but his voice shook as much as his hands. "I told that stupid Crystal I didn't want to talk."

"Crystal says you want her."

Randy laughed, the sound reedy and as sharp as a knife. "Crystal's got those what-do-you-call-'em. De-lusions. Thinks every man in the world wants to get her in bed."

Ben inched closer. "Do they?"

"What do you think?" When Ben dared another couple of steps, Randy slid Tyler onto his lap. "I think Crystal is as nutty as a fruitcake."

"It's a possibility. But you let her leave when you could have kept her here with you and Tyler. I just wondered if maybe that means you gave her a message. If it means that you trust her."

"Trust? Crystal?" Randy's voice teetered between laughter and tears. "No way! Everybody else does, though. Everybody always believes Crystal. Even when she's lying through her teeth. No one sure as hell ever believes me."

Ben glanced down at what little he could see of his shirt and tie above the top edge of the vest. He knew they were stained with black mascara and ruined far beyond what any dry cleaner could ever do to save them. He made a face. "I'm willing to believe you, Randy. At least you didn't destroy a perfectly good shirt and tie. I paid seventeen dollars for this tie." It was an outright lie; he'd paid five times that and the tie was one of his favorites, but something told him if a working stiff like Randy knew what kind of money he squandered on neckwear, he might take a potshot at him just to make a social statement.

"What do you think?" Ben grinned, the better to get Randy to relax a little and maybe, catch him off guard. "You think I'm going to believe a woman who could make such a mess?"

"She got close enough to try, didn't she? That's the thing with Crystal. Don't matter if a man starts out wanting her or not. She just has to get close. Has to get a guy all hot and bothered."

"The only thing she got me is dirty." Ben took a few steps nearer and congratulated himself. So far, so good. He had Randy talking and that was half the battle. Now to worry about the other half.

"I'll tell you what, Randy, it's hotter than hell standing out here. I'd much rather sit down with you somewhere cool so we can talk man to man. Why don't you just let young Tyler there head off to get an ice cream and—"

"You think I'm that stupid?" Randy waved the gun. He didn't aim it exactly, which was why Ben didn't take cover and get in a shot. "The way I figure it, my boy here is the only thing that's keeping me alive right about now."

"How so?" Arms out at his sides, Ben made a great show of looking around before he turned back to Randy. "There's no one here who's going to hurt you, Randy. Sheriff Thompson's over in Plankville. Something about a lost cow."

Randy snorted. "Stupid Bob Prentiss. Always misplacing his livestock. Stupid Crystal. Stupid, stupid me." He blinked back tears and when a couple of them splashed down his cheek, he dashed them away with his gun hand. "I thought I could be reasonable. I thought somebody would listen."

"Two ears. No waiting." Ben pointed. "Talk all you want. That's what I'm here for. To listen. Only, I've got to remind you, you're breaking a whole host of laws here, Randy. I'm willing to negotiate. To cut you a deal. But we can't start until you get rid of that gun."

Randy tightened his hold on Tyler. "I've tried talking without a gun. I've talked to my lawyer so much, he won't even take my calls anymore. Not without charging me two hundred bucks an hour. I tried to be reasonable with Judge Mulgrew, too. He threatened me with one of them restraining orders. I've talked to everybody. Everybody! And nobody will give me the time of day. Maybe they will now, huh? Maybe they'll pay a little more attention when they know I'm serious."

"I know you're serious." Ben stepped onto the platform where the Tilt-O-Whirl cars twirled. For part of the ride, the cars were slanted up on an angle and he had to look up to see Randy. "Never doubted it for a moment, Randy. Knew you were a serious fellow the minute I laid eyes on you. It's just that if you want me to listen, you're going to have to do something for me. So if you'd just let Tyler—"

"No!" Randy's face got blotchy. His voice rose an octave. "No! No! No! I ain't letting go of my boy. They won't let me see him. They say I can't have any visitation."

"And once we have this settled, we can talk to the judge about it, Randy, and—"

"You ain't listening! Judge Mulgrew decided the case against me even before he heard my side of the story. He said I couldn't see Tyler on account of how I'm a bad father, but that's bull. You know why that judge believed I'm a lousy father? You know what Crystal did to persuade him?"

Ben didn't. He didn't even want to think it was possible to sway an officer of the court in the way that Randy suggested. True or not, though, Randy believed it, and right now, that was what was important.

"If that's so, Randy, then I'll look into it. I promise you, I'll see that justice is done."

"Justice?" Randy's voice broke. Tears streamed down his face. "Who's gonna see justice done to me?"

It was hell not having the answer to Randy's question.

The realization filled Ben's veins like ice water. He twitched it aside. "So you don't want to talk to Crystal. You don't want to talk to your attorney. You don't want to talk to the judge. Who's left, Randy? Who do you want to talk to? What do you want me to do?"

"What?" As if he'd forgotten it was there, Randy peered at the gun in his hand. He shifted his gaze to Ben. Blinked. Looked at Tyler. Stared at the gun.

It was an even bigger slice of hell to realize that Randy was so upset, he didn't have a clue what he wanted.

Ben grumbled a curse. Bad enough when a hostage situation involved unreasonable demands, cockamamie conditions, and convoluted terms. Even a bad bargaining chip was a bargaining chip. But when there was no bargaining chip at all...

Ben sucked in a long breath of hot evening air and let it out slowly.

When there was no bargaining chip at all, somebody was bound to get hurt.

No way could Randy be thinking clearly or they wouldn't be faced off across the Tilt-O-Whirl. Still, something told him that Randy was fully aware of the reality of the situation: Not all of them would leave the carnival alive.

There was nothing to be gained from avoiding the obvious so Ben figured he might as well at least try to be the voice of reason. "If anybody gets hurt, Randy, I won't be able to do anything for you. No deal."

"Ain't nobody gonna get hurt except maybe me. And him," he added, glancing down at Tyler. "That way, nobody can keep us apart anymore."

Ben never could understand that sort of thinking. He grumbled his annoyance. "That's not going to help! You want me to help you, Randy, you're going to have to give me something to work with."

Before Randy could reason his way through the logic of this argument, something behind Ben caught his eye. Ben watched Randy's expression melt from wariness to amazement. Too curious not to, Ben looked over his shoulder.

His heart did a somersault and then stopped completely.

It started up again with a jolt when he realized that Lacie—wearing a shimmering silver evening gown, her Miss Kansas Summer Squash banner, and a glistening tiara that caught the evening light and sent it flashing all around her— was headed straight for the Tilt-O-Whirl.

"Hi, Randy! Hi, Tyler!"

Lacie didn't know the first thing about police procedure, but she had watched enough episodes of *Law & Order* to know that she had to prove to Randy that the only weapon she was carrying was her smile. She made sure her wave was nice and big, the kind she usually used when she was up on a pageant stage and the judges were seated in the back row. That way Randy was sure to see that the only things in her hands—or on them—were her elbow-length satin gloves.

"Hi, Ben!" She walked up to where he was standing and added the greeting almost as an afterthought. Not because she hadn't seen Ben there right from the start but because he looked so completely flabbergasted, she figured if he heard his name, he might snap out of it.

He did.

"What the hell—" He ground the words from between clenched teeth and slid her one pointed look before he turned his attention back to Randy. "Are you completely insane? What are you doing—"

Lacie's teeth were clenched, too. Around her biggest and best smile. "I heard there was some mix-up," she said, loud enough for Randy to hear. "And you know what, I know it's just a little bit stuck-up of me, but, well . . ." She put one hand to her cheek, tipped her head, and giggled. "I thought maybe I could help."

"You can help by getting the hell out of here." Ben's voice was a low growl meant only for Lacie's ears.

It gave her the perfect excuse to pretend she didn't hear him at all.

"You know, Randy, you never did get one of my autographed pictures when I was signing them earlier. That got me to thinking. And worrying." She tipped her head the other way. "Randy Holcomb, are you mad at me?"

Randy shook his head furiously. "I could never be mad at you, M-Miss Baxter. You've always been kind to me. You and your m-mother. She's a nice lady."

"I know Mom thinks of you fondly, too. I know she'd never want to see anything happen to you." She gave Ben a look just to make sure he got the message, "That's why I came by just to make sure everything was okay."

"Everything was okay before you got here." Ben's voice was no more than a whisper.

"Uh-huh." Lacie took another step onto the Tilt-O-Whirl platform and answered Ben in a voice that was just as quiet. "That's why Randy's sitting here with a gun. That's why you've probably got one stashed someplace. Oh, yeah, everything's just peachy here at the Summer Carnival. It ought to get even better when trigger-happy Ed Thompson shows up." She batted her eyelashes at him. "What do you say we get this over with before he does?"

"That's exactly what I was trying to do."

"Then, let's get Randy to help. What do you say, Randy?" Lacie lifted her chin and projected her voice like she did when she was onstage. "I'm all for wrapping this up. What can we do for you?"

"We can't do anything, Randy." Ben shouldered Lacie aside and stepped between her and Randy. "I told you before. I won't deal. Not while you're still hanging on to Tyler."

Randy's arm tightened around the boy's shoulders. "I'm not going to let go of my boy."

"Of course you're not!" A lifetime in the spotlight, and Lacie knew how to be the center of attention. She moved in front of Ben. "I don't blame you one bit for not wanting this guy to be in charge of Tyler," she told Randy. "He's irresponsible and quick-tempered. And look at that little piece of dirty tie sticking up over that silly vest of his." Lacie shivered. "I'll tell you what, Randy, you want to talk to Ben, that's fine with me. You boys talk, Tyler and I will take a little walk."

Randy looked toward the midway. "But Crystal—"

"Crystal's not getting her hands on this boy tonight. You know how I can promise you that, Randy?"

Randy leaned forward just a little. Not much in the threatening movements department, but Ben responded instantly. His eyes narrowed and he tensed, ready to spring into action the second the situation called for it. Lacie's job was to make sure the situation never called for it.

She fluffed the banner that hung over her shoulder. "I can promise you that, Randy, because we're old friends. You've known me for a long time. You know I'd never lie to you."

"I know that, Miss Baxter. But—"

"But that's not going to do a thing for the real problem, is it, Randy?" Lacie tapped the toe of one of the sling-back pumps she'd bought online to replace the ones she lost the night of the kidnapping. "You've been done wrong, Randy. By your attorney and by that no-good Judge Mulgrew and especially by Crystal. I can understand that. And so will everybody else, once they hear your story. I called Jeff Parkman," she told him. "The newspaper reporter. Turns out he was right here at the carnival anyway, so that worked out just fine. He's on his way over here now and he says he's going to give you front page coverage. You can tell your story to everyone. Only..."

Interested, Randy leaned forward a bit more.

And Ben's hand went to the back of his jacket.

Lacie swallowed the ball of panic in her throat. "You're going to have to let Tyler come with me," she told Randy. "And you'll have to put down the gun. It's a secret but..." This time, Lacie leaned forward, too. "Jeff's scared to death of guns. Don't tell anyone because he likes to pretend he's not. Does all those stories on hunting and such but don't let that fool you. He sees you with that gun, he's not going to talk to you. And if he doesn't talk to you, he can't put you on the front page of the paper. And if he doesn't put you on the front page of the paper, how is everybody going to hear what you have to say?"

Randy looked at his weapon. "You think—"

"I think folks are going to be up in arms when they hear your side of the story. I think the hardworking people of this great state are going to rally to your cause, Randy Holcomb." Lacie raised a fist, Scarlett O'Hara–like. "I think—" A sound behind her brought Lacie whirling around.

"I think Jeff is here." She smiled, gave Jeff the thumbs-up, and turned back to Randy. "What do you say, Randy? You ready to let everybody in Sutton County know what a good daddy you are?"

"I am a good daddy." Randy nodded and sniffed back tears. "I'd never hurt my boy. I could never—"

"Of course you couldn't, Randy. If you want to prove that, you'll let Tyler come with me." She didn't wait for Randy to think about it. She held out her hand, and when Tyler slipped off his father's lap and headed toward her, Lacie held her breath.

As soon as he was close enough, Lacie scooped Tyler up into her arms. "See? He's fine, Randy." Lacie patted the boy's head and kissed his cheek. "We'll get some pictures of you and Tyler together. That will look terrific on the front page of the *Intelligencer*." Her expression soured. "Except for the gun, of course."

"Except—" Randy looked down at the gun in his right hand. Slowly, he let it slip out of his fingers.

11

"Wiley Burnside, you're a genius!" Dinah had promised herself she wasn't going to lose her focus, but sometimes, a girl just had to follow her gut instinct. At the risk of getting distracted by Wiley's muscles and Wiley's to-die-for body and the way the taste of Wiley's lips against hers always made her feel like she was this close to nuclear meltdown, she stood on her tiptoes and gave him a quick kiss.

One of his muscular arms automatically went around her waist and she grinned. "Grabbing your mom's keys while she's at the stupid carnival! You're the smartest man in the whole wide world." She kissed the tip of Wiley's nose and the little divot above his upper lip. "And the handsomest." She kissed his chipped-from-granite chin. "And the sexiest."

Even though it was already past dark and the light above the back door of the high school was burned out, she could see the way Wiley's eyes sparked.

And she just loved when that happened.

Wiley nuzzled a kiss against her neck. "You want to—"

"Not here!" Dinah laughed and gave him a playful sock on the arm. It wasn't like they'd never done it at the high school—in the boys' locker room and in the music room and even under the principal's desk that time Mr. Fortnoy called Wiley in for detention and then had to go check on the fire alarm that Dinah had tripped. It was just that tonight, they had other things to worry about first.

"You know I do." Dinah traced an invisible pattern over Wiley's skintight T-shirt. "But let's get this over with. What do you say? That way, when we're all done, we can celebrate."

"Celebrate. Yeah." Just thinking about what was in store for him made Wiley's hands shake. When he stuck his mother's key into the lock on the back door, the rest of the keys and her metal World's Greatest Mom ring did a little dance that pretty much matched the way Dinah's insides were jumping around.

Wiley gave her a look. "Ready?" he asked.

Even though she wasn't sure, Dinah nodded. There was no use turning back when they'd come this far. So she wouldn't get scared. Even though they had racked their brains earlier, neither one of them could remember if the back door to the school was wired with an alarm. When Wiley turned the handle and pulled the door open, Dinah held her breath.

Nothing.

No alarm.

She let go a long sigh of relief and stepped inside the school. "Don't turn on the lights," she told Wiley when he automatically reached for the switch. "I brought a flashlight." She reached around to the backpack she was wearing and pulled out the flashlight, flicked it on, and arced the beam over the first-floor hallway.

"I hate this place," she mumbled.

At her side, Wiley laughed. The sound echoed through the empty hallways. "I hate this place, too."

"So we both hate this place." Dinah liked the way her voice sounded when it came back at her. Like it belonged to somebody else. Somebody who was calmer than she was.

Somebody who was holding it together. Somebody who realized that what they were doing could get them in very big trouble.

And was willing to do it, anyway.

"Let's get moving," Dinah told Wiley. Even though she'd dropped out of Sutton County High two years earlier, it was impossible to forget the building. No matter how hard she tried. Dinah remembered the classrooms where she'd done her best to fail every subject she ever took. She remembered the cafeteria, where more often than not, somebody who knew who she was would come up and smile and say something stupid like, "You don't look a thing like Lacie!"

She got rid of the thought with a twitch.

Yep, she remembered the place, all right. She remembered the smell: old socks and chalk dust and the thousands of unappetizing lunches that had been served there over the years. She remembered the way the air always seemed too dry and the halls always seemed too narrow and her skin always felt like it was crawling—just a little bit—every time she walked through the door.

Unfortunately, she'd forgotten about the trophy case.

Just outside the door to the main office, her light hit the glass front of the case and her stomach flipped.

"Lacie." She grumbled the name while she looked over the case that was topped with a brass plaque that said

LACIE BAXTER, SUTTON SPRINGS HIGH
SCHOOL GRADUATE, BEAUTY QUEEN.

She shone her light over the pictures and the trophies and the sparkling crowns displayed there.

"Doesn't it figure? Other schools have trophy cases full of sports trophies. This school has a case full of Lacie. I can't even get away from her here." She passed the light of her Rayovac over the pictures of a high-school-age Lacie.

Holding armfuls of roses. Wearing glittering crowns. Smiling. Always smiling.

"Wiley, I have an idea." Dinah giggled. "Let's take one of her crowns and put it on the skeleton in the biology lab. What do you say? It would be a riot!"

"I don't know..." Though it was nearly midnight and they were alone, he looked over his shoulder. "We should just do what we came here to do and get out of here. Besides, the case is locked and—"

"No. It isn't." Dinah shone the light on the little metal padlock that held the glass cover of the trophy case in place. It was hanging open. "Why would anybody... ?" She passed the light across the case again. "There are a couple of pictures missing. Look, Wiley." She skimmed the light over a series of empty spots in the case. "What does the little card below that first empty place say?"

Wiley leaned in close. "Lacie Baxter," he read, and because Wiley wasn't the world's best reader, he took his time. "Senior Year... Sutton County High School... Miss... Miss Valentine."

"And that one?" Dinah swung the light to the empty space next to it.

"Miss Pumpkin Festival. That's what it says. And the one next to that says Miss Christmas Queen. From the same year." Wiley glanced a look at Dinah. "Why would anybody want old pictures of Lacie?"

"She probably took them herself!" Dinah laughed, and when the sound reverberated back at her and she heard how loud it was, she clamped a hand over her mouth. "She probably took them herself," she repeated, only this time, she whispered. "Like she doesn't have enough pictures of herself all over the house!"

Just thinking about it was enough to get Dinah moving. "Let's get this over with," she told Wiley. "Let's find her files."

Wiley nodded his agreement and led the way into the

main office, a big, square room that contained the table where fat Miss Glenallen handled attendance every day, the desk where Mrs. Burnside worked and over on the far wall, the door that led into Mr. Fortnoy's office. Because it was the beginning of July and the school had been closed since the middle of June, the place was cleaner than usual. No stacks of papers or backpacks that had been left on buses and piled in a corner for their owners to claim. No phone messages or hall passes or report cards ready to be signed and mailed out.

The pizza boxes on Wiley's mom's desk really stood out.

"Pizza?" Wiley lifted the lid and peeked into one of the boxes. "And not that old, by the looks of it. Who would be—"

A sound from inside Mr. Fortnoy's office interrupted Wiley's words and made Dinah's heart leap into her throat.

She grabbed Wiley's arm. "There's somebody in here."

"No." Except when they were in bed together, Wiley wasn't the most imaginative guy in the world. He knew what he knew and he knew that at midnight on a Saturday in July, the school was supposed to be empty.

Supposed to be were the operative words.

They heard another noise from the direction of the office, like the sound of someone walking around, and Wiley slid Dinah a look. "You don't suppose..." He swallowed hard and tried again. "I thought you said that FBI guy was at the carnival with Lacie today."

"He is." Dinah made sure she kept her voice down. "Unless something went wrong and he left early. It can't be him."

Maybe it couldn't, but they heard the noise again.

They didn't stick around to find out who was responsible for it.

Side by side, Wiley and Dinah raced out of the office. They punched open the door and bolted down the steps, headed toward where Wiley had left his truck parked

around the corner. Just as they got to the sidewalk, Wiley
stumbled to a stop.

"The keys." He glanced back toward the door where his
mom's keys—and her World's Greatest Mom keychain—still
dangled from the lock. "We've got to get the keys or he'll
know it was us."

He was right and besides, Dinah knew there was no way
she could talk him out of it. Wiley was not only sexy, he was
brave, too, and while she waited, her heart beating double
time and her blood pumping so hard, she could hear it
swooshing in her ears, he dashed back to the door, turned
the keys in the lock, and shoved the keychain into the pocket
of his jeans.

He moved like lightning and was back in seconds. The
next thing Dinah knew, he'd grabbed her hand and they
were running to his truck. He had it started and in gear before Dinah had a chance to catch her breath.

"That was so heroic!" She turned in her seat and looked
through the back window. As far as she could tell, nobody was following them. "That took courage, Wiley. Real
courage."

"Yeah." Wiley checked the rearview mirror. "But let's not
congratulate ourselves yet. Not until we're far away from
here."

The streets were empty, and even before Wiley turned
down Madison and raced past Linden, she knew they were
headed to Hastings Park. It was the perfect spot to hide out
for a while, mostly deserted at this hour except for the couples who used it as a sort of lovers' lane and a few teenage
boys who thought it was the perfect spot to smoke a little
weed.

Once they were in the park, Wiley skidded to a stop between two tall evergreens and turned off his headlights.
"Anyone?" He looked over his shoulder to the street.

"Not that I can see. I don't think he followed us."

"Good." Wiley slumped back against the seat. "He must know, Dinah. He was there just waiting for us and—"

"It could have been anybody." Dinah didn't actually believe it, she just figured she had to say it. So she didn't look like a wimp. She peeled off her backpack and dropped it on the floor. "There's no way that FBI agent could know—"

"You're right. Of course. You're right." Wiley sucked on his bottom lip. "Only it seems mighty peculiar, doesn't it? I sure didn't tell anyone what we were planning tonight."

"I didn't, either." Out on the street, a car cruised by, and both Dinah and Wiley slouched down so no one could see them. When the car was gone, Dinah sat up again. "Do you suppose he's got our phone tapped?"

"Or cameras. Secret cameras. I hear they do stuff like that. That means—"

"It means we're done wasting time." Dinah was pretty sure that wasn't what Wiley was going to say. Just like she was pretty sure that whatever he was going to say, she didn't want to hear it. "We've been screwing around long enough. We've got to move and we've got to move soon."

"But—" Wiley looked out the back window. "What if—"

"You were brave, Wiley."

Dinah let the words hang in the air for just a couple of seconds before she scooted closer. "You were brave. You were fearless. You could have left those keys, but you went back for them. You risked everything for me, Sugar Lips, and you know I'm grateful."

"Do I?" Wiley slid a look over Dinah's face and down to her tank top, and even though she wasn't breathing hard anymore, she made sure to take a nice, deep breath and hold it long enough for him to see the outline of her bare breasts underneath. She knew it had worked when he took one of her nipples and rubbed it between his thumb and forefinger. "You gonna show me how grateful you are?" he asked.

"You bet." Dinah murmured her approval. "As soon as you agree—"

"That we've got to move and we've got to do it soon."
Wiley tugged her top over her head and tossed it onto the
floor. He bent to take her into his mouth.

"That's not exactly what I was talking about, Wiley!"

He chuckled, the sound of it as warm as his tongue
against her skin. "I know that, Snuggle Bunny. And I promise, we'll get going on that thing. As soon as we're done with
this."

It was a long drive from Rogers to Klaber Falls.

It was even longer when the person you were driving
with didn't say a thing.

Not surprising. Ben hadn't said one word to Lacie since
Sheriff Thompson had shown up from his cow-finding expe-
dition, grabbed Randy by the handcuffs Ben had slapped on
him, and led him over to be interviewed by Jeff Parkman.
He didn't say one word now as he slowed the car to a stop in
front of the Baxter house and punched the gearshift into
park.

Lacie gathered the pink duffel bag that contained her
shoes, her summer squash apron, and the green and white
dress she'd worn for the cooking demonstration. It also contained a pair of khaki shorts and a darling cotton blouse embroidered with tiny palm trees that she'd hoped to change
into after her appearance at the pie and cake ribbon ceremony. She'd never had a chance. Once the excitement at the
Tilt-O-Whirl was over, Ben had hustled her off to the car,
chucked his bulletproof vest and a wicked-looking rifle into
the trunk, and bolted away from the Summer Carnival.

Without ever saying a word.

Lacie opened the car door and looked over at Ben. His
fingers were grasped so tight around the steering wheel, his
knuckles were white. Like he'd done all the way from
Rogers to Klaber Falls, he stared straight ahead, his look as

even as every breath he took. She cleared her throat. "Thank you. I mean, for the ride and for—"

"That was the single most brainless, asinine, insane thing I have ever seen in my entire life." Like lava boiling for far too long just below the surface of some tropical island volcano, Ben's words burst with a vengeance. Just to emphasize them (not that he needed to, since he was red in the face and practically screaming), he slapped the steering wheel. "That was stupid," he said. "It was totally and completely—"

"Yes. It was." Lacie held her pink duffel bag up to her chest like a shield. "You could have been hurt."

"Me?" When he turned to her, his eyes were blazing. "Are you completely out of your mind?" Ben raked a hand through his hair. Not the best of moves, considering that he already had hat hair. Lacie was too bothered by it to simply let it pass. She reached over and smoothed down the cowlick at the side of Ben's hair.

"That's my job," he told her, and just to be ornery, he ruffled his hand through his hair again. "Stepping between civilians and danger. Putting myself on the line. Defusing situations that are too hot to handle. That's what I get paid to do."

"Well, it's what I get paid to do, too." Another thought occurred to her and Lacie amended the statement. The last thing she wanted to be accused of (right after using carpet tape to keep her pageant dresses in place, or a spritz of hair spray to keep her swimsuit from riding up, or petroleum jelly on the inside of her lips to make her smile nice and wide) was deception. "Only, I don't get paid, if you know what I mean. I mean, not paid a paycheck. Not exactly. I mean, I earn the respect of the people of this great—"

"Cut the crap, Lacie." Ben pushed open his door. "You stuck your nose where it had no business."

Though it was obviously a major aspect of Ben's, it certainly wasn't part of Lacie's personality to be argumentative.

But it was also not fair to have to sit and listen to a scathing condemnation of what she'd done.

"That's where you're wrong," she told him. "You're the one who has no business here. If you did, you would have known exactly how to get Randy to listen to you. It wasn't by threatening him. By talking to him about deals and laws and sentencing considerations. What Randy did, he did for Tyler. You'd understand that if you belonged here."

"Don't rub it in." Ben got out of the car, and since there was no use trying to talk any sense into him while he was outside and she was still in, Lacie got out, too. He slammed his door shut. "Just because I don't belong here doesn't mean I can't handle a situation as serious as that one. I'm the professional here. I'm the one who's in charge and in command. I'm the only one who's always calm and in control."

Lacie actually might have been willing to admit that he was right—at least about being able to handle the situation—if over the roof of the car, he hadn't been pointing his finger at her to emphasize his argument.

Carefully, she closed the car door. She set her duffel bag on the newly mown strip of treelawn and stuck out her chin. "The way I remember it, the words I've heard used to describe you are more like *hotheaded, overeager,* and *out-of-control.* That was just the tabloids, of course. The political commentators on CNN and CNBC weren't nearly that kind."

From the other side of the car, Lacie's gown twinkled like starlight in the glow of a street lamp. Her eyes gleamed. Her tiara sparkled. Maybe it was all that twinkling and gleaming and sparkling that caught Ben off guard. Maybe that was why it took him several seconds to figure out what she was talking about.

Unfortunately, it wasn't that easy to forget the day that had changed his life. Or all the ugly media attention that had followed.

He let go a long breath. "What?"

Her lips thinned. "You think we don't get the tabloids out here in God's country? The Pony Express delivers them late, but they do arrive eventually. Sometimes we even see the television news the same week it's broadcast."

An icy dose of reality flooded Ben's insides along with the ugly memories. He scraped a hand through his hair, and when Lacie gave him a look that said she definitely did not approve of the way it was sticking up, he did it again. "I didn't think—"

"That anyone knew who you were?" She nodded as if she understood perfectly. As if she possibly could. "Most of them probably have already forgotten it," she said. "Let's face it, we might be straight out of the cast of *Green Acres,* but we do have our own lives to worry about. Our own little dramas. We don't exactly have time for yours."

"But you haven't forgotten." Ben's insides went cold. "You . . . you've known all along."

"What, you think because I'm a blonde, my brain doesn't work?" If she hadn't laughed when she said it, the comment would have been scathing. Coming from Lacie, it sounded like the most innocent—the most perfect—comeback in the world. "I thought you looked familiar. That first day you showed up here at the house. It had been a while since you arrived, of course—"

"Too long."

"But I never forget a handsome face. And your handsome face was on the front page of every single one of the tabloids on the rack near the cash register at Mercer's. At least until that What's-Her-Name—the singer with the strumpet clothes and the makeup that's way overdone—at least until she got married for the fourth time. Fame is a fickle thing, Ben." She picked up her duffel bag and headed toward the house. "Your fifteen minutes of fame didn't last any longer than all the screaming from that senator's son."

"Well, I don't want to talk about it." Just like when it happened. When his superiors gave him strict orders about how to handle all the media attention and when the reporters were waiting for him at the back door of his office and the front door of his home. Just like then, he refused to be baited.

That didn't explain why he followed along after Lacie.

"Did you hear me?" he asked. "I said I didn't want to talk about it."

"Of course I heard you." She kept right on walking. "You were on the cable news every night saying no comment, no comment, no comment." As if it were nothing at all, she waved one hand. "You might not have wanted to talk about it, but Senator Powell's son, well..." At the bottom of the front steps, she stopped and turned to him. "He did plenty enough talking for the both of you."

Ben's stomach bunched. His fingers curled into fists. "Sean Powell is a punk. He was—"

"According to what he said in all the newspaper interviews and his appearance on Larry King, and his talk with Oprah, and that late-night chat he had with Ted Koppel—" Lacie sucked in a breath. "What he was doing was minding his own business. Out with his girlfriend, minding his own business and along comes Teenage Mutant Ninja FBI agent who throws him against a wall and slaps the cuffs on him."

Ben shifted from foot to foot. "And what about the other side of the story?"

"Other side?" Lacie set her duffel bag on the steps. "The way I remember, it was something about how justified you were to beat him up."

"I didn't beat him up. Believe me, if I had, he would have known he'd been beaten."

"But you did confront him."

"Absolutely."

"And you did intimidate him."

"No more than he deserved."

"And you did arrest him."

"I should have done more than that. That scumbag was—"

"Beating up on a woman." Lacie gave him a level look. "I didn't forget that part of the story, either. That was the official party line, wasn't it? The story that came out of some spin doctor over at the FBI? They said you were—"

"In a restaurant. Having dinner with a cousin of mine who was visiting D.C. from out of town. That part of the story happens to be true." Ben didn't know why, but it seemed important to point that out to Lacie. "I saw Sean Powell and the woman at a table in the corner. They were arguing. They got a little loud and the manager asked them to leave."

"And you followed them outside."

"Damn straight." Ben poked a hand in his pocket and jingled his keys. "I didn't like the looks of the thing from the beginning. By the time I got outside, they were down the block and I saw them walk into an alley. The next thing I knew, I heard her scream. I raced over there and—"

"Smacked around the senator's son."

"I should have done more than that to the little creep. Imagine, hitting a woman." Just thinking about it made Ben feel sick. Just thinking that he'd given Sean Powell nearly what he deserved helped a little. "Yeah, I roughed him up and just for the record, no, I'm not sorry. I'm not sorry I arrested him, either. Even though an army of Senator Powell's yes-men were all over me to say I'd made a mistake and get me to drop the charges."

"They knew, of course. About the publicity. They knew the story was too juicy not to get blown way out of proportion. A senator's son. And a woman who, as it turns out, just happened to be a prostitute."

"He didn't have the right to hit her."

"Of course not." It was the first thing they'd agreed on in as long as Ben could remember and Lacie realized it, too. That didn't take any of the starch out of her shoulders. Or mellow the fire in her eyes. "You weren't sorry even then?

When the media was all over you and the good senator was calling for your resignation?"

"Sorry I didn't hit Sean Powell hard enough to knock out a few teeth, just like he did to that prostitute? You bet. The only other thing I'm sorry about is—"

Ben hadn't meant to say even that much, and at the same time he wondered why he didn't know better and keep his mouth shut, he realized it didn't matter anyway. Lacie knew exactly what he was talking about.

Her jaw tightened. "You're only sorry that because of what happened back in D.C., you got sent here. The land that time forgot."

"They couldn't have come up with a better punishment and they knew it." Thinking back on those days four months earlier, Ben shook his head. He realized his voice was bitter, but then, so was the taste in the back of his mouth. "They wanted me out of the picture; well, they sure managed to accomplish that."

Lacie picked up her duffel bag. "They also got you out of the spotlight. Correct me if I'm wrong—and I'm sure you will—but in your line of work, that must be pretty important. Getting you out of D.C. also took some of the heat off. Sean Powell is still in the news now and then, but your name hasn't been mentioned in months. They protected you. And your job. That tells me you must be very valuable to them."

Ben laughed. "Valuable? Oh, yeah. I'm valuable, all right. Nothing like having Sutton County, Kansas, on your résumé."

"Oh, come on, Ben." She rolled her eyes and set down the bag. "Admit it. It's not so bad here."

"Are you serious?" She couldn't be. Yet Lacie looked serious enough. Maybe she just needed a little reminder. "They do hog calling here," he told her. "They have tractor pulls. I've got nothing to do but investigate a kidnapping that might not really be a kidnapping. Unless it is. Unless you changed your mind again. And—"

Tired of listening, she marched up the steps. "And if you hadn't been there today, maybe Randy and Tyler wouldn't be alive right now. Did you think of that?"

Her words hung in the air, as thick as the moths he saw buzzing around the streetlight. It was nice of her to try to make him feel better, but then again, he didn't expect any less from Lacie. Being nice was what Lacie was all about. Being nice was her business. It was the only reason he gave her a couple of seconds of satisfaction before following her to the front door so he could point out the obvious.

"Randy and Tyler would have been fine. Because something tells me that whether I was there or not, you would have stuck your nose in and saved the day. Or maybe you could have just whacked Randy with your baton. That might have worked."

She looked away. "Not funny."

"Not meant to be. Meant to point out that you could have been hurt today. Or worse." She wasn't listening, so he had no choice but to take her hand in his. When he did, she dropped her duffel bag. Her head snapped around and her eyes met his. Even in this drab light, they were very blue. Ben's voice faltered. "Damn it, Lacie, I wouldn't like to see that."

"Really?" She moved a hair's breadth closer for no other reason than to give him no choice but to loosen his grip. She couldn't have foreseen that when he did, it gave him the perfect opportunity to snake his arm around her waist.

She sucked in a breath of surprise that made her breasts strain against the sparkling fabric of her gown. Even if Ben didn't hear the little tremor in her voice that betrayed her nervousness, he would have felt it in the shiver that cascaded through her. She fought to control her voice and keep her composure at the same time she glanced a look down to where Ben's body just barely touched hers. "Why wouldn't you want to see me get hurt? You said it yourself. I'm brainless and asinine and—"

"Pretty darned brave." It was another thing Ben had never meant to mention. Bad enough when a civilian stuck his (or in this case, her) nose where it didn't belong. Worse when someone who knew better actually had to admit it.

Much worse when that same someone who knew better didn't know better than to do the one thing he'd been wanting to do since the first day he'd set eyes on Lacie.

He pulled her close and kissed her.

12

It wasn't just a bad idea, it was the worst idea of all time.

Something told Lacie it wasn't exactly what she was supposed to be thinking. Not when Ben was in the middle of coaxing a moan out of her that sounded like it was being pulled right out of her most secret desires. Not when the feel of his arm around her, and the taste of his lips, and the little flick of his tongue that tempted her to open up to him were just about the best thing she'd ever experienced.

And just about the worst idea of all time.

Okay, so her brain got the message.

Now all she had to do was convince the rest of her.

It might have been easier if Ben hadn't been so good at what he was doing. Lacie hesitated for just a second, and in that one heartbeat, he somehow found a way to make her tip her head back—just a little more. And arch her back—just the slightest bit. And open her mouth—just enough for his tongue to meet hers.

Murmuring her approval wasn't exactly in her best interests. Then again, neither was linking her arms around Ben's neck. Or not protesting when he slid his mouth from hers and trailed a series of fiery kisses across her jaw and over her neck and down to the hollow at the base of her throat.

"Ben, I—" He nipped her earlobe, kissed her chin, and tunneled his fingers through her hair. "I—" Lacie listened to her own halfhearted attempt at talking some sense into both of them.

"You're talking…" Ben brushed her lips with a feather-weight kiss. "I'm just not listening. I'd rather look at you…" He nudged her back just enough to look down into her eyes. "And taste you…" He grinned, and that little dimple in his cheek grinned along with him.

It was impossible to resist.

It was also impossible to look up at him and not be bothered to distraction by the weird cowlick just above his left ear.

She smoothed down his hair with one hand at the same time she caught her breath when Ben brought his mouth down on hers again.

Another moan. Another step back. And she found herself with her back to the front door and Ben's dirty tie tickling the sensitive skin between her breasts.

It was another thing that should have annoyed her, but all she could think about was how delicious it felt.

And how all she wanted was more.

Ben backed her up another step, and because there wasn't much room to maneuver, Lacie edged to her right. Bad move. She bumped into one of the folding lawn chairs propped near the front door and it tumbled into the chair next to it. That one hit the next one in line. And the entire pile landed on the porch in a heap and a wake-the-dead bang of aluminum arms hitting aluminum legs.

Lacie cringed. Ben laughed.

"We're going to wake everybody up." He glanced toward the house. Except for the nightlight left on in the kitchen and the other one that glowed from the top of the stairs, the place was dark and very quiet.

"Not to worry." Lacie thanked her lucky stars and whatever guardian angel watched over her to make sure she didn't lose her mind along with her discretion. Falling lawn chairs weren't exactly thunder from heaven but they were enough of a distraction to save her neck. And her self-respect.

She bent to retrieve the chairs and Ben helped her put them back where they belonged. It was late and still hotter than blazes, yet now that his body wasn't against hers—now that his arms weren't around her—she suddenly felt chilled. She chafed her hands over her arms and wondered if she weren't telegraphing her thoughts loud and clear.

Mistake?

Oh, yeah, it was a mistake, all right.

Now all she had to do was figure out if she was willing to admit it and strong enough to get herself out of this mess.

Or if she was willing to keep on making the same ol' mistake all over again.

She decided on a course somewhere in between. "Mom isn't home," she told Ben, her voice bumping over the words along with the quick breaths designed to settle her heart. "Today is Ed Thompson's birthday. When he got that call about the cow, he had to leave the luncheon Mom had planned for him. They decided to meet late instead. Ed told me. Back at the carnival. There's a nice little restaurant on the other side of Rogers. A steak and wine sort of place."

"That probably means they'll be pretty late. Ed has Randy Holcomb to take care of." Ben checked his watch. He gave the house another look. "And Dinah?"

"Dinah!" Lacie rolled her eyes. "Out with Wiley, I suppose. I tried to talk her into coming to the carnival but... well..." There was no use relaying the story. Once she cut out all the expletives Dinah had used to describe what she thought of the carnival and everyone who was dumb enough to go to it, there wouldn't be much of a story to tell, anyway.

"This is early for Dinah, but I'll tell you what…" She gave an exaggerated yawn. "It's pretty late for me."

There. She'd just made her decision. And though her body wasn't exactly ready to get with the program and fall into step with what was sensible, her brain was convinced it was the right thing to do.

"Thank you again." Lacie stuck her hand out and then decided it was just about the lamest thing she'd ever done. She pulled it back to her side and hoped the smile she offered Ben was enough to make him understand. Even though she wasn't sure she did. "It was nice of you to come along with me today. And nice of you not to shoot Randy. And—"

Ben's laugh interrupted her. "It's okay, Lacie." He backed up a few steps to give her a little breathing room. "I'm not looking to score, if that's what you're afraid of. Unless you want to…" He raised his eyebrows and gave her a look so filled with wishful thinking that she couldn't help but smile.

"Thank you." This time, she meant it. From the bottom of her heart. Thanks to her new pumps, she didn't need to stand on her toes to kiss Ben's cheek. She gave him a quick smack and backed off fast. Before her body could get in the way of her brain again. "I'll see you soon."

"You bet. Only, next time…" The look he gave her was hot enough to melt metal. Fortunately, it didn't last long. Ben headed down the steps. "You're right. It is late. Good night."

"Good night." Watching him go, Lacie whispered the words along with a firm reminder to herself not to get taken in by the thrill that poured through her every time she so much as thought about Ben.

Like winning a pageant crown.

Only better.

"Don't get fooled by the looks. Don't get fooled by the kiss." She pushed open the front door and headed inside. "Not in your best interests," she reminded herself, closing the door behind her. Because she knew what was on the other end of relationships. She'd learned that from Jake.

And even if she hadn't . . .

Even though she told herself it was way too teenage a thing to do, she hurried into the living room and brushed aside the lace curtains on the window. Standing in the dark where she could see and not be seen, she watched Ben walk to his car.

And tried not to think about what a joy it was to watch the way his nice, tight butt moved. And what a pleasure it would be to feel that—and the rest of him—minus the designer suit.

It was the brain versus body thing again and Lacie grumbled her displeasure under her breath. If she wasn't careful, her body would get the best of her brain. And then where would she be?

Still watching, she saw Ben pause on the sidewalk and look back at the house. Just to be sure he wouldn't see her, she moved a bit to the side.

Even if she hadn't learned the lesson of her life from Jake, she reminded herself, she only needed to listen to Ben to know where their relationship was headed.

And where it was headed was nowhere at all.

Not when Ben couldn't wait to head straight back to D.C.

She dropped the curtain into place and walked to the stairs, ready to climb into a nightgown, pull the covers over her head, and do her best to keep from dreaming about Ben.

She actually might have gotten there if, just as she left the living room, she hadn't run into a big guy wearing a ski mask.

Ben wasn't much for symbolism, but there was no way he could miss this one. Kiss Lacie and walk away? Who was he kidding? He might as well have hung a flashing neon sign over his head: AFRAID OF COMMITMENT.

Afraid? Ben didn't like to think that he was afraid of anything, but like it or not, he figured he must be. Otherwise he wouldn't have backed off so easily. Especially when he wanted—when he still wanted—Lacie so much, he could taste it.

"Afraid." He grumbled the word and pounded down the steps. It wasn't even the commitment that scared him as much as it was Lacie. As much as it was his own crazy reaction to Lacie.

Ben? Want a woman whose most important decision every day was what color of lipstick to wear?

It was the most ridiculous thing he'd ever heard. And the truest.

And that's what made it so scary.

That, along with the realization that he'd found out tonight there was a lot more to Lacie than he'd ever suspected.

Things like loyalty. Friendship. Courage.

Bowled over by the thought, he paused on the sidewalk and looked back at the house, hoping that the reality of the perfect little garden and the darling little window boxes and the straight-out-of-a-hokey-old-movie white picket fence would knock some sense into him and remind him who he was. Where he was.

Then again, if sense had anything to do with the way things were going, he would never have kissed Lacie in the first place.

Uneasy with the thought as much as he was with all it meant, Ben hurried over to the car. He unlocked the door and opened it. He was just about to get in when he heard what sounded like a crash from inside the Baxter house. He paused, one hand on the car door, and told himself he was channeling his overactive imagination from one place where it didn't belong to another. Too uneasy with the fantasies he was having about Lacie—fantasies that were all about her in that sparkly dress and her out of that sparkly dress and what he would do to her and with her when she was out of that sparkly dress—he was all too eager to replace them with daydreams about crime and—

Another crash from inside the house. Ben slammed the car door and took off for the house at a run.

The front door was closed, but there was no mistaking the noises of a scuffle from inside the house. Something got knocked over. Someone grunted. Someone else screamed.

It was Lacie.

Ben hauled back and kicked the door in. He pushed his way through the splintered wood and into the house.

Even though the lights were off and it was impossible to see much but the glow of the nightlight that gleamed in the kitchen, he made out the shapes at the end of the hallway. One of them was Lacie; he saw her dress shimmering in the dark. It didn't take much of a stretch of the imagination to figure out who the other person was.

Ben barreled down the hallway toward the man in the ski mask. Unfortunately, the element of surprise had pretty much been removed from the situation. Kicking down a door had a way of doing that. The big guy knew Ben was coming and he didn't hesitate. He had both his arms around Lacie and was dragging her to the back door. He stopped and lifted her off her feet, then hauled back and threw her right into Ben's path.

Ben saw Lacie coming just as he saw the man in the ski mask head for the back door. Unfortunately, there wasn't anything he could do to avoid a collision in the narrow hallway that led from the front door to the kitchen. He skidded to a stop and braced himself, his arms out to try to catch Lacie and cushion her fall. Even though he was prepared, when Lacie slammed into him, they were both knocked to the floor.

"Are you all right?" Ben rolled to his knees and bent over Lacie. There was a switch on the wall near his head, and he reached up and flicked on the hall light. The cut-glass fixture at the bottom of the stairs was more for style than illumination. It provided just enough light for him to see that Lacie's eyes were wide with terror. That her tiara was missing and that her hair was a mess. There were abrasions on her neck and scratches on her arm.

Ben's gut tightened with anger at the same time his heart squeezed. He scooped her into his arms. "Are you hurt? Did he—"

"I'm—ouch!" Lacie reached behind her and grabbed her back.

"Is it your spine?" Ben acted on instinct and his instinct told him this wasn't good. As gently as he could, he laid her back on the floor. Another wave of pain crossed Lacie's face. "Is it your neck? If that no-good son-of-a-bitch broke—"

"Ben!" The last thing he expected to hear out of Lacie was a laugh. She pushed herself up on one elbow, and reaching behind her, she dragged out her tiara. "I got poked." She made a face. "My crown fell off and—"

"You're okay? The rest of you . . ." He did a quick assessment, glancing from her head to where one of the spaghetti straps of her gown was torn and hanging over one shoulder. From there, he looked to where her gown was tangled up around her knees. "You're not hurt?"

Lacie sat up and plopped her crown back on her head. "Just my pride. And a new pair of pantyhose." She frowned down at the run that went all the way from her left ankle up to her thigh. "And my backside." She winced and rubbed a hand there, offering him her other hand for some help up. "If you'd just—"

"Later." Ben bounced to his feet. They'd worry about Lacie's pride and what her tiara had done to her backside later. For now, he had a bad guy to find.

He raced through the kitchen and slapped open the back door. He was just in time to hear the squeal of rubber and see a car on the street behind Mapleshade when it peeled away from the curb and took off like a bat out of hell.

"Damn!" Ben grumbled a curse and reached for his

phone. He dialed Sheriff Thompson's office and got Clete Harter, who informed him that there wasn't much he could do. Sheriff Thompson was out enjoying his birthday dinner and he had the only patrol car. Since Clete had Randy Holcomb to keep an eye on...

"Thanks for nothing." Ben flipped his cell phone shut. "Son of a—"

"They never would have caught up with him anyway."

He swung around to find Lacie right behind him. One of her high heels was broken and she listed slightly to the side, like a fragile pleasure boat that had, against all odds, made it through a hurricane intact. She kicked off the broken shoe, slipped out of the other one, and set both of them down near the door.

Hands on her hips, she glanced down at the pair of shoes that wasn't much of a pair any longer. "Why is it always the good shoes?"

"Maybe the guy's got a thing about shoes." Ben doubted it. More likely, he had a thing about Lacie, but Ben didn't think this was exactly the right moment to point that out. He watched her pad over to the kitchen sink and turn on the light above it.

"Water?" She got a glass from the cupboard and turned on the tap, and though she was very good, she wasn't expert enough to fool Ben. He saw the way her hands shook. The way she kept her shoulders very rigid, as if it took every ounce of energy she had to keep from crumpling. When she filled the glass, the water sloshed over the side.

"Come on." Ben grabbed the glass out of her hand and turned off the water. "I'm taking you over to the hospital in Sutton Springs. To the emergency room."

"I don't need a hospital." When he put a hand on her arm, she brushed him away. "I'm fine. Just a little shaken up and—"

He pulled a kitchen chair out from the table just in time for her to plop into it. Ben went to the refrigerator for a few ice cubes, added them to the glass, and handed it to her. "Here. Drink this. You'd probably be better off with a shot of whisky but something tells me there isn't a bottle of it in the Baxter house."

"There's cooking sherry." Always accommodating, she started to get up, and Ben put a hand on her shoulder to keep her in her chair.

He watched her drink the water and allowed her a couple of moments after to catch her breath and get her bearings.

"He was here? In the house?" Ben started into the questioning as gently as he could. "When you walked in, was he waiting for you?"

Lacie nodded. "In the hallway. But not when I walked in. I went into the living room for a little while." She looked away as if there were something about confessing to being in her own living room that was embarrassing. "Then when I decided to go upstairs..." In spite of the heat, she shivered, and Ben stripped off his suit jacket and draped it over her shoulders.

"It's all right to be upset," he told her, keeping a hand on her arm to steady her. "You'd be crazy if you weren't."

"I didn't think..." Lacie eyes were bright with tears. She bit her lower lip. "I mean, right in my own home. What if my mom had gotten here first? Or Dinah? What if...?" She blinked, and a single tear as bright as a jewel trickled down her cheek. "What if you weren't here to save me?"

"But I was here. That's the important thing. That, and seeing if we can figure out who this creep is." He paused, wondering if it was fair to subject Lacie to an interrogation when the memory of the attack was still so fresh. It was exactly why he needed to do it. Exactly why he didn't want to. He sat in the chair next to hers and put one of his hands over both of hers where they lay on the table.

"Did he say anything?" Ben asked. "Did you hear his voice?"

She shook her head.

"Then, how about his clothing? It all happened so fast, I didn't see much. Can you tell me what he was wearing?"

Thinking, she squeezed her eyes shut. "Jeans. I couldn't really see but there's no mistaking the feel of one hundred percent cotton. And they were rough. You know, not like stonewashed or anything. Not like dress jeans. More like work jeans. Like the kind you'd buy over at the supply store."

"Good." Ben scraped his chair a little closer to the table. "Shirt?"

She shook her head again. "Didn't see it. His arms were bare, though. When he grabbed me"—a shiver ran over her shoulders and Ben gave her hands a squeeze—"I felt his skin. That tells me he was wearing short sleeves. Like a T-shirt."

"You're doing great," he told her. "Anything else?"

"Anything else?" Lacie sniffled and stretched to get a paper towel decorated with smiling teddy bears off the roll on the kitchen sink. She touched a corner of the towel to her eyes, dabbed in under her nose. "He smelled like pizza."

"That narrows things down." Ben chuckled. Not that there was anything particularly funny about the situation, but he figured it might help lighten the mood. And that might help Lacie feel better. "Did you get the feeling you might know the guy?"

"You mean, was it Wiley Burnside?" She sighed. "I don't know, Ben. I honestly don't know. He was big enough to be Wiley, but—"

"But what?"

She shrugged and the broken spaghetti strap drooped. Lucky for Ben—because he was supposed to be working and not paying attention to the way her gown sagged just enough to give him a glimpse of the top of one breast—she pushed it back up again. When she realized that wasn't going to work—at least not for long—she slipped her arms into Ben's jacket and buttoned it up the front.

"But Wiley wouldn't hurt me. That's but what. He might be dumb but he's not dangerous."

"And this guy was."

Lacie pushed a curl of sunny yellow hair out of her eyes. "Are you always this blunt?"

"Only when I need to be."

"And you need to be—"

"Because it's too important not to be." He closed his hand over hers. "Because you're too important for me not to be."

Talk about being blunt. Ben had no intention of laying his heart on the line along with his philosophy of criminal justice. Hard not to, though, when Lacie looked so vulnerable. Hard not to admit that he cared.

"Don't say things like that."

Not exactly the response he anticipated, and at the same time Ben sat back, surprised, Lacie pushed out of her chair.

"Haven't I been through enough for one night?"

"Whoa!" He held up both hands, and even he wasn't sure if it was in surrender. Or to keep her sudden angry words at bay. "I didn't exactly think I was subjecting you to something so horrible. I simply said—"

"You said that I was important to you. I know what you said. I'm just not sure I like hearing it."

"Fine." Ben scraped back his chair and hauled himself to his feet. "Then I won't say it again. I just thought—"

"I know."

"I don't think you do. What, you think I kissed you earlier this evening because . . ."

"Because it was something to do. Because it was fun and you were bored and I was convenient."

Ben sucked in a breath of surprise. "Do you believe that?"

"What's important is that you do."

"I . . ." It was impossible to keep still when his insides were suddenly roiling. Almost as impossible as it was to keep his hands off Lacie. Ben stalked to the other side of the table. His first instinct was to grab her and kiss her until her head spun.

For once, his common sense got the better of him.

Instead, he took her hand in his. "Look, Lacie, I don't know who broke your heart once upon a time but—" Another thought occurred to him and he gave her a careful look. "Yes, I do. I do know who broke your heart. It was Jake McCallum, wasn't it?"

She stiffened. "I told you, that's ancient history."

"Not so ancient that it still doesn't hurt."

"I—" Whatever argument she was preparing, she simply didn't have the energy. Her shoulders drooped. Considering she was wearing Ben's jacket and it was too big for her, she looked more deflated than ever. She lifted her chin and sniffed back a tear. "He walked out on me," she said.

"He's an idiot."

"Well, duh!" She managed a watery laugh.

"You are brave and very beautiful." It didn't exactly qualify when it came to the making-her-head-spin category, but Ben pressed a gentle kiss to her lips. "I'll sleep down here on the couch," he told her. "Just in case our kidnapper decides to come back. And next time..." He touched a hand to his Glock. "If he tries again, that guy's going to regret it."

Lacie brushed the back of her hand across her cheeks. "I'll get pillows," she said. "And a blanket. And I know there are some brand-new toothbrushes in the hall closet outside the—"

"Good heavens!"

Krissie's shocked exclamation drew them out of the kitchen and into the hallway.

They found her on the front porch along with Ed Thompson. They were checking out the splintered door.

"What happened?" Krissie looked from the door to where they were standing, and when she saw that Lacie's hair was a mess, she stepped over the pieces of what used to be her front door and hurried over to her daughter, automatically straightening Lacie's crown. "Are you—"

"I'm fine. Honest."

Krissie wasn't convinced. She took a look at the scratch on Lacie's neck and tisk-tisked while she mumbled. "It might not heal. Not by National Summer Squash pageant time. Of course, pancake make-up might help, but if they notice, they'll hold it against you. The hair..." She shook her head sadly. "Three oil treatments next week," she told Lacie. "When hair gets treated that roughly, it's bound to result in split ends." She cringed and looked from Lacie to the door and from the door to Ben. "Agent Camaglia, do you want to explain?"

Ben was a federal employee, and he figured the truth was the least the government owed Krissie Baxter for her shattered door. "I saw no other way, ma'am," he said. "I needed to provide assistance and—"

"It's not going to work." Lacie tugged at his shirtsleeve. "Before you get yourself in any deeper, take my word for it. It's not going to work."

"Because..."

She laughed. "Four months in Sutton County, Kansas, and you don't know yet? Get with the program, Agent Camaglia!" She poked him in the ribs. "No one around here ever locks their doors!"

13

"So what do you think?" Dinah took a step back and gave Wiley's incredibly sexy butt a long look. Not so easy to keep her mind on her art when her body was urging her to jump his bones. She managed, but only because the light was perfect and they had the place to themselves. She had to work while she could, she reminded herself. They'd save the fun stuff for later. "You think an Indian chief should have red feathers? Or blue feathers?" she asked Wiley.

"I think I'm tired of sitting like this." Wiley was wearing nothing at all but a stretched-out T-shirt with a picture of Gumby on the front. And Pokey on the back. He was draped half on—and half off—Frank Carson's desk, and he glanced over his shoulder at Dinah. He gave her a hangdog look. "I'm getting muscle cramps. You're not going to work all day, are you?"

"That's what artists do." Just to remind him how exhausting it was to be gifted, she put the back of her hand to her forehead. "We get lost in our work. We get carried away. Besides..." Even before she asked Wiley his opinion she'd decided on blue, so she reached for the right bottle of ink and started coloring in the feathers on the chief's headdress.

"With the sun streaming in through the glass doors on the bays, the light is perfect in here. Way better than it is at night. We should have thought of coming in here on Sundays sooner. Old Frank will never know and—"

"Hope I'm not interrupting anything."

The voice from behind them startled them both. Dinah was just about to add ink to one of the feathers and she missed it altogether. Unfortunately, it was pretty impossible to miss Wiley's butt. Her hand jumped and the needle she was working with went in a little too deep.

"Ouch!" Wiley flinched.

"Thanks a bunch." She looked at the blue mess that was now square in the center of the chief's nose and grumbled a curse. She was holding a paper towel in her left hand and she scrunched it into a ball and threw it on the ground. Disgusted, she whirled around, all set to give the intruder a piece of her mind along with a string of curses the likes of which Sutton County hadn't heard in a good, long time. Especially on a Sunday.

She would have done it, too, if she hadn't found Ben Camaglia standing near the door.

Panic and caution mixed in Dinah's insides, churning up the pancakes Wiley had made for breakfast. When Ben pushed off from the door and closed in on her, she couldn't help herself. She took a step back.

A brief thunderstorm had rolled through in the middle of the night and the temperature had cooled considerably. Ben was wearing a raincoat. He had his hands tucked in the pockets. It was just about the flimsiest attempt at looking casual that Dinah had ever seen. Especially since she remembered an *X-Files* episode when Mulder and Scully used the same tactic to try to catch some bad guy off guard.

Most especially since, hands in his pockets or not, there was a vein bulging at the side of Ben's neck that told her this wasn't a social call.

Dinah swallowed hard and watched him stroll around

and take a look at Frank Carson's cramped and greasy office, and when he was done and came to the desk where Dinah had set up her tattooing supplies, he stopped. "On second thought I take that back." Ben picked up one of the bottles of ink and read the label. "I'm not sorry I interrupted at all. You two want to tell me what you're up to."

It wasn't a question. So technically, Dinah figured she didn't have to answer. And besides, she knew she had rights. All sorts of them. There was the one about being represented by an attorney. And the other one about remaining silent. Of course, that didn't explain why the words just sort of fell out of her mouth.

"Doing? We're not doing anything. Not anything we shouldn't be doing, anyway. I mean—"

"Looks to me like you're running an illegal tattooing parlor." Carefully Ben replaced the bottle of ink where he'd found it. "Unless you're licensed?"

"She's gonna be."

"Shut up, Wiley." Dinah shot him a look.

"No. I'm not gonna." Wiley hauled himself up on one elbow. "You are gonna be licensed. And you're going to be the greatest—"

"Get dressed." Ben tossed Wiley the jeans he'd left on a nearby chair. "There's something about interrogating a guy who's not wearing pants that makes me a little queasy."

"Interrogating?" Wiley's face went pale. He grabbed the boxers he'd left nearby—the ones decorated with yellow smiley faces—and turned his back on Dinah and Ben while he pulled them on. When he was done, he hauled on his jeans. They'd already been hard at work on his tattoo for an hour or so, and his butt felt like it had been snapped a couple of hundred times by a rubber band. Instead of zipping his jeans, he just pulled his T-shirt down over the fly.

"What do you mean, interrogating?" Wiley turned back around and gave Dinah a look that told her not to worry, that he had everything under control. "Why would you want to interrogate us?"

"Looks like you haven't been home yet today." Ben perched on the edge of Frank's desk. He ignored Wiley completely and kept his eyes on Dinah. "If you had, my guess is that you'd know what I'm talking about."

Dinah didn't like the tone of his voice. She didn't like the way he looked at her, either. Like he could read her mind. She tossed the tattoo needle she was holding down on the plastic tray on Frank's desk and grabbed a new paper towel to wipe her hands. "Last I heard, spending the night with the man you love wasn't a crime. Maybe you've been hanging around with Miss Lily White Lacie too long. That would be enough to make any guy forget about sex completely!"

Ben knew better than to take the bait. Which is exactly why Dinah decided to egg him on. Just a little more.

"She's something, huh? My sister . . ." Dinah shook her head, and she didn't have to pretend to be disgusted. Thinking about the way Lacie acted like she was better than everyone else pretty much always made her feel that way. "She wouldn't know a good fu—"

"What your sister knows or doesn't know isn't any of my concern." Ben answered so fast, it made Dinah wonder what he was thinking. What he was hiding. There was a calendar on the wall above the desk that featured pickup trucks, and he turned to look at it.

"Actually, what I'm more interested in"—Ben gave the '64 Chevy on the July page one last look before he turned around and shifted his gaze to Wiley—"is where you were last night at about midnight."

"He was with me." Dinah stepped between Ben and Wiley. "We watched a movie, drank a couple of beers—"

"Ate a pizza?"

Like it or not, Ben's question made Dinah think about what they'd found in the school office the night before. She swallowed hard. "No. We didn't have a pizza, did we,

Wiley?" She glanced at him over her shoulder and saw that he must have been thinking about the school, too. That would explain why he looked like somebody had sucker punched him. "We were going to get a pizza, but then Wiley said we could just live on love."

"That's very romantic." Ben pulled a small notebook out of his pocket and scribbled a few lines. "So you watched a movie and drank some beers. Where did you say you did this?"

"My house."

"Mine."

Dinah and Wiley answered at the same time. They exchanged worried looks that got even more worried when Ben laughed.

"Don't think you can be in two places at once. As a matter of fact, I'm pretty certain of it. So which was it?" He looked at Dinah. "Your place?" He crossed his arms over his chest and shifted his gaze to Wiley. "Or yours?"

"Mine." Wiley stepped forward and grabbed Dinah's hand. He held it very tight. Very romantic. Except that he was cutting off her circulation. "She just said 'my house' because Dinah thinks of my house as her house. You know what I mean? I mean, we're going to get married one of these days and then—"

"Yeah, yeah. What's yours is hers and what's hers is yours." Ben waved away the explanation like he didn't care at all, and Dinah wondered why he'd asked the question in the first place. "And after you watched the movie and drank the beers and ate the pizza?"

"Didn't say we ate a pizza." Dinah would have liked to think that she sounded tough and confident but she was afraid she sounded more like she was feeling. Scared shitless. "We watched the movie and—"

"What movie?"

"Biker Babes of Brazil." She blurted out the first thing she could think of. "You'd love it. It stars—"

"Lana Longlegs. Yeah, I know." Ben got up and did another turn around the office. "Lots of tattoos in that movie."

There were, and at the same time Dinah wondered how he knew it, she saw exactly what he was doing. Trying to sound like he was their friend. Just so he could catch them in a lie. She telegraphed her fear to Wiley with a look.

"So after the movie, you guys took a ride, right? Over to Klaber Falls?"

"Klaber Falls? We weren't anywhere near Klaber Falls. We were at—" At the last second, Wiley caught himself and looked to Dinah for deliverance.

"At Hastings Park." Dinah supplied the rest of the story. "We like to make love in the moonlight."

"And that's more than I ever wanted to know about you." Ben finished walking around and stopped just opposite of where they were standing. He looked pretty calm—except for the vein still bulging at the side of his neck. His hands were out of his pockets and fisted at his side. "I think we need to get something really clear between us, Wiley."

Wiley was a few inches taller than Ben and had a good forty pounds on him. That didn't keep Ben from raising his chin and giving him a look that just about dared him to make a move. His voice wasn't any friendlier. "You do it again, Wiley, and I'm going to have your ass in a sling. You understand me?"

"I—" Wiley ran his tongue over his lips. "I don't—"

"You touch her, ever again, and I'm not going to need evidence. I'm going to wipe every road in Sutton County with what's left of your sorry ass."

"Touch? Her?" Wiley blinked fast. Like he did that time right after they started dating and Dinah was so hot for him, she showed up on his back porch in the middle of the night wearing nothing at all but an old trench coat. And a great big come-and-get-it smile.

He recovered in a moment and his jaw went rigid. "Threats or no threats, you'll never make me do that. Not touch Dinah? Who do you think you are, telling me that? There's nothing that's going to keep me from—"

Ben slapped a hand against his thigh. "What the hell is it with you people around here? Can't you get anything right? Even being a criminal?" He spun away from them, then just as quickly, whirled back around. "I'm only going to say this one more time. Watch your step, Burnside. Watch it really close. Because the next time you come after her, I'm going to be waiting for you. I'm done fooling around. Just like I'm done waiting for you to pop out of some dark corner and grab Lacie. It ends. Right here. If it doesn't, you'll pay the consequences."

Ben turned and stalked out of the office, and a second later, the front door slammed shut. Frank Carson's SERVICE STATION OF THE MONTH award shivered on the wall. The calender with the pickup trucks fell and hit the floor.

"Lacie?" Wiley looked at Dinah in wonder. "Does he think we stole those stupid old pictures of her when we were in the school last night?"

When Wiley finally let go of her hand, Dinah shook it. It took a while for the feeling to return in her fingers, and when it did, the truth dawned. "Wiley!" A slow smile spread over Dinah's face. It was only a couple seconds before she was laughing. "Wiley, he thinks we tried to kidnap Lacie!"

"Kidnap? Lacie?" Wiley wasn't always really quick on the uptake, but even he knew a fucked-up idea when he heard one. "You're kidding me, right? Why the hell would we want to—"

"Who cares!" Sweet relief washed over Dinah and she threw herself into Wiley's arms. "Who cares what he thinks! All that matters is that he's got it all wrong. He doesn't know what we're up to. That and when it came right down to it, you defended me. You stood up for our love, even when he was trying to bully you."

Wiley looked pretty satisfied with himself. "I wasn't going to let some tough guy intimidate me. Not when it came to talking about the woman I love. He was just blowing smoke! Unless..." He looked over Dinah's head at the door. "Unless he's just trying to catch us with our pants down."

"Oh, Wiley!" Dinah pushed back and gave him the sort of openmouthed look of surprise she'd seen Lacie practice in front of the mirror when she knew she was going to win a pageant but had to look humble when her name was announced. She inched his T-shirt up at the same time she tugged his jeans down. "What's that you said about pants down?"

"Really, Snuggle Bunny?" The look of concern on Wiley's face was replaced by a big smile. "I thought you were going to be artistic first."

"Artistic? Oh, I am, Sugar Lips. Believe me. I am!"

"There. That's him. Over there talking to Mayor Crist." Krissie gave Lacie's arm a poke at the same time she snuck a look over toward the gazebo. "That's Lester Zwick. The one I was telling you about."

As pretty as a picture in a red and white sundress, a blue silk scarf dotted with stars draped around her neck, and her hair pulled back in a ponytail, Lacie took a sip of her iced tea at the same time she turned to look toward where her mother pointed. Ben couldn't help himself. He had to look, too. It was the Fourth of July, and Freedom Park in the center of Sutton Springs was crowded for the annual ice cream social. He'd just come back with three hot dogs from the stand that was set up over near the steps of the Congregational Church, and before he slid back into his seat at the picnic table, he waited for the crowd between where they were sitting and the gazebo to clear. When it did, he saw the man in brown polyester pants and a shrimp-colored golf shirt. The guy was short and thin and had a long, skinny nose, a pointed chin, and tiny dark eyes.

"He looks like a rat." From the seat next to Ben's, Dinah

said exactly what Ben was thinking. Only, she said it with a mouth full of half-chewed potato chips.

Krissie clicked her tongue and gave her youngest daughter a fleeting, out-of-patience look. That done, she turned her full attention back to Lacie. "You've heard of Lester Zwick, honey. He's one of the most respected pageant judges on the West Coast. He's from around here originally. Gave me a perfect score the year I won the state Summer Squash crown. We're fortunate that the National Summer Squash folks talked him into coming back here to judge this year. Lester and I are exploring the possibilities of being partners in a pageant coaching business," she added for Ben's benefit. "I suppose that means that technically, it would be unethical of me to fraternize before you're crowned, Lacie. But that doesn't mean you can't go over and say hello. Go ahead." Another poke from Krissie. "Go on over there and introduce yourself. Get to know him a little better."

"Yeah!" Dinah gave her sister an evil grin. "Maybe you can get some extra points in the pageant if you give him a blow job."

Krissie's shoulders shot back. "Dinah! You know as well as I do that Lacie won't need any extra points. She's going to be Miss National Summer Squash. Just like I would have been Miss National Summer Squash if only I'd had the chance."

Ben knew better than to get in the middle of a family squabble. He ought to. He came from a huge family that liked nothing better than a very loud, very animated discussion. He'd grown up with it. He was comfortable with it. Heck, he sometimes even enjoyed joining in.

But Krissie's clipped reply and Dinah's scheming comments and Lacie's refusal to say anything at all made him feel he had to do something to calm the waters. Even though in the Camaglia household, these waters would qualify as placid.

He looked across the table to where Lacie was sitting. "You think you're going to win?" he asked her.

How she did it at just the right moments, he wasn't sure, but she blushed. "The competition's tough," she said. "It always is. But this year . . ." As if she were nervous just thinking of the pageant in two weeks' time, she pulled in a breath and let it out slowly. "There's that girl from Nebraska who sings opera while she cooks. And that one . . . you remember her, Mom . . . the one from Minnesota who can recite the Declaration of Independence backward. There's Susie What's-Her-Name from Ohio who plays the oboe, and that other one, that Robin girl who looks so fabulous in a swimsuit. I think it's going to be tougher than ever."

"Nonsense!" As far as Ben could see, Krissie's entire lunch had consisted of a piece of watermelon and a glass of ice water. She finished both and got up to throw her paper plate and cup away. "Doesn't matter if it's tough," she said, and she picked a bit of lint from Lacie's silk scarf. She gave her eldest daughter a wink. "You're tougher."

"You're tougher." Once Krissie walked away, Dinah parroted her mother in a singsong voice. She grabbed another handful of chips from the bowl in the center of the table and slid off the bench. "See you losers around," she said, and the last Ben saw of her, she was headed across the park toward where Wiley's truck was parked.

Ben slid one of the hot dogs onto Lacie's plate. "Sweet kid."

"You think so?" With one perfectly manicured fingernail, Lacie flicked the onions off her hot dog. "Does that mean you don't think she's a criminal mastermind anymore?"

"Wish I knew." Ben took a big bite of hot dog, and when ketchup oozed out of the bun and onto his chin, he grabbed for a napkin and wiped it away before it had a chance to plop onto his white shirt and maroon and white striped tie. "After our little confrontation yesterday, I'm surprised she's willing to get within twenty feet of me."

"No surprise there." Lacie took one delicate bite and chewed. "Dinah told us at home this morning that she was going to go out of her way to see you today. Just to prove that you don't scare her."

Ben laughed. "True to form. I wish I could figure out if she was being true to form yesterday, too. When I went to have that talk with Wiley. I was sure that one of them would break down."

"You browbeat them."

Ben sat up a little straighter on the backless bench. "I never browbeat," he said, and he was pretty sure it was true. "I like to think of myself as a little more subtle than that."

"So, Mr. Subtle . . ." There was a gleam in Lacie's eyes. "You thought they'd spill their guts, huh? Did you ever think that maybe they don't have anything to spill?"

"Maybe." Ben finished one hot dog and started on the second one. "Wish I knew for sure. That's why—"

"Oh, I almost forgot!" Krissie came rushing back over to the table, her cheeks as pink as the lace-trimmed shirt she wore over white slacks and sandals. As if it were the most natural thing in the world, she reached onto Lacie's plate, broke her hot dog in half, and put one piece back on Ben's plate. The mission to save Lacie from unwanted fat grams complete, she brushed her hands together. "You're doing a baton demonstration at two, remember. And Father Sullivan's niece is visiting from Arkansas. They'd like to get a picture with you. I told them three. That way we'll have time to fix your hair after your performance. And Evelyn Swenson—"

"Don't tell me; let me guess." Lacie swallowed another bite of hot dog. "Evelyn Swenson wants me to teach Mandy how to twirl."

"You've got it." Krissie gave her the thumbs-up. When she saw Jeff Parkman about to take a picture of Lacie, she leaned down so that she could be in it, too. "Says she'll talk to you about it later tonight, after the fireworks display. I said I thought maybe you two could get together next week sometime."

"Speaking of next week..." It wasn't in Ben's nature to be shy about anything. Particularly when it came to his work. Like it or not, though, he felt a little uneasy bringing up an idea he'd been tossing around in his mind. "I was thinking..." He looked at Lacie and at the same time wished her mother weren't hanging around. Not that he had anything to hide, it was just that talking to a woman about taking her away for a weekend was one of those things that shouldn't have to be done in front of relatives. Especially mothers.

"I've got to leave town next week for a few days. My sister is getting married. In Chicago," he told Krissie. He swung his gaze back to Lacie. "I want you to come with me."

"Don't be ridiculous!" He wasn't talking to her. Heck, he wasn't even looking at her. Yet Krissie waved away Ben's suggestion with one hand. "That's just a few days before the pageant. Lacie will be far too busy to go anywhere."

"Will you be?" He looked at Lacie again, wishing he were as much of a mind reader as he always liked suspects to think he was. Did she see the offer for exactly what it was, a sensible suggestion designed to keep her safe? Or was she as intrigued by it as he secretly hoped she'd be?

"Lacie?" He waited for her answer and realized that the waiting made him nervous and that he didn't like the feeling.

"What I think you're asking..." She used the kind of voice he imagined she used in a pageant when she was asked what her plan was for world peace, or how she would make sure that no child ever went to bed hungry. It was thoughtful but not hesitant. Careful, but not so cautious as to make it look as if she were out of her depth. "You're asking because you think that if you're not here, there might be another kidnap attempt."

"Absolutely." Technically true, so Ben didn't feel guilty saying it. He also didn't feel guilty about leaving out the part about how the only thing he'd been able to think about since the night of the carnival was how good Lacie tasted, how right it felt to hold her in his arms, and how he thought that if they could get away by themselves for a few days, they might take things to the next level.

Just thinking about the whole thing made him ache from wanting her.

He couldn't say all that—at least not with Krissie hovering around—so he played it safe instead and told her the other half of the truth. "I thought the change of scenery might do you good. I also thought that if word got out that I was gone for a few days . . . well, there hasn't been an incident since the night of the carnival, but I think we both know that doesn't mean it won't happen again."

He was talking about the near-abduction incident.

The color that suddenly streaked Lacie's cheeks told him she was thinking about the other incident. The one that happened on the front porch right before Lacie went inside and nearly got herself kidnapped.

"It's not really a good idea." Lacie heard the words that were coming out of her mouth, but she just couldn't believe them. Chicago? The shopping? The nightlife? The shopping? The restaurants? The shopping?

Plus Ben?

Just thinking about the possibilities warmed her down to her toes.

The kisses? The caresses? The promise she'd felt in the touch of his tongue against hers? The one that told her he was very interested and that if she were very interested back, what was bound to happen between them was going to be very interesting?

Although her iced tea cup was nearly empty, she picked it up and drank down what was left of the melted ice cubes. "There's a lot of preparation before a pageant," she told him, and she congratulated herself for knowing when to listen to her own common sense. "I'll go from one workout a day to two, I'll need final fittings on a number of dresses, an extra hot oil treatment or two on my hair, and—"

"Last I heard, hot oil treatments were not illegal in Chicago."

"It's very kind of you. Really." Lacie gave him a smile just so he'd realize she meant it. "But I've got to be very careful. I don't know what the change in water and air might do to my skin. I can't take the chance of upsetting my system. I won't even—"

"All right!" Ben put his hands up in surrender. "I just thought it would be safer if you came along with me."

Safer?

It took everything Lacie had not to laugh.

Being out of town with Ben would be anything but safe. For her body. Or her heart.

Kidnapper or not, she was far safer right here.

A couple of old women walked by and said hello to Lacie, and Krissie gave them a wide smile. "Lacie's always sensible," she told Ben. "She's always focused. Let's face it, Miss National Summer Squash is the most important—" Krissie's perfectly plucked eyebrows dipped low over her eyes. She stood on her tiptoes.

"Is that Ed over there?" she asked, and when Ben turned around, he saw it was. "He's coming through the crowd and he looks like he's looking for someone."

The moment Sheriff Thompson saw Ben, his expression brightened. He hurried over to where they were sitting. "Need you, Camaglia. Over at the school."

"School?" Ben was on his feet in an instant. "What's going on?"

"Not sure." Thompson sucked on his teeth. "Not sure at all. Only thought maybe you'd like to have a look."

"Sleeping bag. Girlie magazines. Portable radio. Soap. Toothbrush." Ben looked over the stash of items neatly tucked into Mr. Fortnoy's office. "Looks like whoever is hanging around here, he's planning on staying for a long time."

"Just what I thought." Sheriff Thompson nodded. "Pizza boxes out in the outer office, too. Not ordered from Tony's here in town. They're from some pizza place over near the county line, Antonio's or something."

"You call a fingerprint team in?"

Thompson gave him a sidelong look and Ben knew exactly what it meant. All the way over to the high school, the sheriff had been trying to convince Ben—and probably himself—that this was nothing but a case of some drifter finding a convenient place to sleep for a couple of nights. But for all his sleepy-little-town ways, even Thompson knew there was probably more to it than that.

"You think we need fingerprints? For a squatter?" He waited for Ben to contradict him, and when he didn't—only because he knew if he waited long enough, Thompson would contradict himself—Ben took a quick look around.

Whoever their mystery visitor was, he was smart enough to put his sleeping bag flush up against the wall, right below the windows. Even if someone looked in, chances were, they'd never see him. They wouldn't have found him now except—

"What did you say happened?" Sheriff Thompson was holding a notebook, and with a look, Ben asked him to go over the details. "How'd you find all this?"

Thompson flipped the pages. "Got a call from Bill Hunnicutt. You've seen him around, I'll bet. The guy with the binoculars."

Ben thought back to the first day he'd visited Klaber Falls. There was a man outside the Baxter house with binoculars.

"Good ol' Bill. Carries those binoculars with him all the time," the sheriff said. "Says he's bird-watching, but we all know he's just being nosy. Looks like this time, it paid off. Said he saw a man leaving the school early this morning."

"Did he say what the man looked like?"

Thompson flipped through a couple more pages. "Said he saw the guy from the back and that all he could tell was that he was tall. Truth be told, what that probably means is that it was time for Meggie Randolph who lives over there near the post office to start her backyard sunbathing and Bill had better things to look at."

"And this Hunnicutt called you?"

"That's right. Took us a while to locate Mr. Fortnoy and get a key. Haven't touched a thing since we found it."

Ben did another turn around the room. "I'd like to talk to the guy once you nab him," he told Thompson. "I can see someone sneaking in for a night or two, but this guy is here for the long haul. My guess is he's here waiting for something. Or someone." Just so there was no mistaking what he was talking about, he gave Thompson a look.

"Yeah." The sheriff rolled back on his heels and finally admitted the truth. "What I was thinking, too."

Just to be thorough, Ben sat down in Mr. Fortnoy's desk chair and pulled open his top drawer. There was nothing unusual in it or in the next drawer he looked in. There wasn't anything unusual at all until—

Ben yanked open the last drawer on the left and caught his breath. He'd been hoping to find something. He'd even been counting on it. But hoping and counting on were never actually the same as finding. And what he'd found in the principal's desk was a black knitted ski mask.

One look at Ben's expression and the sheriff hurried around to the other side of the desk. "Will you look at that?" Thompson gave a quiet whistle. "She said a ski mask, didn't she? Lacie said—"

"And she was right." Ben slipped the drawer closed. "Let's leave it," he said. "Let's leave all of it. We'll set up surveillance over near the football field. When this guy comes back—"

The sheriff looked up at the ceiling, and Ben felt a sinking sensation in his stomach.

"What?" He stood and pinned Thompson with a look. "Are you telling me—"

"Ol' Bill didn't mean anything by it, of course." Thompson hurried through the bad news. "He said he was surprised, that's all. When he saw the guy coming out of the school. He yelled at him. Told him—"

"Told him he was calling the police." The sinking feeling morphed into something that felt more like nausea. And it had nothing to do with the hot dogs or the onions. Ben sat back down. "He won't come back here. Not now that he knows we're on to him. We could have had him."

"And now we've got squat." Thompson plopped down on the edge of the desk. "What are we going to do?"

"Do?" Ben didn't even have to think about it. He pushed away from the desk, stood, and walked to the door. "What you're going to do is canvass the area and see if anyone around here saw anything. Then you're going to talk to Bill Hunnicutt and see if he can give us anything more than *tall* to go on. Then you're going to see the folks at Antonio's and find who's been ordering pizza to go. What I'm going to do—" He headed out of Mr. Fortnoy's office, and even when he punched open the front door of the school and headed back toward the park, he was still mumbling to himself.

"What I'm going to do is go to my sister's wedding in Chicago," he said. "And now that I know this guy is here just waiting for another chance at Lacie, there's no way on earth she's not coming with me."

It was the right decision. Logical and sensible.

It didn't explain why another thought occurred to Ben, and he stopped on the sidewalk outside the school and sucked in a breath. Like he'd just been sideswiped by an Abrams Tank.

"It's your job, Camaglia," he reminded himself.

Just like he reminded himself that a few weeks earlier, he was dead set on doing that job so that he could make a name for himself and the Powers That Be back at headquarters would give him a one-way ticket out of the Purgatory that was Sutton County.

And now, all he cared about was doing his job. And doing it right.

So that he could keep Lacie safe.

14

"Here. You need a piece of pizza."

"No one actually *needs* a piece of pizza." Lacie smiled at Ben's Grandpa DiNardo before she looked down at the piece of pizza—complete with pepperoni, mushrooms, onions, black olives, double cheese, and anchovies—that he slid onto her plate. Grandpa DiNardo was a short, wiry man closing in on eighty. He had a shock of silvery hair, a big nose, and laughing eyes. "Thanks, but I have my dinner right here, Mr. DiNardo," she said. "I have salad and—"

"Don't even talk to me, young lady! Not if you're going to call me *mister*!" He shook a finger at her. "Mister! Makes me sound like an old codger. Last time anybody called me mister was a month or so ago when I got pulled over on the Dan Ryan for going seventy-five. Cop let me go." He gave her a wink. "A woman, and I pulled my charming Italian routine on her. Works every time!"

Lacie had no doubt of it. Routine or not, Grandpa DiNardo had the charm part down pat.

"You call me Grandpa." He tapped her arm. "Everyone calls me Grandpa. Everyone around here eats, too." He looked at the salad on the plate in front of Lacie. "Green salad, no dressing!" Grandpa shivered. "Ben said you're from somewhere else. Don't they know how to eat there?"

"Somewhere else is Kansas, Pop." Ben's mom, Carmella, slid into the chair next to Lacie's at the dining room table. "And of course they know how to eat in Kansas. They just never taught Lacie. Here." Carmella reached for the bowl of spaghetti in the middle of the table and dragged it in front of Lacie. "Make room on your plate, honey. You've got to try this. It's Aunt Helen's recipe. Helen!"

How Helen heard her above the din of a couple dozen people talking at the top of their lungs, Lacie wasn't sure. Then again, she wasn't exactly sure how this many people could even fit into any one house.

Ben's parents, Carmella and Anthony, lived in a modest Arts and Crafts bungalow with a slice of the Chicago skyline out the back window and—if you looked real hard and the wind was blowing enough to move apart the leaves of the oak tree just outside the living room window—a view of Lake Michigan out front. The house was bigger than the Baxter home back on Mapleshade, but right now, there were so many people in it, it was easy to feel as if the walls were closing in.

Friends, relatives, in-laws, grandchildren, nieces, nephews, neighbors.

Lacie had been introduced to all of them, and though she had an extraordinary memory for names (after all, congeniality was a big part of her job), even she was intimidated.

A tall, heavyset woman in a navy dress made her way through the knots of people gathered in the kitchen and the other dozen or so shuffling past the buffet table set up against one wall of the dining room, loading their dishes to the breaking point. The woman was, apparently, Aunt Helen.

"Lacie's going to try your pasta, Helen." Carmella had to raise her voice to be heard. "She'll want the recipe. Get one of the blank recipe cards from the box. It's in the kitchen cupboard. Next to the coffee."

That taken care of, Carmella scooped a pile of noodles the size of a small mountain onto Lacie's plate. Right next to the pizza. "Helen makes a good sauce," she told Lacie. She put her arm around Lacie's shoulders and gave her a squeeze. "Not as good as mine, of course!" Carmella let out a laugh that rang against the orange and gold stained glass light fixture that hung above the table. She was a round, middle-aged woman with a sprinkling of gray in her dark hair and eyes that were a duplicate of her father's. She lowered her voice, as if sharing a secret.

"What does your mother put in her sauce?" Carmella asked. "Fresh tomatoes or canned? Helen, she says canned, but I say, only if you can them yourself. She uses fennel seed, too. I never use fennel seed. I like oregano. I can add oregano if there isn't enough in Helen's sauce for you. I've got some in the kitchen if you—"

"This will be fine." When Carmella made to get up in search of oregano, Lacie stopped her with a smile. She looked at the heaping plate of food and at all the people gathered in the house. Through the open archway that led into the living room, she could see people sitting on the couch and on chairs and on the floor, eating with plates on their laps. Over in the corner, Marybeth and Jason—the bride and groom to be—were staring into each other's eyes.

"Green salad. All she was going to eat was green salad!" Lacie's attention was drawn back to the matter at hand by Grandpa DiNardo's exclamation. "Can you imagine! You call that eating?"

Lacie had no intention of hurting Grandpa DiNardo's feelings and she certainly didn't want to insult Ben's mother, or his Aunt Helen. But she wasn't about to be bullied into unnecessary fat grams, either.

"I call it smart," she told him. "The National Miss Summer Squash pageant is next week and—"

"Skin and bones." Grandpa DiNardo was not moved by sensible talk of Summer Squash pageants or fat grams. He ringed Lacie's wrist with his thumb and forefinger, and as if it were some sort of hideous trophy, he held it up for Carmella to see. "Look! She's nothing but skin and bones! A few pieces of pizza will do you good. And don't tell me you aren't hungry. Shopping all day!" Shopping apparently wasn't his favorite pasttime. He grimaced. "I hear the girls ran out of the house first thing this morning and picked you up at your hotel. You must be starving."

Lacie was. She had been all day. But that didn't make one bit of difference. Not with the pageant next week and gowns that still had to fit by the time she got back to Klaber Falls.

In spite of the fact that Ben's sister, Angie, insisted they stop for cappuccino and pastry before they hit the downtown department stores, and Veronica (another sister) convinced them that they needed brunch between Lord & Taylor and Macy's, and JoAnn (a cousin) talked them into having just a little something to tide them over between when they ended their shopping excursion and when they got back home to get ready for this big family dinner....

In spite of all the opportunities and all the temptations, Lacie hadn't had a bite since the dry toast and weak tea she ordered for breakfast and the turkey sandwich (whole wheat, no mayo), that she'd eaten for lunch.

"Don't tell me Ben approves." As if Grandpa DiNardo had stood side by side with Ben in the hotel lobby when he gave her the breakfast-is-the-most-important-meal-of-the-day speech, Grandpa shook his head sadly. "I can't believe he'd let you go through the day living on nothing but bread and water."

"Not exactly bread and water," Lacie said. And then she realized it pretty much was.

She got rid of the thought with a shake of her shoulders. "I've seen Ben eat," she added, more to change the subject than anything else. "Lasagna and garlic bread and cannoli and—" She was sure just thinking about it put her at risk of adding unwanted ounces and unsightly inches. "I don't know how he does it and stays so trim."

"Good genes!" Grandpa DiNardo patted his own flat stomach. "And a couple of glasses of wine every day, of course. Aids the digestion. Plus, it makes you awfully happy." Grandpa reached for a bottle of wine and poured some into a glass. He plunked the glass down in front of Lacie. "That will help your appetite," he said. "You'll see."

"Go ahead," Carmella encouraged her with a little nudge. "He makes it himself. We try not to say anything because we know it will go to his head, but it really is good."

The wine was the color of the gown Lacie had worn in the Miss Jolly Holiday pageant the winter before. Because she didn't know what else to do without looking rude and un-grateful and because she wouldn't be caught dead looking rude and ungrateful to people who'd welcomed her as if she were one of their own, she took a tiny sip. And smiled. "It's delicious."

"Told you!" Grandpa DiNardo liked a good compliment. He beamed a smile that revealed a dimple in his left cheek. "If Ben ever gets back here from wherever he went off to this afternoon, we'll get him a glass, too. Maybe it will help him get rid of that long face he's been wearing since he got sent to wherever they sent him to after that flap with the senator's son."

"Kansas, Pop." Carmella shook her head in frustration, but the affectionate look she gave her father said she didn't hold it against him. "Ben is working in Kansas. Where Lacie lives. That's how they know each other."

The wine in Grandpa's glass was only half-gone, but he refilled it to the brim while he looked down to where the food still sat on Lacie's plate, untouched. "Don't you folks in Kansas know you'll never get through a weekend like this without a little fuel in the furnace? I can't believe Ben hasn't told you that. After all, from what I hear, you're staying to-gether in that fancy downtown hotel."

"Just because we're staying in the same hotel does not mean we're staying together."

Ben must have snuck through the crowd in the kitchen when Lacie wasn't looking that way. He walked up behind her and leaned down so that Grandpa could hear him above the noise.

Automatically, Lacie looked his way. And caught her breath.

Ben in a six hundred dollar suit, a starched shirt, and a designer tie was to die for.

Ben in snug jeans and a black and white golf shirt with a little logo over his heart was...

She swallowed around the thought and the sudden dryness in her mouth.

"Your hair!" Okay, so it wasn't the most polite way to greet a guy she hadn't seen all day. Lacie couldn't help herself. Ben looked astonishing. Astonishingly good. Astonishingly sexy. Like his hair had never had the misfortune of meeting Gib Allen's scissors up close and personal. "You got it cut!"

"Styled." Ben's correction was tempered by a smile that was meant only for Lacie and warmed her inside and out. "Went to a place I used to go back when I lived here. Guy by the name of Dionne. Crazy as a loon but he sure knows how to cut hair. He says he never would have been able to help me if it wasn't for that pumpkin oil you gave me."

"Pumpkin oil?" It was apparent that Grandpa didn't like to be excluded from a conversation. Any conversation. He edged his way back in with all the finesse of Ben's plus-size cousin Gracie, who (in preparation for tomorrow's wedding and with a great deal of laughter and loud instruction) was teaching a group of folks in the living room how to do the Twist.

"What's this about pumpkin oil?" Grandpa DiNardo asked. "And what does it have to do with you two staying at that fancy downtown hotel together?"

"Pop, subtle you are not!" Carmella rolled her eyes and got up from the table. "I'm staying out of this!"

"And I'm not getting into it." Ben grabbed Lacie's hand and pulled her out of her chair. "Come on. I've got a quiet little table for two reserved far away from old guys who are way too nosy for their own good."

"Hey!" Grandpa DiNardo was still talking to them as they wound their way through the dancers in the living room and out to the front porch. "Who you calling an old guy?"

The front door closing behind them muffled the noises inside. Lacie breathed a sigh of relief and instantly felt guilty about it.

"It's not like I wasn't having a good time." She scrambled to explain before Ben could call her on it. "It's just that—"

"They're a little overwhelming. And a lot loud. Yeah, I know."

The front porch of the Camaglia house wasn't anything like the front porch back home. Back home, the Baxter front porch was as neat as a pin, as clean as a whistle, and as color-coordinated as if the *Trading Spaces* team had been there and hard at work. The Camaglia front porch was much like the Camaglia house. And the Camaglia family.

Colorful. Rambling. A little eccentric. A lot interesting. Anything but understated.

There were dozens of houseplants lined up on the knee-high brick wall that surrounded the porch. Some of them were in bright pots. Some were in plain terra-cotta. A few were planted in cut-in-half milk cartons. Three huge pots of multicolored impatiens shared space on the front steps along with one of the grandkid's skateboards, a watering can, and (though Lacie hadn't seen hide nor hair of a pet) a bright red dog leash.

There was a low table in front of the living room window that was packed with more plants, as well as a couple of stained glass candle holders, a portable radio, and a Cubs pennant that was hanging in just the right place to be seen from the street. Up on the ceiling, tiny white twinkle lights were strung around the perimeter of the porch, and though when she'd first seen them the day before, Lacie was sure they must have been left over from Christmas, Ben had assured her that his mom kept them up—and on—all year long. They were on now and as the summer evening light faded, they glowed as bright as the fireflies that danced over the front lawn.

At the far end of the porch and hanging from the ceiling was a wooden swing. Ben pointed toward it and the TV tray loaded with food that was set in front of it. "Table for two. What did I tell you? I got us some dinner from the kitchen before I rescued you from the dining room." He led her over to the swing, pulling a Chicago Cubs baseball cap from his pocket as he did. He put it on and plunked down on the swing.

"You're covering up your nice haircut."

"Style. Hairstyle," he reminded her, and gave her a smile that warmed her down to the espadrilles she'd bought on sale at Marshall Field's that morning. "It's my lucky cap."

"Oh, and are you planning on getting lucky?"

He patted the spot next to him on the swing. "Sit down here and let's find out."

It wasn't like Lacie to take chances, especially when it came to something as serious as what was left of her heart. But even a seasoned veteran of the love wars couldn't resist the smile that gleamed in Ben's eyes. Or the touch of his hand when he tightened his hold on her—just a little—and tugged her closer.

It wasn't like her to tease, either, but it was too good an opportunity to pass up. "I'm not sure I'm that brave." She looked him up and down. "Looks like this is one of those places where you don't wear your gun. Sounds like trouble to me."

"Not to worry, ma'am." He inched up the left leg of his

jeans just enough for her to see he was wearing an ankle holster and a small gun. "Your virtue is as safe as your person."

Lacie sat down and gave the gun—and Ben—a dubious look. "What, you afraid your Aunt Helen is going to twist your arm around your back and force-feed you spaghetti?"

"You never know. I know I'd have a fight on my hands if I ever chose Aunt Helen's sauce over Mom's. Aunt Helen—"

"Uses fennel seed. Yes, I know." Lacie tried to look as serious as Carmella had when she was explaining the complexities of the thing. "I heard all about it."

"But I bet they didn't tell you about this!" Before Lacie could move and long before she could plan a strategy to save herself from it, Ben had scooped up a plastic fork full of the rigatoni on the plate in front of them. He popped it into her mouth. "That's Grandpa's sauce. He's got a secret stash and he made me promise not to let anyone know. If word gets out that he brought a dish of his rigatoni and hid it at the back of Mom's refrigerator, there would be a stampede."

"I can see—" Lacie caught herself about to answer with her mouth full. She chewed and swallowed. Grandpa DiNardo's sauce was thick and spicy and just about the best thing she'd ever tasted. That didn't mean that she was happy about Ben ambushing her to get her to eat.

The way he was looking so pleased with himself, she wondered if he realized that.

Or if he realized he still hadn't let go of her hand.

Lacie couldn't see how he'd missed it. The moment he touched her, an arc of electricity tingled through her, fluttering over her shoulders and warming her deep down inside. If she was feeling it and Ben wasn't, then she was the biggest fool this side of the Mississippi.

Then again, the simple fact that she wasn't protesting, she hadn't made a move to pull her hand away, and she was enjoying the sensations that sparked between them pretty much already proved that.

"Pizza?"

Ben's voice snapped her back to reality. He whisked a plate off the TV tray and like a Food Channel chef, tipped it so she could see it better. "I've got cheese, pepperoni, double anchovy, and—"

"And I've got a pageant next week." Lacie declined, holding her free hand palm out, as if she had the magic power to set up a force field to keep out the unwanted calories. "You've already tricked me into rigatoni, the last thing I need is pizza."

"And the last thing I need is for you to go comatose on me because your blood sugar crashes." He upped the ante, picking up a piece of pepperoni pizza and passing it under her nose. "Gooey cheese," he said. "Thick crust. Melts in your mouth."

It was hard not to look at the piece of pizza when it was only a few inches from her nose. It did have gooey cheese. And a thick crust. It did look like it would melt in her mouth. And it smelled heavenly.

She closed her eyes. "You sound like a commercial!"

"And you look like a hungry woman to me! I'll tell you what . . ." Ben gave her a little poke and she opened her eyes to find him with his mouth open and the pizza held in front of it. "I'll prove it's not poisoned or anything. See." He took a bite, closed his eyes, and sighed. "Delicious!"

Lacie held her ground. "Fattening."

He took another bite. "Then, how about a deal? You eat and I promise I'll dance your feet off at the wedding tomorrow. You'll get so much exercise, you'll lose weight instead of gain it."

"You think so?" It wasn't exactly a white flag, but something told her Ben knew surrender when he saw it. He held the piece of pizza out and Lacie took a bite. She chewed and swallowed and sighed.

"Heavenly!"

Ben laughed. "I don't think I've ever seen anyone enjoy a taste of pizza so much. Must be better than I thought."

"It's just that..." Lacie grabbed a napkin off the tray and dabbed her mouth. "I don't eat pizza. Ever. Too much grease. Too much cheese. Too much—"

"Fat. Yeah. I know." Ben held the pizza to her mouth and she took another bite. "Beauty pageants are a lot more work and sacrifice than I ever thought. I can't believe you're willing to spend the rest of your life not eating just so you can participate."

"Well, I'm not going to do it the rest of my life!" He should have known better, and she told him as much with a look. "As a matter of fact..." She leaned a little closer. Maybe it was the way the tiny twinkling lights reflected in his eyes. Or that Ben had one foot propped against the floor so he could keep the wooden swing moving back and forth in perfect rhythm to her heartbeat. He seemed like the ideal person to share her secret with.

"After the national Summer Squash pageant, I'm quitting. For good."

"Really?" Ben was honestly surprised and just as obviously interested. "I thought pageants were your whole life."

"They are. They were. They always have been." Lacie wasn't explaining things very clearly and she sat back, trying to order her thoughts. The wooden swing bucked and she found herself holding on to the wooden arm of the swing with one hand. To Ben with the other. "It's not like I don't love it," she told him. "I do. I always have. It's just that... well, there has to be more. More to life. You know what I mean?"

"I do." Ben took another big bite of pizza and without even asking, popped what was left of the piece into Lacie's mouth. He brushed his hands together and washed down his pizza with a sip of Grandpa's wine. "I'm just surprised you think so."

If Lacie hadn't been so busy chewing, she would have reminded him that brains and beauty were not mutually exclusive qualities. Ben handed her a second paper cup of wine and she took a drink.

"I just don't want to end up like Mom," she said.

Watching Lacie stare down into the wine in her cup, Ben sat very still. He hadn't been looking for her to bare her soul. Hell, he hadn't been looking for anything but a chance to get her alone and maybe, another chance to kiss her. Yet here she was, offering him something even more intimate.

At the same time it made him feel a little guilty, it also made him realize how privileged he was. She trusted him.

He tipped his head, the better to get a look at her. "You mean—"

"I mean obsessed. With pageants." Lacie cringed. "Did I say that?" As if the paper cup were on fire, she set it on the TV tray. "Must be the wine talking."

"Or maybe it's simply the truth."

She considered for a moment. "It is," she told him. "The truth, I mean. And it's not like I hold it against her or anything. She really wanted to be Miss National Summer Squash. All those years ago. She worked so hard and then to have to give it all up. For me." She sat quietly for a moment, thinking.

"You know, that's the real reason I've stuck out the pageant circuit this long," she told Ben. "I want to give her the Summer Squash title. She deserves it for all she's done for me and it will go a long way toward helping her establish her client base for her coaching business. What self-respecting pageant contestant wouldn't want to be coached by the woman who engineered my Summer Squash victory?" She looked at him out of the corner of her eye. "So you see, I do appreciate all my mom has done for me. I just don't want to wake up one morning and realize I've turned into my own mother. I see an awful lot of stage moms and it's not always a pretty thing."

"I'll bet." It was the first time Ben had pictured Lacie as any sort of mom at all. He realized when he did—when he pictured her with a towheaded toddler at her side and a baby in her arms—he found himself smiling. Especially when he realized the baby had dark hair and a dimple in his left cheek.

"So . . ." He washed away the thought with another sip of Grandpa's wine, and when that wasn't enough to smother it completely, he added a few bites of rigatoni. "What will you do instead?"

Lacie shrugged. There was another piece of pizza on the plate, and when Ben picked it up, ripped it in two, and handed half to her, she accepted it and took a bite. "That's the trick, isn't it? I mean, I haven't exactly cultivated a lot of job skills. I've been too busy being a pageant contestant."

"You could go into modeling. You're pretty enough."

It was the truth, and there was no way on earth Lacie didn't know it. Yet she managed a blush that matched the ribbon of pink sunset Ben could see in the western sky. She shook her head. "I'm too short."

"Movies?"

That suggestion made her laugh outright. "I don't think Hollywood would be the right sort of place for a girl from Klaber Falls. I've thought about opening my own aerobics studio but, well . . . demographics being what they are, I don't know if there are enough people in town to support it. Let's face it, a beauty queen has a lot of talents but a lot of her talents don't exactly translate well on a résumé."

"You have a nice smile."

He didn't even realize he had leaned closer until he found himself already there. Looking at that smile. Caught by its warmth. Smiling back.

"And beautiful eyes. You have beautiful eyes." He set down his wine so that he could cup her chin in one hand. "You have a great body."

"I won't if you keep feeding me." Lacie took another bite of pizza and laughed.

It was the one and only time he'd seen her completely at

ease, and for a moment, Ben did nothing but sit and enjoy. For the first time he realized just how much the attempted kidnapping had cost Lacie. Far away from Klaber Falls and the threat that haunted her every moment there, she had a chance to relax. And Ben realized that being able to watch her carefree smile was like being given a special gift.

"I can see it now," Lacie said. "Big bold letters on my résumé. Right under my name and address. *Nice smile, nice eyes, nice body*."

"That was nice smile, beautiful eyes, great body," Ben corrected her. "And I'm very glad I brought you to Chicago."

"So you could fatten me up?" She laughed again and when Ben leaned nearer, she didn't back off.

"I was thinking more like so I could get to know you better."

Lacie's smile was as hot as the red pepper flakes Grandpa sprinkled in his sauce. "A little better? Or a lot better?"

"I'm hoping for the *lot* part, but let's start with a little and move on from there. What do you say?"

He didn't wait for her to answer because he didn't need her answer. He saw it in her smile. He felt it in the pressure of her hand against his and the way she twined her fingers through his. Right before he kissed her.

She tasted like wine and tomato sauce—with a bit of pepperoni—and Ben had another epiphany of sorts.

He realized he'd never tasted anything so good.

And there was nothing he wanted more than…well… more.

He would have gotten it, too, if someone hadn't knocked on the front window.

Not even trying to disguise his disappointment, Ben looked over Lacie's shoulder.

"Coffee?" Carmella mouthed the word and looked from Ben to Lacie, and even though she did her best to control her excitement, Ben knew better. His mother had that gleam in her eyes, the one that told him that as soon as she had a chance to spill the beans, there wasn't one person in the house—or on the block, for that matter—who wouldn't know that Ben and Lacie had been kissing.

"Sure." Ben raised his voice and waved his mom outside. "We'll have coffee."

"I thought so." Carmella left the pot in the house and brought two steaming mugs of coffee outside with her along with sugar packets and a small pitcher of milk. "I didn't know what you liked in your coffee," she told Lacie. "So I brought everything."

"This will be perfect." Lacie accepted the coffee—black, no sugar—and thanked her with a smile.

"So I gave you the coffee." Carmella backed off, wiping her hands on a small kitchen towel she'd brought along with her and chomping at the bit to get back inside and start the rumors flying. "I'll just go tell Helen—"

"You do that, Mom." Ben grinned. "But tell her not to get carried away, huh? No baby showers. Not yet."

"Baby showers?" When she looked at him in wonder, Lacie's golden brows were low over her eyes. "What are you—"

"Hey!" Ben took a sip of coffee and sat up. "Hey, did you . . ." He figured his taste buds were playing tricks on him. Maybe the heady experience of kissing Lacie just automatically made everything taste better. Just to find out, he took another drink. "It tastes like Consuela's. Back in D.C. I know Mom didn't make this."

"That's because I did." Lacie looked at him uncertainly. "Before dinner. I asked if I could help and your mom asked me to get the coffee ready. Sometimes I make it a little strong. Is it—"

Ben gave her a quick kiss. "There's something you can put on your résumé. Extraordinary coffee-making skills."

Contented, he sighed and took another long drink.

Lacie's coffee was as strong as paint thinner and as tasty as the touch of her lips against his. It was as hot as the tremor of desire she aroused inside him, as delicious as the promise that trembled in her kiss.

And just drinking it while he looked over the rim of his cup at her made him realize something else.

When he'd brought Lacie out to the front porch, all he was hoping for was another kiss.

He had never thought something as simple as a piece of pizza and a cup of coffee would make him see what he should have seen long before now.

That he was head over heels in love with her.

15

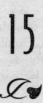

Back home, Lacie would have stopped long before things got out of hand.

Then again, back home, everyone knew who she was. And who they expected her to be. Never once had she disappointed them.

But Chicago wasn't Sutton County. And here, no one knew her as anything except Ben's date for the wedding.

There was something freeing about the whole experience, and though she was no psychologist, Lacie figured it probably explained why she ate far more pasta than she should have at the wedding and why she had a couple of glasses of wine before dinner and a couple more after. While she was at it, she might as well use the whole anonymous-in-a-strange-city-with-a-whole-bunch-of-people-who-were-too-loud-and-too-crazy-and-who-she-really-liked-anyway rationale as an excuse for the way she danced every single dance at the reception. Sometimes with Grandpa DiNardo. Sometimes with Ben's dad. Sometimes with various nephews and in-laws and family friends.

Mostly with Ben.

It probably also explained why, when they returned to

their hotel and he walked her to her room and said good night, she felt a little like Cinderella must have felt. *Before* the coach turned back into a pumpkin.

Light-headed.

Giddy.

Shimmery. As if the magic of the evening were in the air all around her.

There was a knock on her door a couple of minutes later and she opened it to find Ben standing out in the hallway with a champagne bottle in one hand and two long-stemmed glasses in the other. She invited him in.

Looking far too gorgeous for her peace of mind in the tuxedo he'd worn to the wedding (minus the jacket), Ben came into her room only far enough to close the door behind him. He held up the champagne bottle. "I thought you might be thirsty. And..." There was a long, skinny table set against the wall and he set down the bottle and the glasses. Like a bad guy caught in a drug bust, he held his hands in the air and turned all around. "I thought it only fair to warn you. No weapon."

Lacie was standing near the bed and she tipped her head and gave him a careful look. Ben's white shirt made his hair look inkier than ever. Even his pricey haircut (*hairstyle*, Lacie corrected herself) wasn't enough to tame the bit of it that drooped over his forehead. As if he could feel her eyes on it, he brushed it back with one hand and gave her a grin that warmed Lacie inside and out.

"You want to search me?"

She did. Thoroughly.

She was finally ready to admit it.

Only not just yet.

Lacie allowed a slow smile to brighten her expression. She took a couple of steps in Ben's direction. The first thing she'd done when she got into the room was kick off her shoes and strip off her pantyhose, but she was still wearing the floor-length gown she'd worn to the wedding. It was the color of a desert sunset and dotted with sparkles that were dusted like starlight at the top of the straight-across-her-breasts bodice. By the time the glitter got to the hem, it was as thick as a meteor shower. The bell-shaped skirt rustled around her when she closed in on him.

"You're trying the charming routine. You must have learned that from Grandpa DiNardo."

Ben grinned, and putting his arms down, he poked his hands into his pockets. "I learned a lot from Grandpa. You might have noticed, he loves to tell stories. Bet you heard a bunch of them tonight."

"Yeah." She stopped a few feet from him and crossed her arms over her chest. "But Grandpa DiNardo isn't the one who's trying to charm his way into my bed."

"I wouldn't put it past him!" Ben laughed because while they both knew that Grandpa was a frisky old fellow, they also both knew that he would never cross the line when it came to the woman everyone at the wedding had taken to calling "Ben's girl."

He pointed toward the phone that sat on the table next to the bed. "If you're desperate, I could give Grandpa a call."

"I'm not desperate." Lacie grinned. "That's what makes this so special."

"You mean—" Though it was clearly what Ben was hoping for when he walked in, he seemed a little taken aback. A hesitant smile came and went over his expression, tempered by logic, brightened by hope. Logic won.

"It's the wine talking," he said.

Before they had left for the wedding hours earlier, Lacie had arranged her hair in a fluffy concoction of an upswept style, and even this late at night, every hair was still in place. She pulled the pins out of the back of her hair and when she was done, she combed her fingers through it and shook her head, letting it spill around her shoulders.

"Not the wine," she told Ben. "Haven't had a glass of wine for a couple hours."

He took another step closer and his eyes glimmered in the light of the single lamp Lacie had lit over on the desk. He looked over her shoulder toward the window and the piece of Chicago skyline that shone beyond. "Then maybe it's the altitude. We are on the twentieth floor."

"And there isn't anything near this high in Klaber Falls. Except maybe Dinah and Wiley most of the time. Yes, I know about the whole altitude thing!" Lacie laughed. "You think that's maybe why I'm feeling a bit light-headed?"

"Could be."

"Maybe. Maybe not. Maybe it's more like anticipation. You know, like I could start breathing again if you'd just kiss me and get it over with."

"Except that if I kiss you, it won't be to get anything over with. It will be to start something."

Even though she knew that was exactly what she wanted, she pretended to consider while she tugged off his bow tie. From there, she skimmed her hands over the front of the pleated tuxedo shirt and down even farther. As light as butterfly kisses, she brushed her hands across the front of his trousers. "Something big?"

"Oh, Jesus, Lacie!"

It had taken more self-control than Ben knew he had to walk into the room and not throw Lacie right down on the bed. For a guy who wasn't exactly known for his patience, he figured he was doing a pretty good job. Until now.

Too eager to wait a second longer—and way too aroused to endure the agony—he hauled her into his arms and kissed her.

It only made him more eager—and more aroused, though he didn't think that was possible—when she acted just as eager—and just as aroused.

He tasted her mouth and trailed a series of kisses toward the neckline of her gown where all night—because even though he tried like hell, he couldn't help himself—his gaze had strayed, hoping for just a glimpse of her breasts.

Now, when she arched her back, encouraging him to do more than just look, Ben was only too happy to oblige. He slipped the skinny straps of the gown down her shoulders. But when he made a move to slide the straps all the way down her arms in the hopes that the rest of the gown would follow, nothing budged.

It killed him to have to let her go, even for a second. He moved back a step and gave the gown a wary look. "Aren't clothes supposed to . . . ?" He wasn't sure how to explain, so he demonstrated, holding his hands just inches from Lacie's body and slipping them down. "I mean, when I nudge, shouldn't that dress of yours—"

She gave him a smile that was as teasing as any he'd ever seen. "I have to be ready for all contingencies, even a broken dress strap. You wouldn't want me to walk down the runway in the spotlight and have my dress fall off, would you?"

"Only if I was the only one watching."

"But you wouldn't be." There was that smile again. As pristine as an angel's, as tempting as the devil's. "I'm always in front of a crowd and I'm always prepared." She spun around and scooped her hair off her neck. "Unzip me."

"Unzip . . ." It wasn't the first time Ben had ever had the opportunity to help a beautiful lady out of her clothes. But this time when he reached for the tiny pull at the top of the zipper, his hands shook. He hauled in a breath designed to steady them and inched the zipper down.

Little by little, he exposed a sweep of Lacie's bare skin. Patience might be a virtue, but it was an overrated one. Before she could move, he nuzzled a kiss against the nape of her neck. He slid his mouth along her spine. He put a hand on either side of the zipper and tugged the bodice of the dress.

And it still didn't move.

"All right! I give up!" Ben backed away. "I'm hotter than a firecracker and now your dress—"

"It's a pageant dress!" Lacie laughed. She turned around

and folded the front of the gown down just enough for him to see. "Carpet tape. See. It's one of a beauty queen's best-kept secrets."

It was a little hard to concentrate on the strips of tape stuck between the gown and her skin when he also found himself staring at her breasts. He managed. But only because the carpet tape was the weirdest darn thing he'd ever seen. Lacie's breasts, however, just happened to be perfect. Peaches and cream. He thought of the sticky tape up against skin that was made for hot, wet kisses and he made a face. "It looks as uncomfortable as hell."

"Not to worry." She put her hand inside the dress and he heard the little rip-rip sound of the tape coming away from her skin. A couple more rip-rips and she had it free of the dress. Finished, she pulled the strips of tape out and held them up for him to see. "See? Not a problem. I'm used to it. No muss, no fuss."

"But a hell of a tape burn." He shook his head in wonder. "You mean you—"

"You want to see?"

The question sizzled in the air and suddenly, Ben felt like all the oxygen had been sucked out of the room. He swallowed hard. "You mean—"

"I mean, do you want to see?" She didn't wait for him to answer. She slipped the gown off and stepped out of it. She held it up in her arms, the blush-colored fabric reflecting the high color in her cheeks, and for a few seconds, Ben could have sworn she was actually thinking about the hideous possibility of wrinkles and the wisdom of hanging the dress up.

With a sly smile, she tossed it on a nearby chair instead.

Somewhere in the back of his head, Ben knew that some women's formal gowns had built-in bras. Somewhere in the back of his head, he figured that, knowing Lacie, anything she did wear under her clothes would be gauzy and dainty and as feminine as the gentle curve of her hips. After all, it was the way he'd pictured her in a dozen different fantasies a dozen times a day.

But even that wasn't enough to prepare him for the sight of Lacie in tiny white panties.

And absolutely nothing else.

His mouth was dry and he tried to swallow at the same time he looked his fill. Even with the light to her back, he could see that Lacie's breasts were high and round. They were perfect, just like the rest of her. Her nipples were full, and as much as his fingers ached to touch them, he forced himself to stay put. At least for the moment. For the moment, he wanted to enjoy the tightening in his gut, the fire that slashed through him, the incredible, exquisite sight of Lacie's near-naked body.

There was a dusting of freckles on her shoulders and across her breasts and she had the kind of flat stomach that would make a bodybuilder proud. Her legs weren't long but they were . . .

"Perfect." The word slipped out of Ben on the end of a sigh.

Lacie had spent all her life as the center of attention. She was used to being looked at.

But she'd never been looked at like this.

She forced herself to stand still, even though Ben's eyes were wide and his pupils were dark with desire. Even when he trailed a look over her that set off a fire every place it touched. It stopped, finally, on the frothy little French-cut panties she'd bought on her shopping excursion the day before. When she purchased them, she'd harbored a secret fantasy that Ben would get the chance to get a good look at them. Finding that fantasy come to life—and realizing there were plenty more to come—caused awareness to streak through Lacie's body and heat her blood. It was hard to get words out, harder still not to beg Ben to stop looking and start touching.

"Look!" How Lacie managed a tone so light was hard to

fathom, but she figured the opportunity was too good to pass up. She held out her arms and did a flawless pirouette. "No weapon!"

"Yeah, but you're dangerous."

"You think?" She tried for a smile but anticipation blocked her breathing. "You going to stand there all night and be afraid? Or you going to get closer?"

Ben didn't need to hear the invitation twice. On his way over, he kicked off his shoes and unbuttoned his shirt. Fine by Lacie, because by the time he was close enough to touch, she skimmed her hands inside the tuxedo shirt, under his sleeveless T-shirt, and over skin that generated heat and the intoxicating smell of his aftershave.

As carefully as if she were made of porcelain, Ben flattened one hand and touched his palm to her nipple. "You're beautiful." He moved his hand in a circular motion. First one way, then the other. "You're perfect and beautiful and—"

"And you'd better stop talking and kiss me." She unbuckled his belt. Unzipped his pants. Reached inside.

And just as she expected, Ben was done talking.

He bent and took her breast into his mouth and Lacie tipped her head back and moaned. "Bed," she told him.

Ben wasn't exactly listening. While she pulled off his shirt and tugged down his pants, he nuzzled a kiss between her breasts and feathered his fingers down to the lacy edge of the white panties. He dipped his fingers inside and she caught her bottom lip in her teeth. "Bed." Like the rest of her, Lacie's voice teetered on the brink. "We really need to—"

"Fast."

They didn't bother to pull back the bedspread.

Lacie sat on the bed and watched Ben yank off his T-shirt and step out of his boxers.

And much like he'd done to her just a few minutes before, she took a long look, her anticipation growing with every passing second.

Nice, wide shoulders.

She knew that much.

A sprinkling of dark hair across his chest. Strong, slim legs, nice abs. The rest of him...

Grinning, Lacie reached out and touched him, and when he responded instantly, her grin widened.

She was still smiling when he nudged her back against the pillows.

"You're sure?" The what-a-lughead-I-am-for-asking-at-a-time-like-this expression that touched Ben's face made Lacie's heart squeeze with something more complicated than simple affection. More primal even than the aching desire for Ben she'd been carrying around with her practically since the moment she'd met him.

"Sure of this." She touched his lips with a kiss. She flattened her hand against his chest and felt the steady rumble of his heart vibrate through her fingers, each strong, quick beat in perfect time to hers. "Sure of this."

Because she couldn't wait a second longer, she tugged off her panties, and when he settled over her, she guided him inside her. "Sure of all of it," she said. But when Ben stroked into her—once, twice, each movement faster and deeper—she knew it was a lie.

Sure?

She was swept away by a desire so overwhelming, she wasn't sure of anything except that she wanted more.

She skimmed her hands across Ben's back, brushed them over his chest. His breathing was rough. His mouth was on her neck and her breasts. His hands were propped on either side of her and he lowered himself enough to cover her mouth with his.

He shuddered against her and Lacie gave in to the feeling. And to the same, awe-inspiring sensations that left her gasping for breath and holding on to Ben.

Sure?

Heck, she wasn't even sure anymore which way was up and which way was down.

The only thing she was sure about was that right now, she really didn't care.

"What are you thinking?"

Ben's question snapped Lacie out of her thoughts. She was sitting in the passenger seat of his car, watching the familiar scenery between Sutton Springs and Klaber Falls whiz by.

"I just thought..." She'd just finished putting on a fresh coat of lipstick and she clicked shut her compact and put it and the tube of Pink Passion back in her purse. "I just thought it would look different."

Ben's laughter rumbled through the car. By now, it was a familiar sound and it sent a familiar sizzle along Lacie's skin. "We've only been gone for four days. What did you think might change?"

She shrugged. It wasn't like her to be at such a loss for words. But how could she explain?

"I'm different." It was way too simplistic an explanation to cut any mustard with a man as methodical as Ben, but at least it was a start. "I ate pasta. I drank wine."

"You made mad, passionate love to a hot-as-hell federal agent."

"I did!" Lacie's smile reflected the sparkle of heat that ignited inside her every time she thought of it. Every time she thought of Ben. "Which means that everything else should have changed, too." They passed the sign that said WELCOME TO KLABER FALLS and Lacie twisted in her seat to look around. "But everything in Klaber Falls is exactly the same. Look! The stores along Main Street are the same. The flowers are the same. The same kids are hanging around outside the library. The same library they never dare to set a foot into." She plopped back against her seat. "Everything in Klaber Falls is always exactly the same."

"Not everything." At the same time he kept his eyes on

the traffic light where Main met Porter, Ben reached over and put a hand on her knee. "Something tells me things are going to be more interesting than ever around here now."

"As interesting as they were this morning?"

He knew exactly what she was talking about. Practically before they had opened their eyes that morning, they had made love, and they did it again in the shower before they left their hotel for the airport. Remembering it just as clearly as she did, he smiled and gave her a glance out of the corner of his eye. "We could blame it on the champagne."

"We could. But we drank the champagne last night. After we made love the first time."

"And before the second time."

Ben flicked on his turn signal and headed toward the Baxter house on Mapleshade. "Never hurts to get some practice in. Especially when it's something you're planning on doing a whole lot."

"It that a promise, Agent Camaglia?"

"It's a— What the heck!" Ben jammed on the brakes and Lacie jerked forward. Her seat belt ground into her shoulder but she hardly noticed. She was too busy staring at Krissie, who, at the first sign of them pulling up in front of the house, came running down the front steps and just about jumped in front of the car.

Even beneath a coating of expertly applied blush, Krissie's cheeks were pale, and though her hair was wound into a perfect braid and her white shorts and bright orange top were without a wrinkle, Lacie knew something was wrong; she was wearing blue flip-flops. Color coordination notwithstanding, her mother would no sooner wear flip-flops outside the house than pigs could fly.

As soon as Ben stopped the car, Lacie hopped out. Ben was at her side in an instant.

"What is it?" Lacie grabbed Krissie's hand, and something about the simple gesture touched off a chord in

Krissie. She began to cry. "Mom, what's wrong? What happened?"

"What happened?" Krissie sniffed back tears and her voice rose on a note of panic. "Everything's changed, that's what happened. Look! I found this on the kitchen table. Just a little while ago." She was holding a single sheet of paper torn from a spiral notebook and she waved it in front of Lacie's nose, too close for her to see much of anything except for Dinah's loopy handwriting.

"She's done it this time." Krissie fluttered the sheet of paper in front of Ben. He was faster than Lacie and he snatched it out of her hand and read it over quickly.

"What?" Lacie couldn't stand the suspense. "Ben, what does it say?"

He read it out loud. "It says, 'We can't wait any longer. Leaving now. Headed to the La Siesta Motel in Rogers for our honeymoon.'" Ben pursed his lips and whistled. "Looks like your sister and her Incredible Hulk boyfriend have eloped!"

16

"So what are you going to do?"

They had just gotten Krissie settled down on the couch with a glass of cold water and the promise that she'd feel better if she put her feet up, took a few deep breaths and relaxed. Ben thought that had pretty much settled the matter.

He'd thought wrong.

He turned to find Lacie looking at him expectantly, and a little like she was ready to jump out of her skin.

"Do?" He waited for more of an explanation and when it didn't come, he answered honestly. "I'm going to go back to Sutton Springs and I'm going to unpack. Then I'm going to take a shower." He hooked an arm around her waist and pulled her close enough to feel each of the incredible curves that he'd been lucky enough to explore, firsthand, the night before. A smile tickled his mouth in much the same way as just thinking about being skin to skin with her again tickled his imagination. And a few other things. "I don't have to be back in the office until tomorrow morning and it's only seven o'clock. If you'd like to come with me—"

Apparently, Lacie was looking for something more than just an honest answer. She puffed out a breath of annoyance, pulled away from Ben, and looked over her shoulder into the living room. Krissie's eyes were closed, her head was back against a pink pillow embroidered with teddy bears wearing Victorian clothing. Lacie grabbed the sleeve of Ben's suit jacket and tugged him out to the front porch. Quietly, she closed the door behind them.

"That's not what I meant and you know it." Lacie was nothing if not a master at controlling her emotions. At least outside the bedroom. But even she couldn't hide the undercurrent of tension in her voice. As if she realized it and was willing to try anything to control it, she crossed her arms over her white cotton blouse. "I meant, what are you going to do?"

Ben had sisters. He had a mom who was full-blooded Sicilian and as happy as the day was long—as long as no one got her dander up. He knew that with any woman, he had to tread carefully in a situation like this, just like he knew that because of all Lacie meant to him, he was willing to tread even more carefully than usual.

If only he could figure out where to step. Without landing in a minefield.

He yanked off the Cubs baseball cap that he'd put on as soon as they arrived at the airport in Kansas City and started on the long ride to Klaber Falls. "What am I going to do about—"

"About Dinah!" Lacie stopped just short of raising her voice. She looked at the living room window where they knew Krissie was relaxing on the other side of the lacy curtains. "About Dinah," she said again, her voice a whisper that wasn't as gentle as it was impatient. "What are you going to do about Dinah?"

"Looks like she decided to take care of the *do* part all by herself." Ben grinned. It seemed the appropriate response to news about a wedding. "I'll buy a card and send flowers. Or one of those cutesy Christmas ornaments like Marybeth and Jason got. You know, 'Our First Christmas Together' with lots of hearts and flowers."

Lacie's jaw was tight. Her lips—so full and moist and kissable such a short time before—were thin. "In case you haven't noticed, I'm not in the mood for funny even if that was funny. I'm serious, Ben. This is serious. You've got to move and you've got to move fast."

He still wasn't sure exactly what she was asking, but a picture was starting to form. One Ben didn't like. He stepped back, settling his weight on one foot. "Are you asking me to—"

"Stop the wedding! Yes, of course I'm asking you to stop the wedding."

"You've been watching too many old movies. You want me to burst into the church and cause a ruckus just when they get to the 'Speak now or forever hold your peace' part?"

Lacie pressed a hand to her heart as if that could stop it from pounding out of control. "You're teasing. Of course. Don't do that to me, Ben. Not at a time like this. For a minute there, I thought you were serious."

"I am serious." Far be it from Ben to couch the truth in anything less than the foursquare straight talk he expected from everyone else. He rubbed his thumb across his chin and realized he'd missed a spot completely while he was shaving that morning. At the time, he had been distracted by Lacie, who was working magic with a bottle of body lotion and the massage skills she'd learned to relax tense muscles before a pageant.

As much as he would have liked to go right on thinking about that, he had no choice but to get rid of the thought with a shake of his shoulders. "Lacie, what do you expect me to do?"

It was a simple enough question. She didn't give him a simple answer. Instead, she paced to the other side of the porch and back, her hips swaying like heaven on earth inside a knee-length skirt decorated with bright summer flowers.

"All right." As if that would slow things down, she held up one hand. "We're obviously not communicating. Let's try this again. You read Dinah's note."

"Right." Ben nodded. "She said she and Wiley were leaving today. That they were getting married."

"And that doesn't bother you because . . ."

Ben shrugged. "Because it's none of my business."

"But—"

"But nothing." He was tempted to raise his voice—just to make sure she heard and understood—but he stifled the urge and held his temper as deliberately as he curled his hands into fists at his sides. "Dinah's old enough. Wiley's old enough. If they want to get married, it's no skin off my nose."

"Even if it's the biggest mistake she'll ever make?"

"You're being a little melodramatic, aren't you?" Ben laughed. Until he saw the flash like heat lightning in Lacie's eyes. It was a lesson he'd learned a long time ago and he should have remembered it: Never tell a woman who was being melodramatic that she was being melodramatic.

He grumbled a curse, aimed partly at himself for forgetting and partly at her for making him forget. Of course, by then, it was too late to take anything back, and besides, it was the truth and there was no reason he should have to. Instinctively, he found himself squaring his shoulders, and by the time he realized it, it was too late to undo that, too. He tried to brush it all off with an airy "You're overreacting."

She didn't take that comment any better than the others. Lacie's jaw was rigid, her chin high. She propped her fists on her hips. "You wouldn't say it was overreacting if one of your sisters up and ran away with some scummy guy covered with bad tattoos."

There was nothing like assailing the honor of the Camaglias to make a man feel defensive. And nothing like feeling defensive to make an FBI agent—or any other self-respecting guy—feel a sudden rise of heat that, this time, had nothing to do with Lacie's cute little body or Lacie's sweet little lips or the memory of how Lacie had managed to make him crazy again and again in the hours they'd spent alone together.

It had everything to do with Lacie being irrational.

"I wouldn't say it was overreacting if one of my sisters up and ran away with some scummy guy covered with bad tattoos, because my sisters have too much sense to up and run away with some scummy guy covered with bad tattoos," he told her. "And besides, your sister is the one who put the bad tattoos on the scummy guy in the first place. Even if my sisters were dumb enough to—"

"If they were dumb enough to do half of what Dinah has done, you'd be all over them. Deny that. You'd be the first one to stick your nose where it didn't belong."

"That's different."

"No, you've got it all wrong." Her voice broke over the words, and realizing it, Lacie turned away. Impatient, she smacked her hands against the porch railing. "I'm not sticking my nose where it doesn't belong because my nose does belong here. Dinah's my sister. And she's making a mistake. A huge mistake. She's screwing up her life and—"

"And maybe that's something she's got to learn for herself."

"No." It was as simple as that. At least to Lacie. "That's a cop-out. That's the excuse we use when we aren't willing to step in and help other people through hard times. She shouldn't have to learn the lesson for herself. Not when there are people who can help her. People who can talk her out of it. If she was paying attention all those years ago—"

Whatever else she was going to say, Lacie decided against it, and whatever it was, Ben knew better than to stir the pot and call her on it. Things were already getting out of hand.

"Look at it this way…" He poked his hands into his pockets. "Maybe Dinah doesn't want to be talked out of it."

"Oh, come on, Ben!" Lacie threw her hands in the air and turned to him. "You've met Wiley. You've even tried to have a conversation with the man. Tell me she can't see what she's getting herself into. Why on earth would she want to do a thing like this?"

"Maybe she's in love with him."

It was another one of those things that Ben thought was as plain as the nose he'd been accused of sticking where it didn't belong. It was, apparently, not so plain to Lacie.

Her cheeks paled. "No." The single word was as sure as a rifle shot, and for reasons Ben couldn't explain, it felt just as painful.

"No way." Lacie emphasized the words with one quick movement of her hand. "It's not possible."

"What? It's not possible that Dinah could love Wiley? Or it's not possible that anyone could love your scraggly little sister? Come on, Lacie. Isn't Miss Summer Squash supposed to be a little more understanding and tolerant than that?"

"This isn't Miss Summer Squash talking. It's me."

Lacie pushed past Ben and pounded down the steps. She headed toward the garage, where Ben knew her '99 pink Neon was parked.

"Where do you think you're going?"

All right, so it wasn't the most diplomatic way to word the question. Ben wasn't exactly feeling politically correct. Watching Lacie's retreat was just about as uncomfortable as the look she tossed him that made him feel as if they were strangers.

As if Chicago had never happened.

"Lacie!" Ben looked over the side railing of the porch toward the driveway, and when she didn't stop and she didn't turn around, he headed down the steps after her. He planted his feet on either side of the strip of weed-free grass that ran up the center of the driveway and crossed his arms over his chest. Enough of a statement to tell her she wasn't leaving. Because he wasn't moving.

"At least talk to me, Lacie."

She rolled up the garage door, and when she was all set to get into the car Ben realized he needed to up the ante.

"Lacie!" He made sure he raised his voice so she couldn't pretend she didn't hear. "Don't tell me you don't believe in love, Lacie Jo Baxter. You must. You have to. After all, I love you."

Lacie froze with her hand on the car door.

"Don't say that. Don't say that." Lacie closed her eyes and repeated the words like a mantra, sure that if she said them enough, she could somehow convince Ben to stop playing cruel games. She didn't have a clue how long she stood like that, she only knew that when she finally drew in a long, trembling breath, her lungs were starved for oxygen. When she pulled her hand back to her side, her muscles ached. She scraped her palm against her flowered skirt.

It took everything she had, but she managed to leave the relative safety of the garage and march back in Ben's direction—out in the open where, if she wasn't careful, her emotions would be exposed.

She stopped just out of Ben's reach, and though she was hoping to sound more detached and less like she'd been hit over the head with a whole dump truck full of bricks, her words came out sounding just like they sounded to her own ears back in the garage. Shaken. Stirred. Desperate. "Don't say that."

"Why not?" He eyed her like she was an armed suspect and he wasn't sure what she was going to do next. "Why shouldn't I say it? I love you."

It was as if his words were stones, biting into her skin every place they touched. She winced and stepped back. "Because it isn't true. It can't be."

His eyes narrowed. "You calling me a liar?"

"I'm calling you a fool. And here all this time, you've been accusing me of being the one with my head in the clouds."

"So I'm a fool. And I have my head in the clouds. I love you. In spite of it all."

"In spite of—"

"Okay, so that wasn't the best way to word it." He gave her a one-sided smile that wilted beneath the stone-cold look she sent back. "What I meant is that I love you in spite of the pumpkin oil and the Mrs. Allen's Secret Eye Whatever! In spite of the makeup and the never-ending smile and the baton routines and—"

"What's wrong with my smile? And what's wrong with baton routines?" She reared up and took a step forward, and something told her it was the first time Ben had ever given ground. To anybody. He took a step back and instantly, she knew he wasn't happy about the show of weakness.

Realizing it gave Lacie a perverse sense of pleasure. At least until she heard a noise like a growl from deep in his throat.

"Your baton routines are corny," Ben said, and he emphasized his opinion by pointing a finger at her. "That's what's wrong with them. Baton routines went out with Lawrence Welk and lava lamps."

"They're artistic."

"They're boring."

"They're—"

"And while we're at it, your makeup is too perfect. Your eyes are too blue. You smell too much like strawberries." He was still holding his Cubs cap and he slapped it against his thigh. "Your pumpkin oil costs a fortune and we both know you could probably get the same results from cooking oil. But no-o-o." He dragged out the word. "You would never resort to something that ordinary. Your clothes are too cute for words. Hell, you're too cute for words. That's what's wrong, Lacie. That's what's wrong with you."

"Are you done? Actually, I don't care if you are done. I think I've heard enough." She twirled around and would have made it back to the garage if he hadn't clamped a hand on her arm.

"Are you telling me Chicago didn't mean anything to you?"

Chicago meant everything.

Lacie knew it because her heart squeezed at the thought. And her body caught fire. She knew it because one look into Ben's eyes and she knew it meant everything to him, too.

And it was the last thing she wanted to talk about.

Lacie looked away and instantly regretted it. The feel of Ben's fingers tightening around her arm told her that he recognized her sign of weakness, too. She knew him well enough to know that he would use it to his advantage.

"You can't be one person in Chicago and another person in Klaber Falls," he told her.

"Don't you see? That's where you made your mistake." Lacie yanked her arm out of his grip. "I'm exactly the same person in Klaber Falls that I was in Chicago. That's what makes this whole thing so impossible. Besides, we're not talking about Chicago. We're talking about Dinah and what she's about to do to screw up the rest of her life."

"That's funny." Ben sounded anything but amused. "I thought we were talking about the good thing we had going. Or should I say the good thing I *thought* we had going?"

"You had a good thing going with a woman who's too cute and too smelly and—"

"I didn't say *smelly*. I said you smelled like strawberries and nobody is supposed to smell that good."

"So now you're saying I'm a phony?"

"I'm saying that we need to talk. Not about Dinah and Wiley. About us."

"There is no *us*. Don't you get it? There was never an *us*. There never can be. It's a nice dream but . . ." She swallowed hard and somehow, she managed to control the emotion that threatened to tear her words apart. "I acted a little crazy in Chicago. I'm sorry if that sent the wrong message. I'm sorry if you thought it was anything but exactly what it was."

"And exactly what was it?"

She shrugged and hoped the gesture was noncommittal. "It was a good time, that's what it was. It was fun. But what we did in Chicago..." A flush of heat touched her cheeks and she knew he saw it. She had nothing left to lose.

She snapped her gaze to his. "That's as out-of-control as I'm willing to get."

"And hearing me say I love you... admitting that you just might be in love with me, too... that's even more out of control, right?" The anger in Ben's voice simmered down to something less dangerous but far more disturbing. She'd never been witness to a man accepting something he desperately wanted to believe couldn't be true. She never thought she'd see Ben give up.

That explained it, of course. Why, when he backed away, her heart felt as if it had crumbled into a million tiny pieces.

"I can't believe Jake McCallum hurt you that much."

"Jake—" Lacie's voice broke and she scrambled to get herself back on some sort of even keel even though she knew that without Ben holding her—without him standing at her side—that would never happen again. Even she was surprised at how, when it came right down to it, she could lie with the best of them. "Jake has nothing to do with this."

"Right. And I just fell off the turnip truck. What, did Jake tell you he loved you, too?"

"Yeah, something like that." Just looking at the hurt in his eyes—just knowing that she was responsible for putting it there—caused her unspeakable pain. The only thing she could think to do was to get away from it. And from him. And the only way she could do that was to leave.

She spun around and headed back to the garage.

"That's it then, right?" How Ben managed to sound so calm when the entire world was falling apart was a mystery to Lacie. "This is the end?"

"Yes." Right before she got in the car, she gave him one last look. "This is the end. Good-bye, Ben."

She turned the key in the ignition and backed out of the

garage without even bothering to look over her shoulder. She knew if she saw Ben again, she'd fall apart, and besides, Ben might be willing to deal with the situation by getting angry. He might even be willing (unlike Lacie) to hang his heart and his emotions out on the line where everyone could see them and every blip on the radar screen of life could batter them. But he wasn't stupid. He wasn't about to get squashed.

By the time she pulled out of the driveway and chanced a look around, Ben was nowhere to be seen.

It was just as well, Lacie told herself. She didn't have the luxury of wallowing in self-pity. She didn't have time to think about her own worries and the way her insides felt like they'd been taken for a twirl in a food processor.

She had to find her sister.

Before Dinah made the same mistake Lacie had made all those years before.

Why did it have to be the La Siesta?

Lacie pulled her car into the parking lot and found a space just to one side of the pink and orange sign that was blinking on and off atop a tall white pole.

The last place she ever thought she'd come back to was the La Siesta Motel.

The thought sat inside her like a brick, nearly as disturbing and uncomfortable as the emotions that had been roiling through her ever since Ben pulled the rug out from under what she'd been telling herself was nothing more than a fabulous weekend of even more fabulous sex.

"But no-o-o." She dragged out the last word, her voice an echo of Ben's back at the house. "It was supposed to be simple," she told herself. "It was supposed to be uncomplicated."

And then he had to ruin it all by throwing around the L-word.

Getting queasy just at the thought, Lacie slid out of the car and headed toward the motel. It had taken her the better part of two hours to drive to Rogers and it was nearly dark. Most of the lights in the parking lot were burned out, but she could tell that nothing had changed in the last six years.

Heading for the main office, she looked at the same plastic flowers that were poked into the same dusty soil in the flower beds. The same chipped paint on the same cement block walls. The same battered shutters on the windows and the same lights that glowed, here and there, from behind the same cheap drapes.

The same guy was sitting behind the front desk. She remembered his long gray hair pulled back into a ponytail. His bloodshot eyes. If she wasn't mistaken, he was wearing the same Grateful Dead T-shirt he'd been wearing the last time Lacie checked in.

He didn't look surprised to see her.

At the same time a little shot of paranoia made Lacie nervous and a little shot of anxiety made her take a close look around the tattered, dirty—empty—lobby, she told herself she was being silly.

Of course the guy recognized her.

Everyone recognized her.

"Hi!" Just so she wouldn't disappoint him, she gave him one of her trademark smiles. Since he refused to meet her eyes, she wondered if he noticed. "I'm looking for Dinah."

There was a bookshelf behind the man, and it was stuffed to the gills with old newspapers and empty potato chip bags. Teetering on the top shelf was a radio blaring Sixties acid rock. Maybe he was used to the noise; the clerk apparently didn't have any trouble hearing. He fiddled with some papers on the desk in front of him. He took a drag on a cigarette. "Thought you might be," he said. "The second I saw you walk in here. Thought you might be looking for those two."

She only hoped they were talking about the same two.

Lacie's voice bumped over her words in the same way that her heart was thumping. "Big guy, right? Lots of bad tattoos? And a woman? She's short and has a blue streak in her hair. Really bad wardrobe and the makeup . . . well . . ." It wasn't inconsequential. Just irrelevant. At least right now. "Have you seen—"

"Room Seventeen."

The lobby spun, and Lacie found herself clutching the edge of the front desk. Just so she didn't spin with it.

Why did it have to be Room Seventeen?

"Seventeen?" She gulped around the word and the sudden dryness in her mouth. "You're sure it's Seventeen?"

The clerk was seated on a chair with rollers and he wheeled back from the desk, stood, and headed for a coffeemaker that looked like it hadn't been cleaned since the last time Lacie set foot inside the front door of the La Siesta. He brought it back to the desk and poured the coffee into a mug that didn't look much cleaner.

"Coffee?" He glanced up at her just long enough to offer her the cup along with a smile that showed off teeth the same nasty color as the glass coffeepot.

"No. Thank you." Lacie backed away from the desk. "I can't tell you how much I appreciate your offer but—"

She was already pushing open the door before she had a chance to finish.

Outside, she took a couple of seconds to compose herself. She listened to the chorus of crickets chirping in the night air and drew in a long breath. She glanced down the broken sidewalk that led toward the far end of the building. She knew Room Seventeen was all the way down at the end.

Last room. Most privacy.

Wasn't that what the clerk had told her six years earlier?

"That was then and this is now," she reminded herself, and before she could also talk herself out of what she knew she had to do, she headed for Room Seventeen.

There were no lights on in the room. Which didn't seem all that strange.

The door was open a crack. Which did.

Considering what it might mean and what options it left her, Lacie shifted from foot to foot on the scrap of walk in front of the door.

She was sure of one thing. She didn't want to walk in on Dinah and Wiley while they were doing what she knew Dinah and Wiley did every time they were close enough to do it.

What she and Ben had been doing just a few hours before.

The thought snuck up and bit her, and before she even realized she was doing it, she found herself with her arms crossed over her chest. The gesture was defensive, sure, she realized that. Just like she knew that it was a feeble attempt at keeping the pieces of what was left of her heart from crumpling completely.

"Not now," she reminded herself. Partly because it was true and partly because this wasn't the time for regrets or doubts. She'd have plenty of time for that later. Like the rest of her life, when she'd look back on tonight and kick herself in the pants for refusing to take the chance at happiness that Ben had offered.

Because she couldn't even think about it without falling to pieces—and because she didn't have the luxury of falling to pieces at the moment—Lacie tapped her knuckles on the door instead. "Dinah? Dinah, you must be in there because the door is open. It's me, Lacie. Dinah, honey, I know you're probably not very happy to see me but we have to talk. Okay?"

No answer.

Lacie stepped closer to the door and tipped her head, listening.

There was no heavy breathing coming from inside the

room. No creaking of the rusty bedsprings. No sounds of running water or snoring. No sound of anything at all.

"Dinah?" Lacie inched the door open and stepped into the doorway. With all the lights off, it was impossible to see anything, and she felt along the wall to her left for a switch. When she finally found it and clicked on the light, she saw that the room was empty.

No mussed bed, and except for a black duffel bag tossed on the dresser against the wall to her left, no suitcases. No nothing but a room that was less than clean, a newspaper scattered over the gold and green bedspread and—

Lacie craned her neck.

There was something lying just outside the open bathroom door. Something dark and soft-looking, like a cat curled on the worn gold carpet. Curious, she stepped farther into the room and walked over to see what it was.

Too late, she heard the footsteps behind her and heard the door snap closed, then lock.

Right about the same time she realized the thing on the floor was a black knitted ski mask.

Lacie wasn't sure if it was adrenaline or just plain fear that made her spin around.

When she did, she thought maybe she was still spinning. Or maybe just hallucinating.

Her heart crashed against her ribs so hard, she could have sworn she'd cracked them. Her blood whooshed in her ears. Her mouth dropped open and she shook her head and leaned forward, certain that her eyes and the lousy lighting that threw the room into a mishmash of light and shadow were playing tricks on her.

"Jake?"

17

The phone rang almost as soon as Ben stepped into his room.

He eyed it warily, debating about whether to pick it up or not.

After all, it was probably Lacie. Probably apologizing.

Now all he had to do was decide if he was ready to forgive her or not.

It really wasn't much of a surprise when he realized it was no decision at all. He tossed down his suitcase and scrambled for the phone, afraid that it would stop ringing—and he'd miss his chance—if he wasn't quick. Good thing he didn't say what he was thinking about saying—the line about how he'd just started the shower and he'd turn it off to save hot water and wait for her so she could soap him down.

It was Ed Thompson.

"Camaglia?" Sheriff Thompson's voice was strained with excitement. "We've got him, Camaglia. Right here. Right now."

Something told Ben he was supposed to be interested in whatever it was the sheriff was talking about. The same something that reminded him he'd be a whole lot more interested if it were Lacie on the other end of the phone. "Him?" Trying to downplay the thread of disappointment that poured through his veins like ice water, he loosened the knot on his tie and slipped it down. He shrugged out of his suit jacket and crossed the room to turn on the air conditioner. "Who exactly are you talking about?"

"Him." Someone in the background said something to Thompson and he grunted his agreement. "I'm outside the school," he said. "Clete Harter's been here most every night since the Fourth of July. We've got him. We just saw him and another person go inside."

"You mean the guy who was camped out in the office?" A thrill like an electrical shock coursed through Ben's body and he grabbed for his suit jacket and slipped it back on. "I'm on my way over now." He didn't bother to listen to what Thompson said in reply. It might have been something about how there was no hurry because Thompson and Harter were sure they could handle this themselves.

Ben was damned if he'd let them.

If he couldn't give Lacie anything else—if she wouldn't let him—at least he could do this for her. At least he could give her peace of mind and her safety. Her life as she knew it, minus the threat of being kidnapped.

As for the rest of her life as she knew it, a life without Ben in it . . .

He got rid of the thought at the same time he reached for extra ammunition for his Glock and tucked it in his pocket. He'd worry about that later. For now, he had a kidnapper to take care of.

He was out of the house in a minute and at the school in less time than that. He found the sheriff's patrol car parked along the side of the building. Thompson and his deputy were at the back door.

"I saw him go in." Clete Harter was just about Ben's age, a tall drink of water with blotchy skin and a receding hairline. He nodded, mighty proud of himself. "I've been staying there." He pointed. "Under the bleachers. I've been watching. And tonight—"

"Tonight, you did a good job." It was not the kind of compliment Ben would normally offer to another professional, but he knew Harter would appreciate it, and after better than a week spent camping on the rock-hard ground under the football bleachers, he figured the deputy had earned it. "The door's not locked?"

"Looks like our perp has a key." Thompson hooked a finger under the door handle and pulled it open.

Ben made sure to keep his voice down. "Could you tell which way they went?"

Harter shook his head. "Nothing down that way," he whispered, glancing toward the right. "Except the cafeteria. That way..." He looked in the other direction. "That's where the office is. You know, where we found his things. Past that is the library, then the computer lab."

"My guess is the office," Thompson said.

"My guess"—Ben drew his weapon and stepped into the school—"is that we might be able to follow our ears."

He was right. If they kept quiet, they could just hear the sounds coming from the left end of the hallway. Beeps. And a number of clicks.

"Computer lab." Ben mouthed the words and, with a gesture, instructed Thompson and Harter to either side of the hallway and took point.

His heart beat double time and Ben enjoyed every frantic thump. Like the old days, he reminded himself, stepping up to the door of the computer room. It was shut and the only light he could see from under the door was the faint glow of a monitor screen.

Closing in on a bad guy...

Tightening the net around some scumbag...

He signaled to Thompson and Harter to back him up and get the lights on as soon as they were inside. He drew in a breath, reared back, and kicked open the door.

It would feel good to put the cuffs on—

"Dinah and Wiley?" Ben barely heard his own voice beneath Dinah's terrified screeching and the curse of surprise that came out of Wiley.

"What the hell!" Ben looked down the barrel of his gun at the two kids who, at the sound of the commotion, flew out of the chairs they had pulled up in front of one of the computer terminals. They were shaking in their sneakers, breathless, pale.

"What's going on here?" Ben snapped the question at them, along with a look that told them he wasn't kidding. Of course, the way they were staring at his Glock pretty much told him they already knew that. "What the hell are you two doing here?"

Dinah looked at Wiley.

Wiley looked at Dinah.

It was a toss-up which of them was going to faint first.

"Sit down." Ben pointed to the chairs they'd just jumped out of, and it was a good thing. He didn't think either of their legs would hold them much longer. Her cheeks as pale as chalk, Dinah collapsed into one chair. It took Wiley a little while longer; he was too petrified to bend his knees.

Wiley ran his tongue over his lips and gave Thompson and Harter—and their drawn weapons—a wary look. "Nothing's going on, Officers. Sirs." A single drop of sweat trickled down his forehead and into his eye. He didn't wipe it away. "We were just—"

"Just what?" Thompson took a quick look around the room and stationed Clete at the door. "Just looking to set up housekeeping somewhere other than the principal's office?"

A shiver snaked over Dinah's shoulders and made the Japanese *anime* character on the front of her T-shirt jiggle along with her breasts. "Why would we want to do a thing like that? Especially here. I hate this place."

"Right. Like you haven't done it before." Maybe because he realized Ben would keep Dinah and Wiley covered,

Thompson holstered his weapon and instructed his deputy to do the same. He glanced around. "No pizza boxes this time. But then, maybe you haven't been back long enough to make yourselves at home."

"Those pizza boxes..." Like a deer caught in headlights and just waiting to get flattened by an eighteen-wheeler, Wiley blinked. Because he could see that Thompson wasn't listening, he switched his gaze to Ben. "We saw them, too. They...they weren't ours. We didn't leave them in the office."

"And I should believe that...why?" Satisfied that neither Dinah nor Wiley posed an immediate threat—at least not one he couldn't handle—Ben put his Glock back in his shoulder holster. "Are you telling me that wasn't your stuff in the principal's office? The sleeping bag? The shaving kit? The ski mask?"

"Ski mask?" Wiley started to hyperventilate. "You mean a ski mask like that guy wore who tried to kidnap Lacie? You mean you think I—"

"What should I think?" There was an empty chair opposite where Dinah and Wiley were sitting, and Ben spun it around and straddled it. "I find a ski mask in the principal's office and I find you two"—he gave them a careful look that made Dinah reach for Wiley's hand and hold it tight—"I find you two here. If there's another explanation..."

"There is. And it's my fault." Dinah popped out of her chair. She stood up very straight, and though she was clearly scared to death, Ben had to give her credit. She made a pretty good show of looking brave. "I talked him into it."

"But I wanted to be talked into it." Wiley jumped up and stood at her side. "I never said I wouldn't do it. I wanted to help. I had to help. Dinah's an artist and she deserves the chance to let the world know it. She shouldn't be kept out just because of some stupid rule that doesn't have anything to do with—"

"But it was my idea from the start!" Dinah took a step forward. "You can't punish Wiley for something I thought of. Besides, I sort of ... what's the word ... I coerced—"

"Coerced?" Because he was tempted to laugh, Ben coughed behind his hand. It was hard to picture Dinah even knowing what the word meant, much less coercing anyone into doing anything. "Exactly what did you coerce Mr. Burnside here into doing?" he asked her. "And how?"

"Sex." Dinah sounded like it was the most natural thing in the world. Which, now that Ben thought about it, it probably was. "I tempted him. Like a too-hot-to-trot she-devil. And even though Wiley's the strongest and the smartest and the toughest guy in the whole wide—"

"The sex had nothing to do with it!" Wiley's voice cut right across hers. He turned just enough so that he was looking into her eyes, and he took her other hand in his. "It wasn't the sex. It never was. What I did, I did for you. Because I love you."

"Ah, Sugar Lips ..." Dinah's eyes got watery. "That's the most romantic—"

"This is all very touching." Ben stopped them both before they got carried away. "But it's still not explaining what's going on here. I'll tell you what, for now, let's not worry about whose idea it was or who talked who into what. Just tell me. If you two aren't the ones who left the stuff in the principal's office, what the hell are you doing here?"

Now that the moment of truth had come, Dinah glanced away. She sniffed. "We're ... we're hacking into the school's computer files."

Ben glanced at the monitor of the computer that Dinah and Wiley had been using when he burst in. The screen showed a list of student names. The beginning of the alphabet. Including the Bs. "Hacking into the school's files because ..."

"Because Dinah wants to go to tattoo school. Because she deserves to go. Because she's an artist, and an artist—"

Wiley stopped himself when he saw the thunderous expression on Ben's face. "She can't get into a tattoo school," he said. "Not without a high school diploma."

"And you dropped out." Somewhere in the back of his mind, Ben remembered hearing that about Dinah. "So you two simply decided—"

"To get into the files. To change my information." Dinah hurried into the explanation before Wiley had a chance to say a word. "It was my idea, so it's all my fault. Don't blame Wiley. He's a genius, you see. At computer things. But that doesn't mean he should go to prison. Send me instead! I'm the one who deserves it. I'm the criminal mastermind."

Ben sat back and considered. It wouldn't hurt to give Dinah and Wiley a couple more minutes to worry about what was going to happen to them, and besides, he needed a couple of minutes, too. To try to figure out how things had gotten so mixed-up.

He waded back into the interrogation slowly. "So all this time, you two have been—"

"Just trying to get in here," Wiley explained. "Into the school. Into the computer files that my mom maintains. But the last time we tried—"

Dinah took over. "We heard somebody. In the principal's office. We haven't been back since that night."

It all sounded so far-fetched, it was probably true.

"And you didn't see anyone here tonight?" Ben looked from Dinah to Wiley. "No sign of anyone else at all?"

"That's right." Wiley answered, but they nodded in unison. "We got the key. It's on my mom's keyring. She's going to raise holy hell when she finds out we snatched it." He glanced at Thompson. "Does she have to know?"

Ben answered before Thompson could. "That all depends," he said. "On how much you know. And how much you're willing to help."

Nothing like a little incentive to grease the wheels of cooperation.

Wiley understood perfectly. "We figured we'd just come in and take care of Dinah's file," he said. "You know, change it to make it look like she graduated. That way we could send a transcript to Tattoo to You, the school in Kansas City, and she'd get accepted and nobody would ever know the difference."

"You'll never put together a case against us." Apparently, Dinah had missed the part about the grease and the cooperation. Her shoulders shot back. "I won't say anything against my man and you can't make me. Isn't there some law about husbands and wives testifying against each other?"

"Hold on there!" Ben waved her back into her seat. "Did you say husband and wife?"

"That's right." Dinah grinned. "As of two days ago. We're Mr. and Mrs. Wiley Burnside."

"But your note—"

"You know about the note?" Considering the news, Dinah tipped her head, and she would have been as mad as a hornet if she had known that when she did, she looked a whole lot like Lacie. "Then, you shouldn't be surprised. We told Mom we were eloping."

"But you said two days ago."

She nodded. "That's right. Two days ago. Lacie was with you in Chicago. And Mom was over in Sutton Springs for the afternoon. You know, sucking up to those stupid Summer Squash pageant assholes. We figured it was perfect timing. No one would butt in. We left the note on the kitchen table and—"

"And someone took it." Ben sprang out of his chair. "Someone was in the house and took the note two days ago. He put it back today. After he knew Lacie would be back. Because he knew when she saw it, she would head over to the La Siesta to try to stop you."

Ben hurried to the door.

"Hey, you can't just leave us here with them." Thompson called after him. "What do you want us to do?"

"Huh? Do?" Ben's brain was working so fast, his words couldn't keep up. He ignored Thompson and gave Dinah a quick look. "Get a GED!"

It was a funny thing for Lacie coming face-to-face with the thing she'd dreaded more than anything else. The person she had nightmares about. The memories she'd never been brave enough to bring out into the bright light where they could be picked apart like a corpse at an autopsy.

Funny, she wasn't laughing. She also wasn't feeling like she'd always thought she'd feel if her path ever crossed Jake's again.

Breathless. Like she'd always been breathless anytime Jake was near.

Crazy. Like she'd always felt crazy when they were alone together and there was a chance that he would kiss her.

Reckless. Like the one and only time in her life that she'd ever listened to her heart and the urgings of her body and the little voice saying that—just this once—she could be her own person and do her own thing.

Heartbroken.

But then again, that was the price she'd paid for the breathless and the crazy and the reckless part.

Instead, standing across the shabby room from Jake, looking into the brown eyes that had taken up permanent residence in the darkest places of her psyche—like a wolf stalking the fringes of a campfire—realizing that he was here, right here in Room Seventeen, where she'd last seen him six years before...

It all left her feeling...

Nothing.

Dealing with the epiphany was a little like learning to walk again after the world had tipped on its axis. Lacie grabbed for the corner of the battered dresser across from the bed.

"Jake, I . . ." She tried for a smile and she didn't even have to look at the mirror over on her right to know that it wasn't working. She could feel her lips waver. She could practically taste the dust in her mouth. She unstuck her tongue from the roof of her mouth and tried again.

"Jake, it's such a surprise to see you. I guess that's an understatement, huh? I mean . . ." She caught a glimpse of the ski mask out of the corner of her eye, and a mixture of disbelief and outrage twisted her stomach and made her knees feel as if they were made out of Junie Morgan's famous grape jelly. "You're the one who tried to kidnap me!" Lacie wasn't sure if she should laugh or head over to the other side of the room and punch Jake in the nose. "What kind of sick joke is this? And where's Dinah? Dinah and Wiley were supposed to be—"

Jake chuckled. It was not an especially pleasant sound. But then, Jake didn't look especially pleasant at the moment, either.

The last six years had not been kind to him. The boy who had been as tall and as thin as a beanpole was now a man whose shoulders were rounded and whose body had thickened. His face—too rough-cut ever to be called cute, too cute ever to be considered really handsome—was fuller now, as if Jake had sucked on a balloon and the air had gone right to his cheeks and stayed there. His skin had lost its glow. The craggy lines on his face that had always been as much a part of Jake's appeal as his devastating kisses, his cutting wit, and the bad-boy attitude that he wore like a second skin, had been replaced by furrows that told Lacie that he complained a lot. And frowned even more.

In spite of the changes, he was not unattractive. Just different, in a hard-edged sort of way. Like a naughty but cute puppy that grew into a headstrong dog before anybody had a chance even to suggest obedience training.

"You fell for it, huh?" Jake crossed his arms over his white T-shirt, and Lacie saw that he had a scar that went from his wrist practically all the way to his elbow. It shared space on his left arm with the black and white tattoo of a rattlesnake. "I was in your house, Lacie. A couple of days ago. Looking for you. Not exactly easy since you folks started locking your doors, but let's just say I've learned some useful things in the last few years. I found the note and I . . ." He paused, searching for the right word. "I appropriated it," he said, pleased with himself. "And put it back today. After I heard you were headed back to town."

A sick sensation flooded Lacie's insides. "You mean Dinah and Wiley are already—"

Jake nodded. "You always were prettier than you were smart."

It was not exactly the way to begin a reunion, tender or otherwise. For the moment, Lacie set aside the thought of Dinah and what she'd done. Though they could never be erased, even the biggest mistakes were fixable.

And her biggest mistake was standing ten feet from her.

"I was smart enough to get away from you out at the Whipple Farm. Now do you want to tell me why you felt you had to go through with that poor attempt at a kidnapping in the first place? Jake, if you wanted to see me again, all you had to do was knock on my front door."

"And let the whole town know I was back? Nah, that wasn't exactly in the game plan. Then again, neither was my stuff getting found over at the school. I had to buy another ski mask." He glanced at the one he'd left lying on the floor. "Thanks to Thompson and that FBI agent I hear is hanging around. I was all set to try to snatch you again. And then I found your sister's note and realized there was an easier way."

"Luring me here."

"That's right." Jake moved away from the door, and instinctively, Lacie moved back. She told herself it was because the room was small and Jake was a big guy. He needed plenty of room to maneuver. It would have been nice to believe it, too, better than admitting that seeing him close in frightened her. A spark of adrenaline told her to keep her distance.

There was a chair against the wall, opposite the bed and next to the dresser. Jake dropped into it and Lacie breathed a little sigh of relief. "Your mom still running your life?" he asked her.

"She doesn't run my life." Lacie heard the echoes of the words she'd used six years earlier and she cringed. "Mom only wants what's best for me."

"And what's best for you was never me."

Nothing like a cold dose of reality to knock some sense into her head. It was Lacie's turn to cross her arms over her chest and give Jake the kind of deliberate look he'd been aiming in her direction since the moment she turned around and saw him in the room. Maybe he was a better actor than she was. It was a little hard for her to control her disgust.

"I guess you went out of your way to prove that when you walked out on me."

"Don't take it personal." Jake waved away the words and reached for a pack of unfiltered Marlboros. "I never meant it to be anything but what it was. And you have to admit . . ." His gaze slid to the bed and his eyebrows rose. "You had a hell of a good time."

"But you said—" She caught herself on the verge of sounding like it mattered. Hard to break a six-year-old habit. But not impossible. She hardened her voice. "You told me you loved me."

"I wanted to get into your pants."

"And you knew—"

"Oh, hell, Lacie." Jake hauled himself out of the chair. There was a cigarette lighter on the nightstand next to the bed and he retrieved it. It took him a couple of flicks to get the cigarette going, and when it did, he hauled in a deep breath of smoke. He let it out slowly. "You don't actually think there was any other reason that I wanted to marry you, did you?"

"No." Six years' distance did a whole lot to clear a girl's brain. Thinking back on it, Lacie realized it was absolutely true. "You were the bad boy of Sutton County."

"And you were Miss Do-Not-Touch. The girl all the guys wanted. The one we knew we could never have. Because you never said it, but we always knew. None of us was good enough for you. That's what your mama said, right? Your mama said—"

"'Stay away from that Jake McCallum.'" The second Lacie felt her shoulders slump, she pulled them back again. "Looks like I should have listened."

He glanced at the bed again. "If you did, you would have missed a whole bunch of fun."

"Think so?" Lacie managed a laugh. "I hate to disappoint you, but it wasn't exactly the highlight of my life."

"Mine, either." Jake finished his cigarette and stubbed it out on the pressed wood nightstand. "Not that you weren't sweet in your own hokey way. But, let's face it, I don't go for the whole virgin routine. It's fun at first, but after that . . ." One corner of his mouth twisted into something that was close to a sneer. "I got bored, Lacie. You bored me. Didn't take long, did it?"

"Only about as long as it took me to realize you were no prize, either." It was another piece of the truth that had evaded her for as long as she could remember, and even though it brought a flare of anger to Jake's eyes, Lacie was glad she'd said it. "I have to tell you, Jake, the first day was exciting. It was an adventure, you know? And I was a rebel, living a fantasy. By the second day, we'd run out of things to say to each other. As for the sex . . . well, you were the only one having any fun. When I got out of the shower that third day and walked out here . . ." She looked around the room that had changed so little. "When I realized that you were gone, it hurt. But underneath the hurt was a whole lot of relief."

She could practically see Jake's ego bruising. She imagined the black and blue color would pretty much match the unattractive dark flush that stained his cheeks.

"You think you're the queen of the whole damned world, don't you?" Jake hurled the cigarette lighter over Lacie's shoulder. It crashed into the wall behind her. "You always thought you were better than me. Even when you said you'd marry me. You always thought you were just rescuing some poor unlucky scumsucker and dragging him up by his bootstraps."

"No." It wasn't true, and she wouldn't let him go through the rest of his life believing it. "I didn't love you. Not really. I won't pretend I did. But it wasn't like you think. I was young and I thought love was . . ."

Instead of even trying to explain, she made a move toward the door, and when Jake didn't try to stop her, she unlocked it and put her hand on the knob. She turned to him. "I had it all mixed up, Jake. I thought what I was feeling was the real thing. But it was hormones. You were good-looking. You were dangerous. You were the guy I was supposed to avoid at all costs, and I was like a kid who was told not to play with matches. For the first time in my life, I didn't listen to my mother. I didn't care about my pageant career. I took my life into my own hands. It wasn't my finest hour."

"I didn't think it was mine, either. Until I got out."

There was something about the way he said the words that Lacie didn't like. "Out? You mean out of—"

"Prison." Jake said it like it was a given. "That's where I've been, you know. Fifteen to twenty on armed robbery. Early release." He grinned. "Good behavior."

Armed robbery? Lacie swallowed her disappointment. And her disgust.

There didn't seem anything left to say. "Look, Jake . . . if there's anything you need—"

"Cut the crap, Lacie!" He had her arm in his grasp so fast,

Lacie never had a chance to move. He gave her a shake that vibrated all the way down to her toes. "Don't pretend like you don't see where this is leading."

"Leading?" She refused to let him see that she was scared, so she raised her chin and looked him in the eye. "What are you talking about? I'm sorry you were in prison, but there's not a whole lot I can do about that. If you were caught robbing—"

"You're stupider than I thought!" He gave her a little push that sent her staggering back against the door. "I was caught sticking up a gas station," he yelled. "In Nebraska. Two days after I left here, Lacie. Two days after I walked out on you. Just four days after you and me got married."

"But that's not ..." Lacie tried to do the math. She tried to get her days in order and her memories straight. "If you were in jail, how did Mom know? And why didn't she tell me? How did she get in touch with you to sign the annulment papers?"

Jake didn't answer right away, and waiting for him to say something, Lacie thought she would scream. "Jake?" She took a step toward him and another one back when he shot her a look that sent chills up her spine.

"What did she tell you?" he asked.

Lacie stumbled through the memories. "She was here," she said, glancing over at the chair that Jake had sat in just a little while earlier. "When I got out of the shower that day. You were gone and Mom was here. She said ... she said you called her. You told her you'd decided to leave. You knew she was here in Rogers that day because I mentioned that she had a nail appointment with Florence over at that little salon that used to be next to the bakery. She said—"

"Let me guess, she said she knew you'd be upset when you saw I was gone. She said I called her and told her I was leaving and she came right over. Just so you didn't have to be alone in your time of need."

"Yes." Lacie didn't understand why Jake made it all sound like an obscenity. "She told me—"

"She told you a lie." Maybe he knew it was impossible to hear when the blood was whooshing so loud inside her head. He grabbed her arm again and hauled her close enough for her to smell the stale beer on his breath. "Krissie's the one who showed up here while you were in the shower," he told her. "I don't know how she found out where we were and it don't make no difference anyway. She knew. She knew we were here. She knew we were married. She offered me money to walk out on you."

"And you took it." Thinking about Jake taking a bribe to break her heart was less painful than thinking of her mother offering the bribe. "You accepted the money, and all you had to do was leave me?"

"Yeah." As quickly as he had grabbed her, he dropped her arm. "One hundred dollars. I spent most of it right away in a bar over in Elwood. Washing away the taste of you. Needed more money, so I held up a gas station just over the border in Nebraska. That's when I got nabbed and that's where I've been ever since."

"But Mom knew. She must have known. She knew where you were and—"

"Nobody knew." Jake grabbed another cigarette. "Not Krissie. Not nobody. Nobody ever contacted me. So nobody ever knew."

It didn't make any sense. Until she could figure it out, Lacie paced back and forth. "Mom told me you walked out on me. And I believed her. Why shouldn't I? Then a month or so later, she gave me the annulment papers. You'd already signed them and—"

Panic streaked through Lacie's insides and solidified somewhere between her heart and her stomach. Her legs refused to hold her any longer, and she plunked down on the bed.

"You..." Her breath caught and so did her voice. "You never signed those papers."

"Never saw 'em. Never signed 'em."

Through her daze, she couldn't be sure, but she could have sworn Jake was smiling. He dropped down on his knees on the floor in front of her, and she was too stunned to object when he took her hands in his.

"You know what this means, don't you, Lacie, honey? It means we're still legally married."

18

The clerk at the La Siesta was a whole head shorter than Ben, and he never stood a chance. Ben was in the lobby and had the guy by the throat before the door closed behind him.

"Let me guess..." Ben wasn't in the mood to be conciliatory so he didn't even try. "Lacie came here looking for her sister, but her sister was already gone. Somebody else was waiting for her, though, and you sent her to his room."

"It wasn't my fault!" The clerk gulped for breath. "He... he checked into Room Seventeen and he said when she got here, to send her down. He said he'd hurt me if I didn't. He's big enough to do it, too."

"So am I." It would mean mountains of paperwork and hours of explaining to his superiors, but Ben actually thought about throttling the guy. It would teach him a lesson, and besides, he deserved it. Ben actually might have had the satisfaction of finding out how good it would feel if Ed Thompson and Clete Harter hadn't pulled into the parking lot and pounded across the blacktop to the office.

"What the hell do you think you're doing?" Thompson took a look at the FBI cap and bulletproof vest that Ben had already put on. He took another look at the clerk, whose face was red and whose eyes were bulging. "You can't just—"

"Yes. I can." Ben's resolve was as firm as the line of his jaw. He turned his attention from Thompson and back to the clerk. Because of the way he was holding the guy, the clerk could barely talk so he eased up his grip. "Was he carrying a gun?"

"Didn't see one." The clerk coughed and spluttered. He had a duffel bag, though, and I suppose just about anything could have been in it."

"Name?"

"Name?" The clerk wiped a hand across his tie-dyed T-shirt. "Name's Arnold," he said, sticking out his hand to Ben. "Arnold Alvin Whatley. Pleased to meet—"

"Not your name!" Maybe the throttling wasn't such a bad idea after all. "The name of the man in Room Seventeen."

Arnold scraped a finger under his nose. "Didn't ask his name."

"And you didn't ask him to sign in?"

"Not exactly that kind of place where people want to be known, if you get my meaning. Not always my business to ask names. There were two kids who said they just got married that left this morning. No sooner were they out of the office than this guy comes in. Says he wants Room Seventeen and pays me cash. Says he won't be staying long. And that there will be a beautiful lady along to see him."

"And that didn't make you suspicious?"

"Why should it?" Arnold shrugged. "Not that he was any great shakes in the looks department, but like I said, ain't none of my business. Figured if he had a beautiful woman coming over to see him, he was one lucky dog."

Disgusted, Ben turned and headed for Room Seventeen.

He glanced at Thompson, who was walking at his side. "No sign of movement from the room?"

"Nothing we saw when we pulled in. Place looks as quiet as a tomb."

"And no other way out?"

Thompson shook his head. "I've been here before. For business only," he added, before Ben could comment. "There's the door to each room, and the front window. But it doesn't open. And a window in the bathroom at the back."

"Big enough for a person to crawl through?"

"Wouldn't think so, but you never know. When a man is desperate..."

"Right." Ben motioned for Deputy Harter. "You cover the back. Anybody comes out of that window, I want you there waiting. Only, Harter..."

The deputy had already turned away, but when he heard the steel in Ben's voice he stopped and turned around.

"Make sure you know who it is before you risk a shot."

Harter nodded and hurried toward the back of the building.

"Sheriff—" Ben glanced at the older man. "If you'd be so kind as to cover me..."

"You mean you're going in there? You don't want to call him out here? See if he'll come quietly first before you—"

"I'm not going to let him get the jump on us. Not while we still have the element of surprise on our side." Ben adjusted his cap. "I'm going to kick down the damn door and get Lacie away from that crazy man. Before she gets hurt."

"You can't possibly care." Lacie looked into Jake's eyes, hoping he wasn't telling her what she thought he was telling her. "You're not here because you want to—"

"Take you back?" Jake got to his feet, chuckling. "You want me to take you back?"

"No." It was the truth, and she didn't see any reason to deliver it in anything less than the simplest terms. "I don't want you, Jake. And I think it's pretty safe to say you don't want me, either. But then, why—"

While she was talking, Jake went over to get the duffel

bag. He pulled out what looked like glossy eight-by-ten photographs and tipped them in Lacie's direction.

She couldn't have been more surprised if he had shown her a picture of Bigfoot in a wedding gown.

"It's me! They're me!" Lacie sprang to her feet and went over to get a closer look. "Me as Miss Valentine. And Miss Pumpkin Festival and Miss Christmas Queen. Jake, what are you doing with these pictures? Where did you get them? And why do you want them? They're years old!"

"Yeah. Years. Miss Valentine. You remember that, Lacie? That was the pageant you won our senior year of high school."

"Of course I remember. I wore red taffeta. Strapless. With a little—" Jake probably didn't care. "But what does all that have to do with—"

"And right after we graduated, Lacie, you remember what happened then, too, don't you?"

"Like it was yesterday." Lacie's voice was breathless. "My eighteenth birthday. And you convinced me—"

"To elope. And you—"

"I was stupid enough to do it. Stupid enough to believe you when you said you loved me. Jake, we've been over all this. What difference does it make now, anyway? Something got screwed up with the annulment and—"

"*Something* didn't get screwed, Lacie. *Somebody* got screwed. And that somebody was me. While I was sitting in prison in Nebraska, you were being crowned Miss Pumpkin Festival." He side-armed the picture at her and it fluttered to the floor. "And Miss Christmas Queen." That picture came at Lacie, too. Right at her face, and she closed her eyes and ducked out of the way.

"You can see my dilemma here, can't you, Lacie? Here I am, an ex con, fresh out of prison and just passing through Sutton County on my way to I don't know where. I stop for lunch at some greasy spoon over near Ida and I hear your name mentioned. I'll tell you what, I listened a little closer then. I heard you were still competing in pageants. They talked about how you were gonna win Miss Summer Squash. Imagine my surprise! Because I knew something they obviously didn't know. You know me, just had to find out for myself. So I stopped at the high school and found all the evidence I need." He glanced at the photos on the floor.

"When you were crowned Miss Pumpkin Whatever and Miss Freakin' Christmas, you wasn't a miss anything. You was a missus."

"I was—" Good thing the bed was right behind her, because Lacie's knees gave way again and she collapsed on it. "You're right. I had the annulment papers, and I figured that took care of everything. I had gotten married. But the marriage was annulled. I wasn't a Mrs. anymore and that made me still a miss. Oh, my gosh!"

Her stomach clenched. A sour taste filled her mouth. She would have run to the bathroom to throw up but the way she remembered it, the bathroom wasn't very clean.

"All this time... I've been ineligible. For all the crowns. For all the pageants. Jake, I'm not Miss Kansas Summer Squash!"

"Or Miss Anything Else."

She couldn't imagine how he could sound so matter-of-fact about it. Or why he sounded so pleased. She looked up to find Jake grinning down at her.

"We can take care of the problem easy enough," he said.

"We can? Take care of the problem?" It was hard to think when her head was pounding. When her world was spinning with all the velocity of a tornado. She wasn't sure how Jake thought they could take care of the little problem of a marriage that had never been undone, pageant crowns that had been awarded under false pretense, and—

"Oh, my gosh! Ben!" Lacie put a hand to her mouth, barely controlling a sob. "He didn't know. He couldn't, of course. I mean, I didn't know so how could he know? What a lousy thing to do to a guy!"

"I was thinking more about me." Jake's voice snapped her

back to reality. "Like I was saying, we could take care of this, Lacie."

"You mean..." It was impossible, of course, but she figured she had to say it. Just to clear the air. Just so Jake could tell her she was crazy and they could get on to finding some reasonable solution to a problem that was anything but. "You...you aren't trying to blackmail me, are you, Jake?"

Jake didn't laugh often. Even back in the days when she thought she was head-over-heels in love with him, she admitted that he was a sullen sort of guy. All angst and teenage anger. Of course, that was the whole point of falling for him in the first place. But Jake laughed now. Hard. He slapped her on the back.

"You got it, baby," he said, and once he had himself under control he added, "Finally, little Lacie grows up and realizes there's more to life than sparkly crowns and pretty dresses. The way I figure it, I've been handed a gift. In return for all those years I spent behind bars. Maybe you thought we weren't married anymore, Lacie, but the great state of Kansas still considers us husband and wife." The smile left his face and eyes completely. "I figure a couple hundred a month ought to do it."

"A couple hundred! A month! Jake, I don't..." Because she couldn't sit still a second longer—not when her stomach was jumping and her nerves were stretched to their limit— she hopped off the bed. "You'd do that to me? You'd hold this over my head? You'd hurt me? For...for money?"

"Abso-fucking-lutely!" Jake threw his head back and roared. "You've got until tomorrow. Or those pageant folks getting ready over in Sutton Springs are going to hear an earful."

"But, Jake!" It was useless to argue with him, and there was no sense in trying to reason, but Lacie couldn't help herself. She believed there was a spark of good in every person. She had always believed there was one in Jake. He couldn't... He wouldn't...

One look at the gleam in his eyes, and she knew he would.

The truth settled like a lead weight inside her, and even though she knew she'd mess up her lipstick, Lacie bit her lower lip to keep herself from sobbing. "Jake, I don't know what to say. I—"

She was saved from saying anything at all when the door crashed in.

Everything after that happened so fast, Lacie wasn't sure exactly what went down. She saw Ben charge into the room, rifle at the ready and a fire in his eyes that told anybody who was nuts enough to get in his way that they were making the biggest mistake of what could turn out to be a very short life.

Jake wasn't stupid, and he knew the drill. One look at the rifle and the man who was wielding it, and he dropped to the floor, his hands above his head.

"Are you all right?" Ben didn't take the chance of taking his eyes off Jake. He whipped his handcuffs off his belt, twisted Jake's arms behind his back, and slapped the cuffs on. "Did he hurt you?"

"I'm fine." It wasn't exactly the truth, but Lacie didn't think this was the right time to get into the oh-by-the-way-I'm-married part. "Don't hurt him!" When Ben yanked Jake to his feet none too gently, she hurried forward. "This is Jake, Ben. Jake McCallum."

Apparently, Ben wasn't in the mood to be sociable. "Well, Jake McCallum . . ." He shoved Jake toward the door. "You have the right to remain silent and if you're smart, you'll do just that." He stepped outside and took Jake by the arm, hauling him along. "Anything you say can be used against you—"

Before he could finish, a single shot out of nowhere echoed in the night. Ben reacted instinctively, pushing Lacie out of harm's way.

Jake wasn't so lucky.

Lacie saw the way his body jerked forward. He went rigid, then collapsed at her feet.

Even before she saw the red stain spread over the front of his T-shirt, she knew that Jake was dead.

It was Joe Flannagan's summer league night, and Ed Thompson had to call the Bowl-O-Drome three times before Joe actually believed that there had been a shooting in Rogers and that he had a body to pick up. It took the funeral director more than an hour to get there, and every minute of that hour felt like a lifetime to Lacie.

It didn't take long for a crowd to gather, and while Clete Harter kept them back behind a quickly devised barrier made up of yellow tape, trash cans, and—on its farthest end—the sheriff's patrol car, Lacie paced the blacktopped parking lot of the La Siesta. Her brain was working so furiously, she hardly noticed the folks who called out their greetings and asked what was going on and what she was doing there. She didn't even stop to talk to Jeff Parkman, who blurted out something about being lucky enough to just happen to be in Rogers to cover a ponytail league softball game. When he practically got down on his knees and begged her for an exclusive interview and a couple of photos to go along with it, she walked right on by.

She couldn't say a thing. Not to anyone. At least not until she managed to get unstuck from the endless loop of panic, disbelief, and confusion that clutched her insides so tight, it felt as if a hand were in there twisting her soul into a thousand painful knots.

On her first trip past Room Seventeen, Lacie watched Ben set up a perimeter around the crime scene. She supposed it made sense. There were rules that had to be followed and procedures that had to be observed, even with a plain-as-the-nose-on-your-face murder like this one. Jake had been killed by a single shot to the chest, even Lacie knew that. As hard as it was to believe, it was true, and she watched Ben look over the area. His eyes narrowed, the FBI cap he'd worn when he burst into the room missing and his hair a mess, he checked out the hole in Jake's chest and the strange, twisted position of Jake's body. Done with that, he stood and looked around. It was probably the first time he noticed the wooded area across from the motel, and when he did, he pointed toward it and motioned Clete to go have a look.

Lacie kept on pacing.

A couple of minutes later, Clete Harter ran out of the woods with a rifle in his hands. Lacie heard Ben grumble a curse and saw Ed Thompson go over to the patrol car.

Her path intersected with Ed's as he headed back to the motel. "It's ours, all right," she heard Ed say. "Somebody must have snatched my rifle out of the patrol car while we were too busy to notice."

Somebody who really wanted Jake really dead.

Lacie's stomach did a cha-cha. She could have sworn her bones had been yanked out and replaced with Jell-O. Rather than risk collapsing on the blacktop and giving Ben another body to deal with, she sat down—hard—on the cement barrier that separated the parking lot from the sidewalk that ran in front of the La Siesta.

"Put your head between your knees." She hadn't noticed Ben come running over. At least not until he pushed her head down and held it there. He rubbed her back with his other hand. "The nausea will pass," he told her. "Just keep your head down."

Keeping her head down was apparently something she was pretty good at. Way down in the sand. Exactly where it had been for six long years.

Thinking about how blind and stupid she'd been wasn't any more comforting than thinking about Jake lying dead outside the door to Room Seventeen. Rather than think about either when her eyes were closed and her nose was practically brushing the pavement and her flowered skirt was pushed up above her knees, Lacie came up for air.

She found herself eye to eye with Ben.

Right about now, it wasn't exactly a place she wanted to be.

"You all right?" She supposed it was the same question he would have asked any witness unfortunate enough to be front row and center when some poor sucker happened to get in the way of a speeding bullet. Still, she couldn't help but notice that his eyes were warm with concern, that his voice held a note of emotion she suspected no other witness had ever been fortunate enough to hear.

Or unfortunate enough to have to figure out how to deal with.

"I'm..." She'd better find out before she committed herself. Lacie hauled in a long breath, and though the world still wobbled and her stomach still jumped, something told her there was no use waiting for it all to stop. If she did, she'd be there a long, long time. "I'm fine. Really. Just a little—"

"Shaken up. Yeah, I know." Ben sat down next to her on the pitted cement barrier. He slid his arm around her shoulders and pulled her close, and for the first time since Lacie had turned to find Jake McCallum on the other side of the room, some of the tension inside her eased away.

Ben had to go and ruin a perfectly warm and fuzzy moment with questions. "That was Jake?" he asked. "Jake McCallum? The guy you used to date? You're sure?"

"Sure?" She was tempted to tell him that it was pretty hard to forget a guy you thought you'd been married to for a few days. And found out you'd been married to for six years. She didn't. She wasn't sure the words would make their way past the queasy feeling rumbling through her insides. Or that she even knew what the right words were.

"That was Jake." She looked over her shoulder toward Room Seventeen to see that Joe Flannagan was there with the hearse that had FLANNAGAN & SONS written on the side of it in flowing gold lettering. "I haven't seen him in a long time, but it was him. No mistake about that."

"What did he want?"

"What difference does it make?" Her voice held an edge of hysteria. Even Lacie heard it. She fought to keep it in check, and didn't come out the clear winner. "He's dead, Ben. Poor Jake is—"

"That scumbag has been trying to kidnap you all summer!" Ben hopped to his feet and pointed over to where Joe was zipping Jake's body into a big black bag. "You want to tell me how that qualifies him as *poor Jake*?"

She didn't have an answer. Not for how angry she felt at Jake for putting her through everything he had put her through so he could convince her to give him money. Not for how upset she was to think that when he found out the truth, he'd decided to blackmail her. Or for how sorry she was that even though he had been a jerk, Jake was a dead jerk. Not for the life she'd lived for the last six years that had turned out to be a lie.

Or for the words she should have had to explain it all to Ben.

The words that simply refused to come.

Feeling as if she'd been weighted down with cement blocks as long and as heavy as the barrier where she sat, Lacie pulled herself to her feet. She wouldn't have made it if Ben hadn't offered her a hand up. She wouldn't have been able to keep from falling to pieces if she hadn't let go.

She brushed off the seat of her flowered skirt and realized for the first time that there were splatters of blood in among the roses and on her white blouse. Something told her that explained the sticky dots on her face, too. She didn't think it was the best time to think about that. Not if she wanted to keep herself from fainting right then and there.

"He's dead, Ben." Somewhere between the sitting down and the standing up, the emotion had drained from her. Her voice was flat. Her insides were empty. Except for the thread of doubt, the tangle of fear, and the little voice inside her that told her she had some serious thinking to do. "Whatever Jake did...whatever he wanted...can't that wait? He's dead and...I'd like to go home."

"Sure." Ben waved for Clete Harter. "I can't leave right now. You understand. I have to—"

"Wrap things up here. Yeah, I know."

"Clete will take you home." He slanted the deputy a look and didn't get an argument. "And I'll come by later, on my way back to Sutton Springs. We'll have a long talk."

Was that a promise? Or a threat?

The thought wedged itself inside Lacie and sat there, hard and uncomfortable, all the way home.

Ben was going to stop on his way back to Sutton Springs and talk to her.

Now all she had to figure out was what she was going to say.

And how she was going to decide if she should continue to live the lie that was her life.

Or walk away from her chance of wearing the Miss National Summer Squash crown.

And maybe lose Ben in the bargain.

19

"We need to talk."

Lacie didn't bother to ask if her mother felt like chatting. Or even if she was awake enough to do it. It was already past midnight by the time Clete Harter dropped her off, and once she was in the house, she marched straight up to Krissie's bedroom.

Though she was usually an early-to-bed, early-to-rise type, Krissie was just stepping out of the shower. She had a bright pink towel wrapped around her body and another one around her head like a turban.

Krissie reached for the blue satin nightgown Ed Thompson had given her for her last birthday—the one he said matched her eyes to a tee. She carefully took it off its satin hanger and stepped behind the lace-paneled dressing screen next to her bed.

"It's a little late and I'm awfully tired," Krissie said. "But you know you can talk to me anytime you need to, honey. About anything."

"Even about Jake?"

Krissie's head popped up from behind the screen. Because the only light on in the room was the one next to the bed, Lacie couldn't see her mother's face clearly. She could have sworn there was a flash of something very much like anger in Krissie's eyes, but since it was an emotion her mother never indulged in—not even when Dinah was at her worst—Lacie knew she must be imagining it.

Krissie came out from behind the screen. The satin nightgown was trimmed with a broad band of creamy lace at the throat and the cuffs. There were satin rosebuds around the floor-length hem. Lacie remembered that when Ed gave her mother the gown, he'd said she looked like a queen in it. He was right. As regal as a queen, Krissie straightened the skirt. She reached for the matching robe and put it on. She poked her size-five feet into satin slippers she'd had dyed to match the nightgown and robe.

It wasn't until she was done—until she was ready—that she bothered to look at Lacie.

She gave Lacie an indulgent smile, sidestepped her way around her, and headed for the bathroom. She kept the door open, and Lacie watched her unwind the towel from around her hair, comb it through, and spritz in some conditioner.

"Something tells me my little princess is just a tad nervous about the Summer Squash pageant." Krissie used the same singsong tone of voice she'd used so many times when Lacie really was a little princess and she really was nervous before a pageant. As comforting as it had been so many times over so many years, Lacie found something irritating about the comment now.

She stepped back and watched as her mother smoothed age-defying, wrinkle-reducing, beauty-enhancing cream over her face and down her neck. "It's more like I'm nervous about finding out that my marriage to Jake was never annulled like you told me it was."

Krissie's hands froze in midair, like hummingbirds. But only for a second.

The next second, she put the cap on the jar of cream and set it back on the shelf above the sink, right between the pore-minimizing lotion Krissie sent to Paris for and the SPF 45 sunscreen she smeared on anytime she so much as set foot outside the house.

Krissie sailed back the other way. "Looks like we need to brew some peppermint tea," she said, and before Lacie could tell her that a whole ocean of tea wasn't going to help, her mother was out of the bedroom, into the hallway, and down the steps.

Lacie trailed behind her, and by the time she got down to the kitchen, Krissie had the light on over the sink, the radio playing softly, and a candle lit in the center of the table that made the whole place smell like vanilla.

"How can you be worried about ambiance at a time like this?"

Lacie's question made her mother pause, but she should have known it wouldn't stop her.

"It's times like this that we need beauty most in our lives," Krissie said. She got out a tiny porcelain bowl filled with little blue packets of sweetener. "When we're most upset, it's the everyday indulgences that calm us and help us keep our perspective. You know that, Lacie, honey. I've told you a hundred times."

Her mother pulled out a chair for her and Lacie automatically sat down. Krissie crossed over to the sink, filled the teakettle, and set it on the stove. She brought a china pot, tea bags, and two cups to the table and took the chair across from Lacie's. She folded her hands on the table in front of her and tipped her head so that the light of the candle caressed her cheek.

"I imagine you're upset about Dinah," Krissie said. "You know I am, too. That kind of thing is sure to bring back bad memories. Especially when your sister went and made the same stupid mistake you did all those years ago. Nevertheless, honey, dwelling on the past isn't going to change anything."

"It's not Dinah's wedding bells that worry me as much as my own."

"I don't know what you're talking about." Krissie ripped open a package of sweetener and spilled the powder in her cup. "You've obviously had some sort of complicated evening. You're a mess!" She ran her gaze over Lacie. "You'd better get to bed. The preliminaries for Miss Summer Squash start tomorrow, you know, and you're onstage at—"

"I'm not sure I'm going to participate."

The teakettle whistled and Krissie got up to turn it off. She looked over her shoulder at her daughter, and seeing that Lacie was serious—even if she was talking nonsense—she filled the china pot and sat back down.

"You've seen that What's-Her-Name, haven't you? That Miss Texas Summer Squash. The one with the nice hair and the big teeth. Really, Lacie!" Krissie's shivering laugh filled the kitchen. "You can't let a girl like that intimidate you. Yes, she has a nice figure. Yes, she has flawless skin. And, no doubt, she's already in bed tonight so she won't have dark circles under her eyes in the morning." Looking across the table at Lacie and the dark circles she had no doubt were already under her eyes, Krissie shook her head sadly.

"You can't let little things like that stop you, honey." Krissie jiggled her shoulders, getting rid of the thought that anyone could be better than Lacie. "You're tired. Otherwise you wouldn't be talking nonsense. Of course we're going to compete tomorrow. We've been preparing for this pageant for a long, long time and nothing's going to stop us now. We're going to win. You know that and I know that. Another forty-eight hours and you're going to be wearing the Miss National Summer Squash crown."

"Except that I'm not a *miss*. At least . . ." It was another aspect of the whole mess that Lacie hadn't thought of until now, and now that she did, it felt weird. "I suppose technically what I am is a widow."

"What on earth are you talking about?" Krissie's laugh

might have brightened her mood if Lacie had been in any mood to be brightened.

"I saw Jake tonight," she told her mother. "In Rogers. He's the one who's been trying to kidnap me."

"Oh, my gosh!" Krissie was out of her chair in a flash. She headed for the phone that hung on the wall just inside the back door. "We've got to let Ed know. He's got to—"

"Ed already knows, and it doesn't matter anyway. Jake's dead."

"Dead?" With a whisper of satin, Krissie plunked back down into her chair. "You're going to have to explain this better, honey. From the beginning."

"The beginning?" Lacie was as surprised as Krissie was when she laughed. There was nothing funny about it. "I guess the beginning was that day I came out of the shower at the La Siesta and found you waiting for me."

"That's all in the past." Krissie waved away the words and the candle flame jumped. "We've been through all that, honey. Jake called me. He said—"

"You left out the part about how you paid him a hundred dollars to leave me."

"He told you that?" Krissie looked away. She untied the belt on her satin robe and retied it. She smoothed a hand over her gown, and because she was a firm believer in the benefits of air drying over heat, she fluffed her fingers through her hair. "What else did he tell you?"

"He told me it was your idea. The whole walking-out-on-me part. He also told me we haven't seen him lately because he's been in prison. He just got out. Jake's been incarcerated practically since the last day I saw him. Armed robbery."

"I always knew he'd come to no good." Krissie *tsk-tsked*. "Looks like it's time to admit I did you a favor."

"It didn't feel like a favor. Six years ago... when I walked out of that bathroom and saw that Jake was gone... it felt like the earth had been pulled out right from under my feet."

"Oh, come on, Lacie!" Her hands trembling just the slightest bit, Krissie poured tea into her cup. "Jake McCallum wasn't going to do anything for you except get you pregnant and run off eventually so that you could go on welfare and I could raise your baby."

"You didn't know that. Not then. You couldn't have."

"I could and I did. I did you a favor."

It was the truth and there was no use denying it. Besides, Lacie knew her mother well enough. Krissie wasn't about to back down, and she wasn't about to divulge any of the information Lacie so desperately needed. Not until Lacie gave in. "All right. You probably did do me a favor. Now how about if you do me another one? Explain about the annulment papers."

Krissie smoothed a hand over the gingham tablecloth. "I tried to find him," she said. "The day after I went to the La Siesta and brought you home. I went to Rogers to look for him so that I could talk to him about getting an annulment, but no one had seen Jake anywhere. He'd apparently already left town."

"He went to Nebraska. That's where they arrested him."

"My, my...you did have a little heart-to-heart, didn't you?" When Lacie didn't respond to the let's-share-secrets hum in her mother's voice, Krissie *hurumphed* quietly. "Well, that explains why I could never find him. I tried. I practically begged old Sheriff Hennesey to help, but you know what a crank he was! He refused to lift a finger. I did all I could on my own." She reached across the table and squeezed Lacie's hand. "But when I realized Jake was gone and that I was never going to find him..."

Lacie didn't like feeling like she was about to upchuck. And she'd pretty much been feeling that way most of the day, ever since Ben had announced that he was in love with her. Peppermint tea wasn't going to help, but she had to do something to keep herself busy. That, or start screaming like a banshee.

She pulled her hand away from Krissie's and filled her cup. She took it with her when she got up and stood with her back to the sink. "You forged his signature on the annulment papers."

Krissie's shoulders slumped. She dropped her head into her hands. Her voice was muffled and there was a trace of tears in it that made Lacie want to run over and comfort her.

She didn't. There was still too much they had to clear up.

"It was a stupid mistake, honey." Krissie sat up, her eyes bright with unshed tears. "You made one stupid mistake. So I guess I was allowed mine. I didn't want to see you suffer for the rest of your life just because you were headstrong and stubborn enough to—"

Krissie pulled in a deep breath, calming herself. "I couldn't watch you throw your life and your career away."

"So you lied. To me." It was that more than anything else that hurt. "I remember the day you marched in here with the annulment papers, all signed, sealed, and delivered. You acted like it was some kind of gift."

"It was a gift." Krissie scraped back her chair and stood. Her hair was still damp, and it hung limp around her shoulders and made her face look drawn. The light of the candle didn't travel as far as her face, and her eyes were rimmed with shadow. It wasn't often Lacie saw her mother without her lipstick, and for the first time, she realized that her lips were pale and thin. The smile Krissie threw at her daughter was just as anemic.

"I gave you back your life, Lacie Jo Baxter." Krissie's voice was harsh. "After you tried to throw it away by marrying that idiot Jake McCallum. No matter what I had to do or how I had to compromise myself, I knew I had no choice. I did it because I love you. I did it because I had to do it. Just like always. I had to take over and take charge."

"Even though it's my life?" The truth of it tore through Lacie and left her trembling. "It was a mistake, but it was my mistake. You could have at least been honest with me. You could have at least told me."

Krissie drew herself up to her full height and threw back her shoulders. "Funny, I always thought if we ever had this conversation, you'd spend at least part of it thanking me. I put myself on the line for you. Again. I did it because you wouldn't listen when I told you what was right. I did it so that you could be Miss Pumpkin Festival. And Miss Jolly Holiday and Miss National Summer Squash. And don't you ever forget it. And don't you ever let it stand in your way. Now get to bed." She moved toward the doorway that led into the dining room. "We have a contestant breakfast tomorrow morning at nine and after that, the first of the talent competitions. We'll both have circles under our eyes if we don't get the proper rest."

Her words were still ringing in Lacie's ears long after Krissie walked out and went upstairs.

"Were you going to tell me?"

Lacie wasn't really surprised to hear Ben's voice coming from the other side of the back screen door.

Discombobulated?

Sure.

Strung out so tight she felt like snapping?

That, too.

But not surprised.

After all, information was Ben's business.

And something told her that he'd just gotten an earful.

"Was I going to tell you? Not in the parking lot of the La Siesta."

She didn't open the door for Ben and she didn't invite him in. Instead, she dumped her tea in the sink. She watched it disappear down the drain, and when it was gone, she turned on the water and rinsed the sink and her cup. When she turned the water off again, she heard Ben's voice right behind her.

"How about before that?"

"Too late for that." Lacie spun to face him.

"How about now?"

It was technically a question, but Ben didn't sound like he would take no for an answer. He didn't look like it, either. He looked like a guy who'd just been sucker punched by the Easter Bunny.

Because she couldn't stand to face the hurt in his eyes, she pushed off from the sink and stepped her way around him. "What do you want to know?"

"I want to know who really killed JFK. And why the hot dogs at Comiskey aren't anywhere near as good as the ones at Wrigley Field. Someday, I'd like to find out how my mom and my Aunt Helen started the fennel seed versus oregano pasta sauce wars when they both learned to cook from the late, great Grandma DiNardo and she never used either. For now, I'll settle for why you never bothered to mention that you were married to Jake McCallum."

"Because I didn't think I was." Lacie wished she could decipher the expression on Ben's face. He was angry, sure. He was confused. But there was something else there, too. Some emotion that shimmered in his brown eyes, as real as the light of the candle that reflected in them.

It made her sick to her stomach to think he looked like a man who'd been betrayed.

And to know it was her fault.

"It all happened a long time ago." It was a feeble attempt at beginning an explanation, and she was disgusted with herself for even thinking she could get away with it. It wasn't time for reminiscences. Or excuses. It was time for the truth.

For all he meant to her, Ben deserved at least that much.

"It was the one time in my entire life that I did what I wanted to do," she told him, poking a finger at her chest to emphasize her point. "The one time I colored outside of the lines and stepped out of the box and danced to the beat of a different drummer. Unfortunately..." Her shoulders dropped, and though the posture was unacceptable and probably made her look even more haggard than she already did in her soiled skirt and her wrinkled blouse, she didn't make a move to pull back her shoulders.

"Unfortunately," she said, "that different drummer happened to be Jake."

"Krissie didn't approve."

"Understatement!" Lacie's laugh was as thin as her smile. "She had plenty of reasons to think Jake wasn't a good choice. Some petty crimes, a bad reputation, a chip on his shoulder the size of that prizewinning eggplant Zeke Miller grew a couple of years ago. Aside from that . . . well . . . truth be told, I think Mom would have objected to any guy who wanted to take me away from the life we'd built. I was the center of her universe. And I had the nerve to dream of a life of my own."

Even after all this time, the incredible stupidity of the whole thing was nearly overwhelming. Lacie shook her head in wonder. "It was my eighteenth birthday. When Jake suggested we get married, my head said no." She looked at Ben just to be sure he understood that she wasn't totally braindead.

"I didn't listen. I listened to my heart, instead. It was the biggest mistake I ever made."

"Apparently not. Looks like believing Krissie when she presented you with those annulment papers was right up there at the top of the list."

"Thanks for reminding me." Lacie's mouth pulled into a smile that had nothing to do with humor. "You're right. Top of the list." She threw her hands in the air, surrendering to his emotionless assessment. "Call me a fool, I did it again. I believed my own mother who never did a thing in her life except take care of me and help me to use the talents that God gave me to make the most of myself. I actually believed her when she told me she'd seen Jake and had him sign the papers. Imagine anyone being that gullible."

"I can't."

Ben's suit jacket was off. Except for the dark slash over his left shoulder that was his leather shoulder holster, his shirt shone white in the light of the candle. He crossed his arms over his chest. "I would have asked for proof."

"And I should have stopped believing in Santa years before I did! Call me wacky, I couldn't see any reason why anyone would lie about someone as warm and fuzzy as a big fat guy who chuckled a lot and left presents under the Christmas tree for good little kids! What do you want from me, Ben?" Lacie didn't realize how loud her voice was until she heard it echo back at her.

His was just as loud when he answered. "I want to know what Jake McCallum wanted from you, Lacie. Was he looking to get back together? Kidnapping doesn't seem the fastest way to a woman's heart, but then, I'm sort of an old-fashioned guy. He was after something."

"He was after nothing." She slashed her hand through the air. "Nothing but my money. That's what he said. When I told him about the annulment, he figured he had it made. Cash, in return for keeping his mouth shut."

Like it wasn't any big surprise, Ben nodded. "I thought of that. But damn, all the way over here, for the life of me, I couldn't figure out why anyone would want to blackmail anybody as perfect as you."

There was a time Lacie would have taken it as a compliment. She wanted to now, but she knew that Ben was being sarcastic. She pushed past him and headed out the door and into the backyard.

When she didn't immediately hear the door slam, she knew Ben was right behind her.

It would have been easier to head the other way, to walk through the house and go out the front door and get in his car and drive away. It would have been easier—and probably less painful—to go up against a pack of pit bulls than it was for Ben to force himself to follow Lacie outside.

He pounded down the steps without hesitating. By the time she sat down on the picnic table and had her feet up on the bench, Ben made sure he was stationed between her and both the back door and the driveway. Just in case she got any ideas about running out on him before they finished their conversation.

"What was he going to do?" Ben asked. "If you didn't pay, what did Jake say he'd do to you?"

Lacie wasn't in the mood for questions. But then, Ben wasn't exactly in the mood for waiting for answers. When she saw him make a move closer, she shot him a look. "You're the detective, you tell me."

"The Summer Squash pageant?"

"That and every other title I've held in the last six years."

"You agreed to pay to keep him quiet?"

She barked out a laugh. "I didn't exactly have a chance. Before I could say anything, there you were, like Zorro, crashing through the door, waving around that rifle. Then before anybody could do anything, Jake was dead."

"You could be considered a suspect, you know."

Her head came up. "You want to tell me how I could shoot the guy from the front when I was standing behind him?"

"You want to tell me who else knew you were there?"

She stopped for a moment, considering. "You knew. When we were here earlier in the day, I told you I was going to Rogers to stop Dinah and Wiley's wedding." A disgusted laugh bubbled up from her. "I didn't, did I?"

"Stop the wedding? No." Ben moved a little closer. "They were married two days ago. They're already back in Klaber Falls."

"Guess I screwed that up, too."

"You did what you thought was right."

"I did almost exactly what Mom did to me six years ago. And I suppose that, given the opportunity and Wiley's convenient disappearance, I would forge annulment papers, too. Just like Mom did. Just to save Dinah from herself."

"You think she wants to be saved from herself?"

"I—" Lacie hopped off the table. A breeze moved through the trees and the faraway glow of a streetlight played across Lacie's face. "I don't know. I honestly don't know. Not about anything. Not anymore. I don't know who killed Jake, that's for sure. I don't know why anyone would want to. He just got out of prison. That might have something to do with it. You know, bad influences, bad friends. And I'm sorry to disappoint you because I know it would make your life easier if I just up and confessed, but I didn't hire anyone to do it, either. I didn't exactly have time."

She would have walked right by him and into the house, and Ben should have let her go. After all, it seemed a fitting end to the day that had started like a slice of heaven and ended up in the trash can. He would have, if something that refused to give up hadn't made him reach out and take hold of her arm.

Surprised, she looked over her shoulder at him.

"You can't run away forever," Ben told her.

"I can try."

"Maybe it's time to stop trying. Time to put the past behind you."

"And listen to my heart? Is that what you're telling me?" She pulled her arm back to her side but she didn't retreat. Instead, she turned to face him. "The one and only time I listened to my heart, I ended up having it handed to me on a platter."

"You think I'd do that, do you?"

"It didn't stop Jake."

"I'm not Jake."

"And I'm not the Lacie I was then." She turned and headed up the back steps, and she would have gone right inside if Ben's next question hadn't stopped her cold.

"What are you going to do?"

Lacie felt the ice of Ben's words all the way down to her

toes. She shivered and was grateful that it was dark and that he probably didn't notice.

What was she going to do?

What she wanted to do was throw herself in Ben's arms and beg him to forget that she'd ever been stupid enough to let the love he offered her slip out of her hands. She wanted to tell him that she didn't care about anything at all in the world except him, and that if he'd let her, she'd make the same mistake now that she'd made six years earlier. She'd tell the commonsense voice inside her head to shut up and she'd listen to the advice her body screamed with every heartbeat. She'd grab on to what looked like her last chance for happiness and she wouldn't let go. Not in this lifetime.

She didn't. But only because the emptiness inside her proved one thing: Nothing had changed. In Chicago, she'd given in to what her heart urged.

And this is where it got her.

She shrugged. "Do . . . you mean—?"

"I mean about tomorrow." If Ben had taken even one step closer, she knew she couldn't have resisted. But he didn't. He stayed exactly where he was, his body braced as if for a punch. "I mean, the Summer Squash pageant."

As if she could see her mother there beyond the gauzy curtains, Lacie looked up at the bedroom window. "I have to go to the pageant," she said.

"Have to?"

"I owe her." She didn't have to explain who she was talking about. Ben knew. "And I owe myself. I can't just walk away. Not after all this time. It's going to be hard. Would you . . . ?" She hesitated and then decided that if she were ever going to live the rest of her life outside the cocoon she'd built to protect her heart, she might as well start. It wasn't a good time, but it would have to do.

"I'd be more comfortable if you were there with me," she told him.

Ben didn't answer. He backed away, putting even more

distance between them. It was all the answer Lacie needed, and rather than stay and have it confirmed so that her heart could break even more, she hurried inside. She closed the door and locked it behind her.

Funny, but she hadn't thought she could feel any worse than she'd felt that afternoon when Ben announced that he was in love with her, and then Jake had showed up.

She didn't think she could feel more empty than she had when she realized that Ben knew that her entire existence was one big lie.

But the feeling she had now, knowing he wouldn't back her up when she needed him most, was the worst.

That was when she felt it all, all at once. The misery. The emptiness. The pain.

Because that was when she knew, once and for all, that it was over between them.

20

If he hadn't left his cell phone lying on the Formica-topped kitchen table when he went chasing off to the high school in hot pursuit of the kidnapper who wasn't there, Ben wouldn't have had to check to see if it needed to be recharged. If he hadn't checked, he never would have heard the *beep, beep, beep* that told him he had a voice-mail message.

He didn't exactly feel like talking.

Unless it was Lacie.

Especially if it was Lacie.

As disgusted with the thought as he was with himself for having it, Ben tossed the phone back down where he found it and went about his business. He put away his Glock and the extra ammunition he'd stowed and never had to use. He kicked off his shoes and debated about unpacking the suitcase he'd taken to Chicago. By that time, he thought better of the plan. In the mood or not, he had a job to do. And there was a chance—however slim—that the voice-mail message might have something to do with that job.

What was it Ryan had pulled his chain about all those weeks ago? Crop circles? Cow tipping? Racketeering at the local bingo parlor?

Right about now, he'd settle for any one of them.

As long as the case in question didn't involve a woman who wasn't above stealing his heart but was too busy keeping her emotions bottled up like Mrs. Allen's Secret Formula Eye Rejuvenating Emollient to give him hers in return.

The thought tasted sour, and Ben decided to wash it down. On his way over to the refrigerator for a beer, he picked up the phone again and punched in the numbers to retrieve his messages. He already had a Bud Lite out and cracked open when he heard the voice on the other end.

"Ben, it's me, Harlan." There was a pause in the message, and Ben wondered if Harlan Jenkins, his special agent in charge from back in D.C., was giving him time to remember who he was.

"Things have settled down here, Ben. After that to-do with the senator's son. More important things for the press to worry about. I think..." Ben heard the sounds of papers shuffling over Harlan's desk.

"I've got the paperwork all filled out and I'll send it right along. We need you back here in D.C., Ben. The sooner the better. I've got a couple of cases pending and I think they're right up your alley. Looking forward to having you on board again."

Harlan hung up, and because Ben suspected that in the morning he'd wonder if he'd dreamed the whole thing, he saved the message instead of deleting it.

"Back to Washington!" The words escaped him on the end of a sigh that was part relief and part disbelief. Ben toasted himself with his beer. "Back to Washington!" he said again, louder this time. It was what he'd wanted even before he landed in this podunk town, and just thinking that the dream was finally going to become reality and that the reality was within his grasp made him feel as if the weight of the world had been lifted from his shoulders.

There were a thousand details to take care of. "I need to

close up the office," he told himself. "And get myself packed and—"

Tell Lacie he was leaving?

The thought stopped him cold, and the heaven-sent feeling that raced through his insides like a shot of single-malt Scotch settled and solidified. Like a rock in his stomach.

"Stupid," he told himself, and if he'd had enough energy left after what had been a very long day, he might have emphasized the point by giving himself a good swift kick. "Stupid not to be one hundred percent happy. It's what you wanted, Camaglia," he reminded himself. "What you've wanted all along."

He should have been feeling as though he'd just been granted early release from prison. But knowing he was leaving—and who he was leaving behind—left him feeling...

"Like h-e-double-toothpicks."

Ben grumbled the words with all the certainty of a man who wasn't very good at fooling himself.

After all, the *why* of the thing was a no-brainer.

Now all he had to do was figure out what he was going to do about it.

The last person Lacie expected to see at the National Miss Summer Squash pageant was Ben.

That was why she figured she could relax—at least a little—and at least pretend to be enjoying the hoopla that started that morning and would continue to build over the next couple of days. After all, she had always been conscious of her obligations, to her public and to the many fine people who did all the hard work of putting a pageant together. There was no excuse to stop now.

It was that more than anything else—that deep-down, inescapable, ingrained sense of duty—that kept her awake all through the night.

It was that same sense of responsibility that had brought

her to the place she was right now, outside the judges' tent that had been set up in one corner of Freedom Park. Unfortunately at that moment, the judges were in the middle of a meeting around the breakfast table over at the Morning Star. Lacie couldn't do anything but wait. That, and smile at the seemingly endless line of pretty, cheery Miss Summer Squash hopefuls who paraded by.

"Lacie Jo Baxter, darling, it's so good to see you!" Miss New Jersey Summer Squash—a girl whose name Lacie could never remember but whose size 38DDD chest was pretty hard to forget—kissed both of Lacie's cheeks and gave her a smile that was stiff enough to hang clothes on. "You look fabulous! Really. Well . . ." Miss New Jersey did a quick once-over, noting Lacie's denim shorts and yellow T-shirt. Rather than being perfectly arranged in the kind of frothy style the judges expected, Lacie's hair was pulled back in a ponytail and held in place with a blue scrunchie. Miss New Jersey's mouth puckered into a perfect little pout and she ran a hand down the skirt of her lilac-colored silk shantung suit.

"You're not actually wearing that? Today?" Of course, Miss New Jersey knew it was impossible. She laughed. "You'd better get a move on, girlfriend. Get changed! They've got dressing rooms all set up for us over there." She pointed toward the side door of the Civic Center and the hallway that Lacie knew led past the courtroom and the single-room office where Ed and Clete worked. It deadended at an empty office that was usually used for the every-Thursday-morning senior citizen card game. For the rest of this week, it had been set aside for the pageant and reserved for the contestants to use as a dressing room.

"The judges are supposed to be back in a few minutes and that's when we'll get started," Miss New Jersey continued. "A brief interview. Isn't that what the program says? Then the talent competition starts."

"I don't know how our little Lacie can twirl anything at all this morning when she didn't eat a bite for breakfast." Miss Arkansas Summer Squash was a woman named Bianca LaRue. She and Lacie had known each other since they were old enough to enter competitions. And they'd been old enough to enter competitions practically since the day they learned to walk.

Word had it that if Lacie wasn't a shoo-in for this title—and everyone knew she was—Bianca just might have a chance to win. She even looked like a winner, all bright and cheery in a darling little cherry-red designer suit with a matching bag and shoes.

Bianca played with the string of pearls at her throat. "We had a contestant breakfast this morning," she reminded Lacie in the Southern belle drawl she usually reserved for use onstage. "Your dear, sweet mother was there and she looked worried not to see you. Come on, honey, you know how it is with these things. You were expected to be there."

"I'll bet I was." By now, smiling at her rivals was second nature, but Lacie simply didn't feel like it. "I wasn't very hungry this morning," she told Bianca. Which was the perfect truth. She added, "I'm just too excited about the pageant." Which wasn't.

"Well, excited or not, you'd better not let the judges see you like that!" Susie Moore was Miss Ohio Summer Squash. As the Miss Congeniality titles she'd won at more than one pageant proved, Susie was as sweet and as friendly as the day was long. She hurried over and pulled Lacie into a hug. "You look adorable," Susie told her. "But if the judges see ..." She shivered. "I hear that Lester Zwick, that judge they brought in from California ... I hear he's a stickler for making sure the contestants always give the best impression."

"And, sugar ..." Just to make sure Lacie didn't miss the point, Bianca patted her arm. "Best impressions are not made of denim."

Okay, so it was catty of her. Lacie couldn't help herself. She pulled out the big, bright smile she usually reserved for the end of a pageant. The one she always gave the audience *after* she was wearing the crown. This early in the game, it was a low blow, but she figured it wouldn't hurt to remind the girls who the front-runner was.

"Honey..." Since Bianca had never made it a secret that she envied Lacie her long, full lashes, Lacie batted them at her. "Best impressions are made by remembering that a winner is always a winner. No matter what she's wearing."

She slipped away from the little knot of contestants and wound her way in and out of the crowd that was beginning to gather. Jeff Parkman was there with his camera, and when she saw him coming at her down the brick path that bisected the park, she turned and headed the other way. She passed the concession stands that sold everything from fruit smoothies to fried summer squash, and threaded her way through the craft booths where they were selling lamp bases fashioned out of hollowed-out summer squashes and summer squash recipe books and jewelry made from dried summer squash seeds.

All the while, she kept her eye on the judges' tent. If she was quick, she could get in to talk to them before the festivities officially started.

Just thinking about it caused a little quiver to start up in her stomach, and Lacie braced herself against it. The only consolation in the whole thing was that at least she would be alone in her misery. If she paid attention, she could easily avoid Krissie, who, no doubt, was already talking Lacie up to anybody who would listen. And she knew for sure that she wouldn't run into Ben.

Not here.

Not today.

She supposed that pretty much explained why, when she saw her mother at the other end of the park, then twirled around to head the other way and bumped right into Ben, Lacie's heart did a back flip and her insides fused into something that felt like a lump of molten metal.

Only hotter. And more painful.

"I—" Lacie wasn't sure what was going to tumble out of her mouth, so she stopped herself. Right before she figured that whatever it was, it couldn't make things any worse than they already were. "I didn't think I'd see you today."

"You're not dressed." The look Ben skimmed over her was quick and thorough. "Aren't you supposed to be in an evening gown or something?"

"Too early for evening gowns." She pulled in a tight breath and wondered that she could breathe at all when he was standing so close and what felt like a million miles separated them. "Interviews with the judges this morning," she explained. "And then the talent competition. I'm surprised you're here."

"Are you?" It was early in the morning but the sky was clear. Ben slipped a pair of Ray-Bans out of the breast pocket of his charcoal-gray suit and put them on. Slick move—it made it impossible for her to read the expression in his eyes. At the same time she wondered why he'd go to the trouble, she felt a stab like a knife right in her heart. Nothing like feeling cut off to make a girl's morning.

"Ed Thompson asked me to stop over," Ben explained, his voice as devoid of emotion as she imagined it was when he was reporting to his superiors about some case or another. "You know, to help out with the investigation into Jake's murder."

"There's nothing I can tell you that I didn't tell you last night."

"You're sure about that?"

"Jake. Blackmail. Gunshot." It wasn't like Lacie to make light of something so serious, and she wouldn't have even thought about it now except that she wasn't sure how long she could stare at her own reflection in Ben's Ray-Bans and not fall apart. "You know I didn't do it."

"But I don't know if you asked someone to do it for you."

"You don't believe that!" Lacie would have laughed.

Except that she realized that Ben wasn't looking any too happy. After all, it was his job to dot all the *i*'s and cross all the *t*'s. The devil was in the details. And after everything that had happened the day before, she was nothing to him now except one of the details.

"I couldn't have asked someone to kill Jake for me." He knew it, but she figured she'd better remind him. "Because I didn't know it was Jake. I didn't even know Jake was back in town. You'd be better off trying to find out who knew he was here."

"I'm working on that. Just wanted to cover all my bases." He backed off a little, glancing around at the crowd before he turned his attention back to Lacie. "I told Ed it was the least I could do for him before I leave."

The bit about the sidewalk moving beneath her feet must have been Lacie's imagination. The part about her insides aching was real enough.

"Leave?" Her stomach bunched. "What are you talking about? Where..." She was afraid to ask. Afraid not to. "Where are you going?"

"Back to D.C. Got called back last night. Good timing, huh?"

"Great timing. Only—"

"Lacie?"

It was a wonder Lacie heard her mother's voice behind her at all. What with the way her heart was pumping so hard and her blood was rushing so fast inside her head. She wouldn't have turned around to acknowledge her mother except that Krissie sounded as if she'd been punched in the stomach.

She didn't look any better than she sounded. Even in the pink suit designed to give that all-important best first impression of the Baxter family, Krissie looked pasty. She ignored Ben completely, her eyes riveted to Lacie, her top lip curled just enough to let the world know she was expecting Lacie's best turquoise linen suit. And got denim instead.

"Lacie, honey, what in the world are you doing?"

It was bound to come to this. It was part of the reason Lacie hadn't been able to sleep the night before. Now or never, she told herself, and before she could also convince herself that the *never* part sounded like the best thing she'd heard in a long time, she took a deep breath for courage.

"I'm not doing it, Mom," she said.

"Not doing...it?" Krissie's expertly plucked eyebrows arched. She glanced at Ben. "Do you know what she's talking about?"

Ben glanced from mother to daughter. "Can't say I do. And we've barely had time to talk. Actually, ma'am..." He looked at Krissie. "I'd like to know where you were last night. Say, around nine o'clock or so."

"I was—" Krissie answered automatically, and just as automatically, she stopped when she saw where the questioning was headed. "Don't be ridiculous!" She turned away and took Lacie with her, one hand tightly grasping her arm. "If I wanted Jake McCallum dead, I would have done it a long time ago," she told him. "Before he had a chance to break my Lacie's heart."

"Except that he didn't." Lacie shook off her mother's hand and turned back to Ben. Darn it, with those sunglasses on, she couldn't tell if he was looking at her or not. Then again, she didn't really care. She had things to say. And he was going to hear them whether he wanted to or not.

"See, that's what I figured out last night. I was never in love with Jake. I couldn't be. I was too young and I didn't have the slightest idea what real love was. I didn't know that at all. Not until this summer."

Was it her imagination, or did Ben suck in a little breath of surprise?

Before she had a chance to find out—and before he had a chance to say anything—Krissie was dragging her toward the Civic Center. The only way to avoid what was looking like it could turn into a very public scene was to go along quietly. And talk to her mother along the way.

"We don't have much time." Krissie yanked open the side door and stepped back so Lacie could go in first. She checked her watch. "Interviews start in fifteen minutes. If those judges ever get themselves back here." Another one of the contestants—a girl with a big smile and a Miss Idaho Summer Squash banner—came by the other way, and Krissie swallowed her words and smiled.

"You did bring the linen suit, didn't you?" she asked Lacie. "It goes so well with your eyes and—"

"I didn't. I didn't bring the linen suit or anything else. I'm not doing it. I'm not going to be in the pageant."

Krissie's face was so expertly applied, her expression didn't change. "You're not serious."

"I am." Another one of the contestants came racing down the long hallway and out toward the festivities, and Lacie stepped closer to her mother to allow the girl by. "It's a lie. All of it. It has been for six whole years. I can't possibly participate. Because I can't possibly be Miss Kansas Summer Squash. I was married when I won that title."

Krissie's laugh was as light as angel wings. It froze solid when it met the determination of Lacie's chin, the resolve that stiffened her shoulders, and the no-nonsense expression on her face.

"You're not kidding?" Krissie's voice was breathy.

"No, I'm not. I'm just waiting for the judges to get here. Then I'll talk to them. Quietly. There doesn't have to be a scene."

"Of course there does!" Krissie didn't usually indulge in sarcasm. It didn't fit with her reputation or her personality. It didn't match the chichi suit or the just-so makeup or the hair—every single strand exactly in place. "There has to be a scene," she said again, her eyes meeting Lacie's and blue sparks flying. "Anytime a woman is assured of success and is naive enough to walk away—"

"No. Not naive." Lacie fought to keep her voice down. "I

was naive six years ago. Now all I am is realistic. You might as well know, this was going to be my last pageant anyway."

Krissie was breathing fast. She pressed a hand to her cream-colored silk blouse. "Last . . . you mean . . ."

"I mean I'm too old for this. And I've had my fill. I mean I want to find something else in my life. Someone . . ." She glanced back the way they had come, but Ben was gone. "Someone special. It's been great, but . . ."

"I understand."

It was the last thing she expected her mother to say and, relieved, Lacie let go a long breath.

Krissie looked around at the crowd. "Let's talk where it's not so public. We have a couple of minutes before the judges get back."

As far as Lacie was concerned, there wasn't much left to say. But she owed her mom. Big-time. For all she'd done and all the money she'd spent and all the beauty she'd packed into Lacie's life. Lacie headed down the hallway toward the dressing rooms. By now, most of the contestants would already be outside. If they were looking for privacy, that was one place to get it.

"I'll be right with you." Krissie waved her on and ducked into the sheriff's office. "I just want to see if Ed is in."

Lacie couldn't blame her. Krissie and Ed meant a lot to each other, and as she'd learned, there was nothing like having the man you love at your side during a crisis. It was just too bad she had learned it because the man she loved *wasn't* at her side during this one.

Except for the rolling carts where dozens of pageant dresses hung side by side like a fabric rainbow, and the dressing tables and mirrors that had been brought in, the office was empty. Lacie headed inside and waited.

It didn't take Krissie long to catch up to her.

Just like it didn't take Lacie long to see that when she did, Krissie had a knife in her hands.

It was strange to think of her mother—as neatly turned

out as any of the contestants waiting outside—waving around a wicked-looking eight-inch blade with an evidence tag hanging from the handle.

Not so funny when Krissie closed in on Lacie.

"Grab one of these outfits and get dressed," she said. She pointed from the clothes on a nearby rack to Lacie. "I'll be damned if I'm going to let you walk away and ruin my pageant coaching career before it ever gets started."

"You find out anything?" Ben suspected Ed Thompson hadn't, but he asked anyway. If he kept his mind on his case, he just might be able to keep it off the tantalizing comment from Lacie: *I didn't know what real love was. Not until this summer.*

He held tight to the tingle of excitement that threatened to distract him, and though he told himself he shouldn't, he glanced over his shoulder toward the Civic Center where Lacie had disappeared with her mother just a couple of minutes earlier. Still no sign of them, and he turned back to Sheriff Thompson.

"What's that you said?" As if Ben's eyes set off an electrical charge, the sheriff jumped when Ben looked at him.

"I asked if you found anything."

"About Jake?" Thompson shook his head, but he didn't meet Ben's eyes. "Not a darned thing," he said, looking over to where the contest judges were parading up the sidewalk and heading for their tent. "No prints on the rifle. No one saw anything. No one—"

"Anyone suspect anything?"

Thompson looked up at the tree that shaded the place where they were standing. He looked down at the sidewalk at their feet. "No one has said anything to me."

"Then, we'll just have to keep talking to people. There's bound to be someone who saw something. Who knew Jake was in town?"

"Just us. And not until it was already too late." There

must have been a smudge on Thompson's badge; he rubbed his thumb over it. "I mean, who else would know? Nobody even knew it was Jake until he walked out of that room."

"Unless our friend Alvin Whatley knows more than he's saying."

"The clerk at the motel?" Before Thompson even realized it, he was looking right at Ben. "Why would Whatley care? And who would he tell?"

"Somebody knew Jake was going to walk out of that room."

"Maybe someone saw him walk in. You ever think of that?" Thompson rolled up on the balls of his feet. "I made some calls. Ol' Jake, he got in plenty of trouble over in that prison in Nebraska. Made a lot of enemies. If one of them followed him . . ."

It was not the best theory in the world but it was a theory, and Ben knew better than to reject it out of hand. He glanced toward the Civic Center again, automatically looking for Lacie. All he saw instead was a girl with huge breasts who was wearing a light purple suit. She looked as if she'd forgotten something and she hurried into the building. The door slammed behind her.

"I'd like to clear this up before I leave," he told Thompson.

"Sure. Sure." Thompson checked his watch. He scrubbed a finger under his nose. "Only you know as well as I do that we might not ever solve a murder like this. Just might be too—"

Before Thompson could finish, the girl in the purple suit barreled out the door and looked all around. She saw the sheriff and she ran over. "They're in the dressing room!" she sobbed, and pointed toward the Civic Center. "I peeked in when I heard someone talking and I saw them. Mrs. Baxter and Lacie. And Mrs. Baxter . . . Mrs. Baxter has a knife!"

21

Lacie wasn't in the mood for jokes, so she supposed, in the great scheme of things, that it was a good thing that her mother wasn't kidding.

Or at least it would have been. If there hadn't been a gleam in Krissie's eyes that was every bit as deadly as the point of the knife poised just a fraction of an inch away from Lacie's yellow T-shirt.

A beauty queen was nothing if not calm under pressure.

But the way Lacie figured it, since her decision to retire, she wasn't a beauty queen anymore. And since her mother was threatening her with a knife, that pretty much negated the whole grace under fire thing, anyway.

"Mom!" When Lacie looked at Krissie, it was through a liquid haze that made it look as if her mother's face had been painted with watercolors. "You can't be serious. You wouldn't—"

"The hell I wouldn't." Without taking her eyes off Lacie, Krissie reached over to the clothing rack and grabbed the first thing she laid hands on. It was one of the contestants' talent competition costume, a blue gown with a wide skirt and a low-cut front.

Miss Virginia Summer Squash. Having seen her wear the dress before in some other competition in some other city at some other time, Lacie recognized it instantly. Miss Virginia was the one who played the bells.

Krissie tossed the gown at Lacie, who had no choice but to catch it. "Put it on," she said. "Now. We'll make our excuses to the judges—and to whatever loser that rag belongs to—later. For now, the important thing is to get out there in time for your interview."

Lacie crushed the gown to her chest. It wasn't much in the way of protection but somehow, knowing she had the gown—instead of just her yellow T-shirt—between herself and the knife made her feel a little braver.

"There's not going to be an interview." Lacie let out a little gasp of surprise when Krissie stepped forward. There was a smidgen of room behind her and she moved back a step, keeping the knifepoint—and her mother—at a safe distance.

"I'm through," Lacie said. "With the pageants. With the lies. I don't deserve to be Miss National Summer Squash and I'm not going to win the crown under false pretenses, just because you—"

"Just because I what?" Krissie was wearing a stunning pair of strappy slides in a shade of leather that complemented her skin tone perfectly and made the line of her legs look long and sleek. The heels weren't very high. Even so, when she closed in on Lacie, she suddenly looked as tall and as menacing as Jake ever had.

"Just because I've made you everything you are today? Is that what you were going to say, Lacie Jo? Just because you'd be nothing and nowhere without me? Don't tell me you're going to forget that."

"No. I couldn't. I never . . ." If she'd had the presence of mind to think about it, Lacie supposed she would have realized she was more disappointed than she was afraid. A single tear spilled out of her eye and trickled down her cheek, and she wiped it away with one corner of Miss Virginia's costume. "I've always been grateful," she said, and she sniffed. "I'll never forget—"

"You already have!" Krissie's voice was harsh, her words would have shot back at her in an empty room. Here, they died against the fat crinolines, the wisps of lace, the heavy satin gowns. "If you hadn't forgotten, you wouldn't be standing here talking like a fool. Do you think I sacrificed my whole life for you, Lacie Jo, just so you could do this to me?"

"I'm not doing anything. Not to you. I'm doing what's right. I'm doing what I need to do. What I want to do."

Krissie barked out a laugh. "Oh, yeah, just like last time. What you wanted to do last time was marry Jake McCallum. I let you get away with that, too, didn't I? Look where it got you."

"It got me here. To this place. Now." As if it were a road map laid out before her, Lacie could finally picture her life. "If it wasn't for all that, I wouldn't be where I am today."

"If it wasn't for me, you wouldn't be where you are today!"

"You're right. I'm not going to argue with you. But don't you see? What that tells me is that good or bad, mistakes or not, we all end up where we're supposed to be. I'm not supposed to be Miss Kansas Summer Squash, Mom. Once people know the truth, they won't hold it against you. You'll still be able to have your coaching business. They'll just think—"

"They'll just think what? That they can entrust their daughters to a woman who couldn't manage to keep her own in line?"

"I was going to say that they'll think— No, they'll know . . . they'll know it was my mistake because I'm going to own up to it. They'll know you had nothing to do with it. That you—"

"Get real, Lacie, honey!" Krissie's nostrils flared. "Folks have been buying into our line of beauty queen bullshit ever since the day I entered you in your first Little Miss Sutton County pageant. By now, we've got them so brainwashed, they're going to keep buying into it. They're convinced you can do no wrong. That means I'm going to take the blame."

"But you didn't—"

"Yes. I did." Krissie emphasized her words with a twitchy movement of the knife. "I'm the one who engineered the whole annulment scheme. I'm the one who paid Kim Riley over at the courthouse to shred every last little bit of paper that had anything to do with your marriage. I've got forgery and bribery against me. How do you suppose that's going to look on my coaching résumé?"

Lacie didn't have an answer. Not for any of it. But she knew that telling new lies wasn't going to help eradicate the old ones. "We'll work something out. With Ed Thompson. And with the pageant judges. We'll talk to Lester Zwick and—"

"Oh, hell! Lester." With the tip of the knife, Krissie motioned toward the dress, and when Lacie didn't make a move to put it on, her eyes narrowed. "What am I going to tell Lester?" she asked, her voice poised on the edge of hysteria. "He's already sunk thousands into this coaching business of ours. Stationery. Business cards. Glossy photos."

"Lester will understand." She wasn't sure he would, but Lacie figured that wasn't really important right now. Right now, what was important was calming Krissie. And getting her to put the knife down. Before someone saw it. And Krissie landed in even more hot water. "He seems like a nice enough man."

"Lester?" Krissie snorted. "Like everyone else in this world, Lester's biggest worry is Lester himself. Don't believe me? Take a look at your no-good sister sometime."

"Dinah?" Lacie felt another tear splash down her cheek but she didn't dare make a move to wipe it away. Krissie was standing too close. And the hand that she held the knife in was trembling more than ever. "What does Dinah—"

"Oh, stop being so naive!" Krissie's mouth pulled into a grimace. "You think you were Little Miss Kansas Sunflower Girl just because you were cute?"

"I was five. I hardly even remember—"

The truth hit, and something told Lacie it was just as razor-sharp as the knife blade looked to be. "I won that title because—"

"Because Lester Zwick was one of the judges. And he liked me."

Lacie's stomach flipped. "Are you implying that Lester Zwick is Dinah's father?" She shook her head, distancing herself from the whole thing. "I never asked you to do anything like that for me. I never wanted it. If I wasn't good enough—"

"You were always good enough." Krissie's eyes gleamed in the overhead lights. "You were better than all of them. All of them except for me. I should have been Miss National Summer Squash. I wasn't. Because I was pregnant with you and I couldn't compete. Now it's my turn to have some of the spotlight, my turn to get the recognition I deserve. I'll shape dozens of girls into beauty queens. I can't do that, Lacie Jo. I can't do it if you turn your back on this pageant. If you don't win the national crown. I'll see you wearing it." Krissie closed in, near enough for Lacie to feel the cold tip of the knife against her throat. "Or I'll see you dead."

"You don't really mean that."

When she first heard Ben's voice, Lacie figured she was hallucinating. There had been no sound of a door crashing in, no *chunk-chunk* of a rifle cocking. She looked past Krissie to see that Ben was standing just inside the door of the room. He wasn't wearing his FBI hat or his bulletproof vest. His suit jacket was off, his shoulder holster was empty.

He raised his hands and walked a couple more steps into the room, automatically looking past Krissie and over to where Lacie stood with her back to the wall. His eyebrows slid up. His mouth quirked into a smile that sent a wave of relief clear through Lacie, as real as sunshine.

"Told you there were a couple of places where I didn't carry my weapon." Ben came a couple of steps nearer.

"Don't!" Krissie jabbed the knife close enough to draw a trickle of blood from Lacie's neck, and Ben stopped cold. "There's nothing going on here that we can't take care of on our own," she told him. "So you just back off and let Lacie Jo get dressed and get to her interview."

"Can't do that." Ben rubbed a hand over his chin. "There's this ethical thing that keeps getting in the way. You know, how I'm not supposed to let somebody get railroaded into something they don't want to do. Especially at the point of a knife." As smooth as butter, he slid his gaze to Lacie. "You don't want to do it, do you?" he asked. "That's why you're not all dressed up like those other Barbie dolls out-side. You had no intention of participating in the pageant."

"Not after I heard what I heard from Jake." Lacie watched the way Ben slid a look to her left. The first time he did it, she wondered if he might be checking out the rack of swimsuits that was over there. The second time, she realized he was sending her a message. "I can't be part of a lie. I don't want the Summer Squash crown unless I can win it fair and square. And I'm going to relinquish all my other titles, too." The second the words were out of her mouth, she realized Krissie might not take them well, and her eyes darted to her mother.

Though Krissie's cheeks were pale and her eyes were bright, she didn't make a move, and Lacie went on. "I'm going to contact every single pageant I've been in since the day I said 'I do' to Jake McCallum. I'm giving back all the crowns."

The last thing she expected to hear from Krissie was laughter. The noise was shrill and tight with hysteria.

"Are you telling me I went through all the trouble of killing that no-good son-of-a-bitch and—"

Ben and Lacie looked at Krissie in sheer horror.

"I couldn't let him spoil things for me. I couldn't let him tell people that he and Lacie were married. When Eddie called me—"

"Thompson?" Though Ben was ready for anything, he hadn't anticipated this. He shook his head. "Thompson was in on this with you?"

"Don't be a fool!" Krissie chuckled. Her right hand was shaking more than ever, and she grasped her wrist in her left hand to steady it. "Eddie doesn't have the balls."

As if on cue, Sheriff Thompson stepped up behind Ben. He took in the scene with one thorough look and stepped back, Krissie's words ringing in his ears and making him look like he'd been ambushed.

"Eddie's the one who told me Jake was in town," Krissie told Ben. "He heard it from Alvin over at the La Siesta because, of course, Alvin remembered Jake. Everyone remembered Jake. Eddie called me and I—"

"But Jake was shot." It wasn't that Ben didn't believe her, it was just that he liked to get his facts straight.

"I taught her how to shoot." Ed Thompson's voice was as flat as a Morning Star pancake. "I never dreamed—"

"No, you never did, Eddie." Krissie's sneer was apparently even more painful than the truth. Ed winced. "Now if you two boys will get the hell out of here, my Lacie has a pageant to get ready for."

Lacie tossed Miss Virginia's gown on the floor. "I'm not your Lacie. Not anymore."

"Then, you're not anything," Krissie snarled. "Anything but dead!"

Lacie didn't need another signal from Ben. She saw Krissie's arm tense and she dove to her left. There was a clothes rack not far away and she ducked behind it. Just in time. What little composure she had left erupted in a scream, and Krissie slashed into the rack of costumes. Cloth tore and the air rippled around Lacie.

The next sound Lacie heard was a muffled *hurumph* and a squeal from Krissie. By the time she got up the nerve to peek out from between a lime green chiffon and a royal blue silk, Ben had Krissie's arm behind her back. The knife was on the floor, two feet away.

Lacie pulled herself to her feet. It wasn't until she did that she realized she was crying, and she wiped the back of her hand across her cheeks. Because she couldn't bear the thought of standing close to her mother, watching while Ben slapped the cuffs on her, she scrambled toward the door. "What's—" It all seemed so impossible and Lacie's voice broke over the words. "What's going to happen to her?"

"Nothing."

Both Ben and Lacie had forgotten about Sheriff Thompson.

Not such a good idea, considering that when he spoke, they turned and saw that he was holding his service revolver. He aimed it at Ben.

"I heard what you said, Krissie." Thompson kept his eyes—and his aim—on Ben. "About me not having the balls to help you. I would have. I would have done anything for you. You know that. So you just step away from Agent Camaglia here and I'll get you out of here."

"Thompson!" Ben didn't sound any happier than he looked. "You're not going to jeopardize your career for—"

"For what? The woman I love?" Thompson chuckled. "You're damn right I am. Besides, if I play my cards right, I can make the whole thing look like it was just some kind of sad, sad accident. A girl who lost her mind when she realized her secrets had come to light." His gaze slid to Lacie. "A federal agent who made the fatal mistake of stepping in the way." His eyes moved back to Ben.

And Lacie wasn't about to wait to see what would happen next.

Before she could even stop to think it might be the last thing she ever did, she whirled around and punched the sheriff square in the nose.

After that, it was easy for Ben to take over. He had Thompson on the floor with his hands behind his back in a heartbeat. He kicked the sheriff's gun out of reach and put Thompson's own cuffs on him. He left him long enough to grab hold of Krissie, who was too stunned and sobbing too hard to have moved an inch.

Tired of waiting outside as he'd been instructed to do, Clete Harter came puffing around the corner at just the right moment. He'd been out in the hallway long enough to hear everything, and he already had his gun out. While he led Krissie away, Ben yanked the sheriff to his feet.

"Stay here," he ordered Lacie.

But then again, he hadn't had a chance to get used to the new reality. She was her own woman now. And she wasn't about to let him out of her sight.

Good thing the jail block was just down the hall. Krissie went into one of the cells, Ed Thompson into the other. Even before Clete Harter had the doors locked, Ben closed in on Lacie. She might have been a little more relieved if there hadn't been fire in his eyes.

"I told you to stay put!"

Lacie had always been more of a believer in the power of a smile than she was in fire-with-fire. Then again, she'd always believed in Krissie, too, in her mother's absolute love, that she absolutely cared about both her daughters.

Looked like it was time to change her thinking about a whole bunch of things.

She pulled in a shaky breath. Right now, it was too painful to think about her mom and all she'd done, so instead she concentrated on the problem in front of her.

And the problem in front of her looked to be a pigheaded federal agent who was way too used to getting his own way.

She propped her fists on her hips and stuck out her chin, wondering at the same time if Ben realized that it was the first sign that things around here were about to change.

"Yes, you told me to stay put," she said. "And I didn't want to."

Ben took a step nearer. "Just like I told you to get behind

that clothes rack when Krissie was waving that knife around. But instead of that—" He shook his head, and maybe because word had gone around about everything that was happening inside the Civic Center and there was a commotion out in the hallway, he raised his voice.

"I can't believe you could be so stupid, Lacie! What the hell makes you think you can attack a guy with a gun and—"

"Maybe the same thing that makes you think you can confront a woman holding a knife?"

"Maybe I've been trained to deal with situations like that."

"Maybe I've seen you in action and I know the way you've been trained to deal with situations is not to get involved before you're prepared. Where is your bulletproof vest, Agent Camaglia? Where is your rifle? Are you crazy, Ben? She could have—"

"She didn't."

"She could have." Reality struck like a cold ocean wave, and tears welled in Lacie's eyes, and for the first time in her life, she didn't try to hide them. The emotion roiling inside her burst along with a barrage of tears. "She could have hurt you. She could have killed you. And damn it, Ben, if you think there's any way in hell I was going to let—"

"Hell?" Ben's mouth dropped open. "You'd better watch yourself, Lacie Jo. Use language like that and you'll be disqualified from pageants from now until forever."

"Good." It felt so right to say it, she tried it again at the same time she grabbed her sleeve and dragged it up to wipe her eyes. "Good! I don't ever want to be in pageants again. What I want, Ben, is you."

He took another step in her direction. "That's all you want?"

"Well, no." Lacie sniffed and wiped the back of her hand across her cheeks. "There's world peace, of course. And a meal for every hungry child. I want a meaningful career where I can use my considerable people skills. Oh, and a family. How do you feel about kids, Ben?"

A smile touched the corners of his mouth. "Blond kids? Blue eyes?"

"I was thinking more like dark-haired. Brown eyes. You know, the charming Italian type." Lacie inched toward him. "I was thinking if you'd just kiss me—"

He didn't need a second invitation. At the same time Lacie threw herself into Ben's arms, he scooped her close. He slanted his mouth over hers, drinking deep, and when he was done, he smiled.

"Are you telling me—"

"That I love you, Ben. That I always have. That I could never tell you because I just never wanted to take the chance."

"And now?"

"Now?" She sniffed and laughed through her tears. "There's no chance involved, is there? This is a sure thing!"

Epilogue

"Come on, Wiley!" At the top of the steps of the Klaber Falls City Hall, Dinah turned around and waited for her husband. He'd dropped her off in front of the building and had gone around to the back to park the truck. If the parking lot hadn't been so jam-packed, it wouldn't have taken so long. "We're going to be late!"

"I'm hurrying as fast as I can." Wiley took the steps two at a time, tugging at the knot on his tie as if it were constricting his breathing and slowing him down. "You sure you're ready for this?" he asked, and when Dinah nodded, they reached for the door together, pulled it open, and went inside.

They were greeted by the Ladies League from the Congregational Church, who took their coats, and by the Rosary Society of Saint Catherine's parish, ladies who were in charge of the punch and cookies for the day and who (though they might have been inclined otherwise) were kind enough not to mention that spiked hair, nose rings, and the newest tattoo on Wiley's arm (a naked woman who had somehow ended up with three breasts) was not exactly de rigueur for the occasion.

Before they could walk into city council chambers and

find the two seats that had been reserved for them in the front row, Lacie popped out of the sheriff's office. She hurried over and pulled Dinah into a hug. Thinking of Wiley as her brother-in-law was taking some getting used to, but she hugged him, too. Just to show that she was trying.

"I'm so glad you could make the drive all the way from Kansas City!" Lacie beamed. "And I want to hear all about tattoo school, but you can tell me later. We're getting started in just a couple of minutes. You going to be bored?"

"Nah." Dinah's hair was now a color that reminded Lacie of butterscotch pudding. She ran a hand through it. "As long as I've got my Sugar Lips around, I'll never be bored!"

Lacie knew just how she felt.

She watched them head into council chambers and stepped back, pulling in a deep breath to settle the excitement inside her.

"You sure you're ready for this?"

The sound of Ben's voice behind her didn't surprise her in the least. She'd felt him there as soon as he'd walked up. The air heated, just a little. Her heartbeat sped up, just a little more.

She reached for his hand. "I'm ready," she told him, and she smiled. "I've got to tell you . . ." She ran a hand over the lapels of his khaki-colored uniform shirt. "You are the handsomest sheriff this town has ever seen."

"Think so?" The twinkle in Ben's eyes told her that he didn't care as much about the compliment as he did the person who gave it to him. "Handsomer than Ed Thompson?"

Lacie's smile faded a bit. Like it always did when she thought about the things that had happened the summer before. "Poor Ed. Medium security was never his style. And poor Mom. I talked to her this morning."

Because he knew how tough it was for Lacie to think of her mother in the women's prison over in Rock Bend, he kissed her cheek. "I hear she's making progress in therapy. Even so, I'll bet she said you're throwing your life away."

"Something like that!" Lacie laughed. "But isn't that what Harlan told you?"

Ben's smile warmed her down to the toes of the value-priced pumps she'd bought in keeping with her husband's sheriff's salary. "Harlan. Ryan. Everyone else I've ever known at the Bureau. You know what?" He leaned nearer and lowered his voice. "They're dead wrong."

"So's Mom. I'm not throwing my life away at all. Finally, I've found the perfect way to use everything I learned on the pageant circuit."

"And you'll be perfect at it!" Ben pulled her close and kissed her hard, and it wasn't until he was done that he smiled down into his wife's eyes. "I guess we'll have to get used to calling you Madam Mayor."

"It does have a nice ring to it!" She kissed him quickly and with enough heat to tell him they'd have a celebration all their own when the town party was over and they got home. "Even if I do like Mrs. Camaglia better!"

"Well, then, Mrs. Camaglia..." Ben pulled the door open, and as one, the citizens of Klaber Falls who were waiting rose to their feet. "You ready to take your oath of office?"

"I'm ready," she told him, and when he briefly reached out and took her left hand in his, the matching rings they wore touched. He brushed her lips with his, wound the fingers of his left hand through hers, and they walked inside, together.

WAKARUSA PUBLIC LIBRARY

About the Author

Connie Lane has worked as a journalist, editor, and creative writing teacher. In addition to romance/suspense/comedy, she writes historical romances as well as category romance. She has been nominated for the prestigious RITA award by Romance Writers of America and has received the KISS award from *Romantic Times* magazine, as well as a nomination from *RT* for historical romance of the year in the Love & Laughter category. She lives in a suburb of Cleveland with her family. She can be contacted at connielane@earthlink.net.

DISCARD

WAKARUSA PUBLIC LIBRARY